FAMOUS LAST WORDS

Also by Gillian McAllister

Everything but the Truth

The Choice

The Good Sister

The Evidence Against You

How to Disappear

That Night

Wrong Place Wrong Time

Just Another Missing Person

FAMOUS LAST WORDS

A Novel

GILLIAN McALLISTER

wm

WILLIAM MORROW

An Imprint of HarperCollinsPublishers

This is a work of fiction. Names, characters, places, and incidents are products of the author's imagination or are used fictitiously and are not to be construed as real. Any resemblance to actual events, locales, organizations, or persons, living or dead, is entirely coincidental.

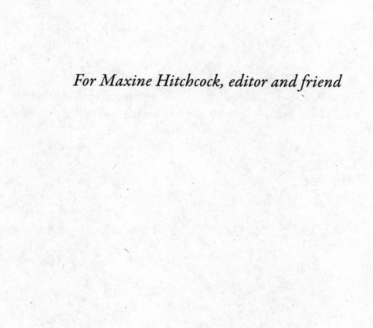

For Maxine Hitchcock, editor and friend

Act I

THE SIEGE

1

Cam

It is one hour before Camilla's life changes, though she doesn't yet know it.

All she knows, right now, as she cleans the high chair while Polly sits on her play mat after breakfast, is that her husband isn't here. He's gone somewhere, left her to deal with Polly's first day of nursery and Camilla's return to work by herself. Has he got a deadline? Has she forgotten some urgent project?

But Cam doesn't forget things. *Luke*, actually, forgets things. So . . . ?

Sunlight enters stage left in her kitchen in three distinct shafts. It's a perfect June day, and Cam woke up a mixed bag of emotions: nervous but excited, sad, happy—her first day back at work after a long nine-month maternity leave. She sometimes longs for words in the English language that don't exist, and today is one such occasion. Trepidation, excitement . . . when she woke up, she thought: Nope, none of them cut it.

And Luke has chosen today to disappear.

He must have some work thing on. He's a ghostwriter, for MPs and celebrities, and has a co-working space he heads to when he needs to think. That'll be it. She won't think about it anymore. Won't ruminate on it—definitely not, absolutely no ruminating, Cam thinks, gripping the dishcloth too tightly.

She watches as Polly leans forward to grasp a toy that's sitting just out of reach. She's so like Luke. Lean, blond, a disposition as sunny as the weather outside. Cam watches as she picks up the toy and throws it, a wobbly, random baby throw that could be deliberate, could be an accident. Funny, Cam's always liked people-watching, but her baby is next-level.

Her phone beeps and she reaches for it immediately, hoping Luke has replied to her, but it's her sister. *Morning*, it says, a selfie of Libby sitting on her sofa, dark hair mussed up in a pile on the top of her head. This kind of message is not unusual: Cam and Libby are engaged in a near-constant text conversation. It doesn't have a beginning or an end, just a regular back-and-forth, a tennis match that never finishes. They've been doing it for as long as they've had phones.

Morning, Cam replies, taking a selfie of her in work clothes, anxious expression on her face that she didn't know she had until she took it.

OMG yes. The big day. Well—to bolster your confidence . . . look! Look who's 12 down in the Times *crossword!?* It's accompanied by a photograph of a clue, which reads *Author of bestselling recent novel about a hot air balloon ride romance (4, 5).*

It's her client, Maya Jones. Cam is her literary agent.

Cam types back: *Wow! I wonder if this is good press exposure? Do they print the answers next week?*

Libby sends a second photo of a very, very small set of answers for last week with a laughing emoji.

CAM: *How many people read this?!*
LIBBY: *. . . Four? What's your cut of four books? LOL.*
CAM: *£8 paperback x 0.1 royalty x 0.15 commission? What's that?*
LIBBY: *Drinks are on me, pal.*

Cam forwards the crossword to Maya, then puts her phone away and yawns. Polly woke her and Luke last night at ten o'clock, one o'clock, and then some other time . . . three, four? Cam promised Luke she would stop looking at the time after he said it only upset her anyway. Polly—old enough now, in their opinion, to know much better—thought it was the middle of the day, and was absolutely, categorically, not interested in sleeping. Luke had looked at Cam, Ewan the bloody dream sheep backlit red behind him, Polly actually chuckling with mirth, and said, "Fancy a suicide pact?" And God, they had laughed, the way they always have. The second Cam met Luke, he made her laugh, and, just like that, she was utterly beguiled despite everything: that he, a writer, was her client, and she his agent. As it turned out, nobody cared about that the way she thought they might.

But where is he? How could he just leave her by herself?

Cam reluctantly gets Polly ready in the sling to walk to the nursery down the road, trying to accept that Luke, wherever he is, isn't going to see Polly before they leave. The house sits quietly around them as she prepares to go, a loaded kind of silence that she tries to ignore: It's the day. The return to work.

Cam has had barely any time to process this change, spent the settling-in sessions stress-walking the streets outside, maternal guilt morphing the inside of the nursery into some awful Dickensian orphanage staffed by ogres. She sometimes thinks she might've read too many novels.

But now it's here, the day mother and daughter splinter into different existences. She said this to Luke only last night, who joked, "Oh, bloody hell, are you not picking her up after?" She'd laughed at that. In every couple, Cam thinks, there is a calm one and an anxious wreck, and Cam is most definitely the latter to Luke's former.

Where *is* he?

She goes to grab her cardigan, and that's when she spots it. On the table in the hallway is a piece of paper with her husband's handwriting on it. As she looks at it, a half-memory of a coffee-scented goodbye kiss from him drifts across her mind, another of him in the shower, the sound of the water running in the distance, both in the veil just beyond deep sleep. So vague she isn't sure that they happened today at all.

Luke once said he would always kiss her goodbye. "I'm never going to be one of those people who just forgets," he once said. "Or, worse, a dry peck on the cheek!"

But did he?

She picks up the note.

If anything is written on one side. Huh? *If anything*? And crossed out? Cam holds the piece of paper up to the light. She turns it over. *It's been so lovely with you both. Lx.*

Maybe the *If anything* is old. The main note is this one, surely? An end-of-maternity-leave note. *It's been so lovely.* A kind of "good luck"?

There's nothing else on it.

How weird. Luke—a writer, after all—is usually clear.

She finds their text thread. She's asked once where he is, called twice, but she'll text again.

As she stands there, overthinking, Polly strapped to her chest, she finds she doesn't know where to start. Everything's so loaded these days. Before the baby, time alone was just that. But now it's a currency. One person's me-time is the other's solo parenting. They're not used to it. They've argued about it . . .

All ok? Sorry to ask again. PS. It's about to happen! The big drop off!! I am to be a working woman once again.

She reads it over, used to proofreading for tone.

She touches the note, just once, sends the text, then leaves.

It is June 21, the longest day of the year, and the hottest so far, too, even at eight o'clock in the morning. The sun is as sharp and yellow as a lemon drop. Cam turns her face to it, apricating in it. Huge flowers have bloomed in the street, big and open happy faces nodding as Cam walks by. She points them out to show Polly (should Polly be understanding gestures yet?), thinking how much she takes the weather for granted lately. It's been balmy for six straight weeks. No breeze, no rain. The same high, blue skies every day, pale at the edges, a deep cyan way up above, as if they're living inside sea glass.

Cam and Luke's lawn has turned yellow and beachy-looking. Each night, once Polly is in bed, Cam takes a novel out there, sits in a deck chair, and just plunges deep into its pages, like diving into a pool containing other worlds. Luke deals with Polly if she wakes. And he knows better than to try to strike up a conversation with Cam, too, during what she calls her introvert hour.

They reach the nursery quickly. A three-story Victorian building sandwiched between a bank and a launderette—very London. Cam feels a dart of dread as it looms into view, that distinctly parental mix of guilt and approaching liberty. The thing about motherhood, it seems to Cam, is that most forms of freedom come with a price. But today, she's just going to pay it, and try to relish it: The return to herself. To the job where she gets to read novels for a living.

Besides, Luke won't be fearing today, won't be imagining Polly not settling or sleeping or eating. Luke is happy-go-lucky, a man who never overthinks. If asked, he would say that the baby will be fine, he's got to work anyway, so what can you do? That's life. Sometimes, Luke tries to reassure Cam by telling her she cannot control situations, and there is nothing that Cam finds less reassuring than this.

And, nevertheless, he clearly is not fearing today, is he? He's not even here. Gone to work, or wherever, without a second thought. How could he?

"Aha, Polly Deschamps," one of the nursery workers says, greeting them at the door. Reflexively, Cam holds her daughter's warm body closer to her chest. "We've been telling everyone about your first day," the woman continues. "We're going to have so much fun."

"Hope so," Cam says. She takes a breath, then lifts and passes Polly into the arms of the nursery worker—a woman whose name Cam doesn't even know or has forgotten.

Polly swivels back and reaches for Cam, just once, their hands momentarily touching for the purest of seconds before she is pulled away from her, and Cam is free, but right now she doesn't want to be.

She grabs for her phone to tell Luke all of this, to say don't worry, I've done the nursery run, something perhaps slightly passive-aggressive, but that's when she looks at his WhatsApp profile: *last seen today at 05:10.* Huh. She didn't notice it earlier when she was busy with Polly and cleaning up. Ten past five is so early, and not online at all since? Unlike him. So strange.

Cam walks into her agency's offices and, immediately, the aroma gets her: books. They're everywhere, and it smells like home.

In the kitchenette, having greeted a few colleagues, glad she used the Tube journey to apply too much makeup, she makes a coffee and thumbs through a historical fiction debut someone else represents. She can feel the pull of the words already.

The streets are so dark they look sooty, lit only by a single oil lamp at its end.

And just like that, she's in: Cam really could stay here, on the Victorian street, standing up in the kitchen, and read this whole thing, the way she has done her whole life—the back of cereal boxes in the mornings; Sweet Valley High books on the school bus.

She closes the cover and breathes out, thinking.

Look. This is fine. It's fine. Luke is doing something somewhere—she's forgotten what, her mind taken up with Polly, that's all. That's *all*. And Cam's here, with good coffee, books to delve into and to sell, *and* she's being paid for it. She's lucky. She's so lucky. She doesn't need to create problems.

But something is creeping up behind her. A kind of dread. That *last seen*. The note.

A beep.

Also.

A text from Libby. This is how she messages. Often one word at a time. This is how *they* message. Well, this or trading mutual insults, usually, anyway.

LIBBY: *I'm baking a cake for this pissing client thing tonight. Is this unacceptable or OK?*

A video of a spinning cake, one side collapsed but repaired with icing.

CAM: *Definitely acceptable.*
LIBBY: *Thanks for lying to me.*
CAM: *Always.*

"Cam!" her boss, Stuart, says, rounding the corner to the kitchen. "Welcome back." Tanned, strawberry blond, mid-fifties. Ostensibly benign and somewhat dithery, he has a list full of bestselling writers that hints at his regular displays of brilliance. He is the sort of person you think isn't listening in a meeting, who then makes the best suggestion of anyone there.

"Baby well? Life feeling on an even keel yet?" he asks.

"Oh yes, better," Cam says, thinking that the house is full of piles of laundry, of unopened bills. The baby doesn't sleep. This morning, Cam showered while shouting nursery rhymes to placate her. When Cam sits in the garden every night, she feels the tasks looming behind her, to-do-list specters that she doesn't have the time to deal with in the way she used to. "All good here," she adds brightly.

"Great stuff," Stuart says. "It all falls into place eventually."

"Hmm."

"Anyway," he says. He raises his arms above his head—he has been, for the past couple of years, that most toxic of things: a gym convert—and starts stretching. Cam finds the best tactic is to ignore him when he does this, and so she pulls the sash window open, overlooking Pimlico below. Gardens out the back, and here, in front, huge white Georgian buildings. She's missed it. The simplicities of a nice view and a hot cup of coffee that she can drink in peace.

"Did you send Adam's novel out?" he continues, two hands braced on the kitchen counter. Cam is worried he's going to start doing squats, but he stops and switches on the kettle instead.

She helps herself to a biscuit, replacing hours unslept with sugar. She discovered Adam's novel while on maternity leave. He'd sent her a query email. She had been checking her inbox, couldn't resist the premise, and asked for the full manuscript. Adam said he preferred to physically post the novel: that he felt like it was no longer his, that way. He'd sent it to her house, since she was off, and she'd offered him representation within three days. The thing is, this work—it doesn't feel like work to Cam. Nothing does that you'd do for free.

"I sent it out last night," she answers Stuart. "Couldn't help myself. I think it's going to go big." She hopes her radar is accurate. Cam knows a good book when she sees one. That feeling you get as a reader, 10 percent in, where you just kind of *sink* into the novel and its world. This one is contemporary fiction about the son of two YouTubers who sues his parents for breach of privacy. She still remembers the moment she opened that padded envelope, read the first line, and thought: *Yes.*

"I want to get a two-book deal, but he hasn't sent me a new idea yet," she says.

"Hmm. You only need a one-line pitch, and it can change. Right, got a crisis meeting," Stuart says, checking his watch. "Author going nuts."

Cam takes some biscuits to her desk and spies more texts from Libby, beginning with *The cake has betrayed me.*

She moves a coaster out of the way bearing the slogan "Main character energy," suddenly wary of her own drama playing out, and opens her laptop. She never shuts it down, and it currently has twenty-five tabs open, almost all of them Google searches.

Baby not finishing meals.
How to stop bickering with husband.
Should my pelvic floor be better by now?

She checks her email. No wild, seven-figure preemptive offers for Adam's book yet. Next, her phone. Nothing from Luke. Should she ring him again, or . . . ?

Cam doesn't know where to begin. Her brain feels so full. Meetings, submissions, novels about to be published. There's a word for this that she recently learned: *fisselig.* A German word meaning "flustered to the point of incompetence."

She was mainlining Jaffa Cakes last night with Luke—who somehow never gains an ounce—lying on top of their duvet. She had been moaning to him about, well, everything really. That Polly wasn't weaning or sleeping well. That she didn't know how she was going to work alongside it all. That she felt a failure most days. Things Cam would only admit in the middle of the night, and only to him, the person who never judges her. Luke had listened and offered her more Jaffa Cakes, not suggesting anything, but she didn't need suggestions, just needed him. "Things feel—I don't know," she had said. "Just like they're not getting any easier."

"I'm chatting to you and eating Jaffa Cakes," he had replied, running a hand through his hair, past the small scar on his forehead that he got from falling off a bicycle as a child. "Seems OK to me."

"We're so unhealthy."

"Junk food is our only defense," Luke had said. "Don't rob me of my pleasure in life. Look—when you go back, why don't you take an evening a week off mum duty? I'll do bedtime. You go and do something. With Libby? Holly? A bar. The cinema."

Cam had grimaced, though she'd appreciated the gesture. Going out would suit Luke, but not Cam. "I like to go to bed with a book," she'd said, sounding meek, but it was true. A paperback novel, pages rough under her fingertips. A candle. Fresh pajamas and sheets. Motherhood, for introverts, is a special kind of difficult, the usual escape routes not available, a thought Cam regularly feels guilty about, but is nevertheless true.

"You do that every night," Luke had said, leaning over to touch her shoulder affectionately.

"I know that. I know I am lame."

"Everyone needs a break. You need . . . space." His expression became more serious. "Cam—you're ever drowning . . . you shout? And I'll rescue you. OK?"

She'd nodded, so thankful she had married a man she could say anything to, but now, she thinks about that first statement.

Everyone needs a break. It contained a darkness within it, didn't it? Is *this* Luke getting *his* break?

Has he actually been slightly huffy recently? Cam ponders it, trying not to spiral. Maybe. She heard him heave an irritated, lengthy sigh the other night when Polly woke; his footsteps as he got out of bed were heavy. When he'd returned, and she'd asked what Polly had wanted, he had ignored her, scrolling on his phone, his jaw tight. Uncharacteristic: Cam has remembered it for this reason.

No, but they went to a wedding last week, and he had been fine then, hadn't he? They'd fallen into their old dynamic. He'd coaxed her onto the dance floor even though she categorically does not dance. "You protest," he'd said, waistcoat unbuttoned, "but you dance so well with me." She'd cajoled him back home at midnight; he had laughed when he saw she'd brought a pair of slippers in her handbag to wear in the taxi home.

God, she can't concentrate. The book on submission, and Polly's first full day away from her, and Luke's absence. They make Cam have that strange but familiar urge to check and check and check again. Emails, the nursery app, authors' Kindle ranks. Anything.

Something comes in from Adam.

Adam@amazingadam.com
21 June at 09:23
Re: Second idea

No, no idea for a second novel yet. How urgent would it be? I have a small-town whodunnit kind of thing on the back burner?

Cam hides a grimace and tells him to keep thinking, hoping he will read between the lines.

She grabs her phone and tries Luke again: "Welcome to the Vodafone messaging service."

She writes another message: *I've had loads of office biscuits as well as those Jaffas! x.*

And this time, she sends it on WhatsApp and watches for the delivered checkmarks.

Luke and Cam met when he walked into her office four years ago. He was a journalist who had ghostwritten a memoir by a football manager about a Premier League team's rise to success: he'd DMed the manager on social media (as a bet on a stag do, he'd later told her) who, to his surprise, had replied saying yes. Cam had enjoyed it a lot more than she expected to. Luke's prose was up-front, transparent, didn't purport to be anything other than what it was: pure entertainment.

Cam had offered him representation. He had replied with a single word: *Shit!* It had made Cam smile. She likes language in all its forms, and a well-timed swearword is the best.

She had sold the memoir to Penguin Random House. His next gig was an autobiography for a singer-songwriter her agency represented and, after that, he was up and running, established and needing a little less agenting, which made it a lot easier for Cam to kiss him several months into their working relationship at a rainy London bus stop after too many glasses of wine. It was late summer, the mornings and evenings just beginning to smell as crisp and cold as apples. Luke had been in a T-shirt that got soaked in the downpour and, to this day, damp clothing reminds Cam of that night, that kiss, that illicit, shouldn't-be-doing-this kiss.

Anyway. Can't concentrate on a word, she continues to Luke. She waits eagerly for his response. *Just have an easy morning today!!* he will no doubt say, but she needs to hear it, needs to see his words to her. Cam makes Luke more sensible and Luke makes Cam have fun. That's how they work. That's the way they have always worked.

The message doesn't deliver. She stares at it: a single gray checkmark. When . . . when do you begin to really worry?

No. He must actually be working hard. Phone off.

But the dread Cam felt in the kitchen rears its head again. She's kidding herself. Something is off.

She calls him again.

Nothing.

At what point is he . . . missing?

Another text from Libby comes through, then a photo. She is running her outfit by Cam, as she often does. She catches one part of it—*It's for a party!! That's where people get together and have fun? Are you aware? LOL*—but she stops reading, because that's when she hears it. Some sort of commotion outside. Is that sirens?

Fear runs its fingertip lightly up her spine, and Cam's imagination fires into action, fueled by fiction. Things that only happen to other people could happen to me, she finds herself thinking. Ambulances, fire engines, warning sirens. Dead bodies and bad news and police hats held in hands and *we tried everything we could* said by kind doctors in green scrubs.

She rises from her desk. She'll just check outside, beyond the foyer. See what's going on.

Their receptionist is sitting in silence, the only noise the television on the wall cycling through news stories. Cam can't hear anything else.

It must be her imagination. Nothing more.

But then everything happens all at once, the way it sometimes does.

"We pause for a moment, here," the news presenter on the television says, something unusual and grave in her tone, "to bring you breaking news from Central London."

As Cam watches, the screen goes black and BREAKING flashes across it in white text. The voiceover switches to a male broadcaster. "Police are trying to end a siege that began an hour ago in Central London." A grainy image appears on the screen. Cam stares at it, but she can't make it out. "A man has taken three hostages in a warehouse in London. We have exclusive CCTV footage from a security guard on duty. Authorities are present at the scene and believe it to be a hostile act."

Before Cam can digest this, she spots them outside: police.

Two officers, one wearing a white shirt and black stab vest, one in a suit, no caps in hands but otherwise just the way she imagined, striding into her workplace. And Cam knows, somehow, in some deep, dark place inside her, that they're here for her. She tells herself she is being stupid, highly strung because of Luke's unread texts and absence, but that's the precise moment that she hears them say her name.

2

Cam's legs feel imaginary, too light. She walks across the foyer and could swear she's four inches from the ground, a ghost floating around a literary agency. It must be shock. Fear.

"That's me," she finds herself saying loudly in the foyer. "Camilla."

"Are you the wife of Luke Deschamps?" One of the coppers turns from talking to the receptionist and looks directly at Cam.

"Yes," she says quickly, thinking that at least it's not Polly. How strange it is the way the order of disasters inverts post-baby.

It's been so lovely with you both. What did he mean by that? Was that—a *goodbye*?

"DS Steven Lambert," one of the coppers says. Late thirties maybe. Pale, freckled. He's accompanied by a woman who introduces herself as PC Emma Smith. She has with her a notepad and pen, just holding them, standing there like a journalist from the '80s.

"Have you got time to have a quick chat?" Smith says, her tone gentle, but in the way somebody has when they've been told to do it.

"What's happened?"

"Is there somewhere we can . . ."

Cam indicates a meeting room off the foyer without thinking, wanting only information, and as quickly as possible.

"Is Luke OK?" she asks.

"Yes."

Cam's shoulders drop six feet. In her relief, she bursts into an occupied room, apologizes and heads to the one next door.

Steven Lambert meets her gaze and he looks tired. He is a cliché of a workaholic. Dark circles, coffee on his breath. "There is a hostage situation unfolding," he says plainly.

"I saw it—on the news," Cam says, blinking. Stunned that these two pieces have connected together: the police and the news story. Maybe she's dreaming. Maybe she's reading a novel.

"A siege. A man has taken three hostages in a warehouse in Bermondsey."

Bermondsey. Luke's co-working space is in Bermondsey, and the word hits Cam with the strength of an anvil. She feels utterly disoriented, *Bermondsey* reverberating around her skull. Cartoon stars appear above her head. Her neck goes hot, a rising tide of blood working its way toward her face like a filling bath. She brings her hands to her chest and feels her pulse in both wrists.

"Oh my God," Cam says. She brandishes her phone. "That's why . . . is he OK?" And then she adds, to explain: "I texted him—he . . . has someone got him?"

Lambert hesitates, and something about the gravity in his expression makes Cam stop speaking. He shifts in his seat, his shirt moving slightly up his arm, revealing a wrist tattoo. Cam can't quite make it out, some swirled symbol or other.

His eyes meet hers. "Your husband hasn't been taken."

"Oh! Good!"

"We believe that he is the person who has taken the hostages," he finishes quietly.

3

Somewhere, in some previously inaccessible part of Cam's brain, a trapdoor opens, and she begins falling through it. "What? No he isn't," she says, the notion so absurd to her that Lambert merely needs to be corrected. As she looks at him, he shifts, and his tattoo disappears once more.

Cam's colleagues have begun clustering in the foyer, because of the news, or the police, she isn't sure, and she becomes momentarily distracted by them. Instead of processing what's being said to her, she is trying to work out what her colleagues must be thinking, in that strange way people in crisis focus on the wrong thing sometimes.

"He's taken hostages?" she says to Lambert.

He wordlessly hands her a phone displaying a video on which he presses Play. It's the same one the news had on.

In the center of the frame are three hostages, sitting silently on three wooden chairs. They have their heads covered with black material, like something from a film. They're so motionless it looks like a freeze-frame, until she sees that they're breathing. The slightest rise and fall of their shoulders. Three sentient, terrified beings, taken.

It's grainy CCTV, hard to make out. For a few seconds, all is still, but then the hostage-taker steps into view.

Tall and slim, all in dark clothes, he moves in front of them, left to right, five, six, seven steps, then pauses, about to turn and move in the other direction. His walk, the shape of his arms . . . Cam sits very still, watching this eerily familiar man.

And then he turns and looks properly at the camera. It's just a glimpse, no more than a second.

But it is him.

It's him.

4

Camilla, it's very important that we go and speak privately somewhere—the station or your house—because we are putting together a strategy to end the hostage situation," Lambert says.

A shivery, fluey feeling comes over her. She holds on to the video and presses Play again, ignoring Lambert. Soon, on this video, she'll notice something different. She knows Luke's face so well. It'll be easy to spot that it isn't actually him. She can screenshot it and send it to him. They'll laugh about it later. *It's been so lovely with you both.*

He comes back into view, pacing, and she thinks it again: It's Luke. That's what her brain supplies once more, the second she sees him. Unmistakably him, the man she's loved for four years. His hair, his walk—are those his *trainers*? They are: the ones with the yellow soles. Distinctive. At this, Cam begins to truly panic.

She waits, then presses Pause when his face is centered right in the frame. It takes a couple of attempts to get it just right. Lambert and Smith watch her dispassionately.

And, eventually, there it is. The scar on his forehead from his bicycle. It is him.

Cam gulps, then looks up. Sunlight outside. Books everywhere: on the table; on the floor; two on a spare chair; one splayed open, propping up a wobbling table leg. Her colleagues in the foyer. Everything looks almost normal.

She blinks, puts the phone down, then plants her face in her hands, not caring what the police or her colleagues think. Her whole body is trembling. Her head judders like she's on a motorbike. Her teeth chatter. She's suddenly so cold.

"Is this real?" she says eventually, head still in her hands, not looking at the officers.

"Yes."

"How do you know it's him? For sure?"

"From intelligence," Lambert says, though that isn't a specific answer. She looks up at him now, thinking how unlikely it must be for a workaholic copper to be wrong. He removes his suit jacket, then stretches his arms above his head, and the tattoo reappears. It isn't a symbol: it's actually upside-down—to her—writing. *Protect and Serve*. Something about it unsettles Cam. This dedication to the cause.

She blinks, wondering when she will stop shivering. She waits, both for that and for an explanation from Lambert. Only one of them arrives. "Number one: his face is a match to the DVLA's facial-recognition system. It's never wrong," he says.

"What?" Cam says, so softly and quietly it's almost a whisper.

"The Driver and Vehicle Licensing Agency," he adds, as though that is what Cam doesn't understand. "This CCTV matches his driving license photograph. We have sophisticated technology that can be sure of this. And a phone is with him and Vodafone have confirmed that it's his."

Welcome to the Vodafone messaging service . . . Luke's provider.

Lambert continues: "He took it into the warehouse, where it pinged a nearby mast at five o'clock in the morning, and then he switched it off." He is unable to keep the satisfaction out of his voice, and some battle line is drawn, right there in a meeting room full of books. He has played his full house of evidence, and Cam says nothing, holding her own cards, a shitty, low-scoring hand.

Lambert seems to make a decision then. "Let's go somewhere we can talk more privately," he says, standing. He leads her out of the meeting room. Through the back of his white shirt, Cam can see another tattoo, a pair of wings spread right across his shoulder blades.

Outside, the road and footpaths are scorched white—holiday pavements. The shadows are short, the sun high, and this is what Cam focuses on. Anything other than the truth. They walk, two coppers and a bewildered woman, and suddenly they're standing by the police car.

Blue lights on silent, two further officers in stab vests, hats, high-vis coats they must be sweltering in. Stuart's voice calling her name in the dim background, but Cam can't reply, can't seem to form any words at all.

Her body is still trembling, legs as unstable as Bambi's. How can her husband be doing this? How?

But he has. He has done it.

The police lead her gently into the back of the car while her colleagues watch on, their mouths agape, their eyes wide in the glass foyer, like visitors at a zoo.

5

Niall

One of the many things Niall didn't count on when he became a hostage negotiator is that hostage situations hardly ever happen. And so, ghoulish as this may be, most of his days are spent waiting for one, like a footballer on the bench. Or, worse, he's called to one that resolves while he's on the way. Niall does more U-turns at motorway roundabouts than he does negotiating.

He is at this precise moment on light duties in the police back office of the Met—he's a detective on the side, though a pretty unwilling one since his hostage training. If he's lucky, he might get a negotiation with a petty criminal who has stolen a bottle of vodka and decided to hold up Tesco Express with a water pistol instead of coming out.

He sifts through the application forms for a vacancy he has in his department, but he can't settle to it today, keeps putting the forms down and buying things on Amazon Prime (a home beer-making kit, a spinning shelf that goes in the fridge that he can put his chutneys on).

It is not especially coincidental to Niall, then, when the call does come, because he's always waiting for it. Vivienne tells him he even answers these calls in his sleep. "'What's the situation?' you say. Some wives would hope you would call their name in your dreams."

"DCI Thompson," he says into the phone as he answers now—fully awake, or so he hopes.

"White male holding up a warehouse in Bermondsey," the call handler says.

He holds the phone between his ear and shoulder and drops the forms, interested. They scatter, drifting off the desk this way and that like feathers, but Niall is much beyond caring what becomes of them. He opens and takes a sip of his Coke—the first gulp of the day is always the best; everyone has their vices—fizzy metal liquid bubbling on his tongue, tilts his head, and says, "What exactly do you mean by holding up?" He stares at the can. He wrote his name on it with a Sharpie, so that nobody would steal it from the work fridge, pathetic as that is.

"He has taken three hostages. Sadly, the media already has it—a security guard being paid to watch the CCTV remotely called 999, which was good, but he also leaked the footage on Facebook."

Niall feels a frisson rush up his body. This is not a domestic. And it's not a shoplifter either. A livestreamed siege.

"He's put bags on their heads." Her voice is deadpan. It's Sheridan, Niall realizes. She took a call for him five years ago, about a man set to jump onto the M4, and she'd said flatly, then, "There's probably nothing anyone can do now, but he's still there . . ." She's bored of the job, and understandably so, but Niall finds it embarrassing when the police do not care enough. He went to the M4, as it goes. Talked him down.

"I have that CCTV for you. Hang on . . ." Sheridan says.

"Just WhatsApp it to me."

"I'm supposed to email it, one sec . . ."

"OK," he says. "We need to get down there. Where in Bermondsey?"

"Behind Shad Thames."

Niall knows it well. Iron bridges in an alleyway that connect apartments above like a Kerplunk! game.

"Perpetrator is called Luke Deschamps."

Niall hears his email beep in his ear. He opens it on his laptop and clicks the link, the phone on speaker.

"I'll be there," he says, watching the video load, standing back from his desk, hands on his hips.

He squints, trying to work out how the perpetrator has power over the individuals in their hoods, and then he sees it: the handgun tucked into his dark sleeve. A Beretta, a pistol.

Bermondsey High Street looks shabby and tired even in the bright sunlight when Niall arrives. He and Vivienne moved last year to the Barbican, at his insistence, to be near work, and now everywhere looks somehow unclean compared to the sanitized holiday-complex feel of his home, a penthouse in a building called Ben Jonson House that looks like something from *Battlestar Galactica*. Viv works for the RSPCA and—from time to time—brings home animals she can't rehome that look kind of out of place in the clean-lined apartment. Niall often approaches the front door with real trepidation, worse than he feels at work, unable to forget the time there was a surprise kestrel in the shower.

He grabs his phone and sends her a text now. *Got called on to a job. No idea how long I'll be,* he writes. *A job or a job job?* she replies immediately. *A job job—proper one!* He smiles down at the phone. She once told him she finds it impossibly sexy when he's on a hostage situation, which Niall has never forgotten.

But today, Viv doesn't reply exactly as he expects. *Right x,* she replies, and that's all.

She will be pissed off with him, Niall thinks with a sigh. They're tussling at the moment, locking horns over work. He got halfway round the North Circular one Friday a few weeks ago to a job that got called off before he got there, but it had made him so late back they had to cancel their weekend away in the Lake District.

But work's work. Policing is antisocial. Everybody knows it.

He ventures down the High Street with a bounce in his step, walking past proper London—corner shops with loose and hot fruit and veg outside, neon Tube signs and graffiti and fire escapes Rapunzeling down the back of buildings.

It's obvious where the siege is taking place, two streets back, on a road comprising mostly industrial units but some clusters of houses too.

"What's going on?" Niall says, hurrying up to James Maidstone, the lead CID detective in charge, known in hostage situations as the silver commander. The gold commander sits in some office somewhere, authorizing things from afar. Niall is the lowly hostage negotiator: here just to communicate.

What most people don't know—and what Niall learned from his training, at a kind of shabby boot camp in Surrey—is that it's not actually about talking. In major terrorism jobs you have two negotiators in: one to talk, and one to merely listen. They're even called that: "the listener." And theirs is the most important job in the room.

Sadly, budget cuts and a lowly three hostages taken means Niall is both today. He takes a sip of the Coke he brought with him. "What's the situation?" he asks.

Maidstone turns to Niall. He's everything Niall is not: a graduate-entry police officer, who's risen quickly through the ranks. He knows things out of textbooks, and looks like it too: wears shoes he shines and a watch he bought in Dubai. Niall, in battered old trainers, feels as old as time itself.

Maidstone takes a vape out of his front pocket and puffs on it. Niall, who quit smoking twenty years ago, still finds he could reach over and inhale the nicotine clouds from it, right there while it rests between Maidstone's fingers.

"Hostage-taker is Deschamps. Thirty-eight. No criminal history at all. A writer. Married to Camilla, who is also his literary agent. They have a nine-month-old, Polly. Not much more information at this time," he says. *At this time* is his verbal tic.

"Right. I need information and fast," Niall says. "What's the deal with the security guard?"

"No suspicion. Wants Facebook infamy, I think."

"Do you think he's involved?"

Maidstone makes a face, then pockets his vape. His black suit shines a kind of burnished hot brown in the bright sun, like a black cat. "I don't think so. He's got loads of followers on there. Alt-right stuff. Put the footage on his feed after calling it in. No connection to Deschamps that I can see."

"Fucking idiot," Niall says. Maidstone's eyes flicker slightly. "And the hostage-taker? Any history of domestics?"

"No."

"Any contact?"

"Nothing at this time."

"So he hasn't levied a threat?"

"No."

"So no idea what he wants?" Niall presses. He checks a clock. Time is already running out. "What I need is eyes on him, so I can see his body language, and a line to him, so we can talk. Find out what his agenda is—and what he's feeling."

"OK. Understood. We have CCTV. Let me see what else I can get you. His mobile's now off, but there's a landline. I'm getting it set up. I want you communicating within the hour." He begins typing—Maidstone gets stuff done, to his credit, and Niall knows he will be getting what he wants soonest.

Viv always says she likes to think his job involves guns and stake-outs and ransoms. She sometimes says things like "And why didn't you blow his brains out?" or "What was the sniper doing?" The reality is, of course, different: it is simply that every person, every single human on Earth, desperately wants *something*, and it is Niall's only job to work out what. He plays along when she asks him, though. It's one of their games. As he thinks of her, he realizes that he forgot to take the bin out this morning—she will be annoyed at him. It's her most hated task, and he left her to do it. The problem with being a hostage negotiator is that everyone thinks you're doing something for some smart, Machiavellian reason. But sometimes, you just forgot the bins.

Maidstone leads Niall across the sunlit street to a van that houses a few laptops. "We have eyes on live CCTV, look."

He grabs for a laptop and hands it to Niall, who watches in silence. It's grainy, hard to make out. A warehouse background of empty shelving racks, only two and a half hostages visible in the frame. They're seated on wooden chairs perhaps grabbed hastily: their angles are skewed. Deschamps is offscreen.

The most significant thing, to Niall, is the silence and the stillness of it: this can only mean one thing—the hostages are terrified.

He brings the laptop closer to his ear and listens carefully: the sound of shoes on cement. Those footsteps are fast and urgent, the movements of an agitated man, which is not good news.

"Let me see the moment of entry," he says.

"We have nothing from the street. Inside, we see one hostage is already there. Then we have Deschamps arriving inside, but only into the main frame. Interior camera doesn't reach the door. And we don't see how he gets his other two hostages in there."

Maidstone finds the footage and starts it on the laptop in front of him.

A woman enters the frame. She walks purposefully on-, then offscreen. There's nothing more for almost thirty minutes.

Half an hour later, Luke Deschamps appears. A small movement at the top of the screen, near the table, and then he walks forward purposefully, holding the gun out in front of him with straight arms. He shouts, to people offscreen, "On the chairs, now, or I shoot!" Gun in hand, directing their actions. He leaves the screen, then drags three chairs into view. He directs each hostage onto a chair, using the gun, then ties them up deftly, with quick hand movements. All three hostages sit rigidly. Deschamps looks directly up at the camera.

Niall pauses it, rewinds, but he can't make out that small movement right at the start. He watches again.

Niall makes a note to run the footage of the hostages through the DVLA database, even though he knows he won't get hits for people with covered faces.

He plays it again, fourth time.

Deschamps is silent as he arrives, and something about it makes Niall shiver. Deschamps does nothing. Merely tracks his targets with the aim of the gun. And then, and only then, does he shout. He likely shepherded them in with the gun unseen, though it's surprising he wasn't issuing verbal directions as he did so.

"OK. Leave it with me," he says to Maidstone.

More and more police are arriving. A couple of uniformed officers are scouting out the area. They will be responsible for assembling the inner and outer cordons. The first steps are to evacuate the few houses and industrial units in the immediate vicinity, telling people in the wider area to get to the back of buildings, far away from possible gunshots.

An officer at a laptop in another van raises a hand. "ID on one of the hostages!" he shouts, getting out of the van. Maidstone whips his head around while Niall listens. The officer comes over quickly to

Maidstone. "Isabella Louis. Forty-two. Her husband, George Louis, has phoned her in."

"George Louis?" Maidstone says immediately—sharp as a tack: George Louis is in the police.

"Exactly. He's on his way here. He worked uniform in Hammersmith before joining the GDPR team. His family owns the warehouse. He couldn't get hold of her this morning. He's pretty sure she was headed there to do some job between tenants. Plus, he's recognized her clothes."

Niall nods slowly. Who takes a copper's wife hostage? Somebody with bollocks, that's who. Not a family man with no criminal history.

"Has George any known connection to Deschamps?" Niall says. "Can we speak to him?"

The officer is standing with the laptop held in one hand, the other typing. "No connection on the force systems. And Deschamps isn't connected to the warehouse in any obvious way. George doesn't know him."

"Get off the systems and onto Facebook," Niall says, his detective instincts bubbling to the surface. "Get on Isabella's social media. We need to know if he took her for a reason. I'm guessing George never arrested him? Not for anything, even speeding?"

"No."

"Got it. We need ID on the others."

Maidstone nods. "We've got nothing at this time," he says. "Look, we need to establish a dialogue."

"We need an RVP," Niall says, gesturing to the copper standing holding a laptop, squinting at its screen in the sun. The rendezvous point: the place they will gather, assess intelligence, be briefed, and, more important, think and strategize. "We can't stand out here. We need to discuss tactics before dialogue. Let's set one up." He points up the road, five hundred yards away—too far for the CCTV to be useful to get a look at the warehouse and Deschamps's arrival—to the pub.

"A Wetherspoon's?" Maidstone says.

"It's better than nothing."

Niall and Maidstone walk up the street together and across the pub's car park, past an A-frame board that says TODAY—TWO FOR ONE PUD-DINGS.

They walk through the double doors, sunlight to gloom, and Niall is immediately relieved that it isn't busy. Wednesday morning, and the heat has driven down footfall. An old man with shaking hands sits at one of the tables with a pint, a betting slip, and a newspaper full of tips. A family of five—tourists, maybe—are nearby with lemonades. Not much else. Fruit machines. Flyers for food offers.

They approach the bar together. Immediately, Niall's eyes flick to the taps. And it isn't Pepsi on draft—it's Coke. How completely excellent.

"I'll set my stuff up there," Niall says, indicating a rickety nearby table. "You talk to the manager and get everyone out," he adds. No one can stay, not even the staff. And Niall finds that most people, when faced with it, don't need the risks spelled out to them.

"I'm aware of the next steps," Maidstone says frostily.

Niall slides his laptop and a designated mobile out of his bag. Nothing more. Some hostage negotiators want the gold commander on the phone at all times, endless discussions, a whole room full of people listening, but Niall doesn't. Just him, the kidnapper, the phone line stretching thin between them. An earpiece he's forced to wear so he can take instructions. He has to record the call for compliance but rather wishes he didn't: experienced hostage-takers recognize the second's delay it causes, though he doesn't get the impression Deschamps is one of these. No criminal history. Family man. Normal job. Though their baby is young . . . he begins to ponder postnatal depression in men leading to some sort of psychotic break just as the patrons begin to leave, shooting curious glances Niall's way.

And George Louis's wife. It's very strange. Niall had assumed Isabella was an accidental hostage, already in the warehouse when Deschamps burst in. But you can never ignore a coincidence in policing, and George Louis is a big-personality copper: aggressive, forthright, and smart too. He could easily have pissed somebody off.

Niall nips behind the bar and pulls himself a Coke, thinking how much he can rack up on the tab they will have to settle later. Anyway. The matter at hand: Usually, by now, a demand has been made. Or a hostage killed.

He keeps the laptop with the CCTV on open, watching it, wanting

Deschamps to come into view. You can learn a lot about someone's emotional state if only you can see them.

Officers begin to trickle into the pub. Police in riot gear, bulletproof shields, holding MP5s and Glocks, then uniformed coppers and yet more detectives taken off missing persons cases and garden-variety burglaries.

Maidstone arrives, and begins his address: "Deschamps is thirty-eight, a writer, a husband, and father of one with no previous. We have no CCTV of him outside the warehouse from this morning, or on the streets: it's an industrial area with limited cameras. The closest is the pub, and neither Luke nor any of the hostages walked by there. All we have is that initial footage, and this."

"You've combed every CCTV?" Niall interrupts.

"We're on it. The CCTV from inside the warehouse suggests Isabella was already there. She behaves like she's alone, and she and George own the building. She waits for half an hour. Then Deschamps arrives. Either the men were already there when Isabella arrived, or more likely Deschamps brought them in, just cut off from the CCTV, given he then tied them up."

Niall raises his eyebrows. He is thinking, forming a plan. Deschamps is a known family man: maybe they should get the wife down here. Use her to engage him.

Maidstone continues: "Isabella is a forty-two-year-old woman who is local to Bermondsey and owns the warehouse with her husband, derelict as it is. Also has no previous and no known connection to Deschamps. Neither does her husband, but he is a Met copper: George Louis. We don't know how Deschamps captured the other two hostages, nor who they are. We have CCTV on him right now and can see his hostages are bound to chairs, with hoods on their heads. Deschamps is offscreen, for now, but is not shouting or making direct threats." He takes a breath. "He is armed, a Beretta pistol, not automatic, but nevertheless dangerous.

"Outer cordon, keep the public out. Inner cordon, aim to control Deschamps should he emerge." He pauses. "At this time, shoot to kill is not authorized, unless—and until—something changes."

Niall has his eyes on the laptop. The only sound is Deschamps's foot-steps.

"The layout of the warehouse is online," Maidstone continues. "There's one door at the front. There is what is deemed a fire escape at the back of the warehouse, up a flight of stairs. It leads only up to the roof—from which there is no external way down, so it is a fire escape in name only. We have a drone up there now."

Weapons click as the officers shift, some perching against tables, some standing amongst the chalkboard specials menus and the fridges full of alcohol. One of the CID gets out a J_2O and uncaps it noisily with a hiss.

And that's when it happens: Deschamps steps back into view on the CCTV, blue eyes right up close to the camera. What is he doing?

The room falls silent. Maidstone comes over to watch Niall's laptop.

All around the pub, laptops display the CCTV, fifty Deschampses, fifty pairs of blue eyes. He reaches one hand up, concentration etched on his features. He's holding something. Is it the gun? No, it's some sort of material . . .

And Niall knows what's going to happen before it does. Deschamps's brow is wrinkled, his eyes wired. And then in one swift motion he covers the CCTV with the material, and the screen goes black. All they have now is sound, the rush of the static.

Next to Niall, Maidstone swallows, loosens his shirt. "Right," he ad-dresses the room. "We have a problem." And then, as if Deschamps heard Maidstone, the sound goes off too. He's switched off the camera. Turned it off at the mains.

6

The squad hums in the unexpected silence.

"We've no longer got eyes or ears on the suspect," Maidstone says. He glances at Niall. "Any ideas on his emotional state?"

"Agitated. Scared face," Niall answers.

"Right—we need the silent drills." Maidstone looks across at the officers responsible for drilling through the walls in the warehouse with equipment so quiet a hostage-taker won't hear. "Please take this as authorization to get started." He turns to Niall. "Anything you want to add?"

Niall sucks in a breath. He really thinks he needs to get Deschamps talking. "I want a line to him. Now, please. And I want the wife here."

Maidstone blinks. It's an unusual move, but not unprecedented. "I need to check the protocols."

"No, you don't; I'm telling you this is what's best," Niall says. This is always the way of it. The protocols. The risk aversion. The "system doesn't allow it." The red tape.

"Let me raise it with the gold commander."

"He's a family man. His wife is his literary agent. They will know how to communicate with each other. They are used to it. I want her here."

"I said I will raise it," Maidstone says shortly. "Meantime—I want you in dialogue with him before I authorize anything further." He raises his hands up. "Your negotiation's going well, maybe I grant you a new privilege."

"I need to get a look at him before I do anything," Niall says. The drillers are already leaving. "As quickly as possible." He needs to see if he's hyped up. If he's calm. Niall's actions will be different if Deschamps looks angry, if he can't sit still, if he is tapping the gun off the back of the hostages' heads . . .

"Yes," Maidstone says. "And see if that gun is pointing *at all* toward the hostages . . ."

Niall says nothing. There are a thousand ways to hold a gun, and only a few of them point to a likelihood of shooting. "Aiming doesn't mean shooting." One of the many things Niall learned on his training is that there are facts and there are assumptions. Niall tries to deal only in facts.

"No, Niall," Maidstone says. "If he's turning off CCTV and pointing a weapon at the hostages, then—then we go in. Armed."

7

___

Cam

Cam is back in Putney after a silent and loaded car journey, back at their house that she left two hours or perhaps a century ago. The police follow her in, not saying anything, just standing too close behind her in the sunlit hallway. She walks past Polly's car seat, and past a stack of mail on the doormat, presumably delivered during the transformation from the before- to the afterlife.

She avoids her own gaze in the mirror by the front door, turns to Lambert and says woodenly, "Living room is upstairs."

Luke calls their house the upside-down house: bedrooms and bathroom on the ground floor, kitchen, living room, and dining room on the first. Cam has always liked the quirkiness of it, a house not like other people's. At night they fall asleep to the sounds of the London foxes in their garden, in the summer to snippets of neighbors' conversations like misheard lyrics.

Or they used to.

They file upstairs and sit down together in an awkward row on the gray corner sofa, next to two manuscripts and a proof of a novel. Cam's eyes are everywhere. Luke's mug on the end table containing the remnants of his cup of coffee. Filter. Two sugars. That coffee-scented kiss. His car key. How can this be? She's seen the video. It's clearly him. So, really, she knows the question isn't *how?* but *why?*

But all the while, Cam is remembering things. More and more and more the longer this goes on. Last week, Luke had banged the top of the coffee machine when it needed more water. The plastic casing had cracked. So unlike him. He was never alpha, never competitive, never physical. A breezy, sunshiny day of a man. The type who couldn't be bothered to make a coffee if the machine had run out of water, not the type to inflict damage on it.

The week before that, he'd received a letter in the post, turned around, and looked at Cam, expression low and furious. "The car was due its MOT three weeks ago," he'd said, but his tone wasn't rueful, or even slightly irritated: it was ice cold.

"Oh, shit," she'd said. She was hanging laundry out in the corner of their kitchen. "I totally forgot."

"Hmm."

"Guess this is life with a baby."

"She's nine months old," he'd said, putting his foot angrily onto the bin pedal and dropping the letter inside. "We should've remembered."

"It's fine. Look—we'll just . . . get it done now," she said, but he hadn't looked at her. Had just stood there by the closed bin, staring down. Cam had put it down to tiredness at the time, but was it?

It was so unlike Luke, Mr. Que Será, Será himself: the man who on their first official date said to Cam he never wanted to waste time worrying when he "could be having fun." Who throws World Cup Final parties at their house. Who turns in projects late because the weather has been nice. Who holds and holds and holds her anxieties, heavy as boulders, and never lets the weight show.

"Camilla, we need some facts," Lambert says urgently now. "We have a warrant to search, which PC Smith is going to commence alongside a team, who is almost here."

"OK," Cam says in a small voice. Her eyes are still roving around the living room, at everything he's left. An Amazon parcel on the dining table just through the doorway. A pair of shoes sticking out from underneath the sofa.

Smith stands and puts on a pair of forensic gloves. Cam looks at her closely. She has a Roman nose, brown hair scraped back from her forehead, eyes that slant downward at their sides. Not a scrap of makeup. Cam feels like a powdered clown in hers. The stupid, optimistic war paint of somebody expecting a good day and getting the worst of her life.

Smith leaves the room, starting who-knows-where, the most humil-
iating and private places, maybe? The bedroom? Polly's nursery? Cam
watches her pass the doorway twice. Her poker face, when she doesn't
know she's being watched, drops. She becomes more judgmental. Looking around curiously, but with an element of Schadenfreude too.

"Camilla, we need to get this information, and quickly. The police
need to know as much background as possible before we get you down
there and get you speaking to him. If, at any point, they have to make
the decision to go in, they need to know who it is they're dealing with,"
Lambert interrupts her thoughts.

"Go in?" she says, without thinking, but he doesn't clarify. Imaginary
scenes come into Cam's mind. Guns. Snipers. Riot gear.

"Let's cut to the chase. Any idea why he would do this?"

"He's—he'll be being forced into this. Or he's having a mental-health
episode . . . he won't be doing it—because he wants to," Cam says, feeling
like she's brainstorming with a client about fictional motives.

"OK," Lambert says easily, clearly not listening to the protestations of
a woman who will always defend her husband. His phone rings, and he
picks it up seamlessly, moving from talking to her to talking to somebody
else. "Yes . . . yes. Fifteen minutes?" he says, then rings off without saying
goodbye, just like they do in the movies.

"All right, Camilla," Lambert says. "We want you at the scene to talk
to Deschamps. Is that something you feel you can do?" he says, even
though it sounds to Cam like he's just agreed to it.

"Yes," Cam says, then feels the need to add: "It's Luke. He goes by
Luke." Her husband is the main character in her life, and what he goes
by matters to her in this out-of-control environment.

Lambert ignores her. She stares at him, this stranger sent to question
her. He doesn't wear a wedding ring, but this is all Cam can glean about
the human behind *Protect and Serve*.

"We'll get you to the scene with our hostage negotiator," he says.
"When we've got the lie of the land here. Fifteen minutes or so."

She looks at the sunlight again, trying to forget, trying to be somewhere else, to be free-falling again, but it doesn't work now. Denial is
over.

A hostage negotiator. Like a movie, with a wire-tapped phone and ten million pounds delivered in a suitcase. A shootout. None of it could possibly, possibly feel any more surreal than it already does.

"No ideas at all here on his motivation?" Lambert barks.

"No."

"The more you tell us, the more we can help your husband," Lambert says dispassionately, and Cam wonders if this is quite true. She is a tool to be used by the police to get to Luke, but will that help him?

"What's the most unusual thing that's happened for you guys in the last six months?"

Cam thinks, then remembers possibly the most significant thing: "We were burgled."

"When?"

Cam thinks. "Six weeks ago. Got home from the park—in the day. Place had been messed up. Luke called the police."

"Right," Lambert says, his eyes already on his phone, finding a contact, and dialing. "You never know what's connected," he says to Cam. "Paul, I need a readout on a burglary. Took place six weeks ago at 24 Bucks Avenue."

Cam dispassionately observes his quick mind working overdrive, while hers is on go-slow. They'd taken Polly to the swings. They'd returned home to their house, which felt cool, the patio doors open in the bedroom. Drawers gone through, kitchen cupboards too. Cam had looked around, holding Polly, at first not comprehending it, until her eyes had met Luke's.

"Jesus Christ," he'd said, and perhaps, *perhaps*, in hindsight, had he seemed more rattled than she would expect? No, not really. A burglary was a horrible thing.

Luke had called the police, had complained about how long he was on hold for, spoken to them out in the garden. Cam had watched him pace, dragging a hand through his blond hair over and over.

That night, Cam couldn't sleep, nor the next, jumping at sounds, imagining strangers' fingers rifling over their things. Yet they hadn't taken anything. Not even a laptop that Luke had left out.

And now look. She watches Smith walk into the kitchen and begin opening her cupboards. Other strangers join her, all searching.

Perhaps her story arouses suspicion in Lambert, or perhaps he always intended to do this, but he sets a recording device down next to Cam. It looks incongruous on her sofa, an old-fashioned black box. "Interview with wife of suspect commencing ten twenty-two, twenty-first June 2017," he says. "When did you last see your husband?"

Something collapses in Cam.

"Last night," she says. "Or perhaps this morning."

Lambert looks at her. "Which?"

The search team arrives. Cam hears them downstairs. Boots on stairs. Lowered voices.

"Camilla?" Lambert prompts, ignoring the team arriving. He is completely and totally focused on her. "We have to get on with this. Get you to the scene. Before something happens."

She pauses, thinking of Luke's note. The cryptic note. This whole situation feels surreal, but this especially so. Could she refuse to answer anything? Is she here—*wife of suspect*—leading the police to her husband?

"He left this morning before I got up. He wrote me a note," she says carefully, knowing that she is not the sort of person who can refuse to cooperate, who can easily lie. "He kissed me. I think." And he did. She really thinks he did. He always does.

"Where's the note?"

"Got it," Smith calls through. She appears again in the doorway—false smile spreading across her features—and the love note from husband to wife is double-bagged. Smith passes it to Lambert, who reads it quickly.

He brandishes it. "What does the back mean? *If anything*? The crossed-out part?"

If anything . . . Did he mean he knew something was going to happen? That he was going to do something? Should she have hidden it? Is this note her thirty pieces of silver, handing her husband over?

"I don't know."

"No idea?"

"No."

"Have you texted him?"

"Yes. They're undelivered."

"What time did he leave here?"

"I don't know. It's a—our baby doesn't sleep well, so it's a blur . . ."

Lambert's eyes catch the sunlight. They're an unusual, patterned camouflage green. Funny, this man must eat breakfast, sleep, get dressed in the morning, but Cam can hardly imagine that he is a human being beyond a detective.

"So he gave you the impression he was heading to work? He's a writer, correct?" Lambert says.

"Yes, he is. He has a co-working space he sometimes goes to . . . It is—it's in Bermondsey," Cam says, knowing the power this word holds. "But he didn't say he was going."

"What's the address? We'll order a search."

"Umm, it's called the Water Cooler co-working space."

Cam's back prickles as she says this. What if he's hidden something there? Some explanation—another note for her? What if *it's been so lovely* was some sort of clue? Cam is used to reading her husband's writing, used to analyzing him, editing him. But this one is lost on her.

What if there's something darker there? Evidence? She is handing her husband over to the police. In the face of him or good citizenship, she's unwittingly chosen.

She went to his co-working space only a few weeks ago, took Polly down to see him one sunny afternoon. "The Water Cooler" was written above the door in brass letters. Luke rented a dedicated office he said he could close the door on—though he never did. While they were there, another occupant of the co-working space arrived to see him, carrying two ping-pong paddles and a ball.

But all Cam really remembers is that he had a framed photograph of them on the shelves. In the evening snow, Cam in a purple hat, scarf, and gloves, he in a black beanie, the light behind them sodium-yellow. Flurries of snow whirled around them, obscuring parts of their faces, some of them blurred, some of them in focus.

How absurd it is that they were once there in the snow together, then in the office, and now here she is, talking to the police about him while he holds captive three innocent people. The shock repeats on her like rolling thunder.

"OK." Lambert fires off an email right in front of her. He doesn't even hide the screen from her, fingers flying across the keys. "Why does he work in Bermondsey?"

"He used to live near there. And the co-working space has good coffee," Cam says honestly, her voice catching. "He likes good coffee." *They* like coffee. Or *did*? It's one of their things. Luke bought beans on subscription just recently for them to share. They're being delivered tomorrow. If he did that—if he intended to . . . ?

"He's a ghostwriter, yeah?"

"Yes."

"Good work ethic?" Lambert receives an email, reads it, then looks back at Cam.

"Tries, but he is extroverted."

"Ah. Prefers to socialize?"

"Yes. Likes the research and interviewing people. Less so the typing."

"Right," Lambert says, perhaps with a slice of judgment. And maybe it's easy to judge Luke, if you don't really know him. If you don't know the way he can make a story about buying a pint of milk entertaining. If you don't know how well he writes, how he knows the precise way to command a story. If you don't know that he cooks their every meal, says he enjoys it, but Cam knows it's because she hates it. Just recently, she'd caught a glimpse of a note called *this week's dinners* on his phone and thought how glad she was that he was hers. The load truly shared, and never resentfully.

"He working on anything particularly . . . interesting at the moment? Anything that might've landed him in some sort of hot water?" Lambert gets out a piece of gum and begins chewing it, offers Cam one, which she declines. His chewing irritates her, adds an air of mania to his fast questioning. Cam wonders how much time they truly have until something escalates in the warehouse.

"He's doing a biography of an MP and researching one for an actor."

"Who?"

"Alan Pastor and Tristan Hughes."

Lambert makes a bemused face. He might not even have heard of them: an under-the-radar Green Party MP and an actor currently in *Macbeth* at the Globe. Could these people have somehow led to . . . all this? Some awful exposé? It would be ridiculous. She can't imagine. Niche, not likely to attract huge sales and certainly won't be of interest to a copper.

"Not worth our time looking into them," Lambert says, and Cam is struck by someone making constant and urgent judgment calls.

"I don't think they're anything big," she says, thinking that these contracts will almost certainly be canceled now, the money handed back. God . . . his income. His reputation. *Her* reputation. The aftershocks of it all keep hitting as she sits there, battered by repercussions.

"Is it unusual for him to be gone before you wake?" Lambert continues.

"Yes."

"He stressed?" he says. Another look at the phone.

"Is something happening?"

"Is your husband under stress?"

"I mean, no," Cam says, but the second she speaks these words, she knows that they are lies. Luke is not ordinarily stressed, but hasn't he been—lately?

Sometime in the spring, Luke had got in late from driving Polly around, then hardly slept one night. She'd been aware of him moving around in the bed next to her, in the small hours. After a while, she'd woken again to him watching television on his iPad, headphones in, the blue flickering of the screen interrupting her sleep. The next day, she'd asked him about it, but he'd said only that Polly had taught him how to be an insomniac. "Really?" she'd said. "I fall asleep the second I'm horizontal."

"Ha, yeah," he'd said, and that was that. None of his usual humor.

The truth is that Luke's been tetchy for a good few weeks, exploding sometimes over undone household admin, nappies, the MOT.

Cam meets Lambert's eyes and something seems to cross between them. He—*Protect and Serve*—wants information at any cost. But these things, these intangible but damning things, Cam is not willing to give to him. There are some lines she cannot cross, and here they are.

Because, despite everything—*everything*—she believes her husband to be good.

Lambert breaks her gaze, looks out of the window. She deflects the question. "Nothing beyond the usual stresses of having a baby."

Lambert's head swivels around like an owl's. He doesn't miss it. "So Luke *is* stressed?"

"No!" Cam says, thinking maybe Luke has had enough of them. Is that it? He's had some sort of mental-health event, his brain broken, betraying him, some sort of split from reality after nine months of propping Cam and her worrisome Google searches up? Of giving her time to herself that she needed? Of cooking every single dinner? God, how selfish she has been, reading a book every night in the garden while her husband carried the load. No other new mother gets that me-time, she thinks viciously about herself.

Or is it sleep deprivation, and everything else?

"Can I see your phone?"

More invasions of privacy. She numbly unlocks her phone and hands it over, reminded—perversely—of childbirth, where after the first examination, all inhibitions were lost. *Look at anything,* she thinks despondently. *Go through it all. I no longer care.*

Lambert scrolls, pen poised in his hand. Cam lets out a sigh. Luke's jacket is on the chair and she has a bizarre urge to go and fold herself inside it, the zip done right up to the top. She's had enough of the questioning. She is peopled out, if nothing else, feels the way she does at the end of a working day, at parties. Sometimes, too, after an evening with her chatty husband.

Lambert is studying her message chain with Luke. They're the ones from yesterday. They'd gone to a café and texted while Luke sat at the table with Polly and Cam had ordered at the counter. A last outing before Cam went back to work.

LUKE: *Chicken salad with mayo or similar? Can't see the menu!*
LUKE: *Unless they have a car quiche? lol*
CAM: *Let me see what they've got.*
CAM: *I'm afraid no quiche!! I can do chicken salad. Caesar dressing?*
LUKE: *DEFINITELY.*
CAM: *Coming up. Coffee?*
LUKE: *Obviously.*

"Car quiche." One of the many in-jokes they have made up. Perhaps due to their occupations, Cam and Luke are more prone than most couples to adopting their own lexicon. Car quiche refers to a quiche they once ate from a service station that they both deemed the best of their life, only afterward they couldn't remember where it was from. They have spent several years trying to track it down.

Cam and Luke have dozens of these words, some of them made up entirely. "Slabbidon," an invented word for when you're feeling jaded and under the weather for no reason. A "Ford Focus moment"—named after a time Cam worked out a problem with her client's manuscript in the car: breakthroughs of any kind were thus called this. "Ordering the fillet steak," that time a friend of theirs checked they were splitting the bill and then ordered the most expensive item on the menu, now a sobriquet for chancers everywhere.

And "sweepy," perhaps their favorite expression, coined by Luke. "I feel a bit woe-is-me," he had said one day, not long after they'd first got together and he still worked in journalism. They were eating out somewhere, the sort of place they went to before kids. Cam can't remember the name, only that they'd sat outside and it had rained unexpectedly, rivulets running off awnings like tassels. They had stayed out there—*Oh, fuck it, I'm not moving now,* said Luke—the night still warm, their arms and ankles occasionally getting splashed.

"How so?" Cam had said.

Luke had gestured with a slim hand, holding his drink. "A bit down on myself. Captain Pete"—how he referred to his boss—"wants me to try and bring advertisers in for the paper."

"And?"

"He wants me to just cold call sponsors up, like a pathetic little . . . I don't know. A chimney sweep, begging people to let me in."

Cam had laughed so loudly it had echoed on the rainy, empty terrace. "Are you now a Victorian? Fancy yourself the new Dickens?"

"The metaphor stands."

And so feeling sweepy became a term used for when one is feeling disheartened, down, or small. Cam felt sweepy when the baby cried too much, when she ran out of day and didn't get to do anything she really wanted to. Luke felt sweepy when, years after his first book came out, his publisher sent him sixty-three pence in royalties, and even sweepier when Cam took her commission off.

"And that was yesterday. So this morning you . . ." Lambert continues, putting her phone down.

"Took my daughter to nursery."

"There someone who can pick her up?" he says, and Cam's heart snaps in two right there like a fortune cookie.

"It's her first day. No, I . . ." Cam says, panicked. Polly will think she's abandoned her. Died.

"You will be needed throughout today, Camilla." And his ominous tone is enough to make her do it.

He gestures to her phone, and Cam scrabbles for it, calling Libby. It connects immediately. Despite their near-constant texts, Cam and Libby do not ever call each other—they both hate the phone—which is why Libby answers with a panicked "You OK?"

"I need you to collect Polly," Cam says woodenly. "From nursery."

"What? Why?" Libby says. This is not something Cam would ordinarily ask: Libby has been trying to have a baby herself for five years. Two years of trying, two failed rounds of IUI, she and her husband Si are now about to embark on their first round of IVF. Cam supposes that the relationship with Polly might be a step too close for Libby, who always looks slightly wounded when she sees her, who once said on text, *I sometimes think she looks like me.* It had been so unexpected, and so loaded for her caustic sister, who only ever deflects pain with humor, that Cam hadn't known what to say back.

"Well, if you think I'm the best person to ask, then . . ." Libby says.

And Libby doesn't know it, but she is. There are friends, there are colleagues, but when the police are standing over you, you really only want your family.

Cam breathes down the line. "Luke is—The police are . . ." She dry gulps on the words. "They're investigating something they say he's done."

Cam sees Lambert's facial expression flicker at her careful wording.

Libby heeds the family emergency and snaps into pragmatism, the way she always does. "What do I need to do?" she asks, and Cam closes her eyes in gratefulness. A heart of gold sits in her sister's chest.

"You need to get to the nursery for five. It's—it's the one on my road. You need a code word. I set it up—hang on . . ." Cam puts her hand to her forehead, trying to think. What was that word? God, Libby will be so triggered by this. She should have asked someone else. "It's 'upside-down,'" she says. "The phrase you need to say." She puts Libby on speaker, then fiddles with the app for the nursery, clicking the button to say someone else will be collecting Polly.

"OK." Libby hesitates, the pause tinny in Cam's living room, and she leans into it, this sisterly, supportive silence that travels down the line to her. "You OK?" she says. Cam takes her off speaker, embarrassed.

"Yeah," Cam lies. "Yeah."

"OK. Stay in touch—if you can," she says, and Cam is so, so thankful Libby doesn't ask what Luke's been said to have done.

Smith walks into the room and picks up Luke's laptop. She's put her hair in a bun on the top of her head, looks slightly exerted from searching, flushed. She is holding several items in clear plastic bags. Cam squints at them. His toothbrush. Two notebooks. But it's the toothbrush that really gets to her: DNA. A private, intimate ablution, swabbed.

Two more officers thunder past her, one of them holding Luke's wallet and passport. He didn't even take his wallet . . . surely that must mean that he didn't intend to leave for long? Or go far?

Or that he didn't intend to go to work for the day at all . . .

Cam suddenly wants to take off and hide everything. Grab their things and go. Keep his secrets for him. This morning, she had a happy marriage. Now she's supposed to hand him over to the police, together with everything she knows about him.

"There," Cam says, pointing to the armchair where his laptop sits. Smith heads to it, but picks up his coat first, searches the pockets. She brings out a clutch of receipts and a letter. She scrutinizes them for a few seconds, then looks at Cam, who immediately stands up and looks at them. Smith doesn't stop her doing so, but she doesn't acknowledge it at all, leaving Cam feeling like a creep at a party.

RECEIPT 21/04

TESCO CLUBCARD FUELSAVE

PENCE PER LITRE DIESEL: 120

POINTS THIS VISIT: 148

SUNDRIES: CADBURY STARBAR

PAID BY CARD ENDING: 4592

RECEIPT 23/04

TESCO CLUBCARD FUELSAVE

PENCE PER LITRE DIESEL: 123

POINTS THIS VISIT: 172

SUNDRIES: CADBURY TWIRL

PAID BY CARD ENDING: 4592

Cam stares at the receipts. And it isn't their contents that makes her suspicious: it's the frequency. Fuel twice in two days, and they live in London. Hardly drive. She tries to anchor the dates in her mind, but can't. Where had he been in order to fill up twice in the spring?

A crumpled-up letter unfurls in Smith's hand. Luke's bank statement. Cam's gaze skims the withdrawals. The two petrol fill-ups are there. Way more than normal. Cash too. But these could mean anything.

Smith's gaze is on her. "Anything jump out?" she says lightly, and Cam suddenly thinks how foolish they are, how stupid to think that Cam might be honest about something like this, something nebulous, where her concerns can hide between the lines of the itemized bank statements.

"Nothing," Cam lies. They'd been driving around to get Polly to sleep, but only for twenty minutes here and there . . .

Smith bags the papers. "Does he have any other computers or assets?"

"No—I . . . No. Just his phone and his laptop."

"Social media?"

"He's not bothered by it."

"Right, Cam," Lambert says, while Smith takes the laptop away. "Anything else unusual happen recently? Anything you can think of other than the burglary? However small."

Cam closes her eyes and sees Polly on a swing in her mind, Luke laughing as she kicks her little legs and windmills her arms. That is real. That is what matters. They stay there for a few seconds in her imagination, sun in their yellow hair.

Cam opens her eyes.

Immediately, she remembers the onions. It was sometime recently, perhaps a month or slightly more ago: she can't find anything to fix it on, and time moves both fast and slow since having Polly. Maybe April: it had been colder, dark after Polly's bedtime.

Cam had been in the bath upstairs, had come down to the smell of dinner cooking. Luke hadn't heard her footsteps. His back was to her, lit by the kitchen spotlights. He was chopping something, chicken sizzling noisily in a wok.

"It was so nice to have a bath and read," she'd said. Polly had suddenly started going to bed. Previously, they'd have to drive her around sometimes to get her to sleep. The difference a few hours to themselves made had been life-changing. A drop of expensive bath oil, a crime thriller, and, most nights, Cam was away somewhere else. Rural Scotland playing detective. Or 1960s Paris. Or just London, but a different London to her own.

"Huh?" Luke had replied jumpily. He'd spun and looked directly at her.

And it was his eyes.

His expression was carefully, deliberately open. Studied. But his eyes. Red-rimmed, bloodshot. And his jaw was set, too, his lower lip tense in that way it is when you're crying but pretending not to.

"Are you OK?" she said.

"Yes?" he'd said, an edge to it.

"You look like you've been crying?"

"No," he'd said, and then, like it just occurred to him, he'd gestured to the chopping board. "Onions."

Cam had thought about it a few times since. In the storm of the baby days, she had told herself that they were normal for feeling frazzled, for grieving an old life, unable to get anything done, competitively tired, but this had been maybe seven months afterward. Unexplained crying. Or perhaps just onions. Who's to say?

But last night . . . hadn't he seemed fine? *I'm chatting to you and eating Jaffa Cakes.* The truth is, the good days with a baby are better than the greatest days in your pre-baby life. They had been a family. A unit. Memories flit through Cam's mind like an old projector movie. Polly's first laugh, like liquid bubble gum. That time she recognized them in the mirror and her eyes went round with shock. The key-in-lock feeling you get when you hold them close to your chest . . .

But had he been somewhere? Been out burning fuel? That night he'd hardly slept? The one she can only just remember, can't place the date of?

Her reverie is interrupted by Smith's appearance in the doorway, and Cam somehow knows from a place deep inside her that she's about to tell her something significant.

"Camilla?" she says. She's holding the laptop. And is there just something slightly triumphant about her expression? Maybe, Cam thinks warily, wanting to shrink away from her like an injured animal.

"What?" Cam says.

Smith pauses. Their eyes lock. "Do you have any idea why this laptop was wiped at just before five o'clock this morning?"

Cam's cheeks get hot. Smith turns, her face catching a slice of sunlight, obscuring her expression momentarily, one side light, one shaded, a Phantom of the Opera.

"No . . . I . . . No. I don't know why."

Her husband is a writer. All of his materials are on there. He'd only delete everything if he intended to . . . Cam can't let herself finish the sentence, not even in her mind. The sentence that ends with something like premeditation, with malice aforethought, with *intent.*

"We'll take it in," Smith says, her words mundane but the tone serious. "See if we can restore it."

She disappears again, and Cam can hear her rustling forensic bags.

Lambert meets her eyes and there's an uncomfortable beat. An awkward silence. Cam thinks it is because of the laptop, but it's actually to do with a revelation of his own.

"Right," he says. "Camilla, there's another piece of evidence missing."

8

What's that?"

"Your husband has a gun," he says flatly. "I assume he bought it and kept it here. But no paraphernalia has been found. No receipt, no box, no spare cartridges. Did you ever see that gun? It would help us enormously to know more about it, and where it came from."

Cam realizes instantly that this is an accusation. "He can't have a gun," she says. "He wouldn't."

A gun. A gun. A gun. She didn't see that on the footage. It was hidden. Had he concealed it?

"I haven't seen a gun," she adds.

"He does have one. If you felt it was best to turn a blind eye until now, that's fine, Cam," he says, misunderstanding her: he thinks she means *in the house.*

Cam looks at Lambert, and then at the recording device, and wonders if actually this has been the point of the interview all along. Perhaps she hasn't been the only one withholding information.

And then the thought body-slams her: poor, poor Polly. She didn't ask for this. Sieges and guns kept in houses and police ransacking her nursery. Cam can hardly stand it. Twinned with this comes anger, maternal anger burning bright. How could he do this? How could he leave Cam to deal with the fallout? To implicate her in it, or at least not exonerate her? To not explain a thing to Cam, to leave his baby daughter?

"*Is* it OK?" she says, incredulous. "To turn a blind eye to a gun? Besides, I haven't. If I saw a gun in my house, the one my baby lives in, I'd . . . I'd . . ." She flounders, can't finish the sentence.

"OK," Lambert says. "Has he been buying anything else unusual?"

"Like what?"

"Hydrogen peroxide, bags of nails . . ."

"No," Cam says, and she almost laughs with the mad absurdity of it. "You think he's made a bomb."

"I have no idea," Lambert says, as though Cam is the one asking insane questions. "But we have to have as much information as possible about what might await us in that warehouse."

Await us. Cam deals in words for a living, and these are not lost on her. They're going to go in. Isn't that what happens? The police go in and shoot? The suspect dies, makes the news, maybe the hostages are rescued, maybe not, and, the next week, everyone's forgotten all of them.

"Who are they?" Cam asks, her voice faltering and hoarse, shame lacing it that she didn't ask earlier. Only cared about the perpetrator. "The hostages?"

Lambert's green eyes connect with hers, then he looks away. "No names yet."

He pauses, seeming to hesitate, but doesn't add anything else. "Deschamps was easier to identify. But he bagged the hostages almost immediately. Hoods make it kind of difficult."

Bagged.

"Are you going to go in?" she asks.

"No firm plans to at the moment," he says. "So long as your husband cooperates."

"OK," Cam says in a small voice, thinking, *Please cooperate, oh please, whatever it takes. Whatever cooperation is.*

"I'll need contact details for all of his friends and family that you can think of," Lambert says. "As part of the profiling, we need to talk to everybody."

Cam mutely starts to write them down on a plain pad with a pen he provides her with. The pen isn't police-issue, has the name of a rock band on the side of it that Cam's vaguely heard of. Her handwriting is strange and jagged, the plastic pen slick with sweat, her phone hot in her hand.

And Cam doesn't know where the thought comes from, only that it arises: there won't be a second child. Not unless there is an amazingly credible explanation for all of this. She almost doubles over in shock from the strength of this revelation. What else won't there be? Won't Luke go to prison, even once the siege is done?

Poor, poor Polly. A criminal for a father.

Cam will be a single parent.

She thinks she might be sick.

She stares at her feet, lost. As lost as if she has landed on the moon, alone. She's still wearing the shoes she put on to take Polly to nursery, when Luke was merely missing.

Lambert's phone rings again, making Cam jump, and he takes the call, uttering only one-word sentences.

"Camilla," Smith says, arriving back in the room. "We've restored a few apps, but most are deleted even from the servers. Anything relevant to you in here? Anything you want to flag?" she says lightly, and Cam is suddenly struck by the thought that perhaps the police are not merely fact-finding, here. Perhaps this is Cam's only opportunity to confess about anything suspicious—or run the risk of being implicated herself . . .

UBER EATS ACCOUNT

Your Orders

Starbucks (Putney)

£9.13 (LARGE) COFFEE X 2

18 Jun 08:02am

DELIVERY CHARGE: £3.40

Starbucks (Putney)

£4.10 DOUGHNUT (CUSTARD-FILLED) x1

18 Jun 08:40am

DELIVERY CHARGE: £2.50

Cam blows a dark, sad laugh out of the side of her mouth. Here he is. Her husband's character. He loves Uber Eats, once said he would Uber a Mars Bar to the sofa if he could.

She looks at the recent searches on his Spotify:

White noise for babies
Lullabies for babies
Music for anxiety

Anxiety.

Cam stares at it. Sure enough, Smith doesn't miss it either. "He usually anxious?"

"No," Cam says.

"Hmm."

"It was probably just—you know. Having a new baby . . ." she prattles. "I've found it hard. It was maybe for me."

"Was it?"

"I don't know. Maybe," she says again, and Smith gives her a hard stare that lasts a second or two too long. Eventually, she moves on, showing her the next set of apps.

ASOS

Recent orders

OUT FOR DELIVERY 24 June 2017: Stonewashed jeans, slim fit, size M

And his Safari search history:

Remove page break on Microsoft Word
Meditation exercises
Krispy Kreme stockists London
Nine month sleep regression?
How to concentrate better

Meditation. Cam stares at that too. Same way she stared at *anxiety*. Luke is not a meditator. Not in any way, has zero interest in it. In fact, likes his busy mind, the way it flits from this to that.

"All pretty benign," Cam says lightly. "Meditation to concentrate better, probably."

"Right."

One final app. Rightmove. One saved search: Grove Avenue, Lewisham. Photographs of a house for sale.

"Ring any bells?" Smith says, and Cam stands at a crossroads once more. At the fork in the road. Here it is: the opportunity. The truth is, Cam doesn't recognize that property, has no idea why Luke has saved it, and on that app.

But she doesn't want the police to go there, to check it out. What if... what if he's hiding something there? What if it's significant, somehow, in ways she doesn't yet know? What if this location is just for her?

Cam stares at the decision, but the truth is that there isn't one, not for her. She is his wife. And, here and now, she tumbles across an invisible line, drawn somewhere between her and Smith, made of loyalty and love for her husband.

"It's a house we thought about buying, but decided not to."

On the other side of the line, everything feels different.

"Right, OK," Smith says quickly, and Cam thinks the second she has a moment, she will go to Grove Avenue herself and find the house. Alone.

"I wanted to ask you," Smith says. "Do you know when your husband last ate and drank?"

"What? Why?" Cam says, still thinking about his Google searches, that house.

"It's just for—so we know a bit more about his physical state," she explains. "And any medical conditions?"

"No. None. Coffee, this morning, I think."

"Right," Smith says. "I heard you say—it's . . . he likes it, right—he likes coffee?" She looks at Cam, and her tone softens slightly, like butter just beginning to melt around the edges, though Cam is certain it is put on.

"Right."

A weighty silence seems to settle between them, though Cam doesn't know why. "That's a good thing for us to offer up," Smith says.

Cam winces. Clearly, they want to entice him out, like he is . . . what? An animal? Prey? Cam feels dirty, as though she wants to shower this grubbiness off—no, go out and wash herself off in rain that, this summer, doesn't seem to want to come. She's giving them information, preferences. Things that they will use to bait her husband. How can Cam be complicit in this? It is these thoughts that she uses to justify it, keeping her secret Lewisham house to herself.

Smith disappears. "OK," Lambert says one last time into the phone, then hangs up.

"This burglary," he says. And oh please, please let him say Luke found out who did it, is teaching them a lesson, something irrational but perhaps understandable, something that, if they can end the situation, he will recover from eventually, serve his time for. These are now Cam's hopes, as surreal as they are.

"Your husband didn't report the burglary," he says, voice low: the tone of a man aware a woman's husband has lied to her.

"What?"

"No phone call was made."

"That's—that's not . . . I was there," Cam says, but she immediately thinks that, actually, she wasn't. He was in the garden: a strange place to make a call.

"Did you ever follow up yourself?"

"No. He did it all. Maybe he—was on hold, and thought he'd try later?"

"I'm sorry. There's no police record of it. No call, no crime number. Nothing."

"He did call. I *saw* him. Surely it's an—an admin error?"

"And Vodafone say no call was made that afternoon."

Cam pauses, stunned. "So—what? He pretended?"

A beat. "Yeah. Looks like it."

The doorbell goes, interrupting Cam's thoughts. "I'll get it. Stay put," Smith says quickly, and Cam is surprised and then shame-filled at the notion that she is no longer at liberty to answer her own front door.

She inches along the sofa and picks up Luke's coat. A scarf is tucked in the pocket. Cam bought it for him. It's merino, navy blue. She pulls it out and it runs between her hands as softly as running water. She holds it to her face. It smells of him. Earthy and clean. She stays there for a few minutes, scarf held to her chest, just trying to slow her breathing against his scent. It's funny, she thinks: it hasn't been coat weather for months.

She looks up, startled, as Smith arrives with Libby.

Tall, broad-shouldered, her sister is as safe a pair of hands as it is possible to be, and Cam can only think of one person she'd rather see more. She stands there on the threshold of the living room, hand still on the doorknob, and says, "Sorry, I—" She looks at Smith, evidently feeling awkward. "I needed to—to grab the sling to carry Polly, when I collect her—sorry . . ." A curl has sprung out from her ponytail, and she grabs at it absentmindedly.

Cam moves toward her. She's standing in a patch of sun in the living room, and molten heat runs down Cam's back as she reaches her, her only other living relative. She feels her shoulders drop several inches. She relaxes into the hug in the way that happens sometimes when surrounded by people who have known you for all of your life.

She doesn't say anything, just makes a funny kind of gesture as she releases Cam, hands spread slightly, like, *What can I say?*

Cam draws a breath in. "They say Luke . . . There's a hostage situation in Bermondsey and they say—he's caught up in it."

Smith stands impassively by the door. Cam darts a look over at her. Is this conversation being observed? Why can't she even give her a moment's privacy?

"What?" Libby says. Her lips blanch. Somewhere deep inside, Cam is touched by Libby's concern for Luke, is ashamed that she is about to obliterate it.

"They say he started it. He's taken three hostages. With a gun." She pauses, then says it again, to affirm it to herself as much as to Libby. "He's got a gun."

"What?" Libby says again, and she says it, this time, bullishly, in the way she only does when truly shocked. Cam is perversely glad to see this surprises her sister as much as her. And something about this, the sunlight, her sister's safe presence in her living room, they make Cam double over, right there in front of Smith.

"Tell me what to do," she says, breathing, panicking, her hands on her knees like an exhausted athlete. "Just tell me what to do." It's a sentence that comes easily from her, the younger to the elder sibling.

"For once I don't know," Libby says, a flash of dark humor in her voice.

She looks like their mother, something Cam finds comforting today. Both of their parents are dead, same as Luke's. Something Cam used to find tragic but, today, she can't quite locate that specific grief amidst the shock.

"I . . ." Cam is, for once, lost for words. "I have to go," she says simply. "To the scene."

"I . . . Jesus, Cam," Libby says, and Cam is unsettled by her seriousness, how changed their relationship feels right now, one that is built on trading stupid texts and unconditional love.

She touches Cam's head, like a vicar. Cam stays there, bent over. Saying nothing. Feeling her sister's hand on her scalp.

"I'll stay here. And I'll get Polly. Please don't worry about anything," Libby says.

"Thank you. I never would've asked you to get Polly if—"

"Don't worry about that. Happy to. I'll stay here until pickup. And sleep here."

"I need to show you—where we keep . . . the bottles, everything," Cam says, straightening up and thinking that, somehow, with a baby, all these things must still keep going. As she thinks of her daughter, she feels a familiar jolt, a kind of yearning, like the notion of going home. It's a simple desire to place her face close to Polly's, to breathe her in, to feel her puffy bottom in her nappy, her chest against Cam's. There is something about it that is like medicine, even on a day like today. Especially on a day like today.

"Yes, do that," Libby says. "It'll be so nice to see her one-on-one," she continues, and Cam is so glad for the kind lie.

9

Niall

With every minute that passes, Deschamps could shoot. But Niall doesn't think that he's going to.

"It's odd we have no ID on the other hostages yet," Niall says as Maidstone's shoes kick up the dust by the side of the road into brown clouds. The warehouse stands in the distance, and Niall begins to sweat. The unknown hostages are troubling him. Usually, they would have been identified by now, reported missing by their families and recognized on the news by their clothes. "It's making me wonder. If all is not as it seems."

"Faces are covered, aren't they?"

"There are all sorts of tells even with covered faces," Niall remarks. "If they're missing, the relatives see the news and recognize what they're wearing. Don't you think it's strange?" he presses. "No one missing them yet. No one phoned it in."

Maidstone pauses. "It is weird," he says. Even he can't deny it. "The force intelligence bureau are on it." He looks at Niall. "What's your first approach going to be?"

"I'm thinking," Niall says.

"Well, think faster. He could take a shot right now."

"He hasn't," Niall says.

Luckily, DS Steven Lambert interrupts them: Niall wants time, is all. He wants to work out what is really happening, and why.

"How's it looking?" Lambert says, arriving from the bar with what looks to Niall like a half pint of cider but that he hopes isn't. "We've visited the wife. Seems very shocked. Nothing suspicious in her behavior so far."

Niall nods. Lambert is a good judge of character but not at when to act. The cordon could be divided into the strategists and what the negotiators would call the knuckle-draggers, and Lambert is most definitely the latter. He likes Metallica, horror movies, and extracting information from people, which he is excellent at. Once, when Lambert was still in uniform and part of an inner cordon, Niall heard him say over the wiring equipment, "We should just kick the fucking door down now and then we could all go home."

"Do you have any idea why no one has claimed the hostages yet?" Niall asks.

"No. It's odd, isn't it? In this day and age . . . with it on the news too. I'd expect people to ring up the second they can't get hold of someone who matches their descriptions."

"I know. And their clothes are obvious." He pauses. "What's Camilla like?"

Lambert turns his mouth down. "Nice," he says. "Scared. Bewildered. Whole body was shivering." He pauses, then adds, "Smart."

"Do you think she's covering for him?"

"No." Lambert places his drink on Niall's table, then puts his hands on his hips, which somehow makes his forearms and biceps look even larger. "But I think that she *would*."

"Why?"

"Loves him," Lambert—terminally single, on all the dating apps— says softly. "It's kind of sad, actually."

"It is."

A woman faces the camera in a TikTok video, holding a handheld mic. She has dark hair and blue eyeshadow.

"So, there's this siege happening in Bermondsey, right. A guy has taken three hostages in a warehouse. However, the news outlets say nobody knows the identity of the hostages. And I'm just thinking—isn't that really creepy?! Here's the footage—do you know them?"

Niall clicks off the video, sighing. The armchair detectives will soon be out in full force.

The silent drills have finally reached the other side of the thick, old warehouse walls, and Niall's been summoned to the scene now to observe it. He's been stripped of his radio, his mobile phone, anything that will make any noise.

"You're not going to like it," Maidstone says grimly to him, shiny shoes bouncing the sunlight around as they walk, and he's right.

The warehouse stands square and sunlit, the inner cordon static around it: a hundred or so armed officers making zero noise or movements, like Niall has walked into a military painting. The police are in riot gear: helmets and shields, MP5s held cross-body.

Maidstone leads Niall across the car park, down a ramp bordered by a small orange brick wall, and to the side of the warehouse that sits in shadow—the sunny side would let too much light in and give them away.

Two officers stand sentry by a tiny hole about a foot off the ground—down low is less noticeable—and they nod to Niall as he arrives.

A recording device is attached to the wall, gazing in through the hole with its electronic eye, and this will be being broadcast in the RVP for people to see, but Niall wants to see it in real time, in the flesh. There's enough room for him to peer in alongside it.

He crouches down. If he so much as sneezes, he will give the game away. Immediately, his knees begin to ache, but he ignores them. They don't have much time. He needs to look, then think, then act.

The hole is less than a centimeter wide, the wall thick, and at first Niall can't make anything out, the view small and imperfect, the inside of the warehouse dim.

But then he sees him, in the fish-eye of the foot-deep cylindrical hole: Deschamps. He is in miniature: at the center of a dollhouse tableau of a horror scene. He is standing in front of his hostages, pacing. Seven steps one way, seven back.

But it's the gun. It's the gun that does it: his arms are as straight as they were on the CCTV, ready to deal with relay, but the barrel is directly and intentionally trained on each of his hostages' heads in turn. The woman then the man then the man. The man then the man then the woman.

Niall's heart descends downward from his chest to his feet. This looks like a person who wants to shoot: he can't deny it. Maidstone will be all over this. This changes everything.

His body language is taut, ready to act, but not especially agitated. No. His shoulders are up, his footsteps quick, now, but he looks . . . what? Niall gets occasional glimpses at Deschamps's features, and he looks . . . well, scared. That's it. He has got scared body language. Furtive and somehow quite meek. Niall assesses the gun. It's aimed but not cocked. But Deschamps's finger is on the trigger.

Niall eventually moves away, and one of the other officers takes his place. Niall touches his shoulder as he leaves. Standing sentry is no easy job.

"I see what you mean," he says in greeting to Maidstone.

"Right," Maidstone replies. "We've got to go in there. He's practically taking aim. Agree?"

Niall hesitates. He *is*. But he's scared. And scared people want a way out. "I *would* like to have a go at contact," he says. He waves his phone containing the email from the coppers searching Camilla Deschamps's house. "I've got some intel, and I've got an idea."

"Are you joking?" Maidstone says coldly. "We said . . . if the gun's pointing at them, we go in." He has sweat patches beginning to form at his armpits and the small of his back.

"No, *you* said that. Body language is made up of more than just a weapon."

"I disagree."

"I think one attempt at contact is reasonable," Niall says, and he can't explain it, but he just doesn't think Deschamps will go through with it. Something about his glossy profile on his wife's agency's website, his books, co-working space—now searched—containing nothing of any note at all, his GP records showing zero concerns.

Despite everything. Despite the captured civilians, the purchased gun, Niall just can't see it. Fear isn't often compatible with malice. Some deep instinct somewhere tells him to wait.

"What's your idea?" Maidstone asks.

Niall pauses. "He likes coffee."

Niall undertook his hostage negotiation course in 2010 in a drafty country manor in Surrey. He was taught—and later mentored—by a DI called Larry who collected old Apple Mac computers. Every weekend he went to some fair or other and bought another, kept them in his loft. It was Larry who taught Niall his cardinal rule: that everybody wants something. Niall—who'd had a harsh Catholic upbringing full of guilt—was pleasantly surprised by the humanity in negotiating, and in Larry.

The first day was lectures that Niall found so dry, he slow-blinked his way through them, texting Viv under the desk to stay awake. The final three days were role-plays: armed fugitives, terrorists, everything. This, Niall needed no distracting from. This was what he was there for.

He sat outside a stately room that an actor playing an armed perpetrator had locked himself inside, and tried to get him to talk with methods he'd only just learned. Open questions, slow and steady, build rapport. *What do you like to do in your spare time? You're having some intense feelings now, but they will pass. Me? I can't wait to get home to my girlfriend and watch* Seinfeld *with her: we're rubbish at modern TV, we are still in the '90s.* Niall always told the truth in these negotiations: he and Viv really do like old telly. Or, rather, they did: When did they last watch reruns together?

They learned about pacing and leading, about priming the suspect to start to agree with you.

They did theory in the mornings, practicals in the afternoons and into the evenings. Eleven-o'clock finishes, sometimes midnight, after which they were encouraged to drink at the bar together, hitting the dorm rooms at three, up again at eight. Niall had at first assumed this was a bonding exercise, but later realized that the instructors' aims were to tire them out. The practical assignments got harder the more exhausted they got, and that's when they transformed: into people who could think fast, people who could hold their emotions at any cost. The only way to learn it was to do it.

On the final day of the course, Niall had walked with Larry to the car park across pale gravel that crunched underfoot and through high autumn winds that rattled leaves. Like every immersive experience, at the end of the week, Niall had felt changed.

"What would be your only tip—if you had to give just one?" Niall had asked him.

Larry had paused for a minute or two as they reached his car—as old as his Apple Mac computers, a 1980s racing-green Mini—then replied: "Above all else, reciprocity: never give up something without getting something in return."

Niall had thought about that a lot in the weeks that followed. But the more experienced he's become, the more he's realized that the rules are just that: rules. And sometimes, they're there to be broken.

And so Niall is going to offer Deschamps some coffee and ask for nothing in return just yet. He's offering it only because he wants Deschamps to know Niall is willing to give, not just take, somebody who wants to listen to him, and to what he likes. His wife says he likes coffee. It's their thing.

"Coffee can be the very beginning of a dialogue," Niall says now to Maidstone. They hurry down the street. "Coffee as an invitation—to open up."

"We are running out of time very quickly here."

Maidstone is the sort of copper who finds doing nothing too anxiety-provoking, would rather take a different kind of risk. He favors action. Niall favors patience, especially with a man who looks too frightened to shoot.

The job of a hostage negotiator, in many ways, is to simply run down the clock. Let the kidnapper become tired, jaded, know that it isn't going anywhere.

Maidstone flicks his gaze to Niall. "You can deliver the coffee," he says. "It's an offer of coffee, left by the door. That's all. You tell him just that. You've got half an hour."

Niall directs an assistant to go and get the coffees. Starbucks, four lattes, four cinnamon swirls. Uncontroversial. Isabella's husband calls in, speaks to Maidstone, says he's heard nothing from Isabella. Says she would have texted if at all possible. Niall closes his eyes for a few moments to think about the hostages. Their fear. Their beating hearts inside that building, relying on Niall to save them.

He heads to stand outside while he waits for the coffees, wishing they'd be faster, and skim-reads a report he's been cc'd on with information Camilla has given, wondering when Maidstone will pull the plug and stop his plans.

Hmm. Interesting: Deschamps has wiped tech and failed to report a crime. See? This is why you wait. You find stuff out with the time that you buy. And all of this points to a man who is hiding something.

He continues scanning the report. *No access to recent internet searches as yet . . . Suspect is not on Prevent list or known to have terrorist associations . . . combing his current contacts now . . . no list of recent iPhone locations visited since April . . .*

Niall stops reading at that and dials the telecoms team who—in situations like this—answers immediately: one of the many reasons Niall likes the dynamism of an unfolding real-time situation.

"Why are Deschamps's locations post-April not available?" he says.

"I know—we're on it," the analyst says. "It's top of my list." It's Claire. He likes her, mum to three, therefore a brilliant multitasker, doesn't miss a trick. "He stopped his phone from location tracking on the twenty-first of April this year. Could just be an iOS update thing."

"I doubt that," Niall says flatly. In his experience, coincidences do not really exist in policing, not as much as people seem to think, anyway. "Twenty-first of April. What time?"

"Just before midnight," Claire says. "Which coincides with an iPhone update while it was charging."

"Or somebody out doing something at close to midnight that they didn't want anybody to know about," Niall replies, wandering into the cool shade of the pub again as he rings off.

Where the fuck are the coffees? Niall grabs a laptop in frustration, begins the research into Deschamps's locations as the clock ticks ever down.

The investigation management system has an old-style display, green text on black, and he's searching for any crime committed on the twenty-first of April this year. It's plausible that something happened involving Deschamps that led him to where he is now: So what was it?

He narrows the search to Putney and Bermondsey, the two places Deschamps is most likely to have been on that day. There's a red spot for every single crime reported, most of them petty. Muggings, burglaries, assaults, batteries: this is London. Niall scrolls and scrolls, hoping that something will jump out at him, scanning for murders, anything very serious, but there isn't one.

He flicks his gaze out of the window to the warehouse. Anything could be happening in there . . .

Concentrate. He goes to the automatic number-plate-recognition database. Somebody in the intelligence bureau will be doing this, but Niall can't resist performing his own search for faster answers.

He types in Deschamps's registration, which pulls up a hundred hits, and Niall scrolls to the twenty-first of April.

Six hits.

22:00: Putney High Street
22:20: an A road in Clapham
22:40: Camberwell
23:05: Whitechapel
23:10: Poplar
23:30: East Ham

Odd place to drive, through Central London—unusual for a native—and so late at night. He can access pictures from each hit, but they're as crappy as ever, near-useless, taken from gantries or poles by the side of the road, dark and grainy. You can barely make out it's a white male, certainly nothing else.

He flicks to the twenty-second of April, but there's nothing, nor on the twenty-third. Nothing comes back on until early May, two weeks later. Now it's the twenty-first of June.

So Deschamps goes out that night but, according to the database, he doesn't come home again.

Maidstone arrives at Niall's table, interrupting him. "Where are your coffees? You're almost fifteen minutes into your allotted thirty."

"Coming," Niall says tightly.

"Growing the beans yourself? We have guns to heads here, Niall."

Niall ignores him. Maidstone is holding a piece of paper: reports of missing persons from this morning in London—sixty of them, with descriptions.

"No matches to our unknown hostages. These guys are both in jeans and white trainers, middle-aged, we think. No one's phoned that in at this time," Maidstone says.

"Lambert was just saying it's weird."

"It is."

Niall points to his screen. "Look at this: Deschamps goes out one night, gets pinged all over the place by ANPR, but then doesn't come home again according to the cameras—and turns off his iPhone location data just before midnight."

"Hang on," Maidstone says. "Let me get the report on the state of the car." He types away on his phone. "See if it's got any evidence on it . . . Finally—your order is arriving," he says, gesturing briefly toward the assistant at the door holding a drinks tray and a brown paper bag. "Get moving. Twelve minutes."

"James."

"What?"

"If he comes to the door to get these, I need an assurance from you that you will do absolutely nothing. And I really mean nothing."

Maidstone shifts on his feet. "That depends what he does."

"I need to be able to give him a cast-iron guarantee that you will do nothing if he gets those coffees. If one of your snipers aims, the rapport will be lost."

"Provided he doesn't aim at us, we won't shoot."

"He may well aim. But I just don't think he'll shoot."

"Hmm."

"Where are the snipers situated?"

He sighs. "One on the door and one on the roof. Do not so much as glance at them, or you will get me sacked and sued."

"I'm not an idiot."

"I'm thinking of the inevitable public inquiry here."

"I need to be able to promise him that we won't harm him. That's my first move always. This coffee needs to be a true offer. Not bait." Niall pauses. "He will think it's bait anyway. I want to prove him wrong as my opening effort."

"Fine," Maidstone says.

"Look at this. Officers have checked the car and the ANPR system for the twenty-first of April. Reg plates got covered in mud, it seems. Stopped pinging the ANPR on the way home. You can see where the mud has crusted off when he starts pinging them again in May.

"At the same time he turned off his location data." Niall's tone slides to frustrated. *Yes*, they need to do the coffees, but they also need to crack the mystery.

"Right," Maidstone says, finally leveling with him. He holds Niall's gaze. "Pretty suspicious."

"It was dry that day," Niall says. It had been dry all spring. "No mud spray."

"Hmm."

Niall picks up the coffees and begins to get moving. He suddenly has an urge to text Viv. She'll be thinking he's staking Deschamps out, wearing riot gear and holding a machine gun. Instead, he's serving coffee.

Niall is ready for contact, holding the coffees and wearing a bulletproof vest.

He is interrupted by Maidstone, talking into his radio. "Engage protocol: negotiator to approach the building in two minutes for first contact."

Niall is wired up. His bulletproof vest is heavy, sticking the sweat to his back.

The coffees are steady in their tray in his hands, probably cold now, but that's policing for you: everything takes longer than you'd think. It tires Niall out, sometimes. Like you have all these instincts and ideas about what to do for the best, and they're culled and culled by red tape and *processes*.

He stares at the warehouse, his gaze narrowing to focus on the black wooden door.

Amazing where the fear goes, when it comes to it: it just disappears. If you do something often enough and don't die, then you somehow think you never will, like when you first learn to drive a car and think about crashing all the time, but within a year are steering with your knees and eating burgers.

The riot squad is ready. The inner cordon is a tidal wave of officers, all waiting, their bodies still, shields up. The road is full of people, but it's utterly silent as Niall walks. Officers part for him like the Red Sea.

The walk takes him one minute. In his ear, Maidstone gives him the all-clear, and Niall stops at the door.

He pauses there, just listening.

He leans closer, clears his throat. "Luke Deschamps?" he says, one ear to the wood. "My name's Niall."

Nothing. He waits five seconds. "I've got a team outside here, with me," he says. "They tell me you've got a gun in there. I wonder if you can help me work out what's going on?"

Nothing.

"Nobody wants to come in. Least of all me. I wanted to talk, really, but first—I heard you like coffee, so I got you some. I'm going to place them—there's four cups here, and some snacks—outside the door. And you have my word that if you open it and pick them up, nobody is going to do a thing. Right?"

On the other side of the door is total silence.

He places them on the ground, on a rubber mat with holes in it, feeling the back of his neck exposed and vulnerable. He straightens up, but still there's nothing.

"Starbucks. Lattes," he says.

Nothing.

"So if you're tired or hungry or thirsty—any of you—they're here. All right?"

He wonders if the hostages can hear his futile attempts.

"So—Luke?" He uses his first name deliberately. "I'll be moving away from the door shortly. And nobody is aiming at you. I don't lie here. So, anything you want to ask me, you know that I'll tell you the truth."

Still nothing. Niall stands back, just waiting, but the coffees go untouched.

"Now, you're in control here, Luke," he says. "You decide whether to stay in or come out."

This is what all hostage-takers want: control, and certainty. Or at least the illusion of it.

Still, Deschamps doesn't speak.

But just as Niall is about to leave, he hears it. A mumble. Nothing more. He raises a hand, knowing the officer with his eyes on Deschamps through the hole will have more idea than him.

A hand is raised back: *Continue.*

Niall steps toward the door again. "Luke—your wife, Camilla, told us you like coffee," he says. "She's very keen to get you home."

At this, he hears something more distinct.

"She's missing you," Niall adds softly.

And there it is: a noise. So quiet, he wonders if his mic and recording device will capture it at all.

"Luke? You OK in there?" Niall asks. "It's tough, isn't it? When we've made decisions we wouldn't ordinarily make. And perhaps for reasons you feel others wouldn't understand."

Now there's silence. Niall turns around. A hand goes up. *Proceed: Deschamps isn't displaying dangerous behavior.*

And that's when he realizes what the noise is: it's sobbing. Deschamps is sobbing.

And this is the bit where it gets easy. The communication channel has opened, and Niall steps into it like it's a fresh running stream that'll carry him away.

"There's always a way out. And it doesn't have to be as bad as you think. I can hear you're crying," he says, and then he starts it: the priming, telling him things he wants him to think. "And I know that's because you care. And I care, too, so let's find a way to get you out of there together."

And then Deschamps speaks.

10

"Niall?" Deschamps calls, a disembodied voice from inside the warehouse.

A rush of relief moves up through Niall like he's a Champagne bottle somebody has just popped.

"Yes?" he says.

Nothing.

"Yes?"

"Can you get a message to somebody?"

"Yes, anything," Niall says, moving even closer to the door. He begins to plant the persuasive seeds. "We've got you coffee here and we're also more than happy to pass a message on." This is the beginning of reciprocity. *Here's what we've done for you . . .*

"OK."

"What would you like to say?"

"Tell my wife . . ."

"Camilla?"

"Yes. Tell my wife that I love her. Her and Polly."

Niall stares at the peeling paint of the door, listens to the silence around him, the desperate, eleventh-hour proclamation of a man trapped in his own actions. What does it mean?

"I will," Niall says. "Anything else you want me to relay?"

Silence.

"Luke? You could come out—tell her yourself. She'd love that."

Nothing.

"Luke?"

Nothing.

Deschamps doesn't speak again. Silence follows silence follows silence. Niall stays there for half an hour, but, just like that, the communication channel is shut off again, the stream run dry.

Furthermore, when Niall gets back to the RVP and watches it all back, he sees Deschamps only held the gun down by his side once: when he sobbed, wiping tears away roughly from his eyes with the back of his hand, like a child. The rest of the time, he kept it trained on his hostages.

"Gold commander thinks we need to go in. And I agree," Maidstone says, arriving by Niall and talking quickly. "Threat to life. He's still aiming at them. He failed to engage. Article Two of the European Convention on Human Rights. These hostages have a right to life, Niall."

Niall heaves a sigh that seems to come right from his trainers. He knows that this is theoretically right, but he doesn't agree on this occasion that their lives are truly under threat. Something in Deschamps is hesitating, and he wants to listen to it. "He said he loves his wife."

Maidstone looks incredulous. "Like a final parting shot? A goodbye? A suicide note?"

Niall appraises Maidstone. How can two people read the same set of circumstances so completely differently? "I took it as a gesture of submission," he says. "He trusted me enough to tell me that. To be his messenger. Of his first message."

"He's issuing goodbyes."

"If we go in, he *will* shoot," Niall says, looking directly at Maidstone. "If we get him talking, he won't. He hasn't shot anyone yet. I want Camilla in."

"We bring the wife in, he says goodbye, he shoots them and then himself. It's Negotiating 101."

Niall stares at his feet, a hand in his hair. He disagrees that negotiating is this simple. The thing is, Deschamps doesn't want to be there. The body language, the sobbing. All of it.

That's what it is. That's what his instincts say.

"At the moment, everyone is alive," Niall says. "We have eyes directly on him. I want to *talk* to him."

"We could hear a shot right now, right this second. We'd get no warning. Bang—and we'd all be done for," Maidstone says. "Our hesitation would not be excusable."

"There are four human beings in there, not three."

Maidstone turns away from Niall, and he thinks he's going to actually storm off like a teenager, but he's looking down at his beeping phone. There are reams and reams of messages on there, emails, calls, texts. Niall ought to be more sympathetic: running a show like this is madly stressful, much worse than being the negotiator.

Maidstone flicks his gaze to Niall. "George Louis has arrived. Wants to be in here." He turns his mouth down, obviously disapproving. "Wants to know what's going on."

"Let him in. It's his wife in there," Niall says. "I'd want to be in the cordon. Wouldn't you?"

"Relatives at the scene is . . . Having Camilla Deschamps here is bad enough," Maidstone says with the tone of voice of an irritated ex-husband.

"He's police. He'll know how to behave himself," Niall supplies.

Maidstone turns away from him, but Niall reaches to touch him on the shoulder. "Besides, we need to interview him anyway. Find out what his wife's like under pressure. If she has any connection to Deschamps. We can speak to him. We might be able to get information."

Maidstone chucks his phone onto a table, where it skitters. "He's on his way. Bring on George. Bring Camilla too. Seems I get no say in the matter. Bring the whole fucking circus."

The Sun

WHO HAS BEEN TAKEN IN THIS ABANDONED WAREHOUSE IN BERMONDSEY?

Three hostages sit on two wooden chairs in a warehouse in Bermondsey. But what is most mysterious about these events isn't the man taking hostages: it's that nobody—not even the police—seems to know who two of the hostages are.

DO YOU KNOW THESE MEN?

Believed to both be six feet tall, broad, white. Look at the CCTV screenshots below and call in if you recognize their clothes.

11

Cam

Cam is numb in the back of a police car, and all she can think is that Polly will be having her lunchtime nap now. She winces as she imagines her in that unfamiliar place. They sleep on floor beds at the nursery, and something about this rattles Cam, like her mind is fixating on this instead of everything else. She tries to pull it back to the mystery at hand.

"I don't understand how you don't have a record of the burglary," she says to Smith. "It *did* happen. It did. He did report it. He said he had a crime number, that you'd look into it."

Smith's sympathy is disappearing, perhaps was faked anyway. "I'm afraid we can only deal with the facts here, Camilla. And he didn't."

"Maybe your systems are faulty."

"Did anybody ever visit? Take fingerprints?" Smith asks with two raised brows in the rearview mirror, and Cam shakes her head no. She didn't think. Was too busy, subsumed into the chaos that is parenting a young child.

"No," Cam replies.

"Is that why you wanted to move? The house on Rightmove?"

"Right," Cam says faintly, thinking how funny it is that sometimes fiction—lies—makes more sense than reality. "Yes."

Smith says nothing, braking softly at some lights. "I'm sorry," she says to Cam, looking at her again. "I know how it feels to be lied to." All Cam sees is those eyes: no other clues in her face. And all she can think is that her husband is a good person. He *is*.

Cam blinks, unsure if Smith means personally or professionally, but doesn't ask. They're on different sides. She's desperate to check out the Rightmove house but can't imagine when she will be able to.

Cam ponders Smith's plain statement, and it is this that makes her truly doubt her husband for the first time. What is it called—Occam's razor? That the simplest explanation is true? Her husband has wiped his laptop. He has lied to her about reporting a crime to the police. He has taken three hostages and held them in a warehouse.

It should be clear that he is not *good*.

They round a corner. They're coming onto the road the warehouse sits on, and the scene is eerie. A fire engine is on the grass verge. The lights of a nearby corner shop are switched off, shut up, a newsstand outside bearing a headline from yesterday. Another police car pulls away in front of them, bumping one wheel at a time off the curb.

The entire street is cordoned off, and the road outside the warehouse is barricaded by police in concentric circles. Cam stares at them, rows and rows of coppers, eventually reaching the building containing the love of her life.

It's a 1970s-style brick building, pitched roof, zero windows anywhere. A single door stands in the exact center, perfunctory, unremarkable, faded black paint become matte with age, like a chalkboard. A single, small boarded-up window in the wood. Cam stares at it, this building with no windows, thinking only one singular thought: that this was planned. Look at it. No glass in the door. No possibility of a witness. Her eyes drift upward to the layers of brick after brick after brick: and no escape.

As she sees it, Cam suddenly and violently misses the before-life. Normality. It's gone forever, her brain helpfully tells her, and she could keel over with the strength of this thought. The notebook she uses to track her reading at work. Her working theory that blue covers sell the most. Her favorite mug for her morning coffee. Her husband's arms around her in bed at night. Gone, all gone.

Smith parks and lets Cam out: her door has a child safety lock on it. The air is hot and close as she stands, and her body unfurls. She's been tense for hours.

She glances across the street. Being led from another police car is a tall, dark-haired police officer in uniform. How strange: two other officers are perhaps restraining him, or at the very least controlling where he goes. He looks exhausted. Their eyes lock, and Cam feels something pass between them. His gaze doesn't leave hers as they walk across the sun-bleached pavements.

"Over here," Smith says, interrupting. She checks something on her phone and leads Cam—much to her surprise—to a pub several hundred yards away. The summer's day continues surreally around them as they walk. Heat rises in fast, jagged shimmers off the tops of police cars, migrainous and sparkling. The air is as sticky as molten butter. Police are milling around in high-vis. It could be a local football derby, a marathon, a festival. Not this, a gruesome crime scene, a negotiation, a place where Cam's communications with her own husband will be listened to with held breaths.

As they walk, she can still feel the man's eyes on her back.

The pub is flat-roofed, a Wetherspoon's with green signage and maybe ten police cars parked in front of it. Three coppers stand sentry, and they stop talking as Cam arrives. Beyond them, toward the warehouse, are the armed police. Cam's eyes keep straying to their automatic rifles. Panicked tears rise up through her throat like boiling water, scorching and painful.

"This is the hostage negotiator," Smith says to Cam, indicating a man just emerging from the double doors, and Cam simply cannot, cannot believe that this is happening. Her sister's voice appears from nowhere in her mind—*An actual fucking hostage negotiator!* she would say.

But nevertheless, he is real, and he is maybe forty-five, tall, lithe—though the sort of person who looks as though he misses meals rather than keeps deliberately in shape—with a closely shaved head and chunky glasses with clear plastic frames. He is carrying a glass of Coke held down by his side and wearing faded jeans, trainers with no socks, and a jaded expression.

He reaches to shake her hand. "Niall," he says. Gravelly voice, Northern Irish. "DCI Niall Thompson."

So he's police. His aim will be to capture her husband. Immediately, Cam begins to distance herself from him.

He has a very direct stare. Gray eyes. As Cam's eyes meet his, she can't help but think of everything of Luke's that she is holding. The crying over the onions. The argument about the MOT. That he shouted at her the other day when his phone rang, then apologized. Ran a hand through his hair, a rattled man. Cam keeps thinking of these things. More and more keep coming to her.

Niall leans against an A-frame chalkboard sign and says, "Let's talk." Cam watches as the authority he has plays out in front of them: the police officers scatter like disturbed insects the second he invites her to speak, leaving them alone in the blazing heat. Niall squints into the sun, then shades his eyes and looks back at her.

"Here's me," he says, passing her a business card. "You need me, day or night, I'm here."

"Thank you," Cam says, taking it. She likes that he's kept her out here, not taken her into a car or interviewing suite somewhere. Just two individuals standing together outside.

Niall pauses, his hands brought together in front of his body. He takes a breath. "I have just made contact with your husband. By the door. I introduced myself to him."

Cam feels her jaw slacken. *Contact.* They've spoken. She had no idea. Nobody told her until now. She wonders if Smith knew. "What did he say?"

Niall looks down at the ground and then back up at her. "He said just one thing," he says, his tone gentle, like he is handling glass with it.

"What?"

"That he loves you. You and Polly." He holds her gaze.

Cam can't speak for a moment. "He said that."

"Yes."

"Only that." Cam can't . . . She can't understand this. Not at all. She's choked up by it. She's angry about it. She's—lost. Just totally lost. What is he doing? What is he thinking?

"That's all he said. *Tell my wife that I love her. Her and Polly.*" Niall removes his glasses, gets a pair of shades out of his pocket, and slides them on. Aviators. They reflect and distort the street around him into technicolored fragments. Suddenly, Cam wonders if he kept her out here so he could easily hide his eyes, his expression. His innermost thoughts.

And she thought she might find his contact with Luke reassuring, but she doesn't. "Did everyone hear?" she adds, and she doesn't know why, only that it feels vaguely unsettling to know that he shouted that out, and that the only people who heard him were police.

"Just me," Niall says, which Cam suspects is a lie.

"Was it some sort of goodbye?" Cam says, fear firing up through her.

Niall seems to appraise her, silent. "Do you think that sounds like a farewell, or an invitation to talk to you?"

"If he wanted to talk to me, I think he would ask," Cam says honestly. "He's a direct sort of person."

"*Is* he."

"Usually."

"I think getting you on the line will be really helpful, given everything."

Cam stares down at her feet. The grass verges are a faded wheatgrass color against the pavement, their edges a fringed old rug. "Niall. Is there a chance he isn't doing this of his own free will? Like—that he's been told to?"

Niall raises his eyebrows, his features arranged into the sort of face you'd make at a dinner party if you met someone who did an interesting job. Mild intrigue. "Let's try and get to the truth together. I'm under pressure to get you on the phone. We don't have much time."

"OK," Cam says in a small voice.

"I have some questions: What sort of person is Luke?" he asks. And Cam's glad of this. Niall has none of Lambert's fact-finding. He is all about character.

He brushes a hand over his stubble, and Cam finds herself wondering the same things about him: Does he have a wife? Kids? How many hostage situations has he ended? Has he ever killed in order to end them? The last question circles in Cam's mind like water going down a drain, around and around and around.

"Happy," Cam says definitively. She finds it easy to describe Luke. "Enjoys his life. Doesn't sweat the small stuff." As she says this last phrase, she wonders if it is quite true now. That is certainly the man she fell in love with. But is it the man who exists today, who shouts about MOTs? And, if not, when did the change truly begin? Was it just this past week or two, or has it been longer?

Tell my wife that I love her.

Niall gestures for her to follow him into the pub. They sit at a table he leads her to that is scattered with torn beer mats. He takes his sunglasses off. Underneath, his eyes look pale and raw.

"Ghostwriter is interesting. He didn't want the public profile?"

Cam blinks. She'd never thought of it like that. "No, I think he just likes writing and researching. Was a journalist. It's . . . it's an easy job. Not great money, but not bad either. You can work for yourself, on your own time. That appeals to him."

"Why?"

"He . . . he likes to do what he wants to do, when he wants to do it."

Behind Niall, two officers begin working on his phone, attaching a recording device. Cam can't stop watching them, the intricate motions of their fingers, the reality of this situation rushing toward her. They're going to call him and try to negotiate. And, if he won't . . .

"Come on, Niall," one of them says to him. "Two minutes."

He ignores them. "Interesting. You think it could be connected to this?"

"How?"

"I don't know. You tell me."

"I don't know."

"I need to know everything he's worked on lately."

Cam pauses. She can't stop thinking about Luke shouting that he loved her. What does it mean? Is this gruesome act somehow dedicated to her? Is he on the brink? About to do something? Is he *sorry*?

"He has an MP and an actor. Then in the past, he's published a book about a Premier League team, a singer, a tennis player, and a biography of a judge."

"A judge?"

"Yes, a district judge."

"Any controversies? Name?" he says.

"I mean—how could writing about a judge two years ago lead to . . ." Cam says, making a hopeless gesture.

"I don't know. But we will find out." He pauses, then says: "You googled arguing with your husband," he says softly, and holds his hands up. "I don't lie, and the Met have checked your Google account's search history. They might not tell you—but I will. It was on your work PC."

"Oh," Cam says, stunned. Those open tabs. "No—I . . . We'd bickered about the night wakes, that's all. Normal post-baby stuff . . . I was looking for reassurance," she says. "That other couples do that too." Her thoughts begin to race about everything she hasn't told them. Could they possibly know? Arrest her too?

"All right then," he says, and it's loaded, but she doesn't speak. "Look. We need to get you on the phone. But does the twenty-first of April mean anything to you?" He begins to clean his glasses on the bottom of his T-shirt.

"Why?"

"Your husband went somewhere into Central London. Around ten, eleven at night. Turned off his location data at that point."

Cam stares at her hands resting on the table, racking her brain. "We had to drive Polly around sometimes, to get her to sleep," she'd said. "We went through a bit of a phase of it. Maybe it was that." And she's so glad that she can provide a credible explanation for this one tiny thing. But it isn't, is it? That fuel bill . . . he'd filled the car up. Twice. He'd come home one night in the spring, and tossed and turned in bed. Was tearful, later, over the onions.

"Ah, the old car nap," Niall says. "So why would he turn his location data off?" As he asks this, he waves away a non-uniformed officer who seems to be hurrying him.

"I don't know? He didn't tell me that he had," Cam says. But all she is thinking about is that something happened to her husband on April 21. Something that made him drive a long way, and cover things up . . . that later made him cry. But what?

She looks at Niall. But she can't tell him. She can't.

"Just to be clear . . ." he says, trying to hold her gaze again, "it was a normal trip out?"

"Yes. As far as I know. I don't remember it exactly."

Somebody outside shuts the doors of the pub. Without the breeze it's too hot. Cam can feel sweat forming along her hairline, can smell stale beer slowly cooking in the carpets.

"What's he like under stress?"

"Doesn't get stressed," Cam says. It's a lie, but it wasn't always. He once got let go from a newspaper and, after receiving the email, opened a Mars Bar with his teeth and said, "Well, that's their loss."

Niall pauses, evidently weighing up how to proceed, then says, "I have met a lot of people through my work and have never known a single one who doesn't get stressed."

"He doesn't. Not really."

"No recent moments of being quick to anger?"

"No."

"No temper, you say?" he asks again and, clearly, he's getting at something here, but Cam's chosen her line.

"No temper," she lies. Because she knows that, when they go in, if they know he is angry, they will be more likely to kill him.

"Right, Cam," Niall says. "Time's against us because the entry team want to go in, as you may have gathered. I'm trying to make contact to avoid that. We have a number for the warehouse, but we haven't called it yet. You get one shot in these situations, and we wanted our ticket with us: you."

"Do you expect him to answer the phone?" Cam is unable to stop herself asking.

Niall spreads his hands in front of him, and then deflects. "Do you?"

She thinks about how much her husband loves to communicate. Usually. They talk much more than other couples, often about total rubbish. And now, nothing. One sentence uttered to Niall. Nothing else.

"He didn't answer me calling his mobile."

"If he's smart, he will answer the landline."

"He is smart," Cam says automatically. "And he likes to talk," she adds quietly.

"Well, then," he says lightly. He looks at her, holds her gaze for a few seconds.

"What if he does? Answer?" Cam says.

Niall looks at the table, then back up at her. "Surrender," he says, "is the only acceptable resolution. So—we work toward that."

Cam stares at the warehouse, just visible through the pub windows. She surveys the walls, Luke just inside, she outside, separated only by molecules of brick and air, nothing more, but a million ideological miles apart. It is absurd to Cam that they can't just go in, unplanned. The way her husband has been available to her for their entire marriage.

"I don't know why he'd do that," she says. "I don't know anything. He's a good person. If he doesn't answer the phone," Cam gabbles, "surely *I* could go in? He wouldn't shoot *me*?"

This is the first time Niall's eyes flash with any kind of emotion, though he covers it up well. "Did you think he'd do any of this?" he says mildly while the sand continues to run down the hourglass.

God, she just wants to do it now. Go in. End this.

Evidently, Niall can read a witness, because he says, "Right, let's do it," seeming to make a decision and sitting up straighter. "We offer you up, and we hope in return—well, we hope for reciprocity, always."

"The release of a hostage," Cam says in understanding. Of course: the police care primarily about the hostages—and about arresting her husband. And she's here to assist with that. Nothing more.

"Exactly," Niall says smoothly. "Let's run through a script of what you say if he answers."

"*When* he answers," Cam says.

"If he answers," Niall replies. "The cardinal rule: you don't lie to him.

If he asks if you're with police, you say yes. If he asks if he will be arrested, you say you don't know."

"Right."

"But don't disclose anything you don't need to."

"But—what should I say?"

Niall moves his phone out of the way and rests his hands, palms up, on the table. "My entire aim is to give him a way out," he says. "So that should be yours too. What does a way out look like for him?"

"I . . ." Cam says, thinking that she is not equipped to answer this, to make this call. She thinks for a few seconds about Luke, about herself, about their marriage.

"I suppose that I will always love him," she says eventually, her voice gloopy with un-cried tears. "That Polly will too. That he's her father. That he can't leave us."

"Exactly. Tell him that. Tell him it's OK to come out. Tell him he hasn't killed anybody yet."

After this, like two people about to jump from a plane, he looks at her, checks she's OK, checks the Met are ready, puts an earpiece in, and then presses Call.

The tinny ring blares out into the pub around them. Two rings. Cam can just imagine him about to answer. Four. His warm voice, his jovial tone. The explanation, whatever it is. Six.

Eight. By ten, Cam knows Luke isn't going to answer.

Only, Niall holds a hand up, then, and says, "We don't hang up. Not yet."

Twelve. Fourteen.

Sixteen.

And Niall was right to wait, because that's when somebody answers.

But it isn't Luke.

12

Niall

Niall's brain works quickly. It isn't Deschamps; it isn't a man at all. Therefore, it is Isabella Louis.

And her police-officer husband is somewhere on the scene.

Shit.

"Hello?" she says again, her voice a whisper.

Camilla's eyes are saucers, staring at the phone, then up at Niall. He needs to get her away from it. He doesn't have clearance for her to speak to anybody except Luke. She could jeopardize the whole thing: relatives often act in unpredictable ways.

And he needs to make sure Isabella's husband, George, isn't anywhere nearby either.

He holds a hand up to a uniformed officer and gestures for him to remove Camilla, feeling regret at her hurt and dumbfounded expression. She looks a lot like young Viv: big eyes, lots of hair, and Niall feels a sympathetic lurch in his gut, but, nevertheless, he turns away from her, needing to concentrate.

Niall scans the RVP for George Louis, but he isn't here.

"Hello, Isabella," Niall says into the phone while the officer removes Camilla. Only ten seconds or so have gone by. He hopes it's not been too long.

Nothing. No response, but the call is still connected.

"Isabella?" Niall says into the phone. "I know you must be scared, but—I need you to talk to me, if you can."

Nothing.

Maidstone approaches Niall and sits down too close to him, clearly unable to help himself, and begins making gestures. Niall waves him away.

"If you can't talk for fear, please tap the handset three times," he says.

More silence at the end of the phone. Niall strains to listen. Nothing. Maidstone drums his fingers on the desk. Niall's whole body is full of adrenaline.

He turns and watches the police: hunched over laptops, fingers to ears. At any moment, Deschamps might grab for the phone. Niall feels a stab of something, guilt maybe, that he's always pretending to be just one man, talking softly to criminals or victims, when really there's a whole team of police there. A tactical commander listening to every word.

He turns again, trying to ignore his audience, the pressure he's under, the resources being directed at this exchange. He gazes out of the window toward where his call is coming from. Armed police surround the warehouse like an ugly gray swarm. The warehouse sits there, impassive in the light.

Maidstone points to the phone. *Isabella?* he mouths, and Niall nods, but he's irritated. He can't concentrate under this scrutiny.

On the line, Niall can hear nothing. No breathing, no shouting, nothing. "In case you didn't hear, it's three taps, if you can't speak," he says.

Silence. Niall turns to look at the phone, to check it's still connected, and as he does so, he hears them. Three delicate taps. Three scared taps.

"All right, Isabella. I heard those," he says, holding a hand in the air.

Maidstone is scribbling on a piece of paper. *Ask her if she'll put LD on.* Niall shakes his head.

Maidstone gestures to Niall, but Niall can't work out what he's trying to say and right now, he needs to be concentrating. He stands up.

"If you are Isabella, this time, tap twice," he says.

Two taps.

Shit. He needs to concentrate. He strides away from Maidstone, who ought to know better than to interrupt him at a crucial moment like this.

"Is Deschamps near you? Two taps for yes." Two taps.

Maidstone rises to his feet, and so Niall steps toward the open pub doors, irritated.

Maidstone catches his eye, looking reproachful, but Niall ignores him. He's just as able to take a call outside as he is in the official RVP.

Niall's breath is held. Deschamps could be right behind her. He could be forcing her to take the call. He could have his pistol in the small of her back. And all Niall has is taps.

Niall looks up at the sky. Cerulean blue, a perfect summer's day. His forehead is sweating as he decides what to do next.

He's gazing down the road, thinking, when he hears it: running footsteps. A commotion of some kind behind him. He whirls around, a finger in his ear, closely listening to Isabella, and stares. And there he is: a uniformed officer, low rank, dark hair and eyes, hands outstretched. It's George Louis, being flanked by two police officers, trying to run toward Niall.

"That's my wife!" he shouts. "That's my wife on the phone! I heard you say her name as you came outside!"

Niall looks at him in shock and has a strange, prescient feeling that this has been his first mistake. They should've kept him away. It was fucking stupid to allow him to come to the scene, a loose cannon. Shit, shit, shit.

"That's my wife! Let me in there!" he cries, and Niall closes his eyes. He shouldn't have taken the call outside.

He gestures for the coppers to control him, to hush him up. They cover his mouth and he strains against them, pulling at their hands. His eyes are round with shock and fear. Niall looks at him for a second, and suddenly he doesn't see a copper: he sees a scared husband, struggling against the authorities, his own colleagues, as they try to contain him and keep him safe.

Eventually, to Niall's horror, he manages to wrench the officer's hand from his mouth. "That's my wife!" he bellows at full volume. "If you're listening, hostage-taker, we're going to come in and we're going to fucking kill you!"

Every single hair on Niall's back and neck rises up. He stays on the line but turns to stare at the warehouse. There is no way Deschamps didn't hear that down the line.

Within seconds, there is a movement at the door to the warehouse. The slightest thing. Something you could miss but that nobody will.

Everybody in the vicinity sees it and holds their breath. It's silent. George is contained. Tens of the police crouching diligently around the warehouse aim their guns toward the door. Radios crackle, but otherwise, the air is quiet and still and blue with police lights, like they're deep in the ocean.

The door moves again.

And then.

In a single, fluid, silent motion, the armed police move forward like army troops advancing at war. Niall stands there, unarmed, in the center of it, the phone still in his hand, just watching the door open slowly, slowly, slowly. The police cock their guns with a collective crack as a figure emerges, all in black, and Niall unconsciously braces himself for gunfire.

13

——

It's Isabella and Isabella alone, emerging gracefully like a ballerina from the dark wings of backstage and into the spotlight.

She has a black bag over her head. She can't see, so moves this way and that, her hands tied behind her back. She emerges onto the police-blue street in the silence. She thrashes, trying to remove the hood by bending over.

An officer moves a torch over her even though it's bright sunlight, looking for weapons. A voice booms out from a police megaphone, tinny and distorted, asking her to stop, to raise her hands. She halts, still blanched in light, and someone approaches and unties her hands, freeing her arms, which spread out, a Christ the Redeemer in the sun. And for just a few, strange seconds, Niall feels as if this moment is only for him.

He moves toward her. He will be authorized to do so: his bulletproof vest is still on; he's the hostage negotiator, after all, and she his first released hostage.

Niall takes five steps, ten, and then he's right next to her. Two officers move out of the way to allow him to get near to her.

A copper pats her down, then removes her hood and steps away, leaving Isabella and Niall alone together. He looks down at her. She has dark hair, is of slight build. Slim wrists and shoulders. She has large hoop earrings in, and something about this makes Niall feel a wave of sympathy for her that is almost painful. How she must have put them in that morning, optimistic, George nearby; maybe he likes it when she wears those ...

She survived, but she will never be the same again. That's the reality.

PTSD, claustrophobia, anxiety, flashbacks. These are what she may experience. Niall forgets this, sometimes, at the height of negotiations, but at the end of every siege he remembers there is always damage done, even to the living. Especially to the living.

"It was me who took your call. Your husband is here waiting. You're safe," Niall says to her. "You're safe now."

"He let me go," she says, eyes wet. "He said he would let me go. He knew I was just caught up in it . . . accidentally, because we own the building."

Niall nods his head. Makes sense. His shoulders drop in relief, relief at having a hostage released. "Do you know anything about the other hostages?" he is unable to stop himself asking.

Isabella doesn't respond immediately. Her hair is staticky and messy from the hood, which has drifted to the floor like a popped balloon, and she pulls her hands to her chest, then her cheeks, then leans right into Niall and sobs.

His muscles untense as he holds her. Maybe they got away with it. Maybe he was correct to ask for more time, to wait, to have Camilla come to the scene. Maybe Deschamps will release the others next.

They stay like that for several minutes, Niall trying to slow her breathing by slowing his.

And just as he's thinking that they will be OK, he hears them.

Two gunshots.

The ones that, ultimately, will end his career. They go off, loud and true, right behind him like a fireworks display that he can't see, only hear.

14

Cam

Cam is waiting on a verge by the side of the road, with two police officers as her keepers. She goes someplace else. All she can think about, see, and hear is Luke, on slow, in her mind. A montage plays out for her as her eyes glaze and she listens to the silence of what might be his own denouement. Luke at a publishing-prize ceremony with her last summer, a man who doesn't care for literary fiction but likes an outing, saying to her, "I don't even know which book this is!" Luke mainlining chocolates last Christmas with her, not moving for hours, turning to her and saying he might just wet himself rather than get up, he was so comfortable. Luke in the labor ward, wet-eyed and quiet and gazing at Polly.

Maybe her mind already knew it was going to happen, and immersed her in these memories, because she hears them while she stands on the roadside in the warm summer air.

The gunshots that everyone has always known would come.

Two gunshots and two echoes, and Luke pops clean from her mind.

She waits for a moment in the quiet calm, the same way you know you will feel pain right after you injure yourself, but it takes several seconds to come. This time, she almost thinks that it won't.

But of course it does. And here it is, a wave of awful closure, of fear. The question of whether he was the shooter or the victim. She thinks she's going to collapse.

Neither of the police react at all. Cam's legs are trembling with adrenaline, jiggling uncontrollably. Gunshots. Gunshots.

"What was that?" she asks needlessly, a hand to her mouth. Her jaw is quivering and she begins to chatter her teeth against her fingertips.

"We'll let you know as soon as we know anything," one of the officers replies.

One of their radios crackles, but no words are said.

Cam stares at the lit-up warehouse, at the drone and helicopter above it, at the hundreds of police around it. But wait. What's that . . . ?

As she watches, it becomes clearer. There's something happening on the roof.

She squints, trying to look, but knowing that if she makes it obvious the police may move her.

The roof is so far away, so high up, they look like moving figurines, but they are yet more police in riot gear, running, shouting, perhaps searching. Against her own moral code, Cam hopes that they're searching for her husband, and that he got away, that he wasn't shot. Against all the things she now knows. That he left this morning, leaving only a shitty, cryptic note. That he went to that warehouse. That he did all this.

15

Niall

The scene erupts into chaos.

"Armed officers in!" Maidstone yells into a radio, which blares out onto everybody's individual radio. "Two shots have been fired. Suspect moved everyone away from the hole in the wall. We didn't see it play out."

Niall whips around, staring at the black door, still banging slightly in the breeze. His head is full of questions he has no time to answer.

He releases Isabella, who stumbles toward a copper who leads her to her husband, and Niall turns to head inside. He ought to arm himself, get some sort of clearance, but the situation has disintegrated into a free-for-all. Police flood into the warehouse like a backfilling tide, and Niall follows, too, not thinking. Not allowing himself to think.

The warehouse is cool inside, a perfume of wet stone and musk, lit by a single fluorescent bulb high above. Niall watches the police scatter, shouting, but he moves slowly, his eyes everywhere. Where is Deschamps? He could have his gun trained on Niall right now. And who'd you want to kill next more than the negotiator?

He creeps slowly forward, watching the police in their riot gear.

Niall isn't looking for the bodies. He intends to find the shooter instead. And how could it not be Deschamps? He had the gun. Niall must find him, because it stops him from looking at the reality.

He needs to find the man who fired the shots despite Niall's instincts that he wasn't going to. The man whom Niall bought time for. Incorrectly, as it turns out. He has that nagging feeling people get when they know something enormous has happened to them but they're not yet ready to fully turn and look right at it.

He needs to find Deschamps and bring him to justice.

His gaze travels upward to the door to the roof. Several police are already going up, the others spreading out in the vast warehouse, and Niall decides to follow them, takes the stairs two at a time.

Sixteen internal steps, one fire-escape door, and soon he is out on a staircase that accesses only the roof. The metal is white hot from the sun and momentarily blinding. His feet pound on the stairs, going up, up, up, the ground far below visible through the grating, the view shifting vertiginously.

The roof is flat and still and quiet, the only noise crackling police radios. Niall guesses an old metal fire escape used to be attached to the building but no longer is.

The roof covering is made of some sort of carbon fiber, flush to the edges, new, bordered by metal railings. There are a couple of extractor fans, old and rusted, but nothing more, and neither of them large enough to hide Deschamps.

His radio blares: "Suspect not in warehouse. He is of unknown whereabouts."

Niall gazes frantically around the roof. If Deschamps is up here, he wouldn't have been able to get down again without being seen.

"You shouldn't be here!" one of the armed officers yells at him from behind a helmet, but Niall ignores him. Where is he? The building is surrounded. The warehouse has one door. On the radio, nobody has located Deschamps. And he isn't on the roof.

Where can he possibly be?

Niall spins in a slow circle, just looking.

There were definitely only two shots. He's sure of that.

Below, Bermondsey glistens in the late-afternoon sun. Beyond that, Southwark, the park just visible, a square knitted patch of dried yellow grass. Police disperse on the roof, heading to the edges, staring downward, but there's nothing. There's no one. No Deschamps. And no bodies yet.

Niall's radio blares again.

"Confirmed hostages' bodies found. Two of them—one bullet wound each to their temples. He'd attempted to quickly hide them—back of the warehouse, behind some shelves, under some tarpaulin."

Niall's head hits his chest.

So Deschamps killed them, then. He knew it, but he didn't want to know it, all at once.

He can't breathe. He looks at the horizon, tries to calm himself, but he can't.

Those gunshots.

Two souls, leaving the Earth.

And this is on Niall. He insisted they wait. He insisted they negotiate. He insisted George Louis be allowed to come, that Camilla be brought down. He bought and he bought and he bought time on credit, in overdrafts, thinking he'd be able to pay it back with interest in talk.

But he couldn't.

Look what happened.

He stares down at the street, at the police vehicles, at the solemnity with which his colleagues have begun to walk.

He is responsible for this mess.

He wants to lie down right here, forehead to the concrete, and sob. Instead, he speaks into his radio. "Status of suspect?"

"Still at large."

Niall walks a slow, ashamed loop of the roof while the police disperse downstairs. He doesn't know what else to do. He knows that, after this, there will be inquests and inquiries and questions asked. He will have to justify his decisions in open court, in police stations, in professional standards offices. And he can't. They are based on two intangible things: instincts and experience. He can explain neither.

He waves a hand and lets it flap by his side, trying to stay mindful. For now, he is here.

This is now a homicide investigation. It's not what he does—he isn't needed. He tells himself he can go home to Viv, to discover an unknown stray animal in their kitchen, to let her stories and her humor wash over him. That this is only work, but he doesn't believe it.

His phone rings: it's Maidstone.

"He's escaped," Maidstone says.

"How?" Niall says into the phone, thinking that this really is the end for his career now. A suspect at large. Two men dead. Maidstone will be questioned; Niall will be questioned. And, slowly, everybody will distance themselves from him and turn against him. Niall has seen this happen countless times to coppers who have had the audacity to make a human error.

"Isabella told us that right at the back of the warehouse is a service lift no one knew about—beyond the view we had of him, not on the plans. It leads from the ground floor to an underground car park shared by an office block three doors down that we also had no idea about. We have surrounded the wider area."

"How did he know about it?"

"Isabella has just admitted in questioning—he said he would let her go if she gave him an escape route. And she did. Her husband didn't know about it. She was the manager of their building."

Ah. Of course. That makes complete and total sense. She saved herself, knowing it might damn the others, and escaped. And who wouldn't do that? He can't blame her.

Niall's voice is too thick to speak back, lined with his tears and sadness. Deschamps's and Isabella's quid pro quo. All the while Niall was waiting like an idiot.

How could he have got it so wrong? He *never* gets it wrong. His instincts are king, and they have never let him down.

Until now.

London sprawls beneath him. Old London, grotty railway arches and ancient buildings, and new London, big, clean, silver skyscrapers glinting in the sun.

So—what? Is he dogmatic? Unable to listen to others? Admit that he's wrong? Did he cause this? Or was it just George, his outburst—bad luck? Would Deschamps have shot without it?

He focuses his gaze down on the street, at the detritus of everything left.

And then he sees her; there she is, a little way down the street, flanked by two officers, looking right up at him on the roof: Camilla Deschamps.

And even though she is in miniature, he feels their eyes lock, and he thinks, *I am going to find your husband. And I am going to bring him to justice.*

And make him pay.

When he arrives home that night, much, much later, Viv has packed and taken two suitcases, left him a note, saying she can't do it anymore, can't be married to him, to somebody who always puts work first.

PS, the note goes on. *It was my birthday today.*

17

Cam

Ten minutes go by, fifteen, as the afternoon sun begins its descent from up high, Cam just watching the roof clear and the warehouse suck up the police and not spit them back out again, the two officers near her not saying a word, or removing her, just doing nothing.

It's sixteen minutes after the shots that Cam sees them. Her body chills as she notices. The crawl of them. The slow-moving non-urgency.

Forensic scene-of-crime officers, all in white, like something from a silent movie.

And then, several moments later, an ambulance, but there's no emergency contained within it.

It's the only vehicle around without its blue lights on.

Cam can only hope it's not for her husband.

18

If you think of anywhere your husband is likely to head, call," Lambert says, his parting shot outside Scotland Yard, where Cam's been held practically all night, answering question after question about her husband, who is now—officially, thank God, thank God?—on the run.

"I will," Cam says, for perhaps the tenth time. "I don't know where he would go," she adds, even though she's said this too. She's given them his friends, his co-working space. She has nothing left. She'd give it if she knew it: she's too exhausted to care.

But she can't deny she's relieved: criminal or not, her husband is alive, and Cam feels a weird kind of shameful relief at this.

The police offer her a lift from a PCSO, but she tells them she wants to walk. They ask her several times, but she only repeats this, thinking that she is not going to go home. Her whole body craves holding her daughter, but she must head to Lewisham. To the street containing the Rightmove property.

It's just after three thirty in the morning, and the air is dark and soupy, the world outside the Uber silent. The sky slowly lightens beyond the car as she travels. It's been night for what feels like only a few hours, the way it is in June. And Cam watches the sky and thinks how somewhere the answer is out there, as obvious as the dawn itself, but still hidden in night.

She winds the window down and it's cooler as they cross the river. The tang of the salt and brine of the water. The air turns from gray to white, a new day beginning.

They arrive at Lewisham. It's easy to find the street, and on that, the exact house she has memorized from Rightmove: a white semi-detached building with an untidy garden and several burglar alarms above the door.

Cam hesitates outside, and the cool air goose-fleshes her skin: she is dressed for a day at the office, not an illegal night-time venture. A security light flashes on, blanching her view, and she stands in its beam, wondering if he is here, waiting for her. It clicks off, then on again when she moves, and she wonders if lights like this will remind her of the warehouse forever. Eventually, a male figure comes to the window. Cam holds her breath, looking up. The address, held deep in an app. Was it for her? Is he here? Her husband, the fugitive?

19

The figure stares down at her for a few seconds. No. It isn't her husband. She's never seen him before. Tall and pale, with gingery hair. After a moment, he opens the window. "What?" he calls. Disappointment throbs through her.

"I'm sorry—I'm . . . I'm looking for my husband," she says.

"What? You've woken me up."

"Luke?" she calls up plaintively. "He had your address. I . . ." she says, feeling pathetic. The Uber driver turns off his engine and looks out curiously at them.

"Piss off, or I'll call the police," he calls back down, closing the window—and her last bit of hope—with a bang.

"Please," she says. "I . . ."

The window opens again, and slams shut even harder. The owner of the house is clear, and the last thing she wants is police contact. But why was this stranger so easy to wake? Was he waiting?

She waits for a minute longer, bewildered, then instructs the Uber to take her home, the leather of the seat cold against her legs. She doesn't think at all on the way home, for perhaps the first time in her entire life. Not a single thought. She keeps them at bay, an ugly dam with water behind it swelling and building.

As she arrives, she sees a police car, two cars back, following her. Cam blushes with shame. Somehow, her last, desperate act being witnessed by the authorities makes it worse. She wonders if they will question her over it or leave it: accept that she has as little idea as them where her husband may be.

She lets herself in her front door, walks straight up to the kitchen, turns off the light, and closes the door, her eyeballs burning in the early-morning dimness. She needs to be completely alone to think, and not be witnessed, not by her sister, not by the police outside, her daughter, not even by the lights above her.

The house must have been nothing. Research for a book. Something accidental.

Nothing.

No clue. No explanation waiting for her.

That house in Lewisham was a symbol of hope on the dawn horizon. And now.

He isn't hiding out. He didn't leave Rightmove as a clue. A stranger lives there. There is no narrative payoff here. No denouement, only confusion.

Well, now. She must face the truth.

My husband is a murderer. She forces herself to think this thought over and over, as though she will burst through some pain barrier and accept it. My husband is a murderer.

She sinks down against the counters to sit on the floor, head lolling backward against a cupboard full of their possessions that were earlier ransacked by the police. Glasses they bought from IKEA. Mugs exchanged for birthdays and Christmases. Polly's sippy cups that, only yesterday, Cam was worried she wasn't using yet.

But Cam can't even hide from the daylight. The very early morning sun lights the appliances silver. The fridge, the range, the toaster. Her husband used these appliances with her until just recently, and now he is a murderer.

She clutches at the skin on her stomach, at her hair. She wants to scream at her broken heart to stop beating. He's a killer.

Cam's head tilts forward onto her knees and she tries to cry, but she can't. She is disgusting. A fool. A scorned woman. There are no tears available. She has hardened, like clay, the moisture dried out of her into cynicism.

She closes her eyes, scrunches them up, but it's futile. She stays there for an age, not crying, not thinking, not doing anything except staring at the grayscale kitchen around her and thinking of standing outside that Lewisham house, alone and abandoned by her husband.

After who-knows-how-long, she walks into the living room.

She checks her phone. She dimly registers that Penguin has offered a six-figure sum in a two-book deal for Adam's novel that she doesn't even open beyond the preview.

She ignores everyone, looks at her texts from yesterday with Luke, from before they went to the café, from before before-before.

CAM: *Are you working very hard or can you have Polly while I have a five minute peaceful wee?!*
LUKE: *Absolutely! Hang on!*
CAM: *It was a good wee. Thank you.*
LUKE: *xx*

But then she spies the volume of other texts she's had. Over sixty.

HOLLY: *OMG—just seen the news. Are you OK?*

STUART: *Don't worry about work. All here if you need us.*

There are more. She becomes quickly overwhelmed by them. They don't make sense to her, don't seem to mean anything. Friend after friend after friend and relatives and distant acquaintances. Holly: her closest friend, a former commissioning editor, now freelance, saying she's seen the news. A text Cam herself might send but is furious at receiving.

The police must have told the media his name. Cam blinks dumbly on the sofa.

So everyone knows. Everyone knows what he's done.

How can she go on? She holds her phone to her chest. How can she? She checks BBC News. There's a live feed.

15:50 Siege ends in dramatic shooting
15:55 Plea for information: Suspect at large and dangerous named as Luke Deschamps

17:01 RECAP: How did we get here?
18:10 BREAKING: Last note left by criminal husband seen by press

Cam can't help but open the final item, and there it is. Her private communication, his last words to her, beamed as large as if projected onto the night sky for all to see. Insult added to injury after injury.

"It's been so lovely with you both" is the cryptic message left from husband to bewildered wife the morning he chose to take three hostages in a siege that gripped London, it reads. Cam clicks off it in disgust. How could they? It might as well be a diary entry. Her cheeks heat with shame. Everyone will have read it. Everyone will know.

#LondonSiege is the top trending topic on Twitter.

Absolutely disgusting, innocent people taken, one user has written.

They should have just gone in and blown him up—terrorists are terror-ists, another comment says. Cam's chest seems to expand and contract, a cartoon heart beating in shock.

Did anyone see THE NOTE he left his wife? WTF?? #LondonSiege

She flips the phone facedown onto the sofa, where it creates a pale white rim of light, and sits forward, unable to bear it.

She wanders through her house. Their belongings are disturbed, put together but not quite right, which makes Cam feel uneasy, like when a hotel room has been cleaned without your knowing.

The search has been thorough, most things looked through. Cam leafs listlessly through a notepad on the hall table, at the John le Carré novel he was reading, at their calendar hanging on the wall in the kitchen. Nothing. No clues left remaining. What did she expect?

She pads downstairs again and into the nursery, where Polly is sleep-ing. On her stomach, bottom in the air, blond hair mussed all over the place like whipped meringues. Cam traces a finger down her cheek, just once, thinking that this is how. This is how she goes on. *Your father is a murderer*, Cam thinks. *Poor, poor you. Worse off than me.*

She picks her up, unable to resist, her daughter a warm, sweet-scented, heavy sack. She still has that newborn scrunch, at times: legs held up near her body like a frog; and Cam presses her baby to her abdomen, the way she grew her, nuzzles her nose into her daughter's neck.

Eventually, she puts her down and walks to her own room, where Libby is sleeping too. She watches her sister for just a few seconds, her face at rest, then gets on the bed and lies down the wrong way, fully clothed. She should sleep, and maybe she will, right here in her jeans. She begins to slow blink. She's alone now. Untethered. Suddenly, she craves the siege, the hostage negotiator, the structure of it. What is she supposed to do now?

Libby must feel her presence because she stirs, opening her eyes.

"Hi," she says softly. The dawn has the bedroom in gray fuzz.

"Hi," Cam says.

Libby sits up. Next to her, on her pillow, Polly's baby monitor whirrs softly. Something about it turns Cam's heart over. How hard this would have been for her sister, yet she did it anyway, to help her.

Cam lies there on her back, looking down her body at her sister, topping and tailing like they used to do as children. "I'm so sorry this has happened," Libby says, a simple sentiment, but one that Cam appreciates. "I can't even think of . . ."

"There's nothing to say."

Libby reaches over and rests her hand on Cam's knee.

"I mean . . ." Cam says, her brain just starting the most tentative beginning of processing. "Like—even if he came back now, he'd go to prison for life." She stops. How could anybody begin to talk about this or truly absorb it?

"What have they said happens now?" Libby asks.

"It's a manhunt. He escaped out the back like someone in—I don't know—*Mission Impossible*?"

"I know . . . Do they know who the hostages are yet?"

"I don't know," Cam says.

"I think you should get some sleep," Libby says gently.

"Maybe."

Libby rolls onto her side, her body close to Cam's, and they stay like that for a long time, awake but silent.

Cam's eyes close completely. The months of sleep deprivation catching up, the past day's adrenaline. She lets herself sink into sleep like a deep, tepid bath, as comforting as childhood. She dreams of Luke, that he's outside, on the street, that he comes back for her, shouts to her—*Tell my wife that I love her*—but when she wakes, she's alone in the afterworld.

Act II
———

SEVEN YEARS
AFTER THE SIEGE

20

Cam

LIBBY: *What date number is this? I've lost count? Gooooood luck!!*
CAM: *Thanks.*

It's the evening, but it's not busy in Côte Brasserie. It's just Cam, Charlie, an old couple in the corner, and a few young people wearing headphones and working at miniature laptops, people who nomadically acquire any old place for the day or night as their office.

There's something plush and nostalgic about it, the quiet and the dimness like a hotel bar or art gallery. "Hook me up to some alcohol. Please. And some fun," Cam says to Charlie.

They are sitting at a table with four place settings, right in the window. Charlie, looking at his phone, glances up at Cam as she says this. He's a newish freelance research assistant, had a career change in his early forties, wanted to try something completely different. They met at a work do in her agency's office, three and a half months ago, right after she made some initial inquiries to sell the house. He walked into their office and she overheard him say, "There's somebody actually sitting reading a novel just in your foyer! Are they on display?" and something in Cam liked that cynicism about publishing, after a lifetime with writers. Charlie is a person firmly in the establishment, not outside of it. He believes very much in working hard. He runs at the weekends. He would never sit and ponder what it was all for. Cam likes this. Someone who's good at life. Who won't put a foot wrong in it. She's enjoyed attending work things with her dark new friend, who says things like, "I'm sorry to tell you, but I hardly ever read."

Cam smiles broadly at him and plays with her hair—a short, messy bob these days, lightened, too, as a way to cover the grays. Sometimes she doesn't recognize herself in the mirror, which she finds kind of thrilling: that was the point.

"Alcohol and fun, you say?" He rocks the chair back on its legs, his eyes on her.

"One hundred percent."

He catches a waiter's attention, then raises his eyebrows to Cam in a question. "The strongest cocktail," she says. "I could—I don't know. I could stay out all night."

"A Bloody Mary—no, two. And a goat's cheese tart," he adds. Cam, surprised he's ordering food already, asks for the same.

"So, what news?" Charlie says.

"Well," Cam says. "So."

"So," Charlie says back. He very deliberately puts his phone to the side, facedown.

"Remember Adam?"

"The big shot—bestselling debut?"

"Yes. Well, his next book is six years late."

"Six *years*?"

"You know publishing."

Charlie rocks back boyishly on his chair, legs stretched out underneath the table, arms folded across his chest. "Six years, though. I mean—what's he been doing?"

"Trying to have ideas." She glances at the menu.

Their drinks arrive, Cam's cold but the glass warm from the dishwasher, and she takes a delicious, tomatoey-alcoholic sip, which hits the precise spot she needed. She closes her eyes, says a silent *cheers* to being here with Charlie at the very beginning of the evening. Maybe they really will stay out all night.

"His publisher checked in with me today." She catches his eye, lets a grin out.

"Crikey—did the publisher rap your knuckles?"

"Well—kind of. Yes. Just said they can't wait *indefinitely*. They're hinting at wanting the advance back, in their own nice way."

"Tricky," Charlie says. "If I were the agent, I think I'd go into hiding."

"Ha."

"Is he stressed?"

"Adam? He writes when he writes. I don't even know if he's started. He won't say. He's the one who will just post it to me when he's ready. It takes as long as it takes."

"Oh yes, the jiffy-bag client!"

"That's the one." Cam smiles. Adam doesn't much like email; he said he liked the remoteness of sending his printed novel in an envelope that he had no idea whether she had received or was yet reading. He had added, when she signed him, that when he wrote the second novel, he'd send it in an envelope too. That it would be his thing. She'd loved this so much she had told everyone. Libby had said he sounded pretentious.

"I mean," Charlie says, "it's just a book." As the words leave his mouth, she avoids her distorted reflection in the windowpane. "Anyway," Charlie says. "So this is why you want to stay out all night. Makes sense, CF."

Camilla Fletcher. She reverted to her maiden name after her married one became infamous. She still remembers the day she signed the form. A kind of somber reverse wedding day. It was surprising how easy it was to change it. And she simply reverted to Fletcher on the agency website; most people got used to it quickly.

"Exactly."

"Must be nice to be able to work precisely when you like," Charlie remarks. Evidently, he can't get past it—sometimes, Cam thinks he doesn't really understand publishing as much as he ought to, because he adds, almost under his breath, "Six years off."

"Oh, trust me," Cam says with a laugh, "he's not been having any fun."

Out of Sight, Adam's debut, was published five and a half years ago. They—Cam's temporary stand-in and Adam—accepted Penguin's two-book offer, and *Out of Sight* had become an international bestseller, in the charts for four straight months here and in the U.S. The second book was expected within the year and is now so late that Cam is sort of half-relieved she's been chased, because the next step is the publisher losing interest entirely.

She leans toward Charlie. "What've you been working on anyway? Tell me something." This is their thing: *Tell me something*.

"I've been working on . . . research about the *Titanic*," Charlie answers with a smile. "Become an expert. Via Wikipedia. But perhaps no one will even read the book."

"Likely," Cam says. "Just a book," she adds lightly.

"Touché," Charlie says. "Nonfiction. Interesting, though." He tells her of various queries and research, and what he's learned.

"Don't you think that sometimes?" he asks. "That no one will ever read it? That it'll just sit on the shelves in Waterstones?"

She raises her glass to that in a silent toast. "All the time," she lies. But something is bubbling up inside. The real her. The one she buries.

Their waiter brings their food. Charlie slices into his tart, a clean cut. He has neat hands, and they eat in silence for a few seconds. There is something nice about sitting with somebody confident. Like you somehow belong in the world.

"So good," Charlie says, gesturing to the food. "I need it. Ran ten before work today."

"You are a better human than me."

"No, I just need to be exercised. Like a horse."

"Yes?" Cam says, ignoring the humor and trying to plumb deeper. She puts her elbows on the table, her face in her hands. Most of all, she enjoys, behind the confident veneer, Charlie's sometimes-vague hints at his own misery: she knows that he is divorced, but not much more. "Or? What?" she says brightly.

"*Or*," he says, expression amused, reaching for the pepper shaker, perhaps as a distraction, "I worry about stupid shit. And don't sleep."

"Join the club," she says.

"There's always running," he says, "even though it's awful."

"Worse than publishing parties?"

"Close second."

He scootches toward her slightly. He smells nice, a subtle expensive aftershave. His knee touches hers.

Cam looks around her. The waitress moves past, carrying a strawberry milkshake and a steak and fries. Cam finds herself watching avidly. She doesn't even know why, until she realizes: it is precisely the sort of thing Luke would order. He would never, ever have a cocktail and a goat's cheese tart. Cam doesn't know why this thought arrives in her mind, or why it feels so forceful, but that is sometimes how it is. She checks the time. It's ten past seven, and she hadn't yet thought of him today. It must be the first time it's happened.

That thought hits her even harder.

No Luke, until 7:10 P.M.

But now she does think of him, and up, up, up goes the pressure in her head.

"One second," she says to Charlie. His eyes dart to hers, confused, like a hurt animal's. Cam tries to care but momentarily can't. She crosses the dimly lit restaurant and pushes open the pink stall door to the toilets. She sits on a green velvet armchair, alone, just for a few seconds.

God.

That steak.

And—just like that—everything she's been pretending falls apart. Her extroversion with Charlie, keeping the conversation going, taking the piss out of publishing, wanting alcohol, to stay out all night. As if.

Funny how some people have a way of pulling a version out of you that isn't really *you*. She catches her eye in the mirror. Stupid haircut. It isn't her.

On the green armchair, alone, Cam places both hands on her heart, closes her eyes, and allows herself to miss him, and the person she was before it all. Content to love herself, because he did. He did. He *did*.

She opens her eyes. The toilets' walls are painted a matte calamine pink, the insides lit with bare bulbs. And she's alone, the way she wants it.

She stares down at her phone in her hands, not wanting to go back in there just yet. And then, for the second time in her life, unexpected news, although she doesn't know it yet, shatters everything.

21

It's a text, flashing up bright in her hands like a spotlight.

<Unknown>
Today 19:16
51.52484054385982, -0.09271149661234793
9 p.m.
Sent from textanon.com

Funny, spam is usually purporting to be someone, isn't it? To get you to do something? Cam replaces it in her jeans pocket, and heads back out to Charlie, telling herself that the text is nothing. That she's rattled by a stupid steak and a milkshake. That's all. And overreacting to spam.

She filled in a form last night, to officially declare Luke dead so that she can sell the house, finally, and move on. That will be why she feels weird. She had to wait seven years to do so. And, as she filled it in, having convinced herself it was the right thing to do, she found herself thinking the thought she never admits to anyone: that, deep down, she thinks he is alive.

She approaches Charlie, and he doesn't look up yet, is immersed in his phone, possibly work. Cam sometimes finds herself thinking, when she is with him, that he is not unlike her.

"Are we seeing Libby this weekend, did you say?" he asks.

Cam winces. She did say that, didn't she? In a moment of generosity to Charlie, she'd offered up a barbecue at Libby's in return for not being committed enough. Because that's the way it is for Cam: a brilliant day with Charlie, then three days full of doubt follow it. God knows what he thinks.

"I don't know—she's struggling a bit," Cam says. "Latest round of IVF failed."

"Oh," Charlie says, his face falling. For two reasons, perhaps: disappointment for Libby but evidence, too, that when Cam receives news like this, she doesn't always reach out to tell him.

"Is she with Polly tonight?"

"Oh yes," Cam says, thinking that, these days, she couldn't keep Libby away from Polly even if she wanted to.

She smiles as she thinks of her. That baby who laughed at everything and threw balls with abandon is now an almost-eight-year-old who laughs at everything and throws balls with abandon. Funny how sometimes everything changes and sometimes nothing does. Polly was Polly from day one.

Charlie nods but says nothing. There is something in his history, Cam thinks, that triggers him. Perhaps he wanted children, perhaps he didn't, but he won't be drawn on the topic of parenthood. She supposes some people might have had that conversation by now, but they haven't. Funny how long you can float along without a plan.

He looks up, smiles, and says: "Maybe we could send Libby something?"

And Cam thinks this is the exact wrong thing to do.

"I don't know," Cam says. "She doesn't like to . . . to show vulnerability, I suppose." The thing Cam wants to say to Charlie is that he doesn't *know* her sister. You can meet someone, be present in their life, even act like you know them well, but he doesn't know Libby the way Cam does; doesn't know that Libby would want to throw a bunch of conciliatory flowers in the bin.

Only the other week, the way that Libby chose to tell Cam that the IVF hadn't worked was to say, "Well, I can eat whatever the fuck I like now, because the bugger didn't stick around."

It wasn't out of character for Libby, but Cam had been surprised, nevertheless, that her sister's cynicism pervaded so deeply. Her words were laced with pain that, clearly, she thought she was hiding well.

"I'm trying to think what I would like if I were in a shitty situation," Charlie continues. "Like, probably just someone to make me my dinner and let me rot in self-pity."

Cam lets out a surprised laugh, thinking that Charlie really understands and empathizes with people's darkness sometimes.

"Let's just do that ourselves," she says.

"It's a date."

Cam's mind keeps going to that text message. It's a strange kind of spam. Nine P.M.? What spam includes a time?

"I just feel for them," Charlie says earnestly. A beat, then he adds: "My ex didn't want kids."

And Cam looks at him, thinking she needs to forget that text, concentrate on him. She can tell that this admission has cost him something. It spills out of him with a wince: unusual for Charlie, ordinarily so slick.

"Oh—I'm . . . I see," Cam says, wondering if she really wants to go here now. Evidently he decided while she was in the bathroom that he did.

"Yes. She left because I wanted kids and she didn't." His gaze lands on hers, an even gaze. It makes sense. His tension sometimes when she talks about Polly . . . "It was an ultimatum from me, really, but she is the one who left—I wouldn't have left her, actually." He sucks his bottom lip in, his expression slightly guarded. "It's her prerogative, naturally," he says, in his typically overtly thoughtful manner. Cam is suddenly struck by the thought that Luke would think Charlie insincere, even though she doesn't.

No. Leave, she commands Luke. *Your opinion doesn't matter to me now.*

Charlie pushes his food aside. "She said I'd end up resenting her. Smart woman," he adds.

"And you didn't find somebody to have kids with," Cam says. This is the first time they've ever discussed anything like this. And all she can think about is why would a junk text message say nine o'clock in it?

She's got to look at it again.

"Yes. And wait for the painful irony—guess who has a child now?" Charlie holds his hands up to her, and she searches his face for sadness, but there isn't any, just a resigned kind of gloom, which she understands entirely. Somebody who has also experienced suffering. Cam didn't want to start dating anyone else, and she certainly didn't want somebody damaged, but there's something nice about it, not tragic. Just somebody weathered, too, by life.

Charlie puts his cutlery down. "The kid looks just like her."

"I'm so sorry," Cam says simply. "I know I have Polly . . . but believe me when I say I really know how it feels when life doesn't go your way."

"Well, I appreciate that," he says. He looks at her. "Let's take these as leftovers and go and rot in self-pity." He gestures to the tarts.

Cam smiles, then nods. But then her phone lights up again, this time an email, but she snatches for it on impulse, opening the spam message again, knowing it's rude, but unable to resist.

And, clearly, her mind was still spinning over it while listening to Charlie, because look: it is far more than just a string of numbers, followed by "9 p.m." The numbers are separated by a comma.

Cam becomes distinctly aware of her heartbeat, which throbs and warps the room as she stares.

They are coordinates.

She's got to go. Forget this conversation, that Charlie is confiding in her.

The light on her phone shuts off, and their eyes meet. She springs to her feet.

"Oh, shit—I'm really sorry, Charlie . . . I need to—look," she says, flashing the phone but not properly showing him a text from Libby, which doesn't exist. "Polly's ill. I'm so sorry. I have to go."

And it's probably obvious—so obvious that neither of them even acknowledges it.

"Oh, for sure," Charlie says, and Cam is ashamed to note he doesn't even seem surprised. "You have to do what you have to do."

"Sorry."

"Take care, OK?" he says. He stays seated. Cam puts a twenty on the table and tries not to look at him. Tries not to admit to herself what she hopes to be true: that that text is from Luke, her long-lost, long-gone husband.

A few hundred feet down the road, stopping dead, she gazes up at the sky, that velvet-blue of June. All around her, London plays out its summer symphony. People smoking, drinking, flagging down taxis. Distantly, she hears a man shout, "No—they've got two-for-ones!"

Cam looks back at her phone. A set of coordinates and a time. Now that she understands it, it doesn't look like a jumble of numbers. It doesn't look like spam. It looks like the most important instruction of her life.

She checks her watch. It's twenty past eight.

She puts the coordinates immediately into Google Maps on her phone. All this time. All this time spent convincing herself to stop looking, to move on. And look: Coordinates. Instructions.

Contact.

The map loads and Cam stares at the location. It's a street in Central London, Islington, an alleyway between two office buildings that has no significance to Cam whatsoever.

But the timescale does. The application she filled in last night. Does Luke somehow know? And want her to know that he isn't . . . ?

No. She can't think this way. He killed people. He *left*. He didn't come back. Sometimes, it's been easier for Cam to believe that he's dead, rather than in hiding. But then, who knows *what* she believes? At times searching for her husband, at times vowing to move on, at times angry, at times sad. Everyone wants Cam to have consistency on his disappearance, and she just doesn't. Who could? The truth is, Cam *is* consistent: she pretends to believe he is dead or bad, while the real, true her believes he is alive and good. That's the truth of it.

Nine o'clock. Forty minutes to go.

She could make it.

She's going to go.

The Tube is the other way down the street, and she has to double back and walk past Côte again. As she does so, feet tripping with hurrying, she sees Charlie, supposedly the new man in her life. He's got his food to go, in a little white cardboard box, and something sad unspools in her stomach as she sees hers untouched. He didn't take it.

Eight fifty-five and Cam is one minute from the set of coordinates. She's fast-walking up the street, eight fifty-six, eight fifty-seven. She can't bear to ponder it, to hypothesize. Like most people prone to overthinking, in a crisis Cam's head is cool. Has become more so, since Luke left: she can rely only on herself.

She arrives near to the spot on Google Maps. It is an alleyway leading off a totally normal London high street. Railway arches, co-working spaces, phone kiosks, and takeaways.

A bus passes, the N19, and she winces. The N19 to Finsbury Park: she'd know it anywhere. Luke's old borough from when they were dating. He once failed to get that bus back there . . .

Cam had been representing him for nine months. After the sale to Penguin Random House, she had gone on to sell U.S. rights to Harper-Collins and by the time she called him with their twentieth translation deal, he'd stopped answering the phone formally and started saying, "Hey, it's the good-news train!"

Calls became five minutes of business and twenty of chat. Two minutes of business and forty of chat. Cam wasn't getting anything done. One-line emails about contract terms had giant personal PSs attached that moved to texts and then to WhatsApps—his avatar gave her a thrill every time it popped up—that didn't, strictly speaking, need sending at all. *Remind me, did you do your Swedish translator queries—I can't find them?* she once sent, then looked around her. Friday, nine o'clock at night, her bare toes at the end of the bathtub, glass of prosecco on the side. She didn't need to know about Swedish queries, and she could've asked her rights colleague anyway. This was not work. This was . . . something she couldn't yet name, or perhaps was afraid to.

But something about him, his effervescence, as bubbly as the drink beside her . . . Luke was more than just somebody she liked a lot, and certainly more than just another author client: he was a gateway to . . . to something more than good times. Luke was relaxation. Luke was "Oh, God, just turn your bloody brain off." Luke was "Look, just have some Jaffa Cakes and forget about it." And sitting behind those fun times was care. Care for her. Something she doesn't have now as she battles bedtime and school-uniform ironing and birthday-card shopping alone, alone, alone.

Their first project together had been a success, the way Cam knew it would be. Friends emailed to say how much they'd enjoyed it. Even

Libby said she couldn't help reading it. Cam found it amusing that everybody's reaction to it was precisely her own reaction to him: Luke was entertaining.

One night, nine months into their working relationship, they'd left a meeting with Simon & Schuster about a new deal for a singer-songwriter's autobiography. They were walking across London Bridge, having gone for dinner and then drinks and then more drinks. It was way beyond a business meeting, and by this stage both of them knew it.

"I'll walk you to the Tube," Luke had said at midnight, his tone light. Cam remembers he had said *ya*, not *you*, an overfamiliarity she liked so much she'd played it back over and over in her mind as they strolled.

It began to rain as they crossed the street. "I'll be fine from here," she said.

"It's cool." Luke indicated a row of bus stops. "I'm going to go from there, anyway." He drew the hood of his parka up with one hand, fur framing his face, and looked at her from within it. "Least I know you're home safe. Or near enough."

And it wasn't about what he said, but somehow the atmosphere changed between them—just like that—as if someone had reached in and wordlessly flicked on mood lighting. The electricity of the weather, maybe: that it was raining was a satisfying pathetic fallacy to Cam, a woman who liked to live in literature where possible. Just as she thought this, the droplets got fatter, striking the pavements with little explosions. Cam was in flimsy shoes, and her feet became squeaky with water.

"That's your bus," Cam said to him as the number N19 pulled in, Finsbury Park emblazoned on its front, but Luke ignored it. And that was the moment Cam knew.

"I'll get the next," he had said, his eyes on hers.

He didn't.

And now here she is alone, watching that same bus speed away.

She walks into the alleyway, her breath held. It bends in a semicircle between two buildings. She thinks of all of the things she knows about the siege and the weeks before it: that the dead hostages were never identified, that Luke never reported the burglary. They are pieces of a puzzle. And there *is* an answer, but it doesn't materialize, no matter how much

Cam tries to put them together. She has just a handful, from a thousand-piece set. Maybe she will never get the rest.

Or maybe she is about to get them all.

The alleyway winds back on itself into a courtyard but it's empty. Nobody here. No windows look into the barren and uninhabited concrete square. All it contains are a few dead shrubs and a bench.

Google tells her she is standing at the precise coordinates. It's twilight: she can't see a soul. On the dim street, in a rectangle of light at the end of the alley where a streetlamp stands, the world continues. For the first time, Cam shivers. It's late. Nobody knows she's here. But what else was she supposed to do?

She double-checks the coordinates and then the time. And this is it. She stands there in the dark, in this weird, closed-off courtyard, closes her eyes, and waits for nine o'clock. Eight fifty-eight. Eight fifty-nine. Nine.

22

Cam opens her eyes and London plays out around her exactly as it was. Another bus passes loudly nearby. A busker down the road plays "Brown Eyed Girl." And all the while, a courtyard with no one in it, only her, alone, the way it always is.

She stares at her feet and waits, doing nothing more than that. It's ten past nine. It's twenty past nine. It's twenty-five past, and nobody is coming. Her heart begins a slow and sad descent down her chest, disappointment made worse by its tessellation with shame. Was it him, and he didn't show? Or was it never him, just spam? Or someone else? Someone who knows something? And if it *was* him . . . was she going to just forgive him for a notorious double murder and seven years' abandonment?

She wanders out of the courtyard, past a locked door that seems to lead to a small basement office, down the alleyway, and out onto another quintessentially London street: Amazon lockers, rows of electric bikes for hire, a Tesco Express. Things are different these days and yet the same.

Cam shivers in the June twilight. In the autumn, as soon as the sun slides lower and the light fades to amber, something in Cam relaxes. But here, walking in the musky heat, it's as if no time has passed at all since that summer seven years ago.

Nine thirty, nine forty, and Cam hurries now, leaving the scene. She walks back down the high street and gets the Tube. She'll tell Libby, if she asks, that Charlie bailed early on her, and then, later, she will get into bed and hide under the duvet, alone. She won't admit she was out, alone on a street, waiting for a ghost from the past, like always.

Of course. Of course he let her down and didn't come. Like always, she thinks angrily while the Underground puffs and shakes its way around London.

It probably wasn't even him, but nevertheless, Cam's anger at her estranged husband flares back up.

She was always a reader but, these days, she buries herself in books and work. The cocktails and the anti-publishing chat with Charlie are not real. This is true Cam: she represents wide-ranging fiction, but her taste could be described easily in one word: escapism. There's a German word for this too: *Weltschmerz*. Translated as "world-grief." To Cam, it is perfect.

She goes through her submissions, tracking the ones she wants to request in her dedicated notebook. She looks at what's at the top of the Kindle store, and finally opens a manuscript she requested yesterday.

Marrakech, 2022

The call to prayer wakes me. A singular man's voice, shortly thereafter joined by a second, then a whole chorus. Pearlescent, early skies, amber at their edges, pink at the top. Flat-roofed, pale-stone buildings. I shouldn't be here. And I don't know it now, but life is about to change forever.

Cam reads and reads. She's in Morocco; she's a male, middle-aged ex-spy called Alfie. She's not separated from Luke; she's not following coordinates. She's not abandoned Charlie to finish a goat's cheese tart alone. She's someone else. Someplace else.

She reads the whole way home, feeling safely ensconced in another world. She barely feels the hot and stale Tube air around her, doesn't see the flickering lights and doesn't feel the jarring carriage.

But as she climbs the steps at Putney, she feels it. Something intangible. A shivering creeping at the back of her neck, like an ice cube touched just lightly to hot skin.

She turns around on the spot. Just beyond the Tube exit are a street artist and two market researchers holding clipboards, hoping to engage pedestrians. Nothing else. She presses her debit card to the barrier, trying to forget. Maybe he's nowhere. Maybe he *is* dead.

Funny. She was so sure it was him, she never considered that it might be somebody else. Somebody sinister. Somebody dangerous. Her back shudders as she thinks it and makes her way home, alone, like she always does. She tells herself she's used to it now. The solo bedtimes and books and television shows she watches by herself and the lone mug she washes up before bed.

But it had been nice to think it might have an end in sight.

23

Niall

Gunshots.

Niall turns over in bed, perfunctorily checks the window to see if they're real, but of course they're not. They never are.

The dream gunshots wake him most nights, now. They started two years ago, infrequent at first. Niall hadn't thought much of them at the time. Strange dreams, from his disaster of a negotiation that meant he went back on detective duties. It's not surprising it resides somewhere in his consciousness, like a deep-sea creature you can only see if you look hard enough.

He tries to sleep again but can't. Time inches ever forward. His room is black, the only light coming from the very edges of the windows—he got blackout blinds last year, to try to help, but they didn't. Eventually, he switches the light on and sits up, rubbing his eyes.

He checks his phone. Four fifteen. Same as ever.

The dream begins to fade from his mind, Niall's heartbeat slowing with it. He was asking for more and more and more time in it. Maidstone refusing. Niall insisting. Niall holding the released Isabella, her body soft and warm against his. Niall changing his mind, racing into the building, and then—always, always, always—the dream ends with the two shots, fired in quick succession, right behind Niall. He never gets there in time to stop them.

And then the bodies. The round bullet holes in their skulls. Their DNA flagged nothing on the police database. Their teeth matched no known dental records nor any on international databases either. No relatives ever, ever came forward for them, despite extensive appeals. It's a mystery with no solution, no ending.

He tells himself it's been on his mind more since the sighting in February. Deschamps, or someone who looks a lot like him, seen near Camilla's house by a traffic officer. They couldn't catch him in time. He got away. And maybe it wasn't him, but . . . the dreams stepped up from there.

Niall gives up on sleep, gets up, and starts the day.

Later that morning, he sits in Jess's office. She is, he is reluctant to say, his therapist. He's been sent to see her—against his will—because he accidentally disclosed the gunshot dreams to Tim, his boss, who phoned it right in. Officers can't be on the verge of PTSD, apparently, not without talking endlessly about it in beige rooms with boxes of tissues on the tables. Niall told them it isn't PTSD, but of course nobody listens.

Jess practices on the first floor of a midcentury block of offices in Lambeth. Her room doesn't smell like a therapist's office: it smells of the bakery beneath it—hot cinnamon rolls and fresh bread and yeast. She is young, too young to be so wise, has blond hair and dimples and a particular contrary tone she gets about her when Niall is saying something irrational without realizing it.

"The same dream as ever?" she says, and she is, Niall thinks, pleased that he's discussing it. He mostly skirts around his two banned topics, this being the first, talking in broad terms about responsibility in policing in general, about the ops he has on, wasting time for the session. Niall is good at talking and good, too, at running down a clock, and he does it every week with Jess.

"When you dream of it—what do you wish you could do in the dream?" Jess asks. She sits forward. She knows what happened in the Bermondsey siege—she was briefed on it by the Met's in-house occupational-health team. But she's never heard Niall outline more than the very basic facts.

"Wake up," Niall says, but Jess doesn't laugh, merely puffs air through her nose and looks down at her lap, then back up at him, waiting for a serious answer that may not come.

It's almost the end of the session, and she leaves it a beat, still expecting some sort of disclosure from him.

"Did you ever see the bodies?" she asks. A surprising question, one that seems to come out of nowhere.

"Yeah. In the station—the forensic pathologist . . ."

"Can you describe them?"

Niall closes his eyes, not wanting to go back there. To the neat temple wounds. Dark hair, brown eyes, blue T-shirts, middle-aged, white, both of them. A Salvador Dalí drip of blood from the neckline downward. Niall used to be bothered by things like this, used to drive home too fast and wake Viv up from sleep to hold her, but he isn't any longer. The truth is, you really can see too much. Until seeing something like this—two people, shot to death—becomes just another bit of admin.

"Do you wish you could stop it?" she suggests. "When you hear those shots?"

"I know that you will say I can't control the actions of gunmen," Niall replies. Another deflection.

Jess smiles. "You don't know what I will say."

"Isn't it that?"

"It is your job to prevent these things as much as is possible"—she holds her hands, palms up, to him—"but you are also a human being."

"I know that," Niall replies. He likes that Jess still talks about his hostage-negotiation career in the present tense. For him, it's all past. The Met didn't take him off negotiations: he took himself off them.

"Vulnerable to mistakes as is anyone." She pauses. "Marital or otherwise."

This is the second banned topic, so Niall ignores Jess's invitation.

He gazes down at his feet, saying nothing. Only earlier this morning he checked Viv's WhatsApp, as he does sometimes. There she was in her profile photo in her pink T-shirt, smiling at him. *Last seen 22:11.* He likes to look at that sometimes. See her continuing on even without him, living her life.

They have some contact. Every few months, one will text the other, something anodyne usually. Viv was very careful last year to let Niall know she is dating an American who—God forbid—has an actual

RSPCA rescue dog. Be still Viv's beating heart. Nevertheless, Niall does, in fact, still feel very close to Viv in that way you do sometimes when you don't see a friend for over a year but when you meet up nothing has changed. Maybe this is a delusion. Probably. Regardless, he hasn't forgotten her birthday since.

"Are you not allowed to make mistakes?"

"I wasn't. As a kid," Niall says sullenly, remembering falling off his bike and getting told off for it by his father, amongst other things.

"Well, you are now," she says. "Trust me."

"Hmm."

"How often are the dreams now?" she asks.

"Only once or twice a week," Niall lies.

It does not exactly surprise Niall when, that evening at seven, working late, he receives the alert from the Met's surveillance team: a text has pinged on Camilla's phone. She's about to be sent a message from a service called textanon.com. The Met had put covert surveillance back on her phone after the sighting. It does no harm and, once in a while, those on the run slip up.

Like this.

Niall springs into action, calling Claire in telecoms. Her kids are in their teens now, and, if anything, she's become even more formidable as her home life has eased.

"I know why you're calling," she says, "and if you let me get off the phone, I will call Text Anon myself and make a release request."

"Fine," Niall says, then waits. He sighs. It's been a long day already, heralded by Deschamps's own gunshots, and succeeded by boring detective work that doesn't excite him. Domestics. Burglaries. Nothing where Niall needs to make a judgment call.

He stares out at London. It's another perfect summer. No rain for weeks, the air crystalline and fragile with the heat, only just beginning to cool down now.

Five minutes, ten, and Claire comes back to him.

"Good news," she says. "It's not sent yet. They're on a delay. We can intercept it."

"Brilliant," Niall says.

"Anon say they hold the message before sending it, so I've asked them to capture it, and not send it," Claire says.

Damn, Niall likes her. She's so smart. "Thank you," he says. Neither of them says the unsaid: That he ought not to be working on this file. Not after he passed it over.

"I'm guessing," Claire says, "that . . . somebody . . . is going to go to the location, instead of Camilla?"

"Right," Niall says, smiling for perhaps the first time today.

"The original text said eight o'clock. At these coordinates," she says, rattling them off.

"Excellent," Niall says, ringing off.

And then, for belt and braces, he sends Camilla a new message, anonymous, identical text, changing the time from eight to nine o'clock tonight: It will be interesting to see if she attends, and what she will do when she thinks her husband might want to meet her. And it will be even more interesting to go in her place and see who wants to contact her so covertly.

Whoever this is—Deschamps?—has chosen a seemingly random location. Unfamiliar, deep in Islington. Niall walks there, the evening light gilding the tops of buildings, the streets in shadow.

They didn't find many answers in the weeks and months following the siege. That the hostages were never identified is a fact Niall found most alarming, most disturbing. It tells him that the situation they dealt with was not normal, but he still cannot work out in what way. Two bodies. No identification. Left in a morgue for three months, then given paupers' funerals, two unmarked graves. Niall has dealt with murder cases where the body was never found. He's never dealt with murder cases where the victims did not appear to exist. It's a clue. He just doesn't know what it means.

They each had on them close to £200 in cash, pay-as-you-go transit cards, and nothing else. No mobile phones. No wallets. No house keys, car keys. Nothing.

Occasionally, over the intervening time, Niall researched things—on the quiet—but they never came to anything. Nothing Deschamps had worked on seemed at all sinister, at all salacious. No salient facts came to light. No visits to counselors, no confessions to friends, not much weird behavior at all, actually. A single suspicious Google search from Camilla about arguing with your husband is not enough to hang a case on.

Niall sat in on interviewing Isabella Louis, after the siege ended and before he left negotiation for good, in a dull police interviewing suite. She'd sat there, small of stature but clear and certain, and told Niall that she'd been cleaning up her warehouse for an incoming tenant to enter the following Monday when she'd heard the commotion. That she'd seen Deschamps pointing the gun at the two hostages, that he arrived with them and that, the second he saw her, he directed her onto a chair too. He didn't tie her hands, only the men's, so when the phone rang, she'd chanced it and darted to answer. She knew the layout of the building well enough. Niall had been vaguely curious about this. "Pretty ballsy," he'd said.

She'd shrugged, looked back at him, and said, "I thought I was dead either way."

"Fair," Niall had replied; other hostages had said similar to him.

The camera in the hole in the wall had captured all of this, but when Isabella answered the phone, Deschamps directed everyone to move. They'd lost sight of them.

Isabella filled in the gaps: when Deschamps had heard George's threat on the end of the phone, Isabella said to Deschamps that she owned the building, and she could get him out of there if he released her.

"I know it wasn't the right thing to do," Isabella said. "But anyone would've done it. To survive."

Niall nodded. Perhaps Isabella took his silence for judgment, because she added, "I know in giving him the escape route I sentenced his hostages to death." Her voice caught on the final word.

"I would have done the same," Niall said.

"We were so thankful for Hamish," she said. "Our security guard who works remotely. He captured it beginning, and therefore alerted you guys."

"And the media," Niall said lightly.

"Well. Yes. But also the police. And George."

She'd looked at him, then, clear-eyed and vulnerable, and Niall had immediately thought that he liked her. "Yes, thank God for him," he said. "What is the most significant thing you remember about it all?" he probed. An open question, designed to pull detail out of her.

"That I wet myself," she said, still looking him dead in the eye. "When he raised the gun to me, to get me to the chair, I wet myself, right then and there." She glanced down at her tiny hands, then back up again at Niall. "Then I had to sit in it. I think it's why he didn't tie me up. Felt sorry for me."

Niall nodded, swallowing hard. "I get that," he said softly. He left it a few respectful beats before asking, "Why do you think Deschamps took his other hostages?"

"I have no idea," she said after a pause. "There was no talk between them."

"Why do you think he killed them?"

"I don't know that either. But I feel like perhaps he was always going to."

"Why?"

"He didn't negotiate with them. He didn't say anything to them. It was like there was nothing anybody could've done."

Niall had winced at that. How had he got it so wrong?

Isabella and her husband George moved on with their lives. She later told Niall she was getting therapy for dealing with a diagnosis of generalized anxiety disorder following her ordeal and was trying to get over that and a fear of confined spaces too. Niall hadn't said he felt exactly the same. When they met again, a few years ago—as part of a victim-support scheme Niall is trying to get off the ground—she asked him if they ever found out who the hostages were. Survivors' guilt, he thought. She told him she'd sold all of their buildings. That she was afraid to go in them.

Niall is almost at the coordinates. He thinks—on balance—that it won't be Deschamps. Wouldn't he send Camilla to somewhere significant—or somewhere very remote? Why the middle of London? He'd be seen by so many CCTV cameras. If he's alive, he's stayed hidden for seven years by not being careless.

Niall arrives sweating at half past seven—he likes to be early; he believes it shows good intent—and he walks a slow loop around the streets.

It's an alleyway that bends on itself, threading between two buildings like a river snake and then into a courtyard. There's a plain blue door leading off the alleyway. He tries it, and it's locked, so he shines the torch on his phone onto the mechanism, but it's a deadbolt, locked from inside. No chance. Using the light, he peers into the cracks, which reveal thin slices of the room to him. It's some sort of storage cupboard. Small, carpeted. A broom, a mop bucket: he can't see much else.

Niall has been waiting professionally for years, and so it doesn't bother him at all to stand in the courtyard for half an hour: you can learn a lot just by looking and—more important—by listening, and so this is what he does to occupy himself, scanning the strange, disused space from the very edge, where he will be unseen when his anonymous texter arrives. It sits in the exact center of a load of buildings, like an empty stomach in the human body. A quiet, calm oasis of concrete. There are two old whisky barrels dotted around, containing long-dead shrubs. A hot metal bench sits in a shaft of sun bounced from somewhere up high. A sprinkling of cigarette butts. And, way, way above him: a square of deep-blue sky. Niall understands now: this could be the most private place in London.

How very interesting. Niall veers once again to thinking it's Deschamps. It's a smart location in which to stay hidden. Not at all overlooked. If you can run the London CCTV gauntlet and get here, you'd be able to do your dealings pretty much anonymously.

Time runs down slowly like sand through an hourglass. At approaching eight, Niall slinks into the shadows even further.

And soon it is eight, then five past. Niall purses his lips, thinking.

He can't imagine they're not coming. Nobody who sends that sort of text would then ghost.

He takes a slow stroll around the cement island, and that's when he sees it. A small envelope tucked into one of the barrels. It's brown; it blended in. Niall picks it up between his index finger and thumb. It's empty inside, but written on the back flap is a mobile number.

He types it into his phone, then sends a message with a simple *I got your note x.*

A text comes back immediately. *Are you there?*

Yes, Niall types back, keeping it simple, giving nothing away. Camilla would presumably do the same.

His phone rings, three times. There's no way Niall can answer, so he merely stares down at it, waiting for whoever it is to ring off.

Speak to me, a text comes through.

I'm too scared to, he types.

I need to know it's you.

Oh, it's me.

Niall paces out of the courtyard, down to the alleyway. He pauses, then another message flashes up. *It isn't you.*

Niall tries to reply, but it says: *Number blocked.*

24

Cam

FORM N208
FEE: £628
STATUS: Submission failed

Cam is at work the next day and—to add insult to injury—the form has already come back, submission failed. *We found some areas where we needed more information*, the government email attaching it says. Cam reads it, her eyes immediately wet, steeling herself against the impersonal questions. She is not surprised to find it's failed. Cam is dashed through with a jaded kind of pessimism these days that has spread and imbued her personality, like a single drop of ink running into water. Just last night, she paused the television during a scene where a man left a woman, and said, "Figures," to an empty room.

Luckily, two junior agents drift by outside her office, distracting her. "Oh, Cam," one of them, Lily, says, stopping. Cam smiles warmly, standing up and slipping into character. Bubbly, happy Camilla Fletcher, formerly Deschamps to people who've been around long enough, who nobody truly notices actually keeps everyone, these days, at arm's length.

"Look, look, look," Lily says, holding out her left hand.

"Aaah, oh! Look *indeed*," Cam says, holding Lily's fingers gently and admiring the engagement ring. It's a princess-cut diamond. Just like Cam's, which lies in the bottom of Luke's bedside drawer.

"Took him fifteen years," Lily says. "Fifteen. Years."

"Worth the wait?" Cam says with a grin that is—she is ashamed to admit—somewhat fake. Behind her, sun hits her desk. Her coffee pipes out delicious smells. And the email about the form looms like a specter, open on her computer.

"Oh, maybe," Lily says, admiring the ring. "We needed to save up, anyway."

Cam closes her eyes. She remembers this phase of life. Engagements and excitement and the delicious notion that you are stepping into adulthood, finally, after all this time. Marriage and houses and kids. So much fun, it felt like pretend-play.

"And will it be literary-themed?" the other agent asks.

"Ha. Maybe. Who knows?" Lily says, smiling at nothing in the way that people in love do.

"Sure, you can get some book proofs for the party favors," Cam says drily.

"That's such a good idea!" Lily says with a squeal.

This is enough for Cam. Too much, in fact. She congratulates her again, then retreats into her office, waits ten seconds for them to pass, and puts her head on its side on the desk, blinking, looking at her computer mouse, thinking about how her marriage ended: with the newspapers speculating endlessly on the note he left her. *Suicide warning or love note?* one said.

Fuck him. *Fuck him.*

It's time to move from the upside-down house. That is what started this process, four months ago. Libby and her husband, Si, both say that she can't sell up without removing Luke from the title. And she can't do that without a declaration that he is dead.

And she couldn't do that until seven years had elapsed. But seven years is too long to have remained there in stasis, her bedroom divided in two: her side, books everywhere. And his: Neat as a pin. Preserved. The only change she's made is that, when his bedside lamp broke, she threw it out and didn't replace it.

She opens the form, and it's overwhelming. Their questions, her answers, and now their comments on her answers.

QUESTION ONE: Please outline the circumstances in which Luke Deschamps *disappeared*. His name is written like that, in a different font. An impersonal insertion, one missing man in a sea of a million.

Cam rereads her answer, covering the siege, the bodies, clearly stating no one ever found out who the hostages were.

Nobody could ever identify the hostages. No DNA match, no DVLA hit, no missing relatives coming forward, no dental records. Nothing. It remains one of the great mysteries of the siege. Cam was told, by Lambert and Smith, that they searched and searched for these people but never found them.

Stuart ambles past her office, his clothes straining slightly at their seams, gym clothes thrown away years back. She glances at him, then hides her screen.

QUESTION TWO: Please indicate the steps the authorities have taken to find Luke Deschamps.

ANSWER: Full homicide investigation—case reference LD36550. Regular contact from police chasing up all of Luke's friends and family, anywhere we spent time together that he might seek refuge in, anywhere at all that he could have been hiding. Not a single sighting. No bank cards used, didn't take wallet or passport. Last police visit was three years ago, except occasional calls from hostage negotiator, Niall Thompson, who said he will let me know if anything significant happens.

There are no comments on either question. Evidently, Cam passed the test.

For those first few years, Cam searched, on and off, for answers. Found the district judge whose book Luke worked on, asked him if there was anything unusual he had exposed. He'd been baffled, said there was nothing controversial whatsoever. He had worked only civil cases, nothing criminal. She'd visited the Rightmove house again—owned by a man called Harry, a tradesman who'd never met her husband in his life. When she asked him why the house had appeared on Rightmove, he said it had been put up for sale but he had changed his mind. Maybe her lie to the police had been the truth after all.

She'd tried to restore Luke's laptop, once she got it back from the police in a ziplock bag. She'd hired a PI to search for him the following summer, who didn't turn up a thing. "He's either very dead, or really knows how to hide," he told Cam—rather insensitively, she thought. That night, she couldn't sleep for thinking about it: Luke wouldn't be good at hiding. He was too flippant, scatty. Liked people too much.

She finds the comments underneath the questions.

PLEASE PROVIDE: *passport and driving license for* Luke Deschamps.

WE ALSO NEED: *names, addresses and contacts details of* Luke Deschamps's: *children, siblings, parents, first cousins, grandparents, aunts, uncles, and any half-siblings, step-parents, second cousins, aunts and uncles by marriage.*

Contact details for Polly. This form is foolish and generic. What is Polly going to say about it all? Cam's heart wrenches for her daughter, who drew the short straw and barely even knows it. She is so like Luke. Painfully so. Gregarious, fun—and funny too. Happy to go anywhere, to do anything, regards a trip to Sainsbury's as a cool afternoon out. Cam used to envisage reading books with her child, but, when she suggested this recently, Polly said, "*Or* we could have a fashion show?" and so they had.

She skips to the parts with more missing information.

PLEASE ALSO PROVIDE DETAILS OF: Luke Deschamps's *GP.*
PLEASE ALSO PROVIDE: *last seen location. Private CCTV not acceptable.*
PLEASE ALSO PROVIDE: *evidence of* Luke Deschamps's *unused credit cards, bank cards, his final mobile phone contract.*

Cam gulps at the last one: she's continued to pay it, all these years, for reasons she's too ashamed to go into on a form. It was easy to allow the

payment to continue to leave his account and, when the money ran out
of that, to transfer it to their joint one.

Their requests are overwhelming. She can't possibly . . . she blows air
out of her mouth, then dials the number on the bottom of the form.

"Probate department," a crisp female voice says after twenty minutes'
Muzak and assurances about calls being important.

"Hi," Cam says, her voice stilted. "I'm—struggling with your form.
I have received some comments back asking for extra documents, but
there are so many—and most don't apply."

"Please give us the form number."

"N208," Cam says, and there's a silence on the end of the line.

"Oh . . . I haven't dealt with that one before," the call-center worker
says, surprise in her voice. "Let me . . . yes, OK, wow. So it's a declaration
of presumed death you're looking for," she says. "Without a death certif-
icate?"

"Right, yes," Cam says, thinking that she doesn't want to be doing this
this morning in her sunny office.

Cam gives her reference. "The thing is—there are a lot of unusual
parts to my husband's case," she says, the words well-worn trauma.

"Okey-dokey," she says. "You will need a designated handler on this
one, who can look into the facts for you, but I think you will need to
make a separate rider statement about—the events."

"OK."

Cam swallows. It has been her New Year's resolution, the last seven
Januarys, to stop going over and over what Luke left behind. His papers
and books and old computers. She's almost stuck to it, this year, and it's
now June. Only had one slip-up after a bad day in February when she
began the process of selling the house. She had a dream Luke came back
for her, was shouting on the street, then disappeared.

But nevertheless, a part of Cam—the whole of her, really—knows
that, one day, she is going to get the answer.

It's why she hasn't told Polly the full truth. When Polly was two, Cam
told her she had a daddy, but he was away. When Polly was four, Cam
said he was pretty far away, but that he loved her very much. When Polly
was six, Cam told her he may never come back, that he didn't want to be

away, but some people said he'd done a bad thing. Just recently, they'd had the same conversation, but this time, Polly had sat up in bed and asked, "What bad thing did he do?"

Cam had puffed air into her cheeks, thinking, This is it. You never get any warning as a parent. Years of *He's had to go away* and *He'd never willingly leave you* had led them here. And what was she supposed to say?

Cam had stared into the middle distance. "Well, the police think that he harmed two men, but I don't think so."

"You don't?"

"No. Your father was . . ." Cam struggled on the tense, her voice treacled around the tough words. "He was a good person. The truth is, I don't know what happened. But I know what he was like."

"What was he like?"

"Fun. Loyal. Loved you."

"Doesn't sound like someone that would do bad things."

"No," and this seemed to be enough for Polly, right then. She'd rolled onto her side, pulled toward her the Jellycat plushie she'd been dressing up in different outfits—Polly *loves* clothes—each morning, and shut her eyes, leaving Cam to think that she was on borrowed time. Soon, Polly would be able to google him. Someone would surely tell her his name, even though Polly now has Cam's surname. Playground gossip would make itself known. The details would come out, somehow, probably this year or next, but Cam couldn't bring herself to force it.

As she'd finished a more traumatic solo bedtime than usual, she passed her own room and stared in at the bed, at the single lamp. "I hate you," she said to Luke, to Luke's absence, to Luke's total lack of explanation. "I fucking hate you," she said again.

Cam had decided to end that day prematurely. She headed downstairs. She moved a three-feet-high stack of books out of the way of her bed, deposited them in two piles onto her bedside table, and got under the duvet, looking up at the underside of it, eyes wide.

She didn't hate him. Not at all.

She reached for her phone, found him, and called. It was why she continued to pay the bill. No rings, but his voicemail. That sweet, sweet voicemail.

"This is Luke Deschamps. Please leave me a message."

She'd called it twice that night. Just to know that he might be out there somewhere, somehow, listening to her.

She finds her own voice is shaking now.

"And was there an inquest for the . . ." the call handler says.

"Yes, but nobody knows who they are."

Cam attended the inquest, all in black, sitting in the public gallery. Listening as the facts repeated themselves like demolitions. Out of character. No explanation for it. A bullet wound in each temple. Two men, aged forty to forty-three. No ID on them. No one reported them missing or identified their bodies.

The day after the inquest had finished, she'd applied to change her and Polly's surname.

"All right, I am going to assign you a handler. She's called Daisy. She will call you back. Are you OK to make the £628 payment on the website?"

"Yes," Cam says, thinking, What's six hundred quid, given everything else that's been taken from her?

Cam and Polly walk through the front door that afternoon, hot sunlight behind them. "How long, exactly, until the holidays?" Polly asks Cam, breaking away from holding her hand and running up the stairs without waiting for the answer.

"Almost a whole term!" Cam calls after her.

"I just want to laze around," Polly calls down, and Cam admires her up-frontness.

Cam flicks through the post. And—ah. As if her emails with his publisher yesterday have conjured it, here it is, in true Adam style. A jiffy bag in her hands, addressed to her.

Inside, a bound manuscript. There's no note. It's the same font he delivered *Out of Sight* in: Baskerville, 12. Cam would recognize it anywhere. No title. Just his words.

Finally! Almost seven years later, but here it is. And just as the publisher was getting irritated too. Cam holds it close to her chest, hoping it's good, hoping it's the one, glad one good thing has happened today, thinking she will read it tonight. When Polly is in bed and the world is quiet, she will sink into fiction, the way she always has.

She takes it into the bedroom, her bedroom, which is still divided in two. Her side and Luke's, his possessions now seven years out of date, but nevertheless still there, waiting.

25

Anonymous Reporting on Camilla

We always meet in a launderette just opposite his apartment. He sometimes thinks his flat or his phone might be bugged, and, otherwise, says the machines are loud enough to cover it. Plus, he says he gets loads of laundry done. He's organized like that, my brother. House as neat as a pin.

It's a small space. Five tumble dryers. Five washing machines. He sits on a wooden bench affixed to the wall. He has closed the door, the one with a little bell above it, and, as I arrive, looks up at me.

"Nothing especially unusual," I tell him. "The house move is still on the horizon, but not underway yet."

He leans his head back against the plate-glass window. He doesn't say anything. "Nothing to report at all?" he says over the thrum of a spin cycle.

"Really nothing."

"No strange visitors, nothing?"

"Nothing. No one coming or going. I've been at the house three times now, watching."

26

Niall

Niall was not surprised to find that Camilla went to the coordinates' location. She waited for forty minutes—a perfectly normal and reasonable amount of time—and then left. Nothing suspicious about that. On her way in, she'd looked harassed and hopeful, and Niall would bet money on Deschamps never having made direct contact with her before. Whatever he's up to, Camilla isn't in on it.

Niall had stood there as she passed, in plain sight but wearing sunglasses despite the evening hour—you can get away with anything in London—just observing her. If he was in any doubt about what the coordinates might have meant to her, he needn't have been: when she emerged, emotions were written across her face. Perplexed, sad, hopeless. He'd not seen her for many years, but she was unchanged facially, though she'd cut her hair into a bob. Big eyes and short hair. Perhaps slimmer than back then, somehow tragic-looking, though maybe he was just reading that into her.

And now it's time for Niall to act. To phone it in. To report it all to the creaking Met, who will impose their bureaucracy on him.

So it is this that brings him to his boss Tim's office on a sunny Tuesday. He knocks once on the dark-wood door, doesn't wait, then enters.

Tim, the detective superintendent, first and foremost, is a genius. Tidy in physical appearance, and with an orderly and structured mind too: he is able to assess a situation and cut through the weeds that pull other people down.

While Niall went into negotiating, Tim favored hardcore policing.

He was the lead on the Deschamps case, once it became homicide, but has now passed over most big cases in favor of management.

Tim is sitting behind his desk. There isn't a single piece of paper on it. Only a laptop and a tall glass of water with—get this—a lemon slice bobbing around in it.

"Can you do something for me?" Niall asks.

"How about *Long time no speak, Tim—how are you?*" Tim replies, folding his hands in a lattice and placing his chin on top of them.

"Sorry. Long time no speak, Tim—how are you?"

Tim wrinkles his nose. "Have you been *smoking*?"

Niall winces. He has replaced Coke with the very nostalgic menthol cigarettes that taste of smoking tobacco covered up ineffectively with chewing gum. They're not sold anymore in England; he has to import them from America on eBay.

"Maybe," he says. "Look—I need a favor."

Outside Scotland Yard, the London Eye spins lazily, the trees in bright-green bloom around it. Beyond that, the river is a purest blue. Summer's turned up the saturation.

"That is no surprise," Tim says, cupping his face and looking at Niall.

"It's quite delicate."

Immediately, Tim's expression changes into something more serious. "Shoot."

"I need to trace a phone number. I suspect it'll be a burner phone, but I want to see first. I could've gone direct to Claire, but I'm coming to you."

"Uh-huh. Understood." Tim spreads his arms. "And?" he says, a small, confused frown on his face.

"I need to allocate it to a file."

"... OK."

"But once I do that, everyone is going to jump on this. And I'm not sure if I'm right here. The file is Luke Deschamps," Niall says.

"Deschamps?" Tim says. "Rearing his head again so soon since the sighting?"

Niall explains the situation to Tim.

"Back from the beyond," Tim replies, an unreadable expression on his face. "Give me the number."

Niall slides it across the desk. Tim glances at it and then begins typing to telecoms, and Niall is so pleased to have a boss who does things just as quickly as he wants them done. Tim waits a few seconds, then reads something off the screen. "It's a disposable pay-as-you-go, as suspected. But it has pinged two masts." Tim's expression changes into more than just mild interest. "One in Central London—needle in a haystack. But then also a mast in Dungeness."

"Pretty remote."

"Yeah."

"A good spot to hide?"

Tim holds Niall's gaze. "Coordinates—*now*—is weird, isn't it? Why not send them seven years ago?"

"I know. Odd."

"We need a team on this."

"Yeah," Niall says. "I think we do."

They pause for several seconds, Niall thinking, and assuming Tim is too. "I suppose we will go down there," he says eventually.

"Southeast coast. Kent?"

"Yes."

"Ask some questions. Knock on some doors. Keep up the surveillance on Camilla."

"Leave it to me," Niall says.

Tim looks up at him, sips the water, then pauses, his expression perplexed. "So you're on this case, are you? Or what?" he asks, then he holds his hands up. "Makes no difference to me."

"I'm not negotiating but I . . . I don't know." Niall turns away from him, looks at the closed door to his office. "I don't know," he says again quietly. "We'll see."

"Sometimes, solving a case stops the demons," Tim says.

"Sometimes, looking for a solution is the problem," Niall says, but he doesn't truly believe it.

"We'll have you on the case until you say otherwise."

The team—including Niall—is leaving for Dungeness in an hour, the force predictably ablaze with excitement at potentially capturing

Deschamps after all this time. One of the PCs just told Niall he was thirteen when Deschamps went missing, remembers watching it on the news, to which Niall said, "Fuck me, I'm old."

Right now, he is walking through the streets surrounding Scotland Yard to buy a new burner phone to contact Deschamps on, and smoking and thinking. He's lucky that Tim is a friend as well as a colleague, who lets him pick and choose what he works on. He overheard Maidstone—now promoted—ask what Niall was doing back on the case, and Tim loyally deflect. He's glad, too, that the Met is springing into action. So often with these things the budget won't stretch, the boxes need to be ticked, and they lose the heat on the lead they have.

There is nowhere better to walk than London. Niall is near to Embankment. It's a windy day, and he gazes at a man sketching the river on a plain pad of paper.

"Niall?" a voice says behind him. It belongs to a woman emerging from the Tube. Niall's eyes meet hers, and it's Rosalind, Viv's sister.

"How are you doing?" Niall says carefully.

She is an avatar of Viv. Same huge head of hair—Niall even now, seven years on, finds strands of them in his flat—but she's different too. Smaller nose, a more contained personality. None of Viv's wildness.

"Yes, great," Rosalind says. She is a person who—Niall thinks—likes to pretend. She's married to a banker called Freddie, who issues putdowns to her in company, which Rosalind pretends not to notice. Oh, or maybe he no longer does—Niall forgets, sometimes, that his information about Viv is long out of date. They keep in touch but not about anything that matters.

Niall and Rosalind haven't yet decided if this will be a ten-second exchange or ten minutes, and Niall stands awkwardly as commuters dodge and weave around them.

"You?" Rosalind asks, perhaps only to be polite. It's been years since Niall has seen her. He remembers a night about a week after Viv left. She went to stay with Rosalind, and Niall turned up at the door on an ill-advised pleading mission. "She's sick of playing second fiddle to a job," Rosalind had said.

"But she never said that," Niall said, standing right there on the doorstep in the rain like some tosser in a movie. "She never said."

Rosalind had half closed the door. "Why should she have to sound the alarm to you?" she said, eyes only just visible in the closing crack. "You should have known."

Two weeks after that, the first lawyer's letter had arrived. Niall called Viv up directly when he'd received it, even though it said to not do precisely that.

"You were not ignored by me in favor of work," he had said, phone cradled into his ear at his desk. "That's what it says here, item one of my 'unreasonable behavior.'"

"Yes, I was. You only had time for me if you didn't have a job on."

"That's the nature of my work. And everyone's work."

"Nothing better to do."

"No, that's not it."

"What did I do that day?" she'd said. "The day of the siege."

"What? I don't know."

"Did *I* go to work? How did I celebrate my birthday?"

"Look: I'll be better," he'd said. "Tell me what you're up to. And I won't—I won't . . ." He couldn't say it. *I won't ignore you or take you for granted.* The thing is, with Viv, like all stinging criticism, it had been warranted. Of course it had. Every copper's marriage suffered.

"Fine," Niall says now to Rosalind. "I don't have long—I'm on a job."

He doesn't know why he says it. To goad her, perhaps. To provoke a reaction. Maybe to make himself feel that he lost it all for something: that work *is* more important to him, even when he is no longer sure of that at all.

And that's when she does it. The slightest roll of her eyes. Niall catches it, the same way that you can only momentarily see a spider's web tracing its way across your path in the sunlight. He says nothing back.

"What job?" she asks. Rosalind is in summer wear, flip-flops and sunglasses, her hair a lion's mane.

"An old siege rearing its head," he says. "How is Viv . . . ?"

"Fine."

"What is she up to?"

Rosalind pauses, clearly wanting to say something but not knowing whether she ought to. Niall stubs his cigarette out on a nearby bin spilling over with rubbish, then tosses it in. "It's fine, Ros," he says. "You don't need to tell me anything."

"She's broken up with Brad."

Brad. The American.

"Oh, why?" he says, feigning sympathy, hot, pleasant hope rising up through him.

Rosalind holds his gaze for a second, there outside the busy Tube. A couple more people push past them, and Niall gestures for them to stand to the side, in the shade of a shop's awning.

Rosalind looks down the street, at a man playing steel drums on Hungerford Bridge in the sun. Eventually she looks back at him and says: "They never stick."

"No." Niall doesn't know what to say. It's gauche to grill Viv's sister. It's unseemly to pester Viv herself. She told him what she wanted, and she got it. Their divorce was finalized four years ago, his unreasonable behavior evidently confirmed and verified by a court, even though he was told they only rubber-stamp it.

And yet . . . sometimes, late at night, he will smoke on his balcony and think of her, and feel sure that, somewhere out there, she is thinking of him, too, right at that exact same moment.

"Well . . ." Niall says, ready to make the meeting two minutes, not ten, ready to stop this conversation and the awkwardness Rosalind is clearly feeling.

She removes her sunglasses and—yes—there are the eyes, those same eyes. Exactly the color and shape of Viv's: the dark lash line, everything. For a few seconds, Niall can only gaze at them and pretend it's her. "She said late one night that she still loves you oh my God I shouldn't be saying this," Rosalind says, just like that, all in a rush.

"Did she?" Niall says. "When?" All of his nerve endings feel alive.

She'd texted him a few months ago. Just a news story about somebody they used to see in the Barbican pushing a pram with two cats inside. He'd replied, and it had ended there, but he'd found it interesting, sad and loaded. The choice of topic: where they used to live together, with the stray animals she collected.

"A few months ago," Rosalind says.

"In what context?"

"Just talk," Rosalind says. "I shouldn't have said that. I've got to go. It's just . . ."

"What?"

"Nothing," Rosalind says. He goes to reach for her, but she waves him off, waves him away. And then, over her shoulder, she throws him a single line: "For a hostage negotiator, you are a terrible communicator in marriage."

A terrible communicator in marriage. This is what Niall keeps thinking as they approach Dungeness, a small coastal wasteland two hours from Scotland Yard. Viv isn't what his mind should be preoccupied with, but she is. The Bermondsey siege and his marital breakdown, forever twinned. Why did she use the present tense? You *are* a terrible communicator in marriage.

He shakes his head. What an idiot, finding a positive in that insult.

He's sitting in the passenger's seat of Tim's car—he hates not driving, makes him feel sick—woozily reading old articles about the Deschamps case.

HOSTAGES NEVER FOUND THANKS TO BUNGLED INVESTIGATION

THE MET have admitted they still do not know, six weeks on, the identity of the men murdered during the Bermondsey siege.

Just over six weeks after the explosive events of a siege in Bermondsey, London, in which writer, husband and father-of-one Luke Deschamps took three hostages and murdered two of them, police still do not know the identity of the dead hostages.

'You would expect dental records, DVLA records, anything,' our expert forensic investigator says. 'These days, it's impossible to not know the identity of a dead body.'

The perpetrator, Luke Deschamps, remains on the run.

Niall sighs, doesn't read the rest of the article, and looks at the straight horizon instead, trying to feel less queasy. It really can be impossible to know the identity of a dead body, despite what the *Mail*'s expert forensic investigator says. If they don't show up on the dental-records website when you search their exact fillings by placement in the mouth and date. If they aren't registered on the DVLA. It baffled Niall, but it's nevertheless true.

The mast the burner phone pinged serves the entire Dungeness estate, a postapocalyptic-looking cluster of beach huts and old radar stations sitting right on the shingled coast. Niall thought it was the UK's only desert, though on the way Tim told him this is an urban myth, that it's "not at all a desert, technically and environmentally."

The sea is rough and tumbling when Niall, Tim, and a small team arrive in unmarked cars. Niall gets out, and immediately a blunted, warm sea wind hits him. It disturbs the marram grass, making it sway and bend and crack. It's hot, but wild.

Niall agrees with Tim: Dungeness possibly is a good place to hide. Not really a small village, more disparate and eerie holiday homes that people pass through week after week, separated by shingle and the sort of stiff plants you'd find in a terrarium, all cut through by a single winding tarmac path.

One lone pub with a swinging sign that sounds like grating metal. A tiny café that, even now, in the high summer, is closed. You could stay anonymous here, for sure. You could see almost nobody.

A lighthouse stands sentry, looking over everything, a single bulb burning at the top. An officer tries the door, but it is locked, the ground-floor window boarded up, empty.

They're in plain clothes. An informal reconnaissance right now. The only way to leave the estate is by road, unless you have a boat, so it doesn't matter that they're conspicuous, in convoy. So far, the text and coordinates could be something and nothing, but Niall doesn't think so. He feels a thrill work its way up his body as they begin to door-knock, officers spreading out in all directions.

The police spiral outward, knocking on the doors of each small holiday home. Niall heads to one of the huts, a small black wooden structure no bigger than most people's bedrooms called "Radar" that stands, angular, on the horizon, like a crow. As he walks toward it, the pub sign squeaks behind him, and he wonders why nobody's thought to oil it. The sound would drive him mad.

He reaches the door of Radar. It's partially clad in corrugated iron, brown, sits right on the coastline, sea stretching out behind it. Niall raises a hand to knock, but just before his fist connects, he sees movement within, through the small round glass window. He pauses, staring, eyes gritty from sea spray.

Nothing more. He squints. It could be him. It really could. On the run for seven years. Imagine if he found him. Brought him to justice.

Niall sends a couple of team members a message, then waits, not moving, not wanting to alert the shadowy form within. He peers around the side of the small hut. There's nowhere for him to escape this time.

Maidstone and another colleague, Robinson, arrive. They look through the glass, then brace themselves.

A single shout—"*Police!*"—and they force the door. And just like one of his dreams, Niall finds he can't go in. His feet and legs stop working. He turns away, staying outside, his shoulders rounded and scared, a coward's stance. Jess formally diagnosed complex PTSD, but Niall dismissed it. Almost every hostage negotiator has some trauma or other, he said, and she said, "Does that make it OK?"

"Come on," Niall says to himself, then takes a breath and heads inside, thinking of that night seven years ago, the shots, Viv's absence, and stares around. Open-plan kitchen, bedroom, living room, all in one.

There's a coat, hung up by its hood on a wardrobe door that is swinging slightly in the breeze of a Dyson fan.

No Deschamps here.

Five minutes later, the owner of the coat arrives back. He's been walking on the beach. That's all.

Niall sighs. He's wrong again. Spooked again. Later, in the pub, they will discuss him, he assumes.

He turns and walks to the next hut; that sentence uttered by Rosalind is still rattling around his brain, and rattling him: *For a hostage negotiator, you are a terrible communicator.* Well, maybe he's a terrible hostage negotiator, too, he thinks. No one has yet found Deschamps on the estate. Niall brought everyone to the very end of Kent and all they found was a coat hanging on a wardrobe, a few holidaymakers, and no Deschamps. He made everyone wait to go into the warehouse, and look what happened there. He sighs, looking up into the arching summer sky, lights up a cigarette, and tries to stop thinking for a while. Just a little while.

27

Cam

Sometimes, Cam thinks she sees him. In a crowd, boarding a Tube. She does it today at the school gate, somebody in a dark-blue jacket and a hat, even in the heat, disappearing behind a flower-lined wall.

Cam blinks. It was nothing. But something about it makes her stop, makes her chest feel hollow and spooked. The feeling of eyes on her, just like at the Tube at Putney. She darts across the pavement, looks up the street, but he's gone.

Polly appears in the distance, distracting Cam, surrounded as ever by a gaggle of friends. "You'll have to give me a tour of your house!" Cam hears her exclaim to somebody so new Cam doesn't even recognize her. She stares at her shoes and smiles at the overfamiliarity of her daughter, the American inflection from too much YouTube, and waits, thinking how interesting parenthood is. That this person was in there all along; even as a baby she found everything funny and happy-making. Cam spent her childhood reading Goosebumps books on playground benches: she sometimes finds she has no idea how to parent an extrovert.

The weather is close, air clouded over, sun only occasionally slicing through like smoke curling underneath a door.

A conversation between two school mums, Kelly Bentley and Isobel Morris, plays out next to Cam, the tone gossipy. Cam pauses, her body as still as an animal in the wild. Nobody at the school apart from the head has yet worked out what Luke did. Many have assumed he's an ab-sent father, an acrimonious divorce somewhere in Cam's past, and Cam never corrects them. She is therefore, as Cam Fletcher, mostly under the radar, but goes on high alert whenever she overhears anything remotely salacious.

Polly has stopped walking now but is still talking animatedly with her new friends.

"I have such awful IBS," Isobel says to Kelly, and Cam relaxes. IBS, not infamy. Well, good. But it reminds her of conversations she used to have with friends . . . her closest friend, Holly, the freelance editor. Their relationship limped on for a year or so after the siege, but Cam couldn't keep pretending her life was normal enough to have a glass of wine with a mate. It just wasn't. They lost touch, texts unanswered by Cam.

Kelly catches Cam looking, and says, "Sorry for the overshare. TMI discussion over here."

"Not at all," Cam says, waving a hand. "I used to have that, but, do you know, peppermint tea really *did* help." This is a total lie, but it erupts out of Cam, nevertheless. This is how she does it. Keep them going. Keep them talking. Never let them know she's weird, and lonely, and fragile. Act natural, so natural, no one ever gets too close.

She distracts herself with her phone. Libby has sent a characteristic string:

So jaded this morning.

Look at this awful house I have to market.

A photo of a messy living room, clothes everywhere, a curtain hanging off the rail at one end.

Also.

How're you?

"You're based on Bucks Avenue, right?" Kelly says, interrupting Cam's reading.

"Where are you?" Cam asks, not answering directly.

"Oh, nowhere as nice as that. I love it there, the little houses with the bedrooms downstairs?"

"That's it," Cam says, and she's got to get out of here. She doesn't know these women, and so the scales are unevenly balanced. They know where she lives: What if they know who she is? She knows it is irrational, but she can't help it. She turns away from them, folding her arms across her body. And she swears she can *feel* it: the look they exchange about her.

Come on, Polly, she thinks, willing her daughter to get moving.

Cam checks her email. She needs more immersion than her phone will afford. She has a submission from a debut author called Jenny, about a woman who discovers her son is a member of an incel group online. Interesting pitch, she thinks, and opens the manuscript right there at the school gate.

It's bone cold on the Saturday when I decided to finally follow Nate. He doesn't notice at all, his lit-up gaze drawn downwards always to the bright mobile phone in his hand. We go like this, me a few hundred yards behind him, for the mile to the bus stop. There is nowhere to hide in the blank-skied winter, but he doesn't look over his shoulder. Not even once.

Cam's breathing instantly slows. She's away from the heat, the school gate, and she's there. Somewhere else, *someone* else. She requests the full manuscript immediately. Anything that grips her she requests: that's her rule. As simple as that. Not worried about genre, about salability. Good books find a home with Cam.

Polly stops talking and eventually arrives, and Cam puts her phone away, rushing to her, squatting down to her level. "What's new?" she says to her, one of their phrases, and Polly beams at Cam.

"Sandwiches for lunch, Sam has a cat, my new friend has moved into a house called the Cuckoo's Nest," she says in her typical Polly way, streams of information bursting forth like a geyser.

Polly reaches her arms out to Cam, and there is something so wholesome about this, so pure, it makes Cam forget everything: parenthood is an exercise in mindfulness that you didn't even know you needed.

Cam holds her to her chest. "And a butterfly came into the class!" Polly exclaims so loudly, right into Cam's ear. Cam's eyes fill with tears as she finds herself having the thought she manages mostly to keep at bay: Luke would love her. He would have loved whoever they made, but he would *love* Polly.

"Right," Kelly says. "I need to get home to chop vegetables. Scintillating life I lead."

As she leaves with her child in tow, Cam thinks that her own behavior is so sad, it's so very sad: Kelly and Isobel probably only want Cam to be their friend.

Miss Ashcroft comes out, now, heading for Cam, who winces, but relaxes as she passes her, off to talk to some poor other parent. Luke has come up only once, in an incident six months ago.

"Got a second?" Miss Ashcroft had said on a freezing-cold December day. It was almost four, twilight, Christmas lights entwined around the school fence, and Cam *felt* those three words so vividly that she could almost see them written in the air, her breath hot-dust white, a warning flare in the night.

They headed inside, down a corridor that smelled of lemon floor wax, plasticine, and stale lunchboxes, and into Polly's classroom.

Polly was still with the teaching assistant, being encouraged to tidy her tray. Cam had eyed the two of them, half-amused. It was not surprising that Polly was messy, and Cam smiled as she watched the TA try to extract loose pencils and wax crayons and curled sugar paper in order to pull the tray out. Funny how genes worked. Somewhere on some DNA strand deep in her husband's and daughter's bodies was coded: *I'd really rather be having fun than tidying up.*

"Fathers came up today," Miss Ashcroft said, as if reading Cam's mind. "Who has daddies, who has two mummies, and so on. One of the kids asked about something they'd seen on TV about single-parent families."

"Right," Cam said.

"So Polly asked if *I* knew where her father was?" Miss Ashcroft said. "She says you say the police say he's bad, that he had to go away. But nothing more? Obviously, Mr. Daniels has advised me . . . but—well. We wondered when you intended to tell Polly the full truth."

And with that, an arrow was fired right into Cam's heart. She remained standing there, listening, but her real self was speared against the back wall in the Christmas bauble display, blood splattered everywhere.

She met Miss Ashcroft's gaze. "When do you advise?" she asked her.

Too direct, too acerbic, but she couldn't help herself. Anger at the police, anger at Luke, anger at even the anonymous dead bodies . . . it all spills out sometimes, onto teachers, her sister, and, most of all, herself. For marrying him but being so lovelorn that she doesn't even regret that. That she lives with hope that he will one day come back, or that she will receive an explanation. The conflicting emotions of it all.

"Why was it being discussed?" she added, an unreasonable question, but she needed to set out her stall: off limits. He is off limits. Cam's stance is not that it didn't happen but rather that he simply still belongs to her. His memory belongs to her. *Don't take him from me.*

Cam had glanced over at Polly. Her eyes were the same as Luke's; her hair was the same. Cam loved it: She could still see him every day. Could pretend he was still here, and, in many ways, Cam is sure that he is. She'd know if he were dead. She *would*.

"It's natural for us to discuss fathers in school," Miss Ashcroft said. "The management and I are aware of your situation and try our best."

Cam had to disclose it when Polly started school. There's a form you have to fill in—another one—when you have an *unusual family circumstance.* That one didn't have the right boxes for Cam to fill in either.

"Obviously," Cam continues, "the truth is very delicate."

"I know."

"What did you say?"

"I said Polly should speak to you."

Cam cringed. Later, she'd brought it up with Polly. Had asked what Miss Ashcroft had said. Polly waved a hand: "Oh, something about dads," she said. The in-the-moment life of a seven-year-old. Cam had let a breath out: on borrowed time, still, but she didn't care.

Nothing happens today. Miss Ashcroft has passed by. Isobel's child comes out with extra spellings to work on and Cam feels a grim spark of Schadenfreude.

As they leave, Polly looks across the street, exclaims, and points. "Look!"

"What?" Cam says, following her gaze. And it's the man. The man in the dark clothes and beanie she's sure she saw ducking away from the school gate.

"He was staring at us!" Polly says, and Cam watches him go, not looking at them, darting back into the Tube station, body language furtive.

"Oh—no, he's fine," she reassures her daughter. She wishes she could believe her own words.

Cam is looking at the many books in her bedroom and thinking that it's funny how she had craved this alone time, this me-time, when Polly was little, and she never got it. And now, single, she has far too much of it. Swaths and swaths of these slow-moving evening hours. She moves Luke's AirPods off his bedside table and fiddles with them absentmindedly.

She drags Adam's jiffy bag onto her lap, her treat, and pulls the manuscript out. She hasn't started it yet, has been saving it in the way you don't quite want to crack open a perfectly smooth Easter egg. But now she peels back the first page.

It started with a task.

Good opener.

The air was cold as gunmetal and the moon was up out ahead, a snowball thrown into the sky and forgotten. I left my house with a job to do set by my father. I'd debated whether to take it, and in the end had decided to. It turned out to be the worst decision of my life.

He's done it. Cam can feel it. The book feels propulsive and intentional to her. And it's so delicious, the slide into make-believe, that she can almost feel it on her skin like a warm embrace.

28

Cam couldn't feel less like going to a publishing do the next night, but it's the launch of one of her newest clients' books, and she can't miss it. She's in the kitchen, with Polly sitting on the counter, swinging her legs and clapping her hands rhythmically in a way so affected Cam is sure it's come from a new friend.

"Auntie Libby's here," Polly says suddenly, pointing to the front door, visible beyond the hallway and down the stairs.

Libby lets herself in and calls out, "I'm here, dudes!"

But Cam immediately notices that there is something odd and careful about her walk. God, it must be exhausting to be Libby. Everyone who knows her always scrutinizing her for signs of pregnancy.

Without saying anything more, Libby arrives in the kitchen and nudges Cam out of the way, then puts two slices of bread into the toaster: Polly's current pre-bed snack. Something about Libby knowing this makes Cam's heart happy. The familiarity, the ease of it. It takes a village, and here is hers.

"Good day?" Cam says.

"Surviving—sold a house. Well, Si did actually."

"Ooh, the messy one?"

"Yes. Pair of rich twats. Too important to clean. Plus, the bin was full of their Deliveroos. Ever think you're in the wrong job?"

"What did they do?"

"They work in oil or something—I pretended to understand."

Cam smiles. "Let's set up an oil rig," she says, and Libby snorts.

"Si would love that," she says. "He described the house as being *full of lovely natural, lived-in accoutrements* on the listing. He'd happily quit. Is it the rom-com book? Tonight? I read the copy you gave me."

"It is," Cam says.

"Boring one," Polly says, though she hasn't read it. But—to Cam's shame—her daughter thinks most books are tedious.

"I liked it," Libby says. "I thought it was very well edited. Although—saccharine ending."

"You're both the wrong readership," Cam says with a laugh. "For different reasons."

Polly giggles, too, though in the way kids do when they don't quite get the joke but want to.

"Who's the target readership? People with books all over their bed?" Libby asks.

"Yes. Exactly," Cam says, suddenly remembering that she was the exact same at university, studying English. Libby had arrived to visit, and said, "Er, why are you sharing a bed with D. H. Lawrence?"

Libby grabs the butter from the fridge. "Crusts off?" she says to Polly. She looks at Cam. "It's good you're going out again," she says, her tone warm and genuine—for Libby—but Cam finds it threatening, like walking too close to an open fire.

Libby is of the view that Cam ought to have moved on. It began as advice *for Cam's own good* but has segued into generalized tension if Cam doesn't appear to be living quite normally, or is maudlin sometimes on anniversaries, or has let friendships slip (all true).

"Well, it's a client," Cam says. "But I appreciate the sentiment: your sad sister, finally getting out."

"No . . ." Libby says, though she doesn't seem to mean it.

Cam studies Libby closely. Is she being slightly tentative about her body, her stomach? She watches her. Yes, she is. It's almost like she's injured . . . and is guarding herself. Cam inhales, saying nothing, only hoping.

Suddenly, Cam wants to stay here. Find out where Libby's at. Sit in loungewear and catch up. "God, I wish I didn't have to go," she says.

Libby throws her a quick look. "No. We just said! It's good for you to go."

Cam shrugs, irritated. She can see the humanity in what Libby wants for her, but Cam was always introverted. Now more so, but it's hardly like she used to go raving.

"Use the babysitter," Libby says, finishing buttering the toast.

"You're not a babysitter," Cam says, and Libby's dimples appear on each side of her mouth. A small smile.

"Libby, do you share a bed with Uncle Si?" Polly says, from nowhere.

"Polly, that's very personal," Cam says.

"It's fine," Libby says with a laugh. "Yes, we do. A big bed."

Cam's body is tensed. Is this some sort of father chat rearing its head again? Or nothing? She glances at her sister, but her face is impassive, relaxed. *It's fine*, she tells herself. *The decision you have made not to tell Polly the full truth yet is fine: it's better for her.*

"Every night?" Polly presses.

"Every night," Libby says, arranging the toast onto two plates. "Though less if he snores. Shall we have this in bed, then brush teeth?" Her tone is bombastic, but she throws Cam a look. Just that, an interested look, but there's curiosity in it too.

Cam is standing next to a bookcase full of leather tomes and an editor from Simon & Schuster. Nearby is a *Mail* journalist, which she's glad for: hopefully they will review Cam's client's book.

They're in Goldsboro Books, one of the oldest bookshops in Britain, hidden up an ancient Victorian street, the buildings out front higgledy-piggledy, clustered like people gathered shoulder to shoulder in the cold. Outside, it's finally raining, tassels of water coming down from the awning. Umbrellas litter the floor by the front door, some opened up to dry, others together like bunches of flowers, glistening wet.

Cam is surprised to see Adam over on the other side of the room—she didn't know he was coming—and she touches his arm as he passes her. "I didn't know you'd be here!"

"Oh yeah—just for a bit," he says. He looks well, tanned: finishing a book suits him. "How's things?"

"Well—very good, obviously," Cam says. "Thank you for your book," she says.

Just as he is about to respond, somebody comes over, interrupts them. A fan, a reader, wanting Adam's signature, and Cam feels a bloom of pride run across her chest.

She turns back to the editor and sees a couple standing in the back, arms slung around each other. She thinks of Charlie. She ought to text him. She should have brought him here tonight, a plus-one. Something deep in Cam cannot bring herself to do this sort of thing regularly. Her mind hardened, seven years ago, around a Luke-shaped wound, never to be the same again. Everyone who has been badly hurt or betrayed must surely have this wound. A deep, reticular network of nerves and impulses within them that says, *Don't get too close. Don't rely on anybody.*

This editor has never acquired anything from Cam, mostly deals in nonfiction, but Cam has always liked her: she is a huge bookworm, always has a paperback she's reading for pleasure in her handbag. For an industry that runs on books, there aren't too many true, bighearted readers like Adrienne, who once told her she read *Dark Places* by Gillian Flynn while in labor. Cam hasn't seen her in years and hasn't spoken to her since before Luke.

Later, Adrienne says, after small talk about the relentless sun and now flash floods, "Look, I wanted to say . . ." She puts her prosecco down on a bookshelf. Her tone is muted, her voice low as the buzz of the launch carries on around them.

Cam braces herself. Unlike the school run, with new friends who post-date her husband's act, Luke is much more of an open secret in publishing. One that she dodges and weaves, and that people are mostly too polite to reference directly.

She meets Cam's eyes. "I knew your husband, a little."

"Oh," Cam says. And immediately, she's looking for the exit, blocked by umbrellas.

But Adrienne stretches a hand out to Cam. "No—no. I really liked him. Our paths crossed because he needed to know a bit about something he was working on. The singer—I was working on a companion book for him, so we had a few meetings."

"I see."

"He was lovely."

Cam sighs. The thing people don't realize is if they ignore Luke, Cam feels bad. But if they mention him, she feels blindsided. They can't win.

She steadies her breathing, looking out onto the street. If you could ignore the people passing by with lit-up smartphones, the hum of traffic a few hundred yards away, you really could be in a Dickens novel, a place Cam finds comfort. Suddenly, she wants to read and acquire some great historical fiction. Disappear into an armchair and into the past.

A passing waiter wordlessly tops up their prosecco, and Cam downs half of it, cool pine needles in her throat.

Cam tilts her head back slightly, exhaling through her nose like a smoker; the room swims slightly. She isn't used to drinking much, but maybe she could be.

"Our last meeting was only a few weeks before—everything," Adrienne says.

Cam glances up at her sharply. "He wasn't working on anything I didn't know about, was he?" she asks.

"He wasn't working on anything controversial at all. He met me to allow me to ask a couple of questions about his singer. He agreed for the free lunch, I think."

"Of course," Cam says, unable to hide a small smile. That sounds like Luke all right.

"He was the last person I'd have imagined to . . . He was—not . . . like that."

Cam, previously breathing in the anecdote like a nostalgic perfume, recoils. The past tense slices through her like a guillotine. Sharp and fast, a clean beheading. *Was.* She wants to tell Adrienne that she really thinks Luke is alive out there somewhere, but doesn't.

"I know," she says quietly. She finishes her prosecco and immediately looks for more. The main lights go off and a few lamps pop on here and there in the bookshop. The dim air smells of old paper, and at least Cam feels at home here.

"He and I had a long chat over lunch," Adrienne continues. "I think about it often. I had had this nonfiction totally tank, lovely author, but it just didn't land. Sold a hundred copies."

"Oh—jeez."

"Yeah, and I chatted to Luke about it, and he said, 'I find it helpful, at times, to think of Cam, and how much fiction means to her. To real readers, sales don't matter, prizes don't matter. She sits in a chair every night and just has the time of her life.'"

Cam shivers there in the warm bookshop. Her husband's unheard observation of her, reported back to her here, years after the event, seven years since he left. The information is old—so, so far in the deep past—but nevertheless, it feels to Cam like Luke has made eye contact with her, somewhere. Tears mist over and then quickly clear. The crying lasts less time these days, but still comes so readily, the same brimming wateriness she's carried for years, like all of her emotions are just closer to the surface: a river perpetually about to burst its banks and overflow.

"That's nice to hear," she says thickly as a waiter tops up her drink again. She stares down into the chain-linked bubbles, eyes wet, thinking of Charlie and his cynicism about publishing.

Cam spots one of her authors' books on a shelf nearby, spine out, and pulls it out and props it up, cover-out. Every little bit does seem to help in these situations. Maybe it isn't pointless. Maybe fiction is one of life's great comforts. Maybe it does matter as much as she feels it does. Maybe Luke is out there somewhere, not just at a lunch in the past, talking about his wife. Maybe their story will get its third act.

"I can't believe you never found out—or you never found . . . what happened to him." Adrienne takes her drink and sips it again.

"No," Cam says glumly. And she can feel herself unfurling, here in the bookshop, out of her sad and hard shell forged in a single day, seven years ago. "You think you will, or you'll get over it, or even that you will learn to live with the uncertainty, but the reality is that you don't. You just remain sad about it." She pauses, then adds: "Still searching." It's the nearest she can come to telling the real, full, embarrassing truth.

"I bet," Adrienne says softly. "I cannot, I really cannot imagine." She puts her hand to her chest, still holding her glass, looking dolefully at Cam. "I wish I'd got to see him again. He canceled our last meeting for that funeral."

"What? What funeral?" Cam says, her voice too sharp. She has no idea what Adrienne means; she is, all this time later, still looking for clues. "When?"

"I don't know," Adrienne says, curiosity crossing her brows, then opening her features in surprise. "Um . . . it must have been very close to—the siege."

"Nobody we knew had died," Cam says, thinking that you don't use a funeral as an excuse. You use a doctor's appointment, a meeting clash, childcare woes. A funeral is macabre, specific and taboo. She looks down, blinks, wants to tip the entire glass of prosecco down her throat.

"Right."

"Is there some way you can tell me when, precisely?" Cam says. "Sorry to ask . . ."

Adrienne holds her glass and works her phone out of her pocket. "Sure," she says. "Yeah. My work calendar will—it'll probably go back that far, won't it? God, sorry about this," she says, and she does look mortified. "I didn't mean to—throw a cat amongst the pigeons."

"It's fine."

Adrienne puts her glass on a nearby shelf and begins typing, two-handed, on her phone. And Cam thinks that something is happening, something is brewing. She can feel it as close as the storm outside.

Nothing for years. Nothing, nothing, nothing—just the steadfast trying to move on, like swimming against a current, putting in all that effort just to get nowhere. Reminding herself of what he did. A double murder of two anonymous souls.

But now this. Coordinates. Information. Cam knows somewhere deep inside her that it is significant.

She stares at Adrienne's hammered silver thumb ring as she types. It throws little diamonds of light over the walls. She's looking at her slim wrists, her purple-painted nails, thinking nothing. Trying to think nothing. Trying not to hope.

"The sixteenth of June," Adrienne says. "Like I said. He said he had a funeral. He got his phone out to check his calendar. I think it said Whitechapel."

"That's five days before the . . . the siege."

"I'm sorry—I . . . I didn't think anything of it." The unsaid lingers in the air between them: *And I didn't think it mattered to you anymore.*

"No. And why would you?" Cam says.

"I mean . . ." Adrienne says, but the sentence goes nowhere.

"I'd better go," Cam says. She's had too much to drink; she's said too much. Suddenly, the quaint surroundings feel menacing. Cam has always cautioned authors about running their mouth at publishing dos fueled by alcohol, and here she is doing just that herself. Oversharing. Asking for information. She's forgotten herself.

"Sure, nice to chat," Adrienne says lightly. "And yeah—I hope . . . I hope I haven't upset you. I don't know."

Cam says goodbye to her client, leaves, and heads out onto the wet, hot street. The air smells of evening petrichor and she takes the long way home, across Waterloo Bridge thinking of those coordinates farther north. Her head is swimming with prosecco and the conversation she's just had. A funeral.

Halfway across, she stops and stares down at where the deep, navy-blue water sits and sloshes. And right there, in the middle of the bridge, she googles it. *Funeral 16 June 2017, Whitechapel.* Maybe it'll show something. Some archive somewhere.

And it does.

29

Niall

The Met has continued surveillance on Cam's house. They've had her phone tapped for four months, but they now also have a small team watching her house on Bucks Avenue, in case Deschamps reaches out.

But that doesn't stop Niall passing by today. Nobody can tell him not to go to Putney. Even if it is incredibly out of his way.

It's five o'clock in the morning. OK—so it isn't out of his way: he isn't going anywhere at all; he got up after his gunshot dream and came. But he feels something, deep inside him. Somebody wanted to get hold of her. And the nighttime is when people act on these impulses. Niall has on a Royal Mail T-shirt he bought off eBay, which comes in handy in these sorts of situations: no one questions a postman.

Besides, he is more observant and more patient than anyone on the Met's surveillance team. That's the reality. So say he comes down here a few nights a week, sits for an hour, maybe two. He might catch Deschamps himself.

From Cam's street you can see an unusual summer mist rising in the distance, coming off the river like ripped-up cotton candy after the wet night. The light at this hour is blue, the air cool, the houses sleeping. Only two lit-up windows on the whole street, night workers maybe, or else insomniacs. Probably police, Niall thinks drily.

He immediately clocks his colleagues' car—unmarked—parked a few hundred yards down the road, and dodges out of its line of vision. Postman or not, he could do without being recognized, without his colleagues finding out that he believes surveillance teams merely sit, talk shit, eat McDonald's, and wait to retire (though they absolutely do).

He stands in the shadow of an alleyway for ten minutes, twenty, just looking and watching. No Deschamps, no visitors at all. Cam and Polly likely sleeping inside, the owner of the Dungeness burner phone given up, for now maybe, knowing they've been traced.

Niall waits there for two hours, standing up. He's not as fit as he used to be, and by seven his knees have begun to ache. He's positioned himself near to her front door, then behind her house, too, checking the garden gate. He's not certain the Met would be this thorough.

Back on the street, near Camilla's door, he stares down an alleyway across the road, his expression blank. Niall knows you have to monitor a house many times until you see something, so he's surprised when he sees a form. No, a movement, at the end of an alley running between two terraced houses, dawn-lit at its opening. Out of the sphere of police surveillance. They will be looking at the house: Niall is looking into places where people might hide.

And just stepping across the alleyway is a man. Tall. Dark hair.

Without thinking, Niall hurries across the street, through the wrought-iron gate, and down the alley.

He reaches the end, looks left and right into the fenced-off gardens, dew on their grass, but there's nobody. There are four more alleyways spiraling off, and he chooses one at random, runs down it, but it's empty, nobody on the other side of it either. He's lost him. He made the wrong decision.

The Deschamps briefings stopped about a year after his disappearing act, and Niall hasn't missed them. This is the first formal one since the arrival of those coordinates, and the mood in the Scotland Yard back board-room is lazy, the dog days of late June, the weather too hot outside. Two DSs are unwrapping frozen fruit bars, the packets leaving orange sticky marks on the table.

He walks in just before it begins. Funny, he still feels self-conscious about this case. In the end, nobody moved him off it but himself, but still, failure is failure, to Niall. That's what his dad used to say anyway.

On the desk is a set of texts and calls Camilla has made. Two are to Luke's number. Hang-ups. To hear his voice, he guesses. Something sympathetic spikes inside him. How sad.

"In short," Lambert says, promoted up the ranks and now leading on this—he lets Niall sit in—"there is no indication the wife knows anything about Deschamps's whereabouts. His passport remains unused, bank accounts closed or inactive, no CCTV sightings, nothing came up in our ramped-up surveillance of Camilla. We'll monitor for another month, if the authorizing officer approves, and then stop again. Even she, herself, is applying to have him declared dead. Not exactly the behavior of someone in touch with him. No need to waste more resources on it."

A disappointed murmur moves around the meeting room. No coppers like cases without any answers at all: they're trained not to. But this is more than that. Usually, there's a working hypothesis. For this one, nothing. A missing man. Two dead, identity-less hostages. It makes no sense to anyone. Did Deschamps target them? How did Deschamps identify a crime that could be not quite victimless but almost?

It's time for Niall to speak up, though he doesn't want to. The push/pull of being here, back on the Deschamps case. He wants answers, and he also wants out. To go to sleep and forget, to never be woken by those gunshots again.

"Just . . ." Niall says, and Lambert looks at him, expression blank: the sort of face that says, *Feel free to speak up, but I'm not going to encourage you.* "I'd rather surveillance don't know, but I was passing there this morning, and I saw someone hanging around. Was it police? Tall guy, dark hair."

"Where?" Maidstone says. He writes something down. Niall hopes he won't pass it on: surveillance are always good to have onside, even if you think they're inadequate.

"At the end of the alleyway opposite Camilla's house," Niall says. "Clearly looking across at her windows, until he saw me. It wasn't Deschamps, but . . . ?"

"I'll relay it, and we'll keep an eye, but only for the next month."

"And that's it—we just stop? Random men watching Camilla. Two dead—still unknown—hostages. The man himself sending coordinates to his wife . . ."

"You might think it was him, but there's very little evidence of that."

"Who else is it realistically going to be?" Niall asks.

"Could be anyone. Literally anyone in the world," Lambert says shortly.

"Yeah, but who does that?"

"We've pursued the lines of inquiry," Lambert says, his tone light, and Niall feels a surge of disappointment that this is who he ended up as. That rock-metal-loving DS who could get anything out of a suspect is now the same as all the others: by the book. "We went to Dungeness. We're watching the house. So far, nothing. This is all expended resources, and it's also heavy surveillance of an innocent woman."

"So that's that then," Niall says.

"What do you suggest?" Lambert says, his tone ice.

"Working a little harder? Or at least a little smarter."

"By which you mean . . ."

"Keep looking for the man I saw. Keep looking for the man we saw on her street four months ago. Keep going back to Dungeness. Ask market traders in the area whether they sold a burner phone to anyone matching his description," Niall says, frustrated. This is how it goes with the Met. He's sure some crimes remain unsolved due to lack of effort, rigid thinking, and red tape. "Does Text Anon have any details of where the text was sent from?"

"A VPN routed to Brazil. A proxy server, designed to hide a location," Lambert says.

"Who would do that but a fugitive? Have you got Claire in telecoms on it?" Niall says, but he will ask her himself.

"Any spammer who wanted anything. A petty dealer who got the wrong number."

"Is that not a crime?" Niall says—a cheap shot, really, one he doesn't even mean.

"Not worth a full surveillance budget," Lambert says humorlessly, conversation closed. "We can't keep throwing good money after bad. If it was Deschamps, he will slip up again one day, if he's out there."

"Yeah, and we won't be looking," Niall says.

Lambert straightens some papers on the table, clears his throat. "Sometimes," he says lightly, "it's best to just accept that some investigations are better off without your input. Speaking generally."

Niall sits back in his seat, disappointed. He's glad he bought the new burner phone the other day: and now's the time to use it. He's given the Met time to trace Deschamps officially, and they haven't. It's time for him to act.

Therapists, another hostage negotiator once told Niall, call it "hand-on-the-door syndrome." When people reveal themselves only as they're leaving, and then bring up the topic that means the most to them.

Jess wants to talk about the gunshots. She wants to get to the bottom of why he hears them. Doesn't seem quite satisfied with the explanation that Niall made a mistake and is haunted by it.

Hand-on-the-door syndrome. Niall does just that in Jess's office today. It's raining, rare summer rain, the world outside her windowpane a watercolor. "Rosalind said Viv never got over me," he says, summer jacket slung on, palm—proverbially only: Jess always opens the door for him—on the handle.

He has nobody to discuss it with, and the conversation keeps moving fast around his mind like a ping-pong ball. He's got to get it out, somehow.

"Oh," Jess says, clearly surprised. "And how do you feel about that?"

She takes her glasses off and begins to clean them on her shirt. Takes one to know one, thinks Niall: she's telling him there's no hurry, inviting him to talk even though the session is over, pretending she isn't listening avidly. "Surprised," Niall says. "She ended it. Said she played second fiddle to my work."

Jess pauses, perhaps weighing what to say, then concluding that Niall can deal with it. She looks directly at him, no glasses, eyes clear. "And did she?"

"Yes."

"Do you regret that?"

Niall turns his mouth down, not saying anything.

"What exactly did she say to Rosalind?" Jess asks.

"I don't know. Rosalind said she'd finished with this boyfriend of hers, the American with the rescue dog"—Jess raises her eyebrows at this—"and that it was because of me."

"Do *you* think it was because of you?"

"I don't know. I have no idea. After she left I . . ." Niall says. His throat clogs as he thinks of that night. It's all tied together for him. The rain intensifies outside. Jess's office roof is flat; they can hardly hear each other over it.

"I told her she didn't play second fiddle to my job."

"But you said that she did."

"I know. But she wouldn't. I . . . I don't know. It's mad," Niall says. "I forgot her birthday, is all."

"Is that all?"

"Maybe. I don't know. No. But sometimes I . . . I just think there's another chance for us." Niall meets her eyes again as he says this, and Jess's face falls in sympathy, perhaps feeling sorry for a deluded old fool.

"Do you think Viv thinks that?"

"I don't know. Probably not."

"Maybe she didn't believe you," Jess says lightly. "When you assured her." She puts her glasses back on. They magnify her eyes, a clear green, not unlike Viv's.

"Believe me?"

"That she isn't second fiddle."

"Rosalind said I am a crap communicator, considering what I do," Niall says.

"Everyone is, about something," Jess says, seeing him out now into the corridor, where it's quieter. "Their Achilles' heel."

"Hmm," Niall says, turning to her as they part, hoping for more wisdom, but it doesn't come. Time's up.

Downstairs, he buys a pain au chocolat from the bakery and gets his new burner phone out. He's going to try to contact Deschamps. He can't leave the case to go cold again, Deschamps to simply remain on the run. Of course he sent those coordinates. Of course he did, and nobody is trying hard enough to find him.

He just needs to bait him with something he cares about, that's all.

Without thinking of the firm boundary he's crossing with the Met—sod the Met and their due processes—he dials Deschamps's burner phone's number. Voicemail. He tries again. Voicemail.

But this time, he sends a text, thinking of himself, and what would get him moving. And it's Viv. It's always been Viv.

If you want to see your wife again, I can help you, he writes.

30

Cam

Cam saved the social media posts about the funerals for here: in bed, early in the morning, by herself. She'd started reading last night, became too spooked, and resumes now. Things feel calmer in the lemonade morning light.

The facts are that one event matches what Cam is looking for: there was a funeral held for a teenager called Alexander Hale on June 16 the year Luke went missing. There was also a funeral for a James Lancaster the week before.

Both teenagers were murdered, their bodies found together on the grounds of a housing estate in east London. It's easy to find the story in the national papers. Their killer was never found.

It feels to Cam like each individual hair on the back of her neck is rising up, until they're standing and quivering.

Alexander—Alex to his friends—was eighteen, a Just Eat delivery driver and amateur footballer, and he was murdered on April 21. Found with a catastrophic head injury at the back of his skull.

James was found with a bullet wound to his temple.

Their bodies only inches from the other.

Their funerals didn't happen for seven to eight more weeks because of the police investigation into their murders.

And Luke canceled seeing Adrienne because of a funeral on the same day. The sixteenth. That was Alexander's funeral.

But . . . April 21 was the date Luke turned off his location data, wasn't it? Didn't Niall say that?

Here is a date that matches when Luke attended a funeral, and a date that matches him obscuring his location data.

She flicks back through her calendar on her iPhone, grateful it still seems to remember every detail of her life, but there's nothing for her on June 16. Not a single entry.

She wonders idly how many funerals take place per day in Whitechapel. She couldn't even guess it. There must be many that aren't so high-profile and aren't on social media. She must be jumping to conclusions.

She puts the date into the photo app on her iPhone, not able to quite admit to herself what her suspicions are, and she starts to scan, hoping to jog her own memory, and she is immediately assaulted with something more painful than a weapon: the past. Nostalgia exists for other people, not Cam, and she physically winces as she sees their family unit of three populate on her phone. Cam, Luke, Polly. Tiny baby feet in laps. A selfie of her and Luke in bed at eight thirty at night.

Her heart hurts with it, feels dense and heavy, like somebody has put their palm to Cam's chest and pressed down. Everything they had, everything they lost, because of him. In the days after the siege and Luke's disappearance, Polly had swiveled her head to the door a couple of times, perhaps looking for Luke, perhaps not. And that had been the only hint that she'd noticed at all: her father gone, before her brain had fully formed. Later, people told Cam to find comfort in this—that Polly *didn't know any different*—and Cam had thought about zoo animals who never knew the bliss of freedom. Later, Polly had started to babble, idle nonsense: da-da-da, like all babies, only to Cam it was extra loaded.

She finds nothing for the date of the funeral or the day in April that can pinpoint where she was, where Luke was, if he was absent.

Jesus. What is she thinking here? That Luke went out for that drive in April, killed two people, with their baby present, turned his location data off, then went to his funeral in June, like some sort of Victorian evil villain?

No.

She's definitely read too much fiction.

She goes back to Google and reads more about James Lancaster, an article beneath a photo of him in sportswear, standing outside a football pitch, one leg up on a wall, broad grin, crazy hair, his mother next to him.

James Lancaster was found bleeding heavily from a single gunshot wound to the temple at midnight on 21st April, heading into the 22nd. Paramedics worked on him for over an hour but he was declared dead at the scene. His parents, whom he lived with, were informed.

No perpetrator was ever found, despite extensive enquiries, CCTV combing, Ring doorbells, car dashcam footage, and door-knocking.

'No expense was spared,' said a spokesperson from the Met.

Then, beneath a school photograph of Alexander Hale:

Alexander Hale was said to be full of a zest for life. He was found with a head injury to the back of his skull, believed to be from a blunt weapon. He is survived by his parents, Michael and Janet.

Cam reads the report, and the stories about the murders, there in bed by herself, shivering as the early-morning wind and the rain rattle past her patio doors.

JUSTICE FOR JAMES, HEARTBROKEN PARENTS' PLEA, headlines the *Daily Mail*. Cam stares at his mother and father, and she recognizes something in their expressions. A kind of heaviness. The thing about grief is that, when it happens to you, you go through the looking glass. Suddenly, everyone else lives one kind of life, with one set of problems, and you another. You're in a different world now, one you can never return from. And you only realize too late how good the first world was.

She keeps reading. The parents of each teenager never appear in the same article. No joint story sold, but then Cam wonders if she would do the same. Maybe they didn't know each other. Maybe that's part of the mystery.

Alex was out alone, walking to the corner shop around eleven at night. It was less than five minutes from the Hales' house in Whitechapel, only he never came home.

James was travelling home from a friend's house.

It is there that the murder case begins: nobody knows who killed them, or why. A head wound and a gunshot.

Both parents were alerted less than an hour later: a pensioner in a house nearby reported hearing shouting, then a gunshot. Paramedics were called to the scene but couldn't save them.

Extensive enquiries were made of the local residents of Whitechapel. Anybody who knows anything is urged to call the designated hotline below.

She googles Alexander Hale's name together with the judge whose book Luke worked on, but nothing comes up. She does the same with James Lancaster. She keeps reading, article after article after article, reaching the depths of the internet, moving on to Facebook posts.

My cousin Alexander Hale was killed on 21st April. Somebody out there will know what happened. The funeral will be held at St George-in-the-East on 16th June 2017.

According to a follow-up post, the funeral was attended by 250 people. And Cam, seven years later, is wondering if one of them was her husband.

And, if so, why.

* * *

FORM N208
STATUS: Under way

Cam is out in the garden an hour later, in the already blazing sun, bare toes warm in parched, spiked grass that rustles like straw. She will miss this house if she ever manages to move, this simple house with its neat garden, her singular deck chair worn to faded in the middle where she's sat and read reams and reams of fiction.

In the sunlight, the rain evaporating off her patio, the Whitechapel double murder and the coincidence of the location data and the funeral no longer feel as frightening or as urgent. She's connected the dots too quickly, too rashly, taking her twos and coming up with five. Luke could've been anywhere on June 16. Adrienne could have been mistaken.

She looks at her phone. Another email update from the government site sits in her inbox, about her application for Luke. It's moved from *Being processed* to *Under way*, whatever that means. The handler helped her to find the documents and stated none were needed where they didn't have them. She sighs, the air close, her breath feeling heavy. Soon, then, he will be declared dead, and Cam will have to stay in the afterworld, alone, questions over coordinates unanswered, like everything.

Her work email is full to bursting with submissions and people chasing her, but she's on leave; it's Friday, Polly has an inset day. She sips her coffee and reads the *Bookseller* and then, as the morning stretches on, Facebook—God, it's so nice that Polly lies in like this!—and then finally WhatsApp. Libby: she's up early.

LIBBY: *???*
LIBBY: *Have you seen the Mail Online?*
LIBBY: *There's a news story there about you? 'Wife of siege-starter speaks out: still searching'*

"Oh fucking fuck," Cam says aloud, standing up in the garden. "Fuck."

She opens it, then closes it, then paces. She walks to the back doors, the soles of her feet damp and warm from the puddles, then opens the article again. Task switching, biting her nails. How has this happened?

It's a whole bloody piece. This is bad. It is so bad. It is worse than when they ran the story on the note Luke left her.

A source close to Camilla Deschamps, wife of wanted Luke Deschamps, who held three hostages in a warehouse in 2017 before murdering two of them and disappearing, says literary agent Camilla, who now uses her maiden name, Fletcher, is still not "over" her husband's betrayal.

Shit.

They have linked her maiden name to her married name in the article. Her clients will see this. Charlie. Her boss. The other school mums.

Her daughter, one day: newspaper articles live forever. Polly's on the verge of being able to search for them herself, and now this.

And Luke, a small and stupid part of her brain adds.

Next to this is a pull quote in bold saying, *You don't get over it. You just remain sad about it*, accompanied by a photograph of her taken from the agency website. It looks as though Cam has sold this article to a fucking tabloid. What will everyone think?

She closes the web page then opens it again, finishing the article.

Who could have done this? She thinks of her conversation with Adrienne at the party. She's sure it isn't her, casts her mind back over and over that night. Why would she?

The *Daily Mail*.

The *Daily Mail*. And—of course. The nearby journalist. The one she hoped her client would get a *Mail* review from. No such luck. She must have earwigged instead, written up the whole story she told Adrienne. How could Cam have been so foolish?

Got a STORY or a COMMENT? the bottom of the article says. *Call us on . . .*

Cam waits, then dials it impulsively. She might be able to get it taken down. If you don't ask, you don't get.

A tinny voice informs her she is in a queue and she puts her phone on speaker on the garden table and stands by the rosebushes, hands on her hips, breathing deeply.

"You are caller number nine in the queue," the voice says, and Cam casts a disparaging glance at it. When, when, when will this ever leave her? This grief. This forever-invasion of her life. This *infamy*.

In a rage, she hangs up the phone. She's not going to tell the call handler who she is, and even if she does, she knows they won't remove the article. They never do. Forget it.

She will ignore it.

Within two minutes, she's back on the website. *RELATED STORIES*, it says underneath, populated by the articles of those first few days of the siege, but one other too. She has never seen it before; she long ago stopped googling herself or Luke. She clicks on it, opens it up.

ISABELLA LOUIS was taken hostage five years ago, and still bears the

scars today, it reads. Cam winces, not wanting to read it. She can live under the delusion her husband is good if she never hears from his victims.

She goes to close the article, but then she sees that Isabella likely
didn't consent to this article either. It bears a paparazzi shot of her
leaving an office with "Hope Therapy" above the door, Isabella clearly
unaware. Cam cringes. Some opportunist photographer, maybe, who
recognized Isabella. How embarrassing. The stories that get told. How
no one knows the truth of things unless they're in them, not really.

She goes inside to get Adam's manuscript. She's only a few pages into
his novel, too tired to read, but somehow savoring it too. He might just
be her favorite client. The prose is beautiful. A young male narrator,
raised into a criminal family who deal in drugs and murder. On his first
familial task, something is about to befall him, Cam just knows it because of the tone of the writing.

*The streets are black, the windows are black, the world is black, and I am
alone.*

It's a departure for him, a real hardboiled thriller, but Cam is enjoying
it, when her brain can focus on it for long enough.

She gets it out to read while the real world tumbles down around
her. She feels her breathing slow as she enters the portal to rainy London.
Streetlights. A misty nighttime outing in winter that goes wrong. She
clutches the manuscript, and she's there. She's there, and not here.

*You're probably wondering about me. Mum and Dad were in old
crime. The sort you don't know about until you're in it too. Money's
like water. If you have it, you pay it no attention. If you don't, you're in
drought. We had nice cars, growing up, but they always had blacked-
out windows. Dad told me my first assignment: 'All you have to do is
stand on a street corner. Literally, that's all.'*

*It wasn't all—I had to supply. Drugs. Stand there with my consign-
ment, waiting for the dealers.*

*The first go, I pretended to myself that I had something else in the
lining of our car: documents, gold bars. Anything but what it was.*

The second time was easier.

Then the third.

Cam, engrossed, writes in the margin: *Right: so this is the descent into drugs of a young man? Bold!*

Her phone trills. Once, twice. Insistent, the same way it was all those years ago, like no time has passed at all. Message after message after message.

Frustrated, Cam puts the manuscript on the table, then flicks around on her phone uselessly, trying to stop them. Acquaintances, school mums. Libby again. She wants to bury the phone deep in the manicured flower beds and run far away. She's *always* been able to use fiction to drown out the real world . . . but not today.

The school gate is worse the following Monday, after a weekend spent in paranoia about the article. Hundreds of pairs of eyes on Cam, it feels like, a torch shone into the woods at night illuminating every creature. It reminds her of the weeks after the siege. The weeks the papers speculated on Luke's note to her.

She stares down at her Kindle, even though it is being splattered by summer raindrops, reading a submission from an unpublished author, blocking it out, telling herself she's imagining it anyway. Her phone beeps, making her jump, but she's not checking it today, can't deal with the prying WhatsApps, the new Facebook friend requests. She will just throw her phone away. She doesn't need it. She doesn't. She'll bin it, live off-grid.

Just as she's thinking these irrational thoughts, a woman approaches her. Older than Cam, early fifties, maybe. The first thing that Cam thinks is that this woman doesn't want to be seen. A baseball cap, nondescript clothes, furtive body language. Maybe because of the rain, maybe not. Cam flicks her eyes to her, then back down to her Kindle, but the woman's gaze pierces through the air toward Cam, like arrows hitting her back, one after the other after the other.

"Excuse me?" comes the voice, and Cam isn't surprised. It'll be a voyeur. It'll be about the article, that stupid, stupid fucking article. "Camilla?"

"Not interested," Camilla says, eyes still down at the Kindle.

"No—I . . . Camilla." She steps closer to her. Cam inches away, goosebumps rising over her arms. "Please."

"What?"

"I need to talk to you. You know me."

"I don't."

"I am the wife," she says. "*Was*. Of one of the hostages."

Cam's head snaps up and, at the too-warm school gate, their eyes meet. Cam can't stop looking at her, this stranger.

"You were . . . ?"

The woman nods quickly, mouth a tight line, eyes wet. "Yes."

And Cam sees now that this visitor is a golden ticket. A key. A clue in the mystery. This woman means that Cam will now know who one of the hostages was.

"What's your name?" Cam says, turning to her.

To Cam's surprise, the woman steps backward, perhaps panicked. "Can you meet? Somewhere not here?" she says. "Somewhere you don't regularly go?" Her eyes flick left and right, and then she takes another step, moving away from Cam, tucking her gray hair further underneath her cap. Clearly, she's compromised her safety to come here today to see Cam. But why?

"Yes. OK."

They pause, the woman clearly wanting to get away, but Cam steps toward her once again. "Wait," she says. "Who was your husband? What was his name?"

"They told us," the woman says, voice hoarse. "They told us not to report them as missing. As dead."

"Who?"

She says nothing.

"When? Shall we meet?" Cam asks, desperate for information.

"Tomorrow?" she says. "Meet at Shadwell station. Nine o'clock in the morning. That isn't on your commute or anything?"

Cam nods quickly, thinking, Oh my God, this woman is a widow because of Luke, but thinking, most of all, that she said *Somewhere you don't regularly go*, which must mean that Cam is being followed.

31

Anonymous Reporting on Camilla

S he met Madison Smith at the school gate," I say in a low voice in the launderette. "I saw the whole thing."

My brother's eyes meet mine. Today, it's raining, long summer rains, and the launderette is cool and dim. It smells of damp clothes and damp weather.

"Noted," he says. A pause, then he adds, "Good work."

I try not to shiver with pride at this statement, but I can't help it. My brother is sparing with praise.

"What was communicated?"

"That I don't know," I answer. "I followed her home from the school, but nothing happened."

"I'll . . . Leave it with me," he says.

As I depart, I hear him making a call about Madison. I wince, just slightly, though I don't show it. It's better not to.

32

Cam

The stranger is not at Shadwell station. It's way beyond nine in the morning, closer to ten, and Cam is tired and pissed off with following clues that dry up, that end up nowhere. She leaves the station after forty minutes, annoyed she didn't get the woman's name or number, but something about her approach has vaulted Cam fully into investigative mode, like the detective novels she represents, and so instead of catching a train and going to work, she walks from the station to St. George-in-the-East in the lime-green summer sun.

Alexander Hale was buried here seven years ago in a plot at the back. James Lancaster was cremated, no grave that Cam can find.

The church is bordered by a park, huge and flat, its grass covered by a sprinkling of leaves already from the too-hot summer, though today it's drizzling. As she rounds the corner, it looms into view, an ancient white building with a crypt out front. In the background, London's housing estates continue on around it, like the church is some mirage. Cam turns around slowly before heading in.

There's nobody around. Through the doors, the church opens up above like a globe. It's a storybook church, the kind a child would draw. She lingers there for a few minutes, looking at the font, the pews, the kneelers for prayer. She heads through it, out the back, to the grave-yard.

A path twists its way through roses, reaching gravestone after grave-stone in the sun. Most are old—from the 1700s—and Cam instinctively heads deeper in as the path winds between two tall pine trees. It's now July, but churches and graveyards never feel like summer to her, the light of a spindly autumnal quality, the graves mossed and in shadow.

And there it is. She finds it easily. One of the newer headstones. Seven years old, but still looks brand-new. White, gold blocky text, the grave laid with fresh flowers.

ALEXANDER HALE. SURVIVED BY HIS PARENTS MICHAEL AND JANET HALE. FRIEND, COUSIN, BROTHER, AND, ABOVE ALL, BEST BOY.

Cam's eyes mist over. To her, now, all children who die are Polly, and all parents are Cam. And here she is, feeling sympathy for them, but she is here for the wrong reasons. Because perhaps her husband stood near here. Perhaps he came to this church, one day seven years ago. Perhaps the reason he did so is because he was responsible for the double murder. Same as killing the hostages. Two men: dead.

On the grave are a handful of photographs. Old-style, Polaroid-type ones. Clearly maintained and replaced often. Cam doesn't pick them up, can't bring herself to, it isn't her place. But she does bend down into the dry grass, sun on her back, and peer closely at them. There's one that might be of the funeral. This very church, heaving with people all in black. It's taken from the back, and they're spilling out, around the pews, out of the doors, down the steps. A wedding photo but inversed, truly a negative. Cam squints at it but can't see Luke there.

But then, if you attended a funeral secretly, you'd be sure not to get in the photograph.

The Hales' address is online, on 192.com, and the Lancasters' is not. They live in a flat in an apartment block called Sarah Carpenter House. Cam doesn't know quite why she's here. Only that it was just down the road. Only that she can't bring herself not to follow everything up.

The communal front door is tired, black paint ancient and crackly, the plastic buzzer cracked and broken, the latch off, and so it's easy for her to let herself inside it and into an even tireder foyer full of rattling mail-boxes, bags of rubbish and a buggy parked up under the stairs. It has a distinct smell about it. The same as in youth clubs, libraries, village halls. Some sort of vague communality, something municipal.

The Hales' flat is number 78, and Cam gets a rattling lift up to the seventh floor based on guesswork. It's a 1930s building, drafty as she walks the corridors, single-glazed sash windows left open, letting summer in. It creates a wind tunnel that whips and tangles Cam's hair. A dog barks at her as she passes one of the flats. Another flat blares a television.

Number 78 has a "Please no unsolicited callers" sticker just above the silver door handle, which Cam has to choose to ignore, though wonders specifically why it's there for these people. There's a spyhole and a door-mat that says "The Hales" on it.

She raises a hand and knocks, and immediately hears movement inside. She's surprised: it's almost the middle of the day, and she had wondered if anybody would be here. Perhaps she hoped they wouldn't.

A man opens the door, his expression blank. Behind him, Cam sees photographs on the hallway walls: clearly of Alexander.

"Sorry—I was wondering if you might be able to help me," Cam says. She takes a deep breath, then prepares to introduce herself with her full name. She wants to observe any reaction. "I'm Camilla Deschamps."

She is used to a response to her old name, but she's not sure if this man has one. He has dark hair, large, expressive eyes, low-set ears. He's in office attire, which Cam finds strange, given he is at home: suit trousers, a rumpled shirt, tie perhaps discarded somewhere, as the collar remains askew. He meets her gaze and raises his eyebrows. "Sorry—I'm not . . . ?"

"I wondered if you might know my husband," Cam says, thinking she has nothing to lose, surely. If Luke has something to do with this family—well. Luke is long gone.

"Who is your husband?" he says. He shifts his weight on his feet. Behind him is an immaculate flat. Midcentury. Expensive-looking furniture, a drinks cart, a rocking chair. Exposed brick walls.

"Luke Deschamps," she answers.

The man turns his mouth down. "No, sorry," he says, taking a quick step back, palms up, and closing the door. Cam hesitates. She can't work out if this was a usual dismissal or a suspicious one, and she doesn't know what to do if it's the latter.

She raises a hand to knock again, but really, what would she say? *My husband went out the night your child was murdered? Possibly he attended his funeral?* She would be as bad as the kind of people who try to get information from her at parties, occasionally at work. The people who pre-date her name change. "I couldn't help but remember . . ." they will say, and Cam will want to close her door too. She can't do it to him.

And anyway, Cam does have things to lose. She acts like she doesn't, she tells herself she doesn't, but she does: the memory of him. That belief she has that is sometimes weak and sometimes cast-iron: that he was good. If he had a hand in a murder before the siege, then she has to stop telling herself that taking hostages was some sort of mistake, something he was forced to do, a no-win situation. It will cheapen his legacy, forever.

She leaves Sarah Carpenter House, and then Whitechapel, rattled, alone. She hurries to the station the way you might rush up the stairs after turning the light out. She tells herself it's nothing, her imagination, reading too many thrillers, but, at the last moment after she has boarded the DLR at Shadwell, a man gets on, too, a full carriage away, all in black. The same man? She can't tell. She tries to look at his face, but he takes off down the crowded train, away from her, his walk quick. As she strains to watch his tall, retreating form, she wonders if it could be her husband, but she'd know that, wouldn't she? Wouldn't she?

33

LIBBY: *Gordon's.*
LIBBY: *Just us two??*
CAM: *Sure*
LIBBY: *Can you be less enthusiastic?*
CAM: *Sure!!!!!!*

It's the beginning of Libby's fortieth celebrations, but as Cam approaches Gordon's Bar that evening, she finds she'd rather be anywhere else. Polly is with a sitter; Libby and Cam always spend their birthdays together, something Luke and Si used to complain about.

Cam's mind is swirling with new information. The unknown woman approaching her, then not arriving at their meeting point, and tenuous links to funerals and the slightly grubby feeling of having been to a graveside that has nothing to do with her.

Libby has already got herself a glass of wine. Cam clocks it and understands immediately: the IVF is not up for discussion. It is a semaphore, a message conveyed without words. Cam feels a guilty stab that Libby feels she has to do this, still, all these years into it. She points to it as Cam arrives. "You and I are going to get fucking pissed."

"Any particular reason?"

"Just birthday."

Cam sits down, her insides cringing. She doesn't want to get drunk, stay out late.

Gordon's is London's oldest wine bar. It is underground, candlelit, the walls porous, the ceilings above great semicircles over their heads, built into the old Tube. Even though it's still light outside, down here it's nighttime, which suits Cam just fine.

"But firstly," Libby says.

"What?"

"We were phoned today about your application. Seems they reach out to everybody to verify Luke is really gone," Libby says, but to her credit she does say it cagily.

"Oh," Cam says. She gestures to the wine. "OK—yes. Load me up. What did they want to know?"

"Basically, if he's ever made contact."

"Oh, great," Cam says drily. "Just stick it on the form if he reaches out to you, right?"

"Sure will," Libby says. "I don't know how you put up with the admin over this—it's so dystopian."

"No choice."

"Still."

"I'll probably never move now. Not for ages anyway. I don't get the impression it'll be a quick process," Cam says, but what she doesn't add is that she's glad of this. That the moving on can be protracted and painful. Let it be so. Let his side of the bedroom stay the way it is, forever.

They sit and sip. Neither of them can hold their drink but, really, Cam just wants to sink into it now that Luke's come up. This candlelit night, this artificial liquid happiness, the past.

"They've asked for our recollection of the events. I guess to check they match yours," Libby continues.

"Hmm," Cam says, and perhaps something betrays her on her face, perhaps her sister just knows her well, she isn't sure which, but Libby says:

"What?" She swirls her drink like a wine taster, red staining the edges of the glass.

"Nothing."

"No. What?"

"Oh, I just got this weird text last week," Cam says. It burbles out of

her, a secret she's found it easy to keep to herself until time spent with
somebody who loves her. Something about the underground location,
the flickering candlelight . . . the fact that Libby is her only intimate acquaintance, everyone else pushed away.

"Show me?" Libby says, grabbing for Cam's phone and scrolling
without permission. "This one?" She waves the phone, and Cam suddenly feels protective of it, of her archive with Luke, but of the spam text
too. The same way she felt when people passed Polly around when she
was tiny. *That's mine.*

"What do you think?"

It doesn't land as she hoped. "I don't . . ." Libby runs her fingertips
up the stem of her wineglass as she reads the text, her gaze lingering on
it. "Sorry—you're not saying you think this was him, are you?" she says,
and it's this precise language that rankles Cam. *You think this was him.*
There's a distance in those words, a severalty. The equivalent of *Sorry if
you think I have offended you.*

"No, I'm not saying anything," Cam replies, defensive. And she isn't,
not really.

Another pause. "Did you go?"

"Yes."

"Cam!"

"What?" she says, irritated.

"Was anyone there?"

"No."

"Obviously. It's clearly spam."

"Have you ever had that kind of spam?"

"I get all sorts," Libby says. "I really like Charlie," she says, very deliberately changing the subject the way somebody might wrench the steering
wheel from the passenger seat. "Hasn't it been almost six months now?"
she asks, and Cam wonders if she makes the error deliberately.

"Not even four," she says, voice clipped.

And, God, *why* did Cam tell Libby, of all people? She knows Libby's
propaganda about moving on. She knows she's a natural cynic too. Cam's
eyes are wet. Suddenly, she wants a girlfriend. Holly, her old friend. A

real, true ally, who would tell her she was right even when she was far in the wrong.

"Not exactly still in first-date territory," Libby remarks.

At the time, Cam had had two dreams in a row that Luke came back for her. The day after the second one, she met Charlie. Literally like some sort of romantic hero, tall, dark and handsome, and she thought it had been a sign. Where's that optimism gone?

"Mmm," Cam says, thinking that she does like Charlie, she *does* . . . "But . . ."

"But what?"

"I don't know."

Libby talks over her. "Declaring Luke dead is just absolutely the right next step. You could even move in with Charlie, in time," she says, and Cam sometimes wonders, the way people perhaps do about their families, if Libby would behave this way with someone she barely knew, a passing office acquaintance. And if not, why is the standard so much lower the higher the intimacy gets?

"It doesn't feel like *the right step*," Cam says, hurt. Her sister may be caustic, but she hardly ever is to Cam. "It feels like second best."

"I get that," Libby says flatly. "You know—I had this dream about you. Ages ago."

"What dream?" Cam says, thinking again of the dreams she has about Luke. Sometimes she just misses him: a figure disappearing into a crowd or boarding a train where the doors close too fast behind him. Sometimes she hears him, wakes, and he isn't there.

"Well," Libby says, and Cam thinks that she doesn't actually want to know, has that feeling of trepidation she gets when around somebody intent on telling her their opinion, collateral be damned. The wine will make it worse. That it's Libby's birthday will make it worse. Suddenly, Cam wants to escape.

"You were with Charlie, properly with him. And you were just—you had moved on. You know? You smiled more. You shopped. You saw friends again. Had a different house. Took the piss."

"I do those things."

"Not like you once did. You still have his socks in his bedside table, Cam."

"I don't need to hear this," Cam says, raising a hand in warning. "I have always been an introvert. And I'll get rid of his clothes when I'm ready."

"And I was so happy for you," Libby continues and—oh. That slices through Cam, cutting her into ribbons. "We had a barbecue, in the dream. We texted all the time again."

"We do text all the time!"

"OK then, you initiated it," and Cam thinks, Ouch. "I was so fucking happy for you," Libby repeats, and Cam is shocked to see her eyes have a sheen to them. Perhaps, in all of this, Libby feels she's lost her sister rather than her brother-in law. "You know what," Libby says, and Cam wonders if she's drunk already. "Don't you think seven years is so long for this?"

And Cam wants to rant, suddenly, words bursting through her as powerful as the heat of the summer. *How, exactly, do you move on?* she wants to say. *Tell me. Tell me how to stop searching for answers. Tell me how to be fine with abandonment. Tell me how to embrace being a single parent. It isn't all it's cracked up to be, not in these circumstances, not when you're alone and disciplining and cooking and bedtiming and lying to your child every single day about who their father truly is.*

But she doesn't say all of this. She takes a breath instead.

A scented summer breeze gusts its way down into the cellar. The candles dart and dance but don't go out, although the rising and falling light lends the bar a confessional feel.

"What does Polly think about moving?" Libby says, evidently trying to push Cam into the future and not back into the past.

"Haven't told her yet—I'm waiting to see what happens . . ."

Libby pours more wine for both of them. Cam wonders, if she gets very drunk now, whether she might be able to forget the things that were said before.

"She will probably google him at some point."

Cam's back prickles in anger and something else. She hates the advice single parenthood attracts, even from her sister. "Well," she says, but then stops, not knowing what to say. "I know that," she adds lamely.

Cam avoids most confrontation and so she stares at her hands, wondering how much time must pass until she can look up and change the subject. She decides a full minute, sitting there feeling foolish, thinking that even though she doesn't have the whole story about Luke, he's still gone, still left, still stayed far away.

"You could just try," Libby says, her voice soft.

"To what?"

"To stop looking. To really, truly move on." She catches Cam's gaze, and Cam thinks she's going to crack a joke, to ease the tension, but she doesn't. Not this time.

"Do you know, I actually don't know how to do that, Libby," Cam says honestly.

"It's a mindset thing."

"I know."

"You could be happy again. Not in limbo." She pauses. "If nothing ever changes—do you think you will still want to be where you are in ten years' time?"

And something about this question and its simplicity actually makes Cam want to change something. This isn't fiction. This isn't a story. Luke really may never come back. Can Cam dedicate her whole life to finding somebody who killed two men—maybe more? Maybe was involved in another double murder, two months before the siege.

To consign Luke to the past, and the secrets he holds with him. To leave him behind.

To stop bothering grieving people in Whitechapel. To leave those loose threads loose and find happiness with someone else. Maybe somewhere else too.

"We could value the house tomorrow. For when the form is sorted."

"Maybe."

"They'll want to know its value to determine Luke's share for his estate."

"Yeah," Cam says.

They lapse into silence.

"You haven't even said happy birthday," Libby says eventually.

Cam bites her lip. "I'm sorry. Happy birthday," she says, shamefaced and sad, trying to inject some heartfelt meaning into her tone.

God, she wants to leave, suddenly, be somewhere silent: the bath, her ears underwater. Something about the bright weather outside up above, the dingy underground, her upside-down house that she is desperate to leave; the inverted world she now lives in, they spook her. Who sent that text? Who killed Alexander Hale and James Lancaster? Why would Luke have attended the funeral? Where is the unknown woman from the school gate?

"When I said the bugger didn't stick around," Libby says, raising her glass, "I meant I was pregnant from the IVF. Two pink lines. Then I lost it. Six weeks. I didn't say sooner . . . I couldn't say. It was too . . ."

"Oh," Cam says, a long, drawn-out emotion that she can't name emerging, which blows their table candle out, dancing this way and then that before dying in a plume of smoke that smells like winter. Happiness, sadness, blindsidedness rushes up through Cam. The way Libby was guarding her stomach: it was due to loss, not life. "I'm so sorry. I'm so sorry. I thought you meant—what they implanted . . ." Oh God, is that wording insensitive? "I'm so sorry, Libby."

"Me too," Libby says. She sinks the glass, pours another. "Least I can drink."

"True."

"Lots."

"Yes. Will you . . ."

"I don't know, Cam. It's like—it's one thing not getting pregnant. It's another thing to lose . . . It's like a death. It *is* a death." Somehow, this is yet more evidence, to Cam, that the world is a mean, upside-down sort of place.

Cam nods, her mouth set in a grim line. "Of course. I understand."

"You don't really," Libby says, but she says it without feeling or resentment in her voice. Cam shrugs, giving Libby the freedom to lash out if she wants to. She understands now. She will talk to somebody else about Luke. Or probably nobody. It doesn't matter.

"It's just been so long," Libby says. More wine down. And it's true. Rounds and rounds of IVF. A few months of the contraceptive pill to regulate a cycle, a procedure to flush out the fallopian tubes, two cycles for that to heal . . . suddenly, years and years and years pass by. "I didn't get all the early scans," Libby says. "Thought it would be buying into fear."

"Well, I buy into fear all the time," Cam says.

"Ha. We tried steroids this time. The guy thinks I've got natural killer cells that attack the embryo. But no dice."

"I wish it had worked out," Cam says simply, thinking how fortunate she is, how tight she will hold Polly tonight, later, when the sitter leaves. She makes a mental note not to mention her to Libby for the rest of the night.

"Yeah. Well. Do you know, I really tell myself I don't expect it to. But the sad thing is, actually, every time I do."

"I do too," Cam lies quietly.

They spend the rest of the evening discussing Si's business, Libby's work, not Luke, and not Polly either.

Outside, in the evening heat, they stand for a few seconds. Just as they are about to hug goodbye, Libby speaks, but a passing bus drowns out what she says.

"Huh?" Cam asks.

"The form asked about the last time I saw him."

"Oh . . ."

"I don't know if I ever told you. You were napping. We called in to see Polly; he said he didn't want to wake you. And all I remember is him there on the doorstep, holding her. His feet were bare and he said he was about to have an ice cream."

Something that feels like home joins Cam right there out on terra firma, the lights of London all around her.

"I didn't know that," she says softly. "But it sounds like Luke."

"I know. Take care," Libby says, something Cam isn't sure she's ever said to her. It's an apology of sorts, an olive branch.

Cam leaves, walks to the Underground, glad she didn't lash out at her sister.

She boards the Tube and thinks suddenly how much she appreciates that small nugget of a memory about her husband. That he had enjoyed an ice cream that day, while holding their daughter close. It was real. It had happened. Something she didn't know about him, didn't know that he had experienced. Something new to her, as though he hasn't gone at all, is just outside, just round the corner, just—somewhere. Waiting for her.

Finally home, Cam stands in her kitchen thinking, Damn Libby. Damn her directness. And damn her dream, too, containing that other Cam existing somewhere, the one who has managed to move on. Attending barbecues with her sister and boyfriend. Somebody who feels joy. Who sends silly texts. Who isn't afraid at the school gate. Ten years from now: Where does she want to be?

And maybe Libby's memory of Luke is a poignant parting shot. Maybe it's a way to say goodbye to him. To feel his existence but to let him go.

Cam lets a huge gust of air out of her lungs and allows it to propel her.

She begins to go around with a bin liner, ridding herself of the last of Luke. She knows it's mad, but she doesn't care. Fuck it, she thinks, finding the things she has been too afraid to throw out. She starts on his side of the bedroom, where his possessions largely lie preserved. She takes the book he was reading and ceremoniously adds it to the bin bag. Partially to prove something to Libby, partially to herself. His old T-shirt he slept in. A box of cufflinks. Take the lot of it.

Say she does proceed with getting him declared dead. Say she does sell. She'll need to move on then. Luke wouldn't even know her new address to find her. No matter that he could find her through work. No matter that they'd reunite, somehow. This simple fact matters to Cam.

She feels like she's motor powered, can't stop. She sweeps through the kitchen, slinging into the bag a pint glass he stole from a pub, his dressing gown, a framed photo of the two of them. She checks his office cabinets, their television unit, the kitchen drawer that's full of batteries and elastic bands and lightbulbs. Anything to do with him. Anything at all. It's gone. And with those objects, Cam is trying to rid herself of herself too. Sad, introverted her. *Be gone, Cam, and get a life.*

And that's where she finds it, at the back of his bedside table, the place that has remained the most *Luke*, tucked between it and the wall. A scrap of paper she's not seen before. And on it, undoubtedly, her husband's handwriting.

H. Grace—0203 1393934.

Cam hesitates. She can't help but trace a finger over the numbers, inscribed by Luke over seven years ago. He was here. He was real, she thinks, touching their blue imprints. So much of their relationship was writing. Representing him, reading him, texting him. And now here is all that remains: a relic.

Cam stands at the fork in the road. Moving on will be hard, she tells herself. Fraught with challenges and decisions. It has to be intentional: Time has not cured this problem in seven years. Behavior will. This is the first challenge, and she must rise above it, throw this note away.

But she can't do it. The compulsion rears up, and she can't resist it.

She googles Grace and the number, but no results come up for it. Without much to lose, she withholds her number and her pride, then dials, standing at the patio doors, looking out into the dark garden.

"Hello," a male voice answers immediately, despite the late hour, despite how much time has passed since her husband must have written it down. Cam paces away from the windows, seeing moving shadows, and speaks. "I wondered—Sorry, I found your number in my husband's things, and . . ."

He waits, saying nothing, which unnerves Cam. "And I . . . I wondered, sorry, because of some circumstances around my husband, I wondered—would you mind telling me . . ." She lets her voice trail off in the silence. "The circumstances in which he was in touch with you?"

He pauses. Cam can hear his breathing. "I wouldn't be at liberty to discuss that," he says. "Sorry."

"Why?" she asks. "Sorry—you're Mr. Grace . . . ?"

"Harry." Something begins to percolate in Cam's brain. Harry . . . Harry.

"Why can't you discuss it?"

"Business," he answers.

"Business?" she echoes.

A dial tone. Cam pulls the phone away from her ear, shocked, calls back, but he doesn't answer. Three rings then voicemail: a dismissal.

There are never any answers. None. She's a fool.

She stands there, her back to the patio doors, still clueless.

God. She is a joke. What does it matter?

She vowed to move on ten minutes ago, and now what is she doing? Calling dodgy businessmen who may or may not have known her husband, the criminal. She's sullied herself once more. Been to metaphorical Shadwell in search of answers. If Luke were here, they'd immediately adopt this as a moniker. Going to Shadwell: when you have a failure of willpower.

The rest of the night heralds the beginning of a downward descent for Cam. Into the history of all of her devices, searching for clues. Googling his number.

And then the rest.

Within seconds, under the sheets, she is existing only in data, and in memories: her old emails to him; their ancient texts. She is no longer searching. She's merely immersing. Everything is preserved in the Cloud—at her end, at least—for her to visit whenever she needs to: a private museum of them.

She scrolls through their iMessages, the last things he said to her, that chicken salad he asked for, and back and back and back through the days preceding the siege. The things the iPhones remember: every thought, every moment of married life, it sometimes feels like.

Crickets chirp outside and what used to be a noisy, traffic-filled road is quieter these days, electric vehicles creeping by like silent cats.

LUKE: *What do you think of these trainers: cool or Sad Dad act?*
CAM: *Sad Dad act.*
LUKE: *No?!*
CAM: *Sorry pal.*

The trainers he wanted—Vejas—came into fashion and then went out again. The café where she bought the salad has now closed.

Cam's eyes begin to burn as more texts load, and she continues to scroll up and up, climbing a ladder to the past, wondering if she might see something hidden somehow, somewhere. Something that connects everything: the burglary, the siege, the hostages, the disappearance, the bodies, Alexander Hale, James Lancaster, Harry Grace, the coordinates . . .

She moves backward through time, through their digital footprint. After half an hour, she has scrolled up so far that her phone has become slow, stilted as she tries to force it to go further. Eventually, it freezes, and she panics. "No, no, no," she says. "No." If it won't scroll up, they're lost forever, that beautiful life that they had thought was mundane, annoying, even.

We got milk?
And:
Bath time is sooo irritating, half an hour of stone cold drudgery x
Is it a black or green bin week?
And:
Yes, always yes to coffee, a caramel latte please, just peeling the potatoes!
And now:
Just this. Blankness.

Nothing before February 2017. It's as far as her phone will go. She sits up, throwing the duvet off her head, her chest clammy with sweat. She can't lose their old texts. There must be some way to export them, somewhere, to someplace safe.

She can't move on. She can't do it. She panics, her phone not responding. She lets it drop down the side of the bed, like a bungee jumper who doesn't return.

34

Niall

It's late at night and Niall is cooking. Well, trying to. He's multitasking. Pondering what to do about suspected-Deschamps, who didn't respond to his text. Chopping chicken, binning irritating pepper seeds, and googling the number Camilla just called. The real-time alerts from O2 will flash up a systemwide message, as she is under their surveillance, but Niall is the only person looking while making stir-fry very late on a Tuesday night. Half of the Met is preoccupied with a murder. Single woman shot dead on her doorstep in north London. No suspects yet. Niall, really an ex-detective, isn't on it.

Google search results: It looks like there aren't many great matches for your search.

Interesting. An office number, or a landline, with no footprint. Unusual these days. Niall hesitates over dialing it, but in the end, after sprinkling his chicken with fajita seasoning, decides not to. Sometimes, you can shoot your shot too quickly.

He had the kitchen done just after Viv left, one of those impulse decisions made by the brokenhearted who think a new kitchen will fix everything. It's space gray and fixed nothing. Awful decision: he doesn't know why he did it. Gray cupboards, gray floor, gray paint. Who decided industrial gray was de rigueur, he thinks, frying up red bell peppers that look aggressively colorful against all that monochrome. It's so late. He doesn't even want to be doing this. This is so dysfunctional. He should've ordered an Uber Eats.

What should he do about this number she called? It could've been anyone, of course, but nobody makes tedious calls at eleven on a Tuesday.

He finds some mange-touts and chucks them in. He notices, lately, as soon as he starts making a meal, he almost immediately loses his appetite. Wants to throw the lot away. Viv used to cook, and it isn't the same without her herbs and spices, and her, too, to share the leftovers with. He surveys the chicken and vegetables. He'll be eating this for days.

A second alert comes in, a low-priority one, so a number Camilla texts regularly. And God, it's weird being privy to this level of a near-stranger's intimate communications.

It's Luke's old mobile number. Niall winces at this, reads the text through half-closed eyes.

I miss you, it says.

Another: *I miss you I miss you I miss you.*

Niall's vision clouds over there in the kitchen. He can feel the pain of those texts. Hell, he could send those texts himself.

Niall is troubled by Camilla. He's troubled by this twenty-two-second call made late at night, he's troubled by her dogged search for her husband, and he's most troubled by the figure he saw in the alleyway near to her house. He's tried to get full surveillance on her, to follow her everywhere—in part, to make sure she's OK—but the budget won't stretch. He's tried to get Claire to harass Text Anon, to force them to dig deeper into who sent the coordinates, and she says she will, but will have to do it on her own time. Deschamps is not a priority. There are other, more current murders to worry about, Niall was told firmly.

Something about it all has an inevitability to it. That Camilla is heading in one direction: toward answers, but perhaps, too, toward danger. He can't explain why he thinks that, only that he does. Something about the shadowy figure . . . funny how he still relies on instincts, even after they let you down. Sometimes, it's the only thing you can do.

He wants to reach out to her, to tell her to be careful, but he can't. It would scupper his chances of catching Deschamps. He might cross some blurry lines, but he can't jeopardize a Met double-homicide investigation. All he can do is watch and wait, and hope she's careful, whatever it is that she's doing. And try to remember whose side he is on: not hers.

His phone goes shortly after the food's ready. It's Tim. "Telecoms have a hit on the number Camilla Deschamps just called," Tim says. "Goes by Harry Grace. He's a heavy. A criminal. Fancy popping by tomorrow?"

"For sure," Niall says.

"He lives at 22 Grove Avenue in Lewisham. The house from Rightmove."

35

Harry Grace does indeed live in the two-up two-down in Lewisham that the police searched right after Deschamps's disappearance. Harry claimed not to know him, and they had no reason to suspect he did. A saved Rightmove property is not a connection. Camilla visited it, right after the siege ended, but gleaned nothing either, though they questioned her about it.

But since then, Harry has been arrested multiple times on petty offenses, nothing connecting him to Deschamps, but slightly suspicious nevertheless.

It looks like a perfectly normal house on a busy road. A bay window at the front, two Velux windows in the roof. The only curious thing is that he has three burglar alarms above the porch, all in a row above the door. Three different brands: ADT. Veritas. Yale. Underneath those, a Ring doorbell.

Interesting.

Niall's been sent out in good faith by his old friend Tim and trusted to talk—the thing he's best at in the world, or so Tim says. And now, he's deciding how to play it. He has no idea why Camilla would call a criminal, only best guesses and hunches. He's meandered this way and that over strategy, enjoying the old detective instincts coming back to life within him, but, eventually, he decided that you can't decide anything until you're in front of somebody.

Niall doesn't have to press the doorbell before a form appears behind the fake stained glass. A man, tall but stooped, gingery hair. Niall doesn't recognize him, hasn't dealt with him or interviewed him, and all he can think as Harry opens the door is that he doesn't look like a criminal. He looks studious, like somebody who might recite poetry at an open mic night.

"Harry Grace—Niall Thompson. Nice to meet you," Niall says cordially.

Harry reacts to this with suspicion, and then he says, "Police?"

Niall nods.

And without a second's hesitation, Harry says, "Warrant?"

Niall cracks a smile. OK, so he is a criminal—and a real pro at that. "No, no," he says, "for once, you're not in trouble."

"Right?"

"A man you know is."

"And?" Harry says. The sunlight illuminates his sallow skin momentarily, burnishing him orange. "Might be nice if I could come in and discuss? Away from the heat."

A quick backward glance into the house tells Niall plenty. No invitation will be forthcoming, and Niall is too fixated on the job at hand to care.

"I'm told you knew a man called Luke Deschamps," he says, deciding to play the first of his cards face-up. And just the name, that distinctive name, it evokes raw emotion on Harry's face. It isn't anger or guilt, or any of the usual criminal fare: it's fear. Something Niall sees often in hostage negotiation, more rarely elsewhere. Harry is afraid of that name, and what it might mean for him. That much is clear.

Still, Niall lays his next cards out carefully, one by one, all facing upward. "I'm told if you pass us information about him, we could very easily make that count positively for you."

"I don't need you: I'm out," Harry says. Shorthand for *not currently in prison*, and Niall is reminded—he forgets this—that a vast section of the British public are in and out of prison, of magistrates' hearings, on bail, on remand, and that they treat this with as much significance as going to Tesco Express.

Harry paces a step backward into the house, moving his face into shadow. Niall can't work out whether this is an invitation to come in, so assumes it isn't.

Their eyes meet, Harry clearly working out whether it's better to discuss Deschamps in the open or let a copper into his home where, clearly, there is evidence of something.

He chooses the latter, which tells Niall he is more afraid of someone seeing him with Niall than he is of talking to him in private. He steps aside and leads him into a small kitchen that seems to be partway through some sort of renovation: tired pine cabinets and linoleum floor on one side, brand-new bifold doors on the other. A stack of new, modern, dark-green kitchen units teeters in the corner. There are no appliances, no kettle, no toaster. Renovations mean money, and Harry doesn't work: he recently stated to the magistrates' court he was *between jobs*.

He doesn't gesture for Niall to sit, and so they stand there, by the pots of paint samplers and boxes of tiles.

"Farrow & Ball," Niall remarks. It's a lighthearted and loaded statement all in one, one that he's proud of. Here's leverage. Harry is doing something to fund an expensive paint habit, and Niall is on the tail of quite what that is.

"Builder says it's a con, needs tons of coats," Harry says.

"My wife swears by it, and she has good taste," Niall says back, wondering if he's fully in character himself or just enjoys the delusion of pretending Viv is still married to him. "Did you know Deschamps?" Niall asks, his voice low, telling Harry: *I understand your fear.* People work on the basis of these small exchanges. Not the words used, but everything else. Human interaction is twenty percent words, eighty percent *other*. Body language and tone.

"I didn't have anything to do with what he did," Harry says carefully, turning his back to Niall and running the tap. He fills a mug, doesn't offer Niall one.

So he knows exactly who Deschamps is, and what he's infamous for, just as Niall suspected.

"Nobody's saying you did." Niall leans his weight back on his feet, giving Harry space. "I definitely haven't been briefed that you did."

"No?"

"No, not at all. In fact, I've been told only that you're one of the best-placed people to tell us what was going on with Deschamps. First, we knew he saved your property on Rightmove. You denied any connection. But now—we know he had your number." Niall leaves a pause. "If only you had told us he'd come to view your house, rather than saying nothing at all, and incriminating yourself, years later."

Niall stands back, his tone soft, his inquiring mind satisfied. That old negotiator training. He's played his full-house hand, right here, face-up.

Harry weighs his options. Niall can almost see the cogs spin; he's holding a piece of bait out to a wild animal and waiting.

"I don't know much," he says. "Not really."

"Do you know if he's alive?"

Harry turns away again, sifting through a stack of sandpaper with a B&Q label attached to it, his head bowed downward.

"Tell me exactly what you're offering me, here," he says, looking up, and the deflection isn't lost on Niall.

"Depends what you know."

"What I know depends on what you can offer me."

"Immunity from future prosecution."

"Sure," Harry says sarcastically.

"I never lie," Niall says simply.

"Ha, yeah," Harry says. "Feds never lie, right?"

The street slang surprises Niall: Harry looks to be about forty, nice house. Unkempt, sure, and he's served time, but even so. "I'm a hostage negotiator," Niall says. "Different to a fed."

"Oh, right—you were his negotiator then?" Harry says, eyes interested. He puts the sandpaper down.

"Yes." Niall fixes his gaze on Harry.

"Didn't do a very good job of it."

It's like taking a bullet, but Niall covers up his wince. "How did you know him?" he asks.

"I would give your name, yeah? In the future." Bingo! Harry is clearly considering Niall's offer.

"Sure thing."

"For any crime?"

"Within reason . . ."

He draws a breath. "Deschamps"—he pronounces the French name perfectly, so well Niall wonders if he is bilingual—"came to me for protection."

"Protection?" Niall says, but the second the word is out of his mouth, he understands. "He bought protection."

Protection. An ancient commodity. Purchased by criminals and desperate people. From personal security all the way up to—well, worse, and mostly at prices you can never pay. Things you can never part with.

"Why?"

"He came to me for help. He was in hot water. I can't say more than that."

"Did you? Protect him?"

"I did protect him. Though not very well."

And Niall can tell he's lost him. His stare becomes evasive, looking behind Niall at nothing.

"Harry—why did he need protection?" Niall asks.

Harry ventures forward now, steps right into a sunbeam, which illuminates his shabby black clothes and strawberry-blond hair. He pauses, stares down at the floor, evidently thinking. He's wearing mismatched socks.

Harry's a criminal, but here he looks vulnerable. So slight, his voice with the sort of watery tone of somebody full of regret.

"I do business," Harry says. "And I keep people's business private. That's the deal."

"Even with immunity on the table?"

"That's the deal," he repeats, but it didn't seem like the deal earlier, not until Niall really started probing.

"He's a wanted man, right?" Harry says.

"Yup."

"So . . . it's not a deal, is it? That you're offering me. It's a threat."

"No, it isn't," Niall says, but, actually, *really*, it is. This guy is no idiot. "Did you offer him a safe harbor? The night of the siege?"

"No. Hang on," Harry says, and he exits the kitchen without another word. Niall can hear his footsteps on bare-wood stairs, and cocks his head and waits. A minute passes, two. Above, he hears the flush of a toilet. He has no doubt Harry is stalling for time, but time is good for Niall, too, who goes to the kitchen counter and scans it. He opens drawers—empty, due to the renovation—and begins a slow loop around the kitchen. By the back doors is a hip-height desk housing all the accoutrements associated with work. Pieces of paper, notepads, pens, elastic bands, drawing pins. Niall moves some of them around, quietly, trying to pretend they are things he could have noticed incidentally; things he doesn't need a warrant to uncover.

A scrap of paper sits in a wooden bowl along with some golf tees and loose change. Niall holds it up to the light while he waits, and reads.

Username: Sully018747450
Password: 84hfkHdn[]
URL: jsudnj283738ndjh.onion.forum

A dark-web login for a forum. Niall would know that kind of onion URL anywhere. He takes a photograph of it, then replaces it in the bowl. Upstairs, all is silent, and Niall waits for five more minutes before he accepts what he already knows to have happened.

He calls out, "Harry?"

Nothing. No running water, no footsteps.

Niall heads out into the sun-blanched hallway and up the stairs. Sure enough, the bathroom window—a large side-opening one—is wide open. It drops down onto the back of the living room, a flat roof that juts sharply into the garden. The back gate is open, still swinging. Niall thinks of the fear when he mentioned Deschamps. And clearly, Harry doesn't think he is saving himself from the police by escaping—he's no stranger to police interviewing suites—but from somebody else, instead. Somebody more important. Somebody more dangerous.

This is the second time somebody has escaped from Niall on this case, he thinks as he watches the gate blow on the breeze.

It's late, after dark, and Niall heads to an internet café called ONLINE NOW. As he walks, his mind naturally turns to Viv—her house is just around the corner from here—and everything Jess said, and some things she didn't too.

He takes a detour, up two side streets and onto a main thoroughfare, and there it is. Viv's house, in darkness. Why is he here? He feels like a creep standing there looking at the house she now lives in. Three windows across, two large ones downstairs. An ancient cat sits in the living-room window.

I miss you I miss you I miss you, said Camilla, and Niall could text the exact same thing, right now, right here. His eyes are wet with it. Her pots and pots of tea and the way she came home with bloody stray cats all the time, the way she must have sat alone on that day, her birthday, and hoped for a single text acknowledging it from her self-involved, arsehole husband.

He doesn't know what to do, he doesn't know how to make the gesture he wants to make—I fucking regret it, I regret it, I regret it—so he gives those windows one last look, willing it to come. How can he tell her, seven years too late, the truth? That he wishes he'd treated her differently. Better. The truth, also, is that he loves his job, and will probably do it again, one day.

Her bin is out. He lifts the lid like a psycho, and sees that it's empty, the rubbish collected. Looking both ways, he grabs it by the handle and pulls it back up her path, leaving it in the bin storage area. He won't tell her he did it. And it wouldn't make any difference to her view of him if he did. But it might make her life easier, save her doing a small task that she hates, and that's worth it to him.

He enters the internet café to an electronic beep. There is nobody here at all, not even anybody behind the counter, and he waits until they emerge.

It's not the kind of person Niall was expecting—an old man, late sixties maybe, with two pairs of glasses on: one over his eyes and one nestled in his hair. It smells of coffee in here: instant, cheap, take it black or white. Niall feels a pang of nostalgia for something he can't name. Maybe it's just the past. The simple bygone time where internet was dial-up and coffee was coffee.

He can't access the dark web easily at work, so here he is. A fleeting visit on his way home, to attempt to find out a little more about Harry Grace and Sully. He's glad the Met is caught up with the woman shot on her doorstep, Madison. Someone is murdered every three days in

London, but, lately, deaths seem to depress him more than they used to. Another life lost needlessly.

It's warm inside the café, and Niall takes off his jacket. Last night, beginning of July, it got darker slightly earlier than the previous, and Niall found himself looking forward to the end of summer, to autumn and to something new. Sometime in the future, when all this is over, where the gunshots may live in the past.

The man leads him over to a surprisingly modern-looking desktop Mac, which he pays fifteen pounds cash to use for forty minutes. "Let me know if you need anything," he tells Niall, but he says it listlessly, not looking at him. He takes a seat behind the counter and opens the front page of the *Guardian* on an iPad. It's his coffee Niall can smell. Brown-gray, half-finished.

Niall takes a seat and tries the login on four dark-web forums without finding a hit. The URL was a dark-web URL, but one temporarily generated, that will have only worked for a period of time. So he needs to try the login manually on as many forums as he can find.

Outside, the leafy London street is black and neon, the color of an '80s disco. Lit-up shops and headlights and streetlamps and dark air.

Four more forums, still nothing. He heads down and down and down the whirlpool of the web, searching more and more nefarious places. He isn't put off—of course criminal enterprises have to hide themselves well from police—and, after a while, Niall pays for a second lot of forty minutes and orders his own instant gray coffee too.

Nobody else would do this. Maybe Claire in telecoms, but that's it. It's old-school work, grunt work, but it almost always pays off.

Ninth forum, tenth, and there it is, on the eleventh. The login works.

He heads straight to the inbox, taking photographs of each message as he goes.

SULLY018747450: *I can do that for you. Meet at my address? 22 Grove Avenue, Lewisham.*

As Niall suspected: Sully is Harry: *Sully018747450—protection 4 all ur needs.*

He clicks *all messages in thread* and lets them load. Then sorts them by date, earliest to latest.

And there it is. In June 2017.

Bingo.

Not only has he found Harry: he's found Deschamps himself, he's sure of it, typing in the past. He shivers, moves his chair back, takes a breath, then begins to read those words from long, long ago that might finally provide answers.

LD47503038: *Can you sell me a gun?*
SULLY018747450: *Yes. What type?*
LD47503038: *A shotgun.*

Niall scoots back from the computer. So this is where he got the gun.

LD47503038: *How long?*
SULLY018747450: *Two days.*

Niall's eyes flick to the date. Except it isn't right. And it's the wrong gun. Luke had a Beretta. This is the day before the siege: Deschamps didn't have two days.

And Niall can feel it, that it is about to happen. An explanation is about to be provided to him from the mists, from all those years ago.

36

LD47503038: *I need it sooner.*
SULLY018747450: *What's the urgency?*
LD47503038: *I need some personal protection. I think somebody is going to murder me.*

And there it is. The reason.

Deschamps thought that he was going to be murdered.

And he was right. He tried to arm himself in readiness.

Jesus Christ. It isn't as it seems. Not at all. He stares out of the plate-glass windows, at the inverted "ONLINE NOW" sign, the world deepening blacker the longer he looks.

He keeps reading.

LD47503038: *How fast can you get me the gun? Somebody knows something about me. They want me to meet at a warehouse, in Bermondsey. I don't know if they want to talk, or . . . I have to meet them though. They'll come to my house if I don't. They've been once already.*

Ah. The burglary, Niall thinks, reading.

SULLY018747450: *Or what? Why don't you tell me what happened?*
LD47503038: *I can't, really. They have found out something about me. They want me to meet with two men at a warehouse.*

SULLY018747450: *Two days for the gun. I can show you what to do. How to overpower and surprise people. But the gun will take two days.*
LD47503038: *It's tomorrow.*
SULLY018747450: *Or I can help to hide you. Come and see me in Lewisham.*

They knew something about him. They wanted him dead.

Niall watches the case as he thought he understood it invert in front of him, right there on an Apple Mac in an anonymous café. The hostages are the perpetrators. The hostage-taker acting in defense. Deschamps didn't start the siege: they came for him. And nobody saw how it began, so nobody knew. All Deschamps knew was that he was going to be murdered. He tried to arm himself in readiness.

LD47503038: *I'm at the warehouse. I need help.*
SULLY018747450: *The gun ain't here yet.*
LD47503038: *I know. I've got to go in and meet them. Sully, they want me dead.*
SULLY018747450: *Can you see in?*
LD47503038: *Yes. They're in there already. They're here to kill me. They are masked, black sacks on their heads with holes for eyes. Can you come and help me??*
SULLY018747450: *I don't deal direct with this stuff. Observe observe observe. Wait. Pause. What can you see?*
LD47503038: *I've got to go in or they're going to come for me at my home, with my family.*
SULLY018747450: *If they're going to kill you, they will have a weapon. Can you get it?*
LD47503038: *They've got it. A pistol.*
SULLY018747450: *Bide your time. Better to be late but with the advantage. Wait.*
LD47503038: *They're talking.*
SULLY018747450: *Wait.*

There's nothing more. Niall puffs his cheeks out, agog, then heads to the Met, downloads the archived CCTV footage, and rewatches it.

Deschamps arrives on the camera, hostages unseen.

And then—that quick movement at the edge of the screen. Niall pauses, rewatches, and he sees it: it's Deschamps's hand reaching for something.

He stops it again, then thinks. The hostages were already there. They must have come in the back, the place Deschamps himself escaped from.

Deschamps turned up unarmed, watched from the outside. Just like Harry said to do.

Then he went in, and waited until they put down their gun. The hand movement is him taking it from a table in the very corner of the footage. The Beretta the police thought he had—it was the hostages'.

Another inversion. Funny how things look different depending on what you know to be true.

He closes his eyes. It all makes sense. It *all* makes sense. It wasn't a siege. There was no siege. It was the attempted murder of a man that turned into the death of two.

The best way to police is to be relentless with it. Harry will not be expecting Niall back so soon, and this is why Niall shows up, past midnight, and rings the bell.

Harry answers the door in dark clothes, shoes on, clear shock on his face.

"Nice to see you, Sully."

And just like that, the threat is made: *I know your criminal identity. I may know your business. I may know every single illegal thing that you're doing.*

Harry wordlessly lets him in. "And?" he says.

"And what?"

"Nothing on the dark web ever gets to court." He leans against his kitchen counter. "Can't trace it. And what if I am Sully?"

"*And* I am perfectly capable of getting your internet dealings to court."

"Don't care," Harry says, but Niall knows that he does. Businessmen can't work when they're inside, after all.

"All right then: unless you tell me what you know about Luke Deschamps, you're under arrest."

A pause. Niall treads so carefully with his words, you would never be able to hear his footsteps. What he's musing on is why, if Deschamps murdered his enemies, he has disappeared.

"What do you want to know?" Harry says reluctantly, then thumps his weight back against the cupboards, the sort of power play a toddler might make.

"Why don't you tell me what you know—and then we'll go from there," Niall says.

"I don't know where Luke is," Harry says, and Niall notes the familiarity of using Deschamps's first name.

"Is he alive?"

"Don't know."

"What *do* you know?"

"Not much."

"Who was sent to murder him?"

"I don't know who ordered the job," Harry says.

Niall's mouth forms a perfect O. "'The job'?"

"Yeah."

"I don't understand," Niall says, though he thinks he does.

"Luke told me when he came to see me that his enemies—I never knew who—were sending two contract killers for him."

Niall's head hits his chest. Of course. *Of course.* The identityless hostages have no ID because they are experienced hired criminals. Had only cash on them and Oyster cards registered to nobody.

They didn't have a personal vendetta against Deschamps. They were on a job, sent to kill him on behalf of someone else. Deschamps's enemies are elsewhere. Niall has been looking in the wrong places.

And this means that Deschamps's existing enemies are alive and well. He merely shot their messengers.

37

Cam

I t's late, and Cam's in bed still clothed, reading Adam's manuscript.

The problem is, I suppose my dad would say, I had too much heart. If the drugs got queried, I took them back. If people couldn't pay the full fee, I let them off. In the end, profits dropped, and Dad found out.

Cam can't concentrate, and not on something so dark. Drugs and gangs. A kid getting mixed up in it because his family made him. Men being bad men, the way they are. She puts the manuscript aside.

Sometimes, Cam thinks access to the internet from a formative age gives her the impression she can solve *anything* on Google. A small part of her thinks she might find Luke out there, hiding in some virtual tab or other, his address written somewhere, or shown as a red pin on a map, and it's this impulse that leads her, after brushing her teeth and closing the curtains on the patio doors, to Google. She intends to search, as she hasn't done for years, for a description of her husband on Reddit. Posters detail missing persons on there, and other people who might have seen them reply. Tall, blond men are not in enormous supply, and hope surges up through Cam every time she does it. Misguided, toxic hope. She'd given this up. She was doing better. And now look.

But what's that? In bed, face washed and shining, neat half of the room on her right, patio doors and her books on the left, Cam starts: the security light has clicked on outside, in her back garden.

It has never once gone on by itself. Not for foxes or swaying trees or anything: only if you're out there. Her arms and legs throb with her heartbeat. She ought to look. She ought to get out of bed right now, rip open the curtains, but actually, she simply freezes in fear, thinking of what the stranger at the school gate said: *Somewhere you don't regularly go.*

And then she indulges in that most toxic of habits: she pretends. Just for a few seconds, the same way she does when she hears car engines idling outside or unexpected knocks at her front door or missed calls from strange numbers. Ordinary occurrences are no longer so, for Cam.

She pretends it's Luke. Come back. Returned. Just for a few moments.

Eyes open, pretending over, she heads upstairs, to the living room, where she can peer out from a vantage point. The curtains open a bright, floodlit slice of white, and she blinks as it hits her.

Nothing. Nobody in the garden: she stares out for a full five minutes, the tension slowly leaving her body, her heart rate coming down.

The light clicks off, and she relaxes. She heads downstairs, reaches the door, and opens it. Cool air pipes in, and Cam ventures out, barefoot, onto the still-warm patio. All she can hear is crickets, the distant sound of traffic. Nothing else. The light reilluminates as she walks a slow loop around her garden, picking out the green bushes and the parched grass. Cam glances at her neighbors' houses, no lights on, and shivers, alone there in the night.

Just as she turns to go back inside, she hears it: the crunch of gravel underfoot, on the path that runs to the back of their gardens.

She freezes, listening, stays still so long she lets the light click off.

Another crunch. Another step. Somebody trying hard to be quiet. Cam's breath is held. She stands in indecision, wanting to find out but not wanting to do so alone. Her head is telling her this is too many coincidences, too many occasions when she thought she was followed. Her heart is telling her it's Luke, come back for her.

No. She won't check alone. It would be foolish. Polly needs her. She needs to be careful as the only remaining parent. Even if it might be Luke. Especially because it might be Luke.

She heads inside, then locks up carefully and goes back upstairs to look into the alleyway from above.

As she watches, a form becomes clear, standing at the back of her fence, stock-still; she had missed him the first time around. Without hesitation, Cam's heart speeds up and she calls 999.

"There's somebody outside my house," she tells the operator.

"OK—have they attempted to break in?"

"Well—no, but they're—they're by my fence, I think they might be scouting the property," Cam says hurriedly. "Please send someone—I'm alone."

The call handler takes her details, and Cam stands at the dark window, looking down. The light clicks off, and, by the time the police arrive twenty minutes later, the person is gone.

"Do keep an eye out," a friendly PCSO tells Cam. "And you could even get CCTV."

"But that won't stop them coming back, or getting in," she says.

"If your house is secure, that is very unlikely," he says. "Most burglars are opportunists."

"I don't know if it is a burglar or ... I ..." she says. The PCSO watches, standing there in her kitchen with his notepad. "I feel like I'm being watched."

He nods, just once, and doesn't dismiss it, which Cam likes. "Any idea why?"

"No," she says, not disclosing her identity. She's sure the police must already know. "But there was someone at my daughter's school—a man. And then someone on the Tube ..."

"All right—keep a log of that, too, and here's my mobile number," he says, and passes it to her. "Any problems, you call, OK?"

Cam takes the card gratefully, her hands shaking, wanting to prolong the meeting so that he doesn't leave her alone again. But he does leave, heading to other jobs, for other vulnerable people, she supposes.

She keys his number into her phone, adds it to favorite contacts, hoping she will never need it.

In bed, later, not expecting sleep, Cam recommences her googling. But before she can, she sees it: a headline, on the news tab of Google, and a photograph.

A photograph of the woman at the school gate.

Cam stares at it in shock. FORTY-SEVEN-YEAR-OLD MADISON SMITH FOUND DEAD AT HOME IN SHADWELL.

And then more: *Dead at not-yet fifty: the London murder that has police FLUMMOXED. Madison Smith: Who was she?*

There in the night-dark room, Cam's chest becomes hot. A woman approached her, saying she was related to one of the hostages, and now she's dead. Cam looked into her eyes just the day before yesterday, but now she's gone.

And there was somebody in Cam's garden just now.

She paces across the room, hands to her cheeks, panicking.

Madison was killed yesterday morning. Cam would've heard about this soon enough, without googling at all, and she wonders if that might have been better than this. A clandestine Google search late at night, alone.

THE FAMILY of Madison Smith have spoken out after she was murdered on her doorstep early yesterday morning. 'We lost a bright and beautiful mother, sister and friend today,' her son, Joseph, told the Metropolitan Police at noon today. 'If anybody knows anything, please, please call in.'

DCI Timothy Young from the Met confirmed that Madison opened her door early yesterday morning, while her adult sons were still in bed, and was shot in the chest and died immediately. Paramedics attempted to revive her but were not successful. CCTV and residential camera footage have captured her killer on film below.

Cam loads up the video, thinking: A woman who found me is dead. A woman whose husband was murdered by my own seven years ago. She can't begin to fathom what it means, only that another person is dead. Alexander Hale. James Lancaster. Two hostages. And now the wife of one of them. Five souls now gone, and all connected to Luke.

She shivers.

There is no mention of Madison's husband in the papers, but there's a video of her assailant. It's grainy and blurred. Two cars pass. A woman walks a poodle across the screen. A man steps into the frame. A man wearing a balaclava, his hood up. He reaches with a black leather-gloved hand to knock.

The door opens.

The back of Madison Smith's head appears.

Then the video ends.

Cam watches it again and looks at him. She doesn't think it's Luke. It's not his walk. But she can't know for sure.

She tries to find Madison's husband online, on the marriage records, on births and deaths, but there's nothing.

She pauses.

Surely, surely, she's got to tell the police of this contact they had? Cam might be the only person in the world who knows she was married to one of the anonymous hostages.

But Madison reached out to Cam, and was then murdered. Cam stood right by her, at the school gate, so close to Polly.

And now she's dead. How can Cam involve herself in this?

Somewhere you don't regularly go.

She shivers again by the doors to her garden, feeling alone but wondering if it's worse: that she's not alone, only thinks that she is.

38

Niall

"No more news here." The next day, Lambert is at the front of the boardroom, one hand on the edge of the whiteboard, the other on his hip. "Niall was sent to grill Harry Grace, so over to him." He turns to Niall, expression expectant.

Niall pauses. He relays briefly his conversation with Harry and what he found on the dark web. He talks fast, excitedly.

When he's finished, Tim seems to be considering things, turning his mouth down, thinking. He's in on this briefing—usually, findings are reported up to him—and seems mostly unable to stop himself from interjecting. "That is a lot of information," he says eventually.

"I know," Niall says, and there begins a creeping thud of disappointment.

"So he was come for by hit men?"

"Exactly," Niall says. And right then, he gets another bad feeling about it. The room isn't reacting as he wanted.

"And your only proof of this is a conversation on the dark web? You have no idea who sent them?" Tim's voice is imbued with skepticism.

"Yes . . ."

"What evidence do you have of what Deschamps needed protecting from?" Tim says.

"Only what he wrote."

"I'm thinking about self-defense," Tim says, a barrage of questions beginning now.

"Clearly he needed help." The feeling of unease grows: he is the only one trying to turn a tide. He's standing there, at the shore, doing it all himself.

"Well, Deschamps could've easily written anything he liked on the dark web, to cover up what he wanted to do," Tim says mildly. "Proving self-defense is a high bar. The threat has to be to someone's life, and an immediate one."

"He asked for help on there in a panic."

"No: all we really know is he posted on the dark web—and then he still went into that warehouse and shot two men."

Niall shakes his head. "That is not what we know," he says. "What about the stuff that isn't hard evidence? That here's a guy with *zero* criminal history, who never wanted to kill anybody, who was begging for help. That here's someone who could've picked up and used their gun, in self-defense."

"Instead he tried to buy his own," Tim says. "Which doesn't look a lot, to me, like self-defense. It looks like pre-meditation."

"He didn't get it in time."

"Despite trying. Look—we are nothing without evidence," Tim remarks, while the rest of the team watch the tennis match of an argument, looking awkward. Conflict hums in the air like a piano key depressed and then released, the air almost silent afterward. Niall shifts slightly away from his boss and jiggles his foot in irritation.

"We have no idea whether Deschamps used their gun," Tim says. "As I recall it, the footage doesn't show it."

"Exactly. It doesn't. I think the men turned up in their balaclavas," Niall says. "I don't think Deschamps bagged them. But we can't tell. They arrived off CCTV, only stepped into the frame once it was done."

"Or, Deschamps herded them in, also off-camera. Look—we can keep the file open. We can look for hit men who were operating then," Tim says, and it's a weak compromise. No direct action. No reinvigorating of the whole case. No desperate search for Deschamps, to find and exonerate him.

"OK—next steps," Lambert says. "I am not minded to throw a lot of resources at who did what in that warehouse: Deschamps is long gone."

"Camilla is not in touch with Deschamps, that's very clear," Claire

says. "Her call to 999 last night about the figure in her garden is probably something and nothing. Paranoia. But she wouldn't do that if it was
Deschamps."

Niall is worried for Camilla, and he can feel where this is going. As he
sinks his head to his chest and tries to take deep breaths, his anger begins
to simmer. They're giving up. Leaving a mystery unsolved. A woman perhaps in danger. They ignored him about what he saw in the alleyway off
her street.

Lambert continues: "I still think we leave surveillance on Camilla for
another month. We can see if we can figure out the basics of who the
contract killers were and who hired them. But nothing more than that.
There isn't the money here to chase this around London for another
seven years on the off chance that this wasn't Deschamps's fault. He fired
the shots. That's the main thing."

There's a murmur of assent around the room.

"What?" Niall explodes. "Hang on—I mean . . . are we not trying to
solve a mystery here? Does the *why* not matter? Or self-defense?"

Tim's eyes flash, but he says nothing, doesn't back Niall up.

"I was sent to get information from Harry Grace, and I did. I got you
all the information you wanted," Niall continues. "And for what?"

"Information, maybe, but all of it insubstantial," Tim says.

"No, it's not."

"We can't verify that it was even Deschamps typing on the web. Imagine," Tim says, his voice now slightly raised too—as incensed as he ever
gets. "Imagine if we acted on this, Niall. Let's say we find him. We go in
with the wrong tactics, because we believe him not to be dangerous, but
instead—some sort of victim."

Niall's sitting slack-jawed at the table, though, really, he ought not
to be surprised. This sort of game-playing has gone on his entire career.
If this, then how will it look? If that, then how will we cover our own
asses? The police are only ever interested in toeing the line. If something
doesn't fit with their narrative, they're not complying.

"Anyway," Lambert says, "it is so unlikely Deschamps is alive. In seven
years, not a single sighting, no slip-ups, no passport pinged, no bank
cards used. What would he even be living on?"

The windows are open, the summer sweeps its smells in, and Lambert concludes the briefing. An end-of-term feeling settles around the room. Any further activity on the Dungeness burner phone will be called in, but that's all. A perfunctory search for the contract killers' real identities that Niall knows, without big budget, will yield nothing: How could it?

"Sometimes," Lambert says, wheeling the whiteboard to the back of the room, then rolling his shirt sleeves up, "you just don't get the answers." Possibly he thinks this is some sort of pitch-perfect ending to the briefing but, really, he just sounds like he's in a hokey cop movie. Niall catches Tim's eye, who gives him a small, sad smile full of pity, and they leave the briefing together.

Outside in the too-warm corridor, Tim stops at a translucent-blue water dispenser, pours himself a drink, and sips it neatly. "You know, I did think we would one day get answers on this one. Pains me to end it, but it's so expensive and I don't think it would achieve much."

"Sure," Niall says, and Tim's face falls into relief. Niall grabs his own cup and fills it. He thinks, these days, that he likes to have a drink on him partially to buy time. That was what the Coke was about: thinking time. He gulps the water down now, fingertips on the ridges of the plastic cup. "Just the small matter of justice."

"Oh, Niall, don't be like that," Tim says. "Two people are dead. Possibly three. We're never going to find out exactly what went on in that building, no matter how much we read on the dark web. It would only ever be Deschamps's account of it."

"You're no longer interested, then. On to the next?"

"I am never not interested in my old cases."

"I didn't mean the case," Niall says coolly. Tim waits. "I meant the truth," Niall says.

They're in an anodyne place for such a significant moment in their relationship. The water cooler. A gray-carpeted corridor. A fake plant at the end that the cleaner sometimes absentmindedly waters.

Deschamps might be innocent. Niall believes that he is.

Deschamps knew two men were sent to kill him. And Niall knows, deep somewhere in his heart, that Deschamps might therefore have been acting in defense of himself. The problem is, he'd never get off on self-defense. For that, his life would have to be under immediate threat. Somebody pointing a gun at him about to fire it. If he took their gun, it won't work. In so many ways, Tim is right, but that doesn't mean you stop trying to find the truth, does it?

There must be an answer, now that Niall knows the two men were sent to kill him. Why were they there? Why did Deschamps decide to shoot after so long?

He has to find out.

The police don't care at all. They won't care that he murdered two men because they were sent to kill him.

They'll simply go after him, and, if they find him, charge him, let a jury decide on self-defense.

And if, when they try to arrest him, he even appears to be armed, they will probably kill him.

That is what Tim meant by his statement: *Imagine . . . we go in with the wrong tactics, because we believe him not to be dangerous.*

This is the Met. This is what Niall's struggled with all along. The due process, the red tape, the by-the-book attitudes. If he complies, it sentences Deschamps to life.

I miss you. I miss you I miss you I miss you. The texts to Deschamps's old number, sent by Camilla out into the ether.

How could he? When he knows Deschamps may now be the victim?

"I care about the truth," Tim replies, but he says it reflexively.

"Yeah, well," Niall says, thinking that nothing can stop him from looking into this by himself. And nothing can stop him from trying to find Deschamps, and get the right ending for him too. Off-record. He buys a new burner phone later, calls the number again. This time: phone not in use. Deschamps, if it is him, has ceased using it.

It's funny, Niall is thinking as he climbs the stairs to Jess's consulting room that evening, he wanted nothing to do with therapy, and now it's the first place he wishes to come tonight, when in need. As though his brain has begun to exist outside of his body, a ball of yarn being unspooled by a professional, someone who only wants the best for him. Who takes the knots out and gives him back his thoughts in neat, segmented strands.

It's a later session, the bakery below shut up, but also the other consulting rooms too. Jess lets them both in with her own key, and they sit down in her room, which is chilly from lack of use. She clicks a small heater on and places it between them.

"The gunshot case," Niall says carefully. It's the very first sentence he utters to her.

"Yes . . ." Jess says, her expression as sharp as a bird's. Finally: her topic.

"This is confidential, right?" he says, blowing a laugh out of the side of his mouth.

"Right," Jess says. The heater begins to glow orange at her feet, pumps out the smell of burnt toast.

"No ifs, no buts?"

"The only *but* is if you might be thinking of murdering somebody," Jess says, and she means it in a completely offhand way, but it gives Niall a shiver. No, he's not. But, with policing, with hostages, you never quite know where someone might end up.

"Of course not," he says, deadpan.

"What about the gunshot case?"

Niall looks down at his hands, folded in his lap, and then back up at her. "I found something out," he says. "And I've fallen out with work over it."

Jess pauses, perhaps thinking that this goes far beyond a therapist's job.

She reaches to straighten her notebook on the desk. "OK. So. What's going on?"

"The man who shot his hostages . . ."

". . . Yes."

"Two people were sent to murder him," Niall says. "The hostages were hit men. That's why he killed them. He wrote online, before it all, that he knew he was going to be murdered. It makes sense to me that it was self-defense. Or that he had no choice. He knew they were there to kill him, so he got in first. They knew something about him, but I don't know what."

Jess seems to shudder, just slightly, looking at Niall. He's never seen her nervy before.

"Horrible, isn't it?"

"It really is," she says. "So . . ."

"So?"

"This is the case where you made the police wait to enter, because you thought the hostage taker wasn't going to kill?"

"That's right."

Niall wants advice. He wants to focus on practicalities, on what to do next. He isn't sure why she's saying this. But as always, Jess is smarter than he is.

"Well—isn't this kind of good, then?" she says.

"Huh?" Niall says dumbly. "I mean—I've now lost the support of the police in looking into it."

"Not that. I meant . . . that—after all—your instincts about Deschamps were nailed on." She sits back in her chair, crosses her legs at the knee. She's so young. Maybe only thirty. She's so young to be so wise. "You weren't wrong, after all."

"I . . ."

"You were right to stall, even if it didn't work out like you expected. He was not the perpetrator everyone said he was. And, somewhere deep down, you knew this."

Niall closes his eyes, stands up, then sits down again. Something feels like it is bubbling up through him. Something that feels like relief. In all the murkiness.

He had been right.

Outside, it begins to rain. A fat patter of raindrops that are the way they should be in summer: huge and loud, a tin of marbles being emptied on the roof above them.

"It always rains when I'm here," Niall says.

"Hey, Niall," Jess says. "Stay with it. Lean into it."

"Hmm."

"You did nothing wrong. You can trust yourself."

He opens his eyes, and Jess is still looking at him. He thinks about his own correct instincts, and he thinks about the off-record call he's going to make to tell Camilla that her husband was good.

Jess wordlessly scoots the box toward him. It's the first time he's needed the tissues in a session with her.

39

Cam

Cam has not told the police about Madison. She's too scared to. A woman has died because of her. What if going to the authorities makes it worse? Instead, Cam buries herself in Adam's manuscript. She's now a quarter of the way through it, and it is really, really good.

Twenty-five percent in, he kills the narrator: *And that's me, gone. Pissed off an enemy of the family. One shot. Bang. And then, that's me dead.*

Cam draws a red exclamation mark in the margin, eager to carry on, but Charlie is coming over. *Wait,* she adds. *So who's narrating? A ghost?*

I knew this might happen to me one day. This is the way, when you grow up in crime. And, afterwards, as I sat high up above, watching my body give up, I started to make a plan for those left behind.

Say someone in my family wanted out. Say my death drew a line for them: enough.

In that case, I hoped those dear to me would find my instructions, hidden deep within the words I'd left them. That, if anything . . . if anyone ever wanted to escape the family business, the weapon I always used was buried in the garden. That important items were in a lockup under my name.

She lays the manuscript down softly on the sofa and thinks of the narrator, dead, making provision for those left behind. Something about it makes Cam shiver, makes her think of Madison, also gone. And Madison's husband, and the other hostage . . . and she can't help but wonder who will be next.

"'Where is my car quiche?'" Charlie remarks to Cam, fifteen minutes later, holding up a mug with this emblazoned on its sides. He'd texted her earlier, saying he was passing, asked to come in. Cam is glad for the company with Polly in bed, tired of checking her windows and doors are locked. And she was especially pleased he made the suggestion given that she'd left him by himself in Côte. So far, he doesn't yet seem to have seen the article online about her.

She prickles now, though, as he brandishes the cup. It was a gift from Luke, of course. One of the few things she just couldn't bear to throw away in her so-called moving-on session.

"Long story," she says weakly, not wanting to explain, not wanting to discuss that shared lexicon with him yet.

Her stomach aches slightly as Charlie picks it up and starts making drinks. A new man's hands where his predecessor's used to be.

It's early evening, sun slanting onto grass, rain temporarily stopped, smell of barbecues in the air.

Charlie spots the hot-water tap hanging over the sink and begins to try to make it work himself. He does this sort of thing sometimes in her house, confident things, proprietorial things, but she doesn't dislike them. It's nice to have someone to take the lead when you are lost.

"Jesus, this seems to be beyond me," he says. "Help a man out, CF?"

"Press down twice then turn," she says, and she reaches too. Their hands brush for the briefest of seconds, and she remembers what Libby said about moving on. She could throw this mug out—the memories, too—and move forward, with him. Stop trying to solve the mystery, which, as much as anything, has become habitual. Something she simply unconsciously wonders about daily, like how some people think about their hobbies or their job.

Still the tap does nothing. "A reluctant boiling-water tap!" Charlie says. "All technology hates me. You ever just feel like a proper old bloke?"

"Not really," Cam says drily.

"Ha. Well, I do. Useless," he says, and there it is again: that slice of sharp vulnerability, an open wound that Cam could almost reach out and touch. She recognizes it in him because it lives within her too.

Just as she's thinking this, across the kitchen island, her phone lights up, she initially thinks with a text but then sees that it's a call. She crosses the room to get it.

No Caller ID.

Slide to answer.

She reaches for it, telling herself that it'll be nothing. It'll be yet more spam. A wrong number. Nothing.

And yet. She can't help it. She is a helium balloon of hope. *It's me*, he will say. *And I can explain everything.*

But what if it's to do with Madison? What if it's the police?

"Like, there's this bastard key-card system at the office," Charlie continues, oblivious to her silently ringing phone, then looks at her, sees her expression. "OK?"

"Yeah," Cam says, mechanically, gesturing to the phone. "Hello?" she says, taking the call. Charlie looks interested, then pretends not to.

"Camilla Deschamps?"

"Yes."

"It's Niall Thompson here. I was . . ."

Cam's body fizzes with surprise, as though somebody has plugged her right into the mains, lightning bolts around her head, hair shocked and standing on end. It's physically painful, her limbs jangling and aching with the surge of it.

Shit.

It *is* the police. It must be about Madison. Why was she so foolish as to not disclose it?

". . . The hostage negotiator," she says to Niall. On the other side of the kitchen island, Charlie glances up, but he keeps his face impassive. As polite and kind as ever. He turns away from her and busies himself folding her tea towels. It doesn't need doing. It would never need doing.

"Yes, Camilla, would you be able to come and—have a chat?"

Or—worse. They've found him. They've found him. They've found his body. She clutches the edge of the kitchen island. It's all over if they have. She thinks she might be sick.

"Have you found him?" she says, her voice shrill.

She crosses out of the kitchen, still holding her phone, and into the living room, where she closes the door.

"Camilla," Niall's voice says calmly, clearly, and everything comes back to Cam. The heat. The Wetherspoon's. The forensics officers, the slow progress of the ambulance.

"Have you found him?" Cam asks again. She glances at her living-room door. God. What must Charlie be thinking? She rakes her hair back from her forehead, paces this way and that, in the same room the police interviewed her in all those years ago. She should've moved. Changed her number. He's going to be dead, and her heart is going to be fucking broken. She had no idea of the hope she had been holding. Imagining she saw him at the Tube. Imagining a spammy text came from him. Everything.

A pause. And then an answer: "No."

Cam leans forward over the sofa, her body a ragdoll thrown on a heap. "Thank God," she says, thinking how stupid it is that she would rather this call be that the police want to investigate her for what happened to Madison than be told her murderous, absent husband is dead. Sometimes, the way we react to things can reveal so much about ourselves.

"Don't worry. It's not . . ." Niall starts.

"Do you know something?"

"Yes."

"Is it where he is?"

"No."

"Is it about Madison?" she says, the words rattling out of her mouth before she can stop them. Relief: the most potent of emotions.

Another pause, this time longer. "Can we meet to talk, Camilla?"

"So it is about Madison?"

A pause. "Yes," he says.

And that's it. That *yes*. It is about Madison. And it is clearly about Luke. And maybe it's about the worst of all things: that Luke is alive and killing his enemies still.

"But I'd really like to do this in person."

"Yes. OK. Whenever. Now," Cam answers, her head hitting her chest. She's not thinking logistics. She's numb.

A soft, understanding laugh. "Tomorrow? I'll send you the address of a place where we can talk privately."

"Tomorrow," she agrees. She will have to ask Libby to have Polly.

Niall rings off, and Cam just sits there. She has somehow landed on her floor, though she doesn't remember how. A candle is lit—she and Charlie were going to come in here—and she watches the flame bend and bow left and right.

It will be that Luke murdered Madison. She draws her knees to her chest, watching the wick and the wax.

Niall hasn't found him, and he doesn't know where he is. He is still a fugitive, on the run, her husband.

But perhaps for more than one crime.

"I'm very sorry," Cam says, ten minutes later. The tea Charlie made her has cooled, and Cam knows she's been rude, sitting there in the living room, silent and alone. "I had to take that."

"Everything OK?" he asks. He's finished his tea, is looking at her with an open expression, the way you might after somebody has embarrassed themselves. Been sick from too much wine on a first date or called you by the wrong name.

"Sort of . . ." she says. She sips her tea and then swallows, deliberating. "I think I probably need to fill you in on something."

"Well," Charlie says, turning away from her, "I enjoyed my tea so much I'm going to make a second. So I'm all yours."

And it's that sentence that does it. He's been so patient. Four months of sporadic dates and closed-off conversations and abandonments in Côte Brasserie.

She thinks about what Libby said in Gordon's, and about what Niall might be telling her tomorrow about a woman shot at point-blank range on her own doorstep, then looks at Charlie's open face, those sweetly folded tea towels, and takes a tentative step toward him. She could tell him. She could just confide in him, and see what happens. She could use an ear, anyway, if nothing else, tonight, while she waits for bad news once again, once more.

"It really *is* a long story," she prevaricates.

"Always best told over tea," Charlie says, raising the mug in a kind of apologetic gesture. "Shall we go out? It's so warm now . . ."

Cam nods. "Yes."

Together, they head down and out into the garden, through Cam's bedroom, one half stuffed full of books, one half empty that Charlie glances at in surprise. It's awkward; they ignore it.

Outside is warmer than the house and humid, too, and they sit down at the table together. Charlie's face is slightly expectant in the last of the evening sun.

"I mean—you really wouldn't believe it," Cam says.

"Try me."

"Do you remember," she says, hesitating, the shame of it still weighing on her like the close air, set to storm again, "a siege in Central London in 2017, where the hostages were found dead?"

Charlie's brow furrows, lowering, then clears in understanding. Cam is used to this sequence as people try to recall what to them was a news story they may or may not have read that took up less than two minutes of their life. "Maybe—yes. I don't know. What happened?"

"One was released. Two died. And the kidnapper disappeared."

"Oh," Charlie says. "Yes. I *do* remember. I had a very boring job at the time. Even more so than now," he adds, his tone gentle, aware that the conversational topic is difficult. "I remember refreshing the news."

"Well, I'm the wife."

He holds her gaze, saying nothing.

". . . Of the kidnapper. Of Luke," she adds. "Deschamps." She hesitates. "It's my married name."

Charlie blows a breath out of the side of his mouth. "Right. I see." His eyes flick this way and that. Cam waits patiently, lets it land.

He pauses for a beat, working it out. Then his eyes meet hers. "Fucking hell," he says. She isn't sure she's ever heard him swear like that.

She explains the full story. The siege, the aftermath, the coordinates just recently, the phone call from Niall, while Charlie listens, his expression concerned. The only things she leaves out are Alexander Hale, James

Lancaster, and Madison. The darker, weirder things that she doesn't want to—and can't—explain. The things more closely associated with present-day criminality.

"Put off yet?" she ventures when she's finished. "I mean—there's baggage and then there's *baggage*."

"No, not put off—never put off." Charlie's voice is soft and serious on those syllables, and Cam sets her tea down on the table, still unfinished, and looks at him.

"It's—I . . . I've . . ." she says, tired now. "It's been a hard seven years."

"I get that. So, you're not CF, but CD."

"Sort of. It was easier to go back," she says.

"I see."

"I think Niall is going to tell me something bad tomorrow," she says.

"Why?"

"I don't know. I think Luke was into something pretty dark," she says, deliberately vague.

Charlie nods. "You don't need to—you don't need to be embarrassed, Cam," he says, his voice muted, low-key, empathetic. The perfect reaction. "I understand. It happened *to* you."

Cam gazes at him. She didn't expect this. That this would feel so intimate, and so right, while Niall is out there with some unknown piece of information. Funny how things happen sometimes. Maybe she really will move on, and maybe she will get answers, too, and maybe one of those things will aid the other.

Cam closes her eyes, draws her cardigan down over her hands, and sits back in the chair. "I'm exhausted," she says. "I'm exhausted by it."

"I can only imagine."

"Tell me something dysfunctional about you."

"I'm attracted to baggage," he says, quick as a cat, and she lets out a surprised burst of laughter.

"Something real," she says.

"Well, I'm childless even though I didn't want to be, I'm a researcher even though it's boring. I think"—he clears his throat—"that maybe it's easy to regard yourself as *other*—and obviously what happened to you is huge. But actually, may I remind you that most everyone feels utterly fucked up by life."

Cam pauses. "That might be the nicest thing anyone's ever said to me," she says.

Charlie laughs. "Oh dear—a very depressing message from me."

"Really not."

"What do you think he knows—this Niall?" he asks, after a few seconds' pause.

"I have no idea. It could be anything. But I've never had good news about it, you know? It's always been something worse. First that he had taken hostages. Then that he'd killed them. Then that he'd disappeared."

"Understood."

The air cools to a scented chill later. They switch to red wine. "Inside, or stay out?" she asks when it's become too dark to see.

"Out, I think, don't you?" Charlie says. He tilts his head back, the orb of London sky above them fading from worn to new denim.

"I have no lights. Just a horrible security one," Cam says, thinking about it clicking on the previous night. She's glad Charlie's here.

"None needed."

Charlie moves from the table and onto Cam's back step, the door to her bedroom open behind him, his legs stretched out in front. He pats the space next to him. There is an unopened bottle of white wine lined up ready. Cam hesitates, then joins him, shifting a tall planter out of the way.

Charlie waves a hand in the darkness. The security light clicks on eventually. "This is very not ambient," Cam says when it blinds them.

"Kind of industrial," Charlie says with a small laugh. "But better than nothing. You said you read out here?"

"Sometimes. In the summer," she says.

"Kindle and wine?"

"Bliss."

Cam wants to keep him here. She's not felt that before, but she does tonight. Telling him has unlocked something for her, and on the strangest night too.

The light pops off again and they're back in the swampy dark. Charlie leans over and tops up their wine. That aftershave. His closeness. "Nice to layer the white on top of the dregs of the red, as all wine connoisseurs would say."

Cam laughs. "I can't even see the glasses."

Charlie hands her hers. The night air is sweet and dark, and Cam suddenly feels safe here, with him. The loneliness she carries around with her has frayed just slightly at the edges into softness.

"What was your very boring job? The one in 2017?"

"It was my job to look after a set of masts. It was called project management, though I have no idea why. It was really, really fucking dull." The wine has loosened his tongue, and she likes it.

"What did you actually do?"

"Honestly, Cam, I have no idea," he says with a small, self-deprecating laugh. "All I remember is being so bored that one day I changed my email signature to a different name, just to see if anyone would notice."

"And did they?"

"No." He sets his glass down with another sniff of a laugh.

Cam gazes at him, thinking that she doesn't like him as much as Luke, but that doesn't mean she doesn't like him at all. That there can be shades of gray here, in the afterworld.

"You know," she says, "I wish I'd told you about the coordinates."

"You should've," Charlie murmurs.

He looks behind them, up at the house, and she's glad he doesn't push it, wanting to know more about Luke, the way a lot of people might. "So you're declaring him dead to move from here? I bet you'll be happy. I moved after Saskia left. Was nice to just—put a stamp on somewhere new. You know?"

"I know," she says softly. "Maybe. I don't know if I'll move yet."

"You will." Charlie is drinking quickly, maybe preparing to leave. "You know," he says, "I know what it's like to . . ."

Cam waits, but he doesn't continue. "You know what it's like to . . ." she prompts.

He pauses for a second, his eyes down, then looks straight at her. "To not ever have any answers," he says simply. He hesitates, his fingers on the base of the wineglass, then adds, "Saskia, I mean. It's not the same as what you went through."

"But . . . ?"

"I don't know whether she just didn't want a baby *with me*. You see? Did she need to meet someone else, or . . . did she just change her mind, down the line?"

"I see."

"It was just—well, I imagine you know exactly how I feel."

"I thought he was alive for the longest time. Maybe I still do."

"Yeah?"

"I don't know. But, anyway, he didn't . . ."

Charlie nods. "I know. Even if he's out there," he says, "even if he didn't mean to do it, he never came back to you."

"That's it," Cam says. "Really, I can never forgive him. There can't be an excuse for what he did. For staying away so long."

She leans against Charlie then. His shoulder next to hers, his body warm, his arm around her. And for the first time in forever, she doesn't want to go to bed and read and shut out the world.

Maybe it's Charlie, or maybe she's simply putting it off, the way you feel sometimes the night before test results you're expecting the worst from. She wants to stay up, with him, and let tomorrow be damned. Let them come for her. She doesn't care: she has him.

Anonymous Reporting on Camilla

I stand and look up at Camilla's house. A typical London home on a typical London street. Chimneys on the roofs, bay windows, street parking.

But I'm not paying much attention to any of that. No, I'm going over the conversation in the garden. How very fascinating, I think, hitching my bag over my shoulder as I take one last look at the house. All information is good information. Especially all that, straight from the horse's mouth.

I turn to leave, to go back, to report to my brother: he will want to know this.

Niall

Camilla is waiting for Niall the next evening at the entrance to the Inner Temple.

She is indeed as pretty as she was then, but Niall hadn't imagined the fragility last time he saw her. It's there in her plainer clothes, her lack of jewelry—no wedding ring—and the lines around her mouth.

She says nothing as he approaches her, just watches him. She's wearing a plain white T-shirt, jeans, and an apprehensive expression.

"Sorry it's so late in the day, and such a strange place," he says. "I will explain."

"We're going in here?" she asks, and she looks nervous. And Niall thinks, Shoot, he didn't mean to cause her worry, or force her into a situation that made her uncomfortable.

"Weird spot, I know, but it's very private," he says. "A good place to discuss . . ." He lets his sentence trail off, unfinished.

The Inner Temple is a gated precinct where lawyers and judges work and sometimes live, and it hardly ever admits members of the public. It's as safe as could be: neither of them can be followed in, on the off chance the Met are still tailing her. You need a pass, which Niall got via a friend of a friend.

It's the perfect place to betray the police, and to tell Camilla what he knows. Niall lets them in. She glances at him as the wrought-iron gate closes behind them but says nothing further.

The buildings are a Christmastime model village—even now in the height of summer it looks like there ought to be snow surrounding the hundreds of tiny orange windows. It's quiet here, and populated, Niall hopes, by good people. A golden Pegasus sits on the top of a weather-vane, and Niall stares up at it, thinking about freedom and taking risks and doing the right thing.

They head through an archway and into a courtyard. He lets a breath out when he sees that it's empty. Onto a narrow, cobbled street lit softly from below, columns of golden light beaming upward.

"Look. Thanks for coming," Niall says. "And for bearing with me. Cryptic as this is."

"I just want to know what you know," Camilla says, perhaps rather shortly.

They continue to walk through the courtyard. The night is quiet and calm around them, scented with wild garlic and that wind-burnt smell people get when they come in from the outside.

"It's delicate," Niall says. "But first: Will you tell me what you know about Madison?" He doesn't add anything further. He bluffed to Camilla last night when she asked him if this was about Madison. If she thinks he knows everything already, she will talk. That's how negotiating works.

And they've both been looking for Deschamps for so long that, surely, their information may be able to help the other?

Camilla visibly winces. Her skinny shoulders go up. Niall feels a lurch of sympathy for her. That she's come out here, met a virtual stranger, late, all on the promise of information. That most precious commodity.

"Once a negotiator . . ." she says.

"Tit for tat."

Camilla sighs. "Madison Smith found me at the school gate—she was wanting to meet to talk properly. I guess she saw an article a paper wrote about me," she says. "You see it?"

"The *Mail*. Yes."

"They overheard me oversharing at a work thing." She waves a slim hand. "Obviously I didn't sell my story to them."

"No. What did Madison say to you?"

"She said that she was married to one of the hostages my husband murdered. We arranged to meet, but she didn't show. She didn't tell me her name. So I didn't know anything, until I recognized her in an article and saw that she'd been murdered. I didn't tell anyone." She drops her voice to such a low register that Niall can barely hear her at all. "I didn't tell the police. No one. I . . . I feel so wrapped up in something that I don't even know what it is. The—the *shadow* he has cast over me," she says, clearly meaning Deschamps. "I know I should have told someone—but I was terrified."

Niall shivers with the shock of it. Knowledge. Fuck. Madison's husband was one of the hostages. So much for the Met doing its paltry research. Look: the answer was waiting for him here, all along. "Who? Who was the hostage?" he asks, ignoring Camilla's anxiety. She has nothing to be anxious about with him, anyway.

"I don't know. She said—'*they* told us not to tell anyone they were missing or dead.' I tried to find her husband but couldn't . . ."

"I'll look." He pauses, then says: "And now she's dead."

"I know," she says softly.

Niall cocks his head, then says: "What do you mean by *they*? 'They told us not to tell anyone'?"

"I don't know. Am I going to be—"

"The Met is investigating her murder," he says softly. "But I'm not. And I'm not really here in my capacity as the Met."

"No?"

"No," Niall says. His mind is reeling. Who the hostages were might be within reach, finally . . .

Nobody in the world except these two, here, in a private courtyard in London, know the connection between the two cases. And it's here, and only here, maybe, that Niall can admit to himself where this is heading. He is off-record. He is off the books. And that almost always ends badly.

"Well," Camilla says, landing at the exact same place as him. "Is that why you wanted to meet here? To discuss something—without other officers?" She glances up at him.

He gestures to a bench. In the late hour, it's become dotted with dew, little pearlescent spheres sitting on black metal. Camilla sits and crosses her legs. "Will you tell the Met I withheld information from them?"

He almost laughs. "Not if you don't," he says, thinking of the secrets he's keeping from the Met. And from Camilla too. He ought to tell her about the surveillance on her but wants to omit the sighting several months ago. She would only go looking for him. And it could have been nobody at all.

He takes a breath. He has decided precisely what to tell her: he will tell her what he knows about her husband. But he isn't going to tell her about the stranger outside her house. He doesn't want to worry her, and anyway, if they are both trying to find Deschamps, he can protect her that way instead. Keep in touch with her. Make sure she's OK. Nor does he want to tell her he intercepted her coordinates. He wants her trust. And he is trustworthy. He just needs her to know that.

Camilla stares up at him, somewhat surprised-looking. "OK. Deal," she says, holding his gaze.

Niall raises his eyebrows. They're under the golden glow of a street-light. It's warm, the crickets are out, the air humming and shivering with the sound. He pauses, wondering how best to word it. "The Met doesn't know I'm here. At all."

"OK?" she says, eyes still scared.

"I've been digging into your husband's case."

Camilla blinks. "And . . . ?"

"The two hostages were sent to murder your husband. They were contract killers."

"What?" Camilla says. Her hands are in a mess of knots in her lap. "Sorry—what . . . I don't understand what you mean?"

"Your husband wrote on the dark web that he thought he was about to be murdered."

"Luke did?" Camilla seems to fold in on herself. A small, reflexive clutch of her hand to her chest. Her body goes completely still.

Luke. Not Deschamps. Something about the name, the way she speaks about him, that movement her hand made . . . empathy surges in Niall's chest. Camilla loves him, knows him, that much is clear. And Niall knows how that feels.

"He . . ." she says softly. "He thought that he was going to be murdered?"

"He said that two men were being sent to kill him. He asked somebody to protect him, he wanted to buy a gun, but he couldn't get one in time. If you look at the CCTV, he reaches for something—and I think it's the hostages' pistol, not your husband's. They were there before him, put their gun to the side. Deschamps observed them for a while, outside, then took it."

"He . . ." Camilla seems speechless. She still isn't moving at all. It begins to rain, another summer storm that seems to come from nowhere, the rain sliding white rods, a Van Gogh painting. Camilla doesn't seem to notice at all.

"We never saw the point of their entry. It was off CCTV. We just heard Deschamps enter, then yell," Niall says, holding her elbow and steering her to her feet. Rain runs down the back of his neck, making him shiver. "But I think they were there waiting for him. He knew they wanted him dead, so he tied them up. They already had the sacks over their heads—to disguise themselves. Just makeshift T-shirts with slits for eyes. They were about to commit a crime. They were trying to kill a man. Your husband."

And there's the moment, right as they're standing there. Camilla closes her eyes. When she opens them again, they're wet, and not with rainwater. Instinctively, it seems to Niall, the first movement she makes is to lean into him, but she quickly pulls away again. "They came for him."

"Yes. I'm pretty sure."

"Contract killers. Hit men."

"Yes."

"He thought he was going to be killed. That's why he—the gun . . ." she says, working through it all. "Do you think that's why he eventually shot them? He had no choice?"

"Yes. Maybe." Water splashes up around her ankles as they walk, but she doesn't seem to notice. "I don't think he had many choices available to him."

"He was good," she says, tilting her face upward. The rain lands on it, illuminating her in silver. Niall doesn't answer. She says it again, almost to herself. "He was good."

Niall lets her have this moment before revealing anything more.

Camilla turns away from him, Niall assumes so she can have her moment in private. Her husband was good.

In the distance, two other figures stand on a rooftop bar: pinpricks on the horizon. They must be half a mile away. Niall squints at them through the rain. The people will be soaking. He smiles as he looks at them and thinks that they won't care. Not at all.

SEVEN YEARS
AFTER THE
ATTEMPTED MURDER

42

Cam

Relief. A high, tidal sort of feeling, rising up through her body and washing her clean from the inside out. He was good. He was the man she married. Night after night, she slept next to him, and she *did* know him. The circumstances of the siege, though still unknown, were not as clear-cut as they seemed. She had been right about him. And that is what matters most.

Cam and Niall walk under a bridge that joins two buildings. The rain is so loud it's like white noise. Her feet might be wet. She doesn't know, doesn't care. She can't yet bring herself to speak properly.

A police officer says men were sent to murder her husband.

That he retaliated.

That, all this time, they were the ones sent to kill, and he the one who defended himself.

She blinks. Niall is looking down at her.

"You don't think he wanted to kill anyone," she says softly. Just checking and checking and checking again.

"No," Niall says. A pause. "I never did, actually. Which was why we didn't go in. I wouldn't authorize it."

"But . . ."

"I know. There's a lot to unpack. I don't think the rain's going to stop—hang on," Niall says, and he leads her across a courtyard, then lets them inside a wooden door and up to the rafters. "I know a barrister who knows the caretaker," he explains.

The corridor is old-fashioned, royal-feeling, deep red carpets faded up to rose pink, portraits on the walls, iron knockers on old-fashioned doors. Niall opens room number 5.

The room is chilly inside, like a church, and Niall perches by the windowsill. Cam lets a breath out and holds her information close to her. Her husband was a victim. He was good.

She chokes on the thought. A storm of emotions: relief; a happiness she hasn't felt in years; sadness too.

And fear. Somebody wanted her husband dead. And he knew it, and told nobody. The dread he must have felt, alone with it, chopping onions and hiding his tears . . . Cam had dismissed that clue from seven years ago, put it down to stress, but now she holds it up in a new light. The sunlight strikes it at the exact right angle, finally, and it fragments out into a rainbow. Somebody wanted him dead. He was a man with few options, desperately trying to find some before they came for him.

Cam's head begins to clear from the shock of it, and she starts to try to work out what she needs to do. How much to tell Niall. Which parts to keep to herself.

But there is liquid happiness in her chest, gloopy as childhood medicine and just as comforting. *He didn't want to do it. He is not, he was not, bad.* Cam swallows it down greedily. *He took their weapon. The one they wanted to murder him with.*

"How did you find out?" she asks him, her heart happy/sad.

"He contacted a man called Harry Grace just before the siege. You're aware of him?"

"Yes, I am," Cam says in surprise.

"Well, Harry lurks on the dark web. He's a criminal from Lewisham. People use him when they want protection. Deschamps reached out to him on there."

"Lewisham," Cam says. Harry in Lewisham.

"Yes. The Rightmove house. Very clever, to obscure a meeting point in that way. When questioned, Harry said he didn't know him."

"Why did someone want him dead?"

"I don't know that, Camilla. But I'm working on it."

"And why would he go on the run? He'd face the police if it was only the police who wanted him. I know he would," Cam says. He'd come back and serve his time. We'd visit him. "The people who want him dead—they killed Madison. They're still at large."

"I know."

"How did you know? To contact Harry?"

"Look—the Met have been surveilling your phone," Niall says softly, slowly. "They wanted to be sure Deschamps wasn't using you to hide. I shouldn't be telling you that. I could be sacked."

"You've been looking at—at my communications?" Cam says, reeling. Seven years on, and she still is under suspicion.

"The Met was surveilling you after you were sent the coordinates. Briefly. It enabled them to try and get some answers."

"Right," Cam says, trying to digest this, trying to work out how she feels. "I didn't know you knew about those."

"Sadly," he says, sympathetically, "it yielded nothing."

She pauses. "I don't care about the Met," she says. "I care about the truth."

The truth. "I know. Me too." Niall kicks his trainer against the old carpet. It's cold in the room, and Cam is beginning to shiver in her wet clothes. "They don't know I'm here. They were not interested in what I found out. They want only to catch your husband."

Cam nods in understanding. "I see," she says, grateful for a copper who will go out on a limb.

Cam walks over to the windowsill and joins Niall. She closes her eyes. London disappears, replaced momentarily by blackness. She opens them again and there it is, still shimmering below. "Do you think he's alive?" Cam says, looking at the cityscape beneath them.

"I don't know," he says, and Cam is again grateful—for his honesty.

Thunder rumbles somewhere in the distance.

A beat. Lightning brightens overhead like a flashbulb.

"I don't know," Niall says again.

"I can feel it," Cam says. "I can feel it." She looks at Niall, hoping she can trust him. Hoping that this is the beginning of the end. That two heads are better than one and, eventually, they can find out what happened, once and for all.

Niall seems to hesitate, just slightly. The information begins to free-fall, as fast as the rain outside. "The man on the dark web—Harry. He told Deschamps he could hide him, if necessary—way back when."

London tilts beneath Cam as though she is in a lift. "You think he could still be hiding."

"Maybe."

She puts a palm to the glass, for a second pretending Luke is just beyond it, his palm against the other side, looking in at her, waiting for her.

"I'm going to keep working on this. Off-record." He looks directly at her.

This opens the floodgates for Cam. As the rain whirls around outside, she tells Niall everything she knows. The funeral, Alexander Hale and James Lancaster. Alexander's father and the frosty reception she got at their flat. Luke going out that night in April. His outbursts in the weeks before the siege. The things she's never told anybody. This man who is betraying the police must be on her side.

She pauses, then says: "When Madison asked to meet me—she said *somewhere you don't regularly go.*"

These words seem to have an effect on Niall, who clenches his jaw. "And she was still killed," he says softly. "Even though, clearly, it was you who she thought may be followed."

Cam looks at him, thinking. "Right," she says eventually.

"I think whatever Luke was caught up in clearly wasn't something he felt he could report," Niall says, looking at her directly. He leaves a pause.

"And he hasn't killed his enemies, after all. He killed their heavies," she fills in.

"Yes," Niall says, his expression knowing and sad, eyebrows raised, mouth turned down.

They both know the implication of this, though they don't say it. Whoever wanted Luke dead is still out there somewhere. They have killed Madison Smith. They may even have killed Luke.

And they might want Cam dead too.

Niall and Cam stay in Room 5 for a long time, watching London's lights glow and pulse beneath them. They talk about the past and the future, about the man Cam thought she saw in her garden, about the coordinates, and about the siege that only lasted for a day but changed several lives forever, Niall listening avidly, just as he did way back when.

43

Anonymous Reporting on Camilla

I have a lot of intel," I tell him as soon as I arrive in the launderette for my report.

My brother looks mildly interested, but that's all.

"Tell me it's something big," he says, folding a sheet from the dryer.

"She's in touch with the hostage negotiator," I say. "They met up, but I don't know what they discussed. Couldn't follow them in."

"Try harder next time."

44

Niall

Saturday night and Niall is the only person in the office. His room is fluorescent lit; the lights hurt his eyes. He's on The HOLMES system, and on Madison Smith.

HOLMES is open-source to every single officer in the police and, one day, somebody may notice Niall has been poking around in files that don't belong to him, but that's a future problem, not a today problem, and so, late, Niall grabs a Coke for old times' sake and begins to dig.

It's still light out, even though it's gone nine at night, and Niall shuts the blinds and begins, his computer humming near silently in the background, nothing else.

He double-clicks the *murder* next to Madison Smith's name, and the summary window opens:

MADISON SMITH, 47, FOUND MURDERED ON HER DOOSTEP BY HER SONS WHO WERE INSIDE THE HOUSE. SHE WAS A STAY-AT-HOME MOTHER, NO KNOWN ENEMIES. HUSBAND IS SUSPECT NUMBER 1: SHE IS ESTRANGED FROM HIM AND HE HAS NOT SO FAR COME FORWARD.

Husband is a listed suspect along the nominals tabs, and Niall clicks it, revealing a new information sheet.

ANDREW SMITH, 52, SELF-EMPLOYED BRICKLAYER. ESTRANGED
FROM WIFE FOR THE PAST SEVERAL YEARS—HER SONS DON'T
KNOW PRECISELY HOW LONG AND NOR DO HER FRIENDS. HE
HAS NO PASSPORT, CRIMINAL RECORD OR DRIVING LICENCE.

There he is. A contract killer. For this reason, Niall supposes, Andrew
Smith has no entries on HOLMES. Nothing comes up on 192.com, the
marriage-and-death register, or social media. Niall spends two hours
looking: to try to find him, to try to find who hired him, but all he comes
up against are dead ends.

He searches next for Alexander Hale and James Lancaster. Found
murdered on the street together in 2017, no suspect ever arrested.

But it's the weirdest thing. Isn't it? Niall sits back in his chair, hand
to his chin. A motorbike rumbles by outside, disturbing his chain of
thought, and he gets to his feet and begins to walk a slow loop of his
office.

Hang on. The murders took place in Whitechapel, on the exact route
Deschamps took that night, the night he turned his location data off.

Only, they never popped up on HOLMES when Niall searched the
crimes that night. He would have noticed. He *would* have. An unsolved
double murder, no suspects, on the night Deschamps went driving,
covered his number plate in mud on the way home, and turned off his
iPhone tracking? Of course he would have fucking noticed. He remembers seeing a few burglaries and assaults, but nothing more. No murder. Certainly not this one. How could that be? And why is it back on
HOLMES now?

45

Cam

The last thing Cam wants to do is dress Polly up and go to her sister's house on a Sunday afternoon, with school the following day, but she has no choice. This is the way it is when you have no other siblings, no parents and, for Libby, no offspring. Cam's absence would be too loaded, even though she went to Gordon's on her sister's actual birthday. Even though Libby seems to want multiple birthday celebrations. Cam is needed, and so she throws on a dress and heads over there with Polly.

She hasn't told a soul about her meeting with Niall. About his revelation. His theory. She's in a hinterland, afraid to hope, aware that it's all deep past anyway. That is what Libby would say: *What do the semantics matter, the exact turn of events? He's still gone, still abandoned you.*

Cam keeps the truth close to her. An embrace she doesn't otherwise have.

It's still early July, and yet there's just the most indistinct autumn chill in the air, hardly yet noticeable, except to Cam, who looks forward to it. Blustery green leaves rustling up ahead, a glass fragility to the blue sky, an orange tint to the light.

She scurries down the street toward Libby's, trying to hurry Polly but also trying not to spook her, thinking of the men who wanted Luke dead, of Madison too. Of the stranger who stood at her garden fence several days ago, so still and quick and quiet she wonders now if he was even real.

"Mum! What's the rush?" Polly says, of course not missing a trick.

"No rush." Cam glances over her shoulder, just once, before Libby's house looms into view.

"You're here!" Libby says when they reach it, and Cam immediately spots it: lemonade in a wineglass in her hand. It's colorless. Her eyes stray to it, then to Libby, who says nothing, and so neither does Cam.

"We are here," Polly says to Libby. "The best guests of your life."

"Polly!" Cam guffaws.

"It's true!" she says, and Cam thinks how funny she is. Her daughter, grown into this happy sunbeam in the most shitty of circumstances; her asphalt flower, pushing up through the dust in a bright pink explosion.

It's 4:30 on the dot. *A late-afternoon sort of thing*, Libby had said. *Tea and cake, etc., whatever*. Libby wanted Cam to invite Charlie, and so Cam had texted earlier, hoping he might read it too late to come, hoping he might arrive too. The mixed-up emotions in the upside-down world with a husband who might be dead, and who might be bad, and who might be good. Charlie's coming, anyway, and Cam is glad of it.

"Happy birthday," Cam says. "How're the stress levels?" she adds, peering beyond her sister and into the throng. You'd be forgiven for thinking it was a kids' party: Libby's friends all have children. Cam doesn't know how she can stand it. Cam was blessed with fertility and still had to quit their parents' WhatsApp group when everyone's babies slept except hers.

Cam follows Libby in and gulps at the crowd, feeling embarrassed, a very special toxic kind of celebrity feeling, same as at the school gate. A couple of people glance over at her, Libby's friends whom Cam half knows but doesn't see often, and Cam drops her gaze.

"God, feeling very sorry for myself," Libby says. "We dropped the cake on the floor. Then we realized M&S didn't deliver the wine, so, feeling a bit woe-is-me."

"Ah, very sweepy," Cam says immediately, using her and Luke's term without thought.

"Huh?"

"Woe-is-me. Luke and I used to call that sweepy," Cam says, unable to resist. "Feeling sweepy."

Libby's brow lowers and she steps aside, beckoning Cam and Polly in. Perhaps it's the esoteric word, perhaps the evidence that Luke is still alive and well in Cam's memory, but Libby says nothing further. A criminal husband is more taboo than death and divorce put together, a fact Cam finds astonishing. Grief is not a permitted emotion within macabre mysteries.

"Is Charlie coming?" she asks Cam, perhaps pointedly.

"Yep." Cam grabs a non-M&S wine and stands underneath a red-and-white awning that her sister has erected over the patio, then sips the wine, alone. Behind her, she hears one of Libby's friends say, "Her. I think her husband is in prison?" And Cam sort of wishes he were. That she could visit him sometimes—Saturday mornings: she wouldn't ask for much.

Charlie arrives later, around half past five. "Welcome," she says, stepping aside to let him in, and as the word leaves her mouth, she sees his face change from impassive to optimistic, pleased. He makes a gesture toward her, both hands on either of her shoulders. Not a hug. More the kind of greeting you'd give a small child, one whom you were excited to see.

Later, much later—have only hours gone by, or actual years?—most of Libby's friends have left, and it's just Cam and Charlie, Libby and Si, and Si's brother, Max. Cam is leaving. It's late. Polly has gone to sleep on a bed upstairs because it's a school night, and something about that simple fact fills Cam with nostalgia for her own childhood. Other people's spare beds and the cold crunch of a sleeping bag and midnight feasts that they had to keep hushed.

She's in Libby's Victorian living room. Libby paid an interior designer to do her whole house up—*I can't be bothered myself; I have had enough of houses by the end of each day*—something Cam had laughed with her over but which she is actually quite jealous of. The walls and ceiling are a dark navy, the lights brass, the mirror a sunburst—Cam knows it's hung too high for Libby to look at herself in it, but she doesn't move it because it *kind of looks right and I don't care.*

"God, I'm bloody knackered," Libby says, flopping onto the sofa and topping up Cam's wine. None for her. Cam wants to ask, is so desperate to ask, but doesn't. "Stay if you want."

"No, it's fine," Cam says listlessly, "we're going, I need to get Polly now," she adds, glad it's walking distance.

"I'll walk you home," Charlie says, "then go to mine."

Cam throws him a grateful glance, trying to ignore the fact that what she's grateful for is his lack of imposition.

Si crosses and uncrosses his legs. He's about eight beers down. And, God, Cam misses those carefree times. She doesn't drink often now because she's always in sole charge of Polly, but she also doesn't drink because she thinks she would cry and overshare her secrets. Again.

"Not seen you in ages," Si says to Cam. Indeed, the last time they spoke was about the form.

"Mmm," Cam says in response. Libby gets up and wanders off down the hallway, leaving them alone together. Suddenly, the sitting room feels sinister. The dark walls and ceiling like a night sky, the air black outside beyond the window. Cam shivers with it, with something, some feeling that she can't name.

"How're you doing?" Si adds, Cam thinks warmly. She looks up at him. His cheeks are pink, like a teething baby's.

"Not bad," Cam says, feeling exposed, sitting there in front of Si, who knows she tried to get her husband declared dead recently, but won't broach that directly. In front of Charlie, who knows the full story, although Si doesn't know that.

Si turns his mouth down and tips his head toward her slightly, perhaps a grim acknowledgment of what she is talking about, perhaps not.

Charlie lowers himself gently onto the sofa next to her, a calm and kind gesture of support. She reaches to touch his knee lightly, just once, thinking of their talk in her garden, his stoic understanding.

And why can't they be? Why *can't* they be a couple? Luke's gone, whatever happened in the warehouse. He's gone.

Charlie's body is warm next to Cam. He smells of that very specific male-just-showered scent. She thinks of him agreeing to come and showering hurriedly, and something sympathetic awakens inside her.

Tentatively, he drapes his arm along the back of the sofa. And something slots into place for Cam. They can be a united front. Maybe her pain isn't a block standing in the way of her relationship with Charlie. Maybe he can help her with it. Maybe she could talk to him about it and be supported by him.

She leans her body against his.

"Ah, a pair of lovebirds," Si says. Not the kind of thing he would say when he was sober, and his teasing unsettles Cam. That they're all rooting for her, but to do something which feels somehow wrong, at times, to her. Incorrect.

Just across from him, on the oak of Libby's rustic mantelpiece, is a photograph of Libby and Si on their wedding day. Behind that is a piece of blue cardboard that says "Window to the Womb" on it. An ultrasound clinic. The lack of drinking was one thing—Libby is often not drinking—but this is another. She calculates it. Is it too soon after the last loss? Cam thinks, *Oh, please, please, please let it happen for them. Please don't let it be an old one.*

Libby arrives and goes to top up Cam's drink again—though she hasn't had any herself—and Cam covers the rim with her hand. "No, I'm leaving," she says.

"Right," Charlie says, getting to his feet, and Cam's grateful for the show of support.

"I'll get Polly," she says to him.

She walks up to where her daughter's sleeping. It's not a nursery, exactly, but neither is it a guest room. Cam supposes it's a nursery-in-waiting. Pale-pink walls, high ceilings, two small windows—dollhouse windows. Black beams across the ceiling—God, Polly used to be fascinated by those as a baby; Cam had forgotten until just now. And now she's enormous, four feet long in a sleeping bag, her baby.

Cam shakes her shoulder gently, then picks her up.

Her body yields into her mother's like a warm sack of flour, and as Polly's legs briefly hit Cam's knees, she longs, suddenly, for those dreamy newborn days when her feet wouldn't even reach Cam's hips. A little hand dangling casually between her breasts. The puff of milk breath by her ear. She didn't appreciate them when she had them, was so ready for them to be over, to be onto the next stage. Weaning. Walking. Sleep. She didn't realize she was rushing it, rushing her, didn't realize that they would only ever get those discrete nine months as a family of three before everything shattered. The bittersweet sadness that always sits alongside motherhood, the notion of gradually losing time, of letting go, is even more pronounced, for Cam. Newborn Polly, with her silken blancmange thighs, gone forever. Two-year-old Polly, who would squat in a demi-plié to inspect bugs in the garden, gone too. You can't keep them. You can't stop time.

Polly stirs, rubbing her eyes, blond hair all over the place the color of wheat right before its harvest, streaked naturally with highlights of July sunlight. Her daughter, born in the autumn, looking like the height of summer. "It's OK," she says, carrying Polly out.

Confusion crosses Polly's features, then she settles again in her mother's arms. For a moment, she looks like Cam, but then she relaxes and is Luke once more. "Hi!" she says.

"Hi."

"Is it the morning?"

"No," Cam says, stroking that flaxen hair, looking at her beautiful daughter. Pink cheeks. Peach fuzz. Still the pout of a toddler, ever so slightly, around the lips, the bottom lip disappearing underneath the top. Soon, she'll lose it all, will grow up fully.

"Are we going to sell our house?" she asks, eyes still closed, and, God, children. Cam really does miss her non-sleeping baby who wasn't capable of overhearing anything, who didn't have a psyche like this: one that could be damaged with a few badly chosen words that Cam alone has to pick.

"Who said that?"

"Uncle Si."

Cam rolls her eyes. Bloody Si, speaking without thinking.

"Maybe, but we'll live somewhere much better," she says. "If we do move."

"Will we sleep upstairs, like here?"

"Possibly."

"Other people's dads live with them, don't they?" Polly says, and the words hit Cam square in the chest like a swinging pendulum. As ever in parenting, the moments you fear happen suddenly, without warning, and you have to fudge it, or it feels like it.

"Yes," she says carefully.

"And mine had to go away. So he won't know about the new house too?" Polly says, and she's confused. She's so confused. Cam leans her head against her daughter's, there on the landing, her heart hurting with it. Should she have given her the straight truth, then? Is that what other people would've done, rather than these vagaries? But would she have been able to handle it—and what it might have meant about her?

"You know what?" she says softly. "You know what I do know?"

"What's that?"

"Well," Cam says, and she shifts Polly on her hip. She hasn't held her like this for months, maybe even years. "Two men didn't like your dad. They tried to hurt him, so he hurt them back. He had no choice. And he left and we don't know where he is. But," Cam says thickly, her throat closing up with emotion, "here's what I know: He loved you so much. And he never wanted to do anything bad, at all. I know that."

"That's nice," Polly says, a tired smile crossing her features. "I didn't know all that. That he—that he had to go away to escape the men who didn't like him?"

"Yes, exactly," Cam says, though really, who knows?

"So he didn't want to leave."

"No."

"I like hearing that."

"I like saying it," Cam says.

"Sometimes people do bad things for good reasons. We learnt in school," she says, sounding about twenty years old. "So is he one of those people?"

"Yes," Cam says thickly. "He didn't ever want to do anything bad."

"Sounds nice. My dad."

"I think so," Cam murmurs, and they rest their heads together for a few seconds, both silent. And she's so glad. She's so glad she held out for the truth, or a piece of it, anyway, so that she could tell it to her daughter. Tell the truth about Luke's legacy, and who Polly is a part of.

"We need to go home, but go back to sleep, I'll carry you," she says to Polly, and Polly looks at her, blinks once, then slides a little bit down Cam's body in her sleeping bag, comedically, cartoon-style, and closes her eyes. And that's that.

As she walks down the stairs, she hears the conversation explode with laughter, hears her husband's name. Surely not, not with Charlie there?

She stops, unconsciously, not wanting to go any further. Drunk people and their gossiping. Her sister and her opinions that Cam ought to move on. She is tired of it all.

"No, he was so rich, we are quids in on the commission," Si says. "Despite his weird habits."

Ah. Just gossip about their estate-agenting business. Cam's shoulders relax. She will go home, later, to Adam's wonderfully dark gem of a book—the protagonist has just told the reader that somebody does know the identity of his killer—and then sleep. Maybe this life isn't so terrible.

"I don't know it—is it a wealthy area?"

"Yeah—near Islington."

"Is it?"

"Look—let me show you," Si says, his voice loud and exuberant. Cam is in the hallway, now, and can hear everything. "It's a tiny borough, hang on . . ." He speaks as he types it in. "St. Luke's." Ah. That is why she thought they were discussing her husband.

But . . . St. Luke's, near Islington. And Cam knows before she gets her phone out, before she googles it, what she's going to find. She knows she's just glimpsed a truth, like a prism that shines the light in the exact right place, just for a second, until it disappears again to darkness.

She types the coordinates in, then zooms out and out again. And sure enough, there it is: those coordinates she was sent were in the St. Luke's Borough of London.

Surely they can only have been sent by one person.

Her husband. He chose them because they contain his name: it was a clue.

46

Niall

"Oh, it's you," Viv says to Niall as she opens her door. As she says this, her face drops, and the evening sun scorches the back of Niall's neck like a blush of shame. He's calling in on his way to a little reconnaissance mission in Whitechapel, just to watch and wait. Swung by Viv's on a whim.

Viv is in full off-duty mode. Bare feet, two toe rings on. The hammered silver catches and fragments the sun into thrown diamonds across the front path. He can't stop looking at those bare feet. Pink polish. She's wearing an oversized white something—he doesn't know the term, but it's the kind of thing you'd throw on over a swimming costume on holiday. It comes to her slender mid-thighs. She has what he knows will be a Chablis in her left hand. She stands on one foot, the other rubbing her ankle as she looks up, perplexed, at him.

"I'm on my way somewhere," he explains. "Thought I'd call in."

Viv blinks, evidently surprised, which is not at all the emotion Niall intended to evoke. "Where?" she says blankly.

"Quarter of a mile away, on a job."

"Rather you than me," she says, still standing partially blocking the doorway. "When are you due there?" she asks, as sharp a negotiator as anyone Niall has trained up.

He dodges the question. "I wondered if I might say something to you."

She glances over her shoulder, just once, but Niall clocks it immediately. "Is somebody here?" he says.

Viv raises her eyes heavenward, saying nothing, but she turns away from him, heading inside, and he takes this as an invitation. He walks through her hallway, living room on the right, kitchen on the left, and out into the back garden. Nobody here except the old cat he saw the other day, and a second one with one eye.

"New cats?"

"New old cats. Owner died," she says.

It's nothing like their place in Central London. Viv moved here seven years ago, into rented, which is at least temporary, which keeps Niall's hope alive.

"Drink?" she says sharply, gesturing with her Chablis. The bottle's sitting on a wrought-iron table he doesn't recognize.

"This new?" he says, tapping it. She sits down heavily in the chair.

"Came with the house. Old tenants didn't want it."

He pauses in her garden, almost fully dark now, but still hot, humming with crickets that he's sure weren't in London a few years ago, and he tries to calm his mind, think about what Jess would say. He thinks she would say that it doesn't matter whether he gets her back. Only that he says the right thing. His truth. The important thing. So that he is more able to live with himself. To move forward without her, to somebody new, whom he might treat better.

She pours him a glass and sits back. God, she still looks lovely. Just—lovely. Blond hair, no grays yet, lines on her forehead, sure, but they look kindly.

"Do you remember my siege case? In the London warehouse?" he says, and then takes a sip of the wine. It explodes in his mouth—she always picked good wine. Cold, as clean and fresh as a bite of an apple that comes away in one neat slice. It slivers down his throat and zings through his bloodstream. Let her offer him another, let him be over the limit, let him have to stay . . .

"Obviously," she says, the word loaded. Viv crosses her feet on the empty chair opposite her and next to Niall, and the case goes clean out of his mind: suddenly, all Niall can think about is those bare feet.

"Well, I wanted to say I'm sorry. That case has reared its head again and—well. So have . . . other events of that night."

"Like?" she says, voice as sharp as the wine.

"Like me being a shit husband."

She blinks, perhaps surprised. She looks at her feet for a few seconds, twitching her toes back and forth, evidently thinking. "I didn't expect that," she says. "It was always that you'd done nothing wrong. That you had to work."

"I see now that I was single-minded. Am. And I know it wasn't about the birthday."

"The bloody birthday was the final straw."

She rises from her chair just slightly, tucks the foot with the toe rings on underneath her, and resettles herself like a contented cat.

"It was seven years ago, Niall."

"I haven't forgotten another birthday since."

"I know that," she says, but she says it gently.

"I heard you broke up with the American."

"How do you know about that?" she says, and Niall can tell, now, immediately, that he's lost her. She's become testy with him, prickly body language. God, who was he kidding? It isn't about being *able to live with himself*, not at all. Of course it's about being with her. And then she adds, "Don't call him that."

"Rosalind told me," he says.

Viv sighs, looks into the distance, then sips her wine. "He wasn't for me," she says flatly.

Because I am, Niall thinks, emboldened by the beautiful dark-green summer evening, the wine, and her.

"Niall," she says, her voice gentle, empathetic. Everything. He loves everything about her. That, later, she will drink two pots of tea right before bed and get up twice in the night to wee. Her mad rescue cats. How long she put up with him, despite everything. "You are obsessed with work," she finishes, verbalizing what has gone unsaid.

"Yes."

"You obsess over things generally," she says. "You won't change."

"I know, and I'm trying—Viv, I really am—to work out how I might do both."

"Do both?"

"Be with you—and with my job."

She pauses for a long while, then reveals her truth to him. "I was your first obsession," she says, and Niall can't help but find that interesting, as well as upsetting.

"I see."

"I was."

"Look." He takes a steadying breath. And here it is, his truth, communicated—he hopes—well. "I'm so sorry I didn't put you first. It is the biggest regret of my life, in fact." He's chosen his words carefully, and Viv's green eyes are immediately wet, but she doesn't open her mouth; she clamps it tightly shut like a baby about to sob.

And he's so vulnerable here. He had no idea this is how people feel when they're telling the full, whole truth. "I'm so sorry. It was not fair on you."

"Thank you for saying that," she says tightly, bottom lip wobbling. She casts her gaze downward, long lashes fanning over her cheeks. The one-eyed cat ambles into the garden, bumps into the table.

"I'm sorry I didn't before. If we were—if we were ever together again—it would be . . ."

"Don't say that. But thank you."

They lapse into a silence that might be companionable and might be a hopeless kind of closure. Ten minutes later, she sees him out.

Ten minutes after *that*, a work text comes through.

CLAIRE: *Text Anon has confirmed the coordinates were sent by an account linked to Deschamps's email. I'll leave it with you.*

47

Anonymous Reporting on Camilla

I t's stale," I tell my brother. "I am really trying, but the information isn't coming easily."

"What have you tried?" he says.

We're walking today. London moves and sways beneath a patchwork blue-and-white sky. The sun on the water, the tourist shops and the narrow alleyways. Funny how hardly anyone knows just how much crime is carrying on all around them.

"Been through her rubbish, even," I say. "I don't know if she's just an excellent secret-keeper, or what."

"This is taking a very long time," he says, and it's the kind of blended menacing and factual statement that everyone around him fears him making. "If she's in contact with him, and we miss it . . ."

"I won't miss it."

"How much of the time are you on her tail?"

"As much as is possible."

"She have any idea?"

"None."

48

Cam

Cam is about to leave for a work-drinks event, but, first, is reading Adam's novel jumpily on her sofa.

The thing nobody knew is that someone else was killed that night. And our killers are not the same person. Things in crime are never as simple as they seem. I was ordered by Dad to kill our dealer. And then some-one else killed me.

A text comes in from Libby, who is going to have Polly for the night while Cam and Charlie go to the work event.

LIBBY: *You left yet?*
CAM: *Almost.*

Cam goes to put Adam's book away.

It might be perhaps too dark, but it's *really* good, and Cam has that feeling when you know you have a sale on the horizon. It's a different genre, but it's a good book, which is all that ought to matter. She reads a paragraph more:

The supplier killed me, and then a bystander pulled him off me, punched him. And, in doing so, threw him backwards, onto a street bollard which injured the back of his head.

He would've got away with it if he'd left then, but he didn't: he came back. His conscience got him, the way it does with good people.

Cam shivers and puts it away. She needs to take Polly to Libby's.

It's a clear evening but cooler, and Cam can't help but feel that autumn is beckoning its fingers to her and Polly, the breeze sharp. Libby's house is white-rendered, its front covered in a shaggy honey monster of ivy, and Cam takes a second to stare at it, her sister's life contained within.

As Cam watches, she feels a longing for something she can't name. This happens all the time, and she sometimes wonders if it is for the other life that might have played out. A bigger house, then another, then another. A sibling for Polly. A lit-up orange window in a family home, a row of shoes at the entrance. Or maybe it's not that, and it's just some-thing everybody feels.

"I shouldn't be eating this," Libby says, opening the door and gestur-ing to a Mars Bar in her hand. "Come on in," she says to Polly.

"Can I have one?"

"No," Cam says. "Dinner soon."

"But . . . ?" Polly says, but is quickly distracted by Libby's nursery-in-waiting upstairs, where she heads to play with the dollhouse. As Cam watches her daughter ascend the steps, the heels of her bare feet fuzzy peaches, she feels a dart of guilt at her self-sufficient daughter, the only child.

In Libby's hallway, their eyes meet. "I suppose it doesn't matter if I gain weight anymore. I can be as fat as I like," Libby says.

"You're never fat."

"Yeah. Well. Anyway. I can do what I want," Libby says.

"Oh?" Cam says, the topic opened, as it often is, at random, unex-pected moments. Some people invite conversation, Libby drops it right in your lap.

"Doctor thinks I'm in peri—my levels are all dipping. I had a late pe-riod, was so excited I stopped drinking, but it was that." Her voice is low. Just off the hallway, her downstairs shower is running, a rain-forest sound in the background. Beyond them, the TV hums on some house-hunting program Si was watching and left on. She looks directly at Cam. "Isn't that just fucking typical? Early menopause, to top everything off."

"I'm so sorry," Cam says sincerely. She's blindsided. Jesus. She can't go now, can she? Just head to the drinks as planned. *Sorry about your menopause and infertility.* "I wish there was something I could do," she says.

"Yeah, well," Libby says. They lapse into silence.

"It never matters if you gain weight," Cam eventually adds, and Libby shrugs equivocally. "For fertility treatment or otherwise."

"I can't do it anymore. You know?" she says. And they stand there in Libby's hallway and Cam wishes they weren't having a conversation this important in these circumstances. Snatched time. She wishes she had gone to the appointment with Libby. Been a better sister to her.

"I do know."

"And everyone talks about—I don't know. Other options, like they're easy and simple, but they're not."

"Don't listen to them," Cam says. "Do what you want to do."

Libby shrugs, then says, "Not everyone gets their happy ending, right?"

"Right," Cam says softly. But something is bugging her, like a floater at the edge of her vision . . . something nagging . . . her mind imploring her to make some connection or other.

"Anyway." Libby motions her inside, and Cam steps into her living room, unable to refuse. On a drinks caddy in the corner of Libby and Si's living room is a vase of fake bright-pink flowers and a golden pineapple ornament. This cabinet changes seasonally. It will be a knitted pumpkin soon.

"I'm sorry about the hormones," Cam says, and she is about to say she's experienced the same, recently—a feeling of mounting anxiety, sometimes; feeling hot at night; periods late and early—but she doesn't. Sometimes, you have to put aside your own feelings when someone else's are worse, that's all.

"Yeah. Me too."

Cam can hear Polly's footsteps above them.

"Weird to think this saga has been rumbling on since you had Polly, and she's upstairs playing by herself," Libby says. "You can achieve a lot in seven years, or nothing at all."

"You have achieved a lot," Cam says. And she doesn't know whether it's the right thing, but she says it anyway, "You tried really, really hard to have your baby."

"I know," Libby says.

"They would have been lucky to have you," she says, and Libby reaches over to grasp her hand, just briefly.

Libby sits down on the sofa, gesturing for Cam to do the same. "I think I've been a bit of a bitch to you," Libby says, looking directly at Cam.

"What?" Cam says, surprised.

"About everything. I don't know. Giving up on IVF has—I don't know. It's made me feel like I can reflect."

"I see."

"I'm sorry. I know it wasn't easy for you to just give up on Luke. I know I made it seem—like it should be simple, maybe."

"You helped a lot, actually," Cam says, which is a lie. The frantic de-cluttering was born out of wanting to move on, but she hasn't actually done so. "You knew I needed to move on. You were right." A second lie.

"I was harsh with you," Libby says. She sinks back into the sofa, her arm slung along its back. "I was . . . well. Do you know something?" she says, and she laughs a little, but it isn't a genuine laugh. It's sardonic: darkness contained within it.

"What?" Cam says, wary, knowing she is not telling the whole truth to her sister and not wanting to receive the opposite in return, not ready to.

"I was expecting you to move on from what is a grief. But the truth is . . ."

"What?"

"I am so fucking jealous of you," Libby says. "Infertility makes you just—so jealous. Some days, my whole body hurts with it. You know?"

"I know," Cam says, watching her sister mess with a pale fluffy throw.

"I guess . . ." Libby continues. "It was—like, before Luke, you had ev-erything."

"Did I?" Cam says.

"Yeah."

And Cam could argue that things are not always how they seem, that everyone has problems behind the scenes—that *look* how she and Luke ended up—but it would be the wrong thing to do. Doesn't she know more than anyone that she really *did* have it all, if only for the briefest of moments? Nine sweet months, then gone.

"I wanted to hurt you," Libby says. "I don't know. I'm sorry. You had the great job and the baby." On this last word, her voice cracks, and Cam fully feels it.

"I don't think either of us has had a good hand," she says truthfully, thinking she knows who she'd rather be: she'd choose this life every time, with Polly. And something about this realization helps her. Whatever happens, she's still got her daughter, singing something tuneless upstairs to herself.

"Well, I'm sorry regardless," Libby says. "You can talk to me about Luke. You can."

"It's fine," Cam says, thinking, It's not that simple.

"I wanted him not to come back," Libby says. "At times. I'm sorry. Infertility—it really fucks you up. Makes you wish for bad things to happen to everyone all the time. Or maybe that's just how I am."

"It's not you," Cam says, truthfully this time. "I have wished for that a lot, too, over the years." After all, who hasn't sat and wished for bad things to happen to other people, beautiful people, successful people? It's just that people don't usually admit it, that's all. "That's just grief, I think," she adds, hoping the use of this word might be held by her sister in the way that she intends it.

"I bet," Libby says, and she scoots closer to Cam on the sofa. "You deserved better than cantankerous old me, in those years."

"Likewise, I'm sure." She hesitates, wanting to tell Libby she was jealous of her, too, but decides not to.

"And I know there are options," Libby continues obliviously. "That's what everyone says."

"*Have* you thought about that?" Cam asks tentatively.

Libby goes to answer, but Polly interrupts, walking into the room, holding her hairbrush out. "Can my *mane* be brushed, before dinner?"

she says. "It feels tangled." For a second, Cam thinks she's asking Libby, but she isn't: she's asking Cam, of course she is. Her mother. "What're you talking about?" she asks, and, internally, Cam cringes.

"Well, why I don't have any children, and what I'm going to do about that," Libby says, her voice matter-of-fact.

Polly's footsteps stop, her hand extended, frozen in the air, holding her hairbrush out, and Cam thinks about the power of honesty. About how they've tried to cover so much stuff up, but look: Isn't it better to just be honest? Polly's nearly eight, not two. She can handle more than Cam thinks.

"Oh," she says slowly. "I see. I didn't know you wanted to have children."

"Very much."

"Oh no," Polly says, her expression verging on horrified.

"But do you know what?"

"What?"

"If I had had my own, I wouldn't have spent quite so much time with you."

Cam's eyes mist over, right there in Libby's quiet and calm sitting room. Seven years of trying, but look. Look at them. Polly crosses to Libby, hands her the brush instead, Libby in loco parentis to Cam's fatherless daughter. Perhaps sometimes you can make the best of things. It doesn't mean you didn't want something else, but . . .

"Well, that's—what's that word? Like when something good happens out of something bad?" Polly asks, and Cam smiles, thinking of all of the years and years and years that have rushed by in what now feels like an instant.

"A silver lining," Libby says, and Cam thinks about how Libby and Polly wouldn't be so close if Luke hadn't gone, thinking about how Libby feels as if Polly is her own in a way she might not otherwise, wondering if Luke misses Polly, if he is alive out there somewhere, and thinking, thinking, thinking whether all this pain has been worth it, or if that is just something people who experience tragedies tell themselves in order to survive.

Later, on the street, Cam looks up at the house. In the window, Libby

bends her head down toward Polly's. Cam stares for a few more moments, looking in at the dimly lit room. They have the same profile. She'd
never noticed.

The drinks reception is less salubrious than a *rooftop party* sounds: a few
neglected plants in pots, a small area. Nice views, but, really, a few concrete slabs. The agency has done its best, and a man at an ice-cream-style
cart is serving cocktails.

Stuart is there, Charlie not yet, and Cam wanders over to him. Not
only because she feels unsafe all the time these days but because she
wants refuge from her own thoughts.

"Adam's here," Stuart says, pointing. He grabs a miniature doughnut
from a passing waiter. "Not big enough," he says, gesturing with it.

"So he is," Cam says. "He's delivered the next," she says in a low voice.
"It's really good. Kind of experimental."

Stuart looks at Adam, and Cam sees him through Stuart's eyes in the
way that you do sometimes. She isn't sure her boss ever met him properly.
Adam is slightly scruffy, but in a good way; Luke once described him as
a bit neurotic-looking. The kind of person who looks self-conscious doing
nothing.

"How?"

"Not his style really. A very dark thriller. I hope they will like it,
though, and he can just be . . . who he is. One of those writers who can
do it all."

"How dark is dark?"

"Fairly. A kid from some crime family mixed up in drugs, then is murdered and narrates his own investigation," she says, thinking how funny
it is how art sometimes mirrors life, but something is creeping up behind
her, some insistent, niggling thought. "He's just revealed that someone
killed his killer too."

"A double murder," Stuart says, and something begins to tick in Cam's
mind, an insistent, metronome-like sound. "Well, crime sells," he adds,
smiling impassively. Cam sips her Bloody Mary and gazes at London's
skyline, not saying anything. She doesn't care enough about what sells.
She cares about what is good.

"I hope the next gap won't be as long."

"I've seen worse," Stuart says. "Plus, when they've written the tricky second novel, they often regain the confidence, you know? Third comes quickly."

The rooftop is beginning to fill up. Cam sees Charlie arrive, a tall, thin form who helps himself to a drink somehow ironically. Cam hides a smile: he doesn't want to be here either. Her cynical sometimes-boyfriend. It's just past seven thirty, still warm, and one of Cam's colleagues has put fairy lights up, winding them around the railings at the edge of the building. They are white, bright, the sky blue behind them. Cam lets a breath out.

"Have you finished it?" Stuart says.

"No!" Cam says. "I might have to go into hiding. I've been so slack with it. It's been—I don't know. It's quite a scary book. But I've been busy." Stuart—famed for his brilliant notes that sometimes take months—nods, takes another canapé from a waiter who offers them. He swallows it whole, unselfconscious, while Cam's eyes keep going back to Adam. He's standing, looking out over London, his back to her, body language somewhat tense-looking, which is normal for him. He's wearing a messenger bag slung cross-body, holding a proof he must have picked up. "I'd better go and fess up," she says. "Notes to follow, as they say . . ."

Stuart raises his eyebrows to her, and she says, "I'll come and find you in a bit. Rescue me, if it escalates!"

"Ha." He moves off to talk to somebody else, taking another dough-nut for the road.

Charlie joins Cam as she is moving through the throng to Adam. "How long before we escape?" he says.

"I reckon we need to do an hour," she says, struck by how nice it is to know someone who is not unlike herself. Luke would have wanted to stay at this party until the very end. "Then to mine?"

Charlie dimples a smile.

"Come meet Adam," she says.

"The jiffy-bag client!"

"The very same."

"Adam," Cam says, arriving at his side. They're seven floors up, the drop to the ground beneath them vertiginous. Tiny cars and people move below them, appearing slow, their details blurred, and Cam will never not think of warehouse roofs.

"Aha," Adam says. "I'm sorry—I've been in hiding."

"This is Charlie," she says. She doesn't add further detail. To categorize him is overly complicated.

Charlie shakes Adam's hand, and Cam thinks how overwhelming it must be to post your soul through someone's letter box. "How's things?" she asks him. And something about seeing him—he is the most reclusive of her clients—brings it all back. That manuscript she first read on maternity leave, in snatched nighttime hours. The bidding war from almost every imprint in the industry that she missed in the aftermath of Luke disappearing. Its publication day just after her return to work, the bittersweetness of it. Mired in grief, Cam had been almost surprised—and perhaps slightly relieved—that she had been expected to carry on with life. Launching books, doing laundry, making dinners. And that book— that book Cam had seen like a nugget of gold in the rubble. The book she found on maternity leave. The book she launched after the siege. That book that became so huge, that everybody had loved so much. It had been like a little party every day at work for a while, but obviously much more fun, for Cam.

"It's odd," Cam says. "I have been thinking about *Out of Sight* a lot, lately. Kind of life-affirming, when you look back." She glances to Charlie. "It was a real ride."

Charlie raises his palms. "I've actually read it," he says. "Loved it."

"Oh God," Adam says, grimaces. "Sometimes I hate that book."

"No!" Cam says.

"No, really. I think all novelists feel that way about a huge, huge hit."

"Well, you shouldn't," she says. "You wrote that book and you're still you, so you can do it again."

A slightly awkward silence seems to settle between the three of them, and Cam decides to acknowledge it head-on, rather than ignore it. This year, no matter what happens with Luke, has been about facing things. Moving house, moving on. Telling Charlie her biggest secret. Working with Niall. They've tried their hardest to find the truth, and maybe that is what matters most.

"I'm loving what I've read so far," she says to Adam.

"She really is," Charlie backs her up. "Reading at all hours."

"I'm sorry," she says. "I have no feedback for you. Yet."

Adam sips what looks like a mojito, saying nothing, but doesn't take his eyes off her. "What d'you mean?" he says eventually, his tone strange. He gestures to the view. "Was hoping for some inspiration here."

"Inspiration?" Cam says, wondering why this conversation feels so confused, and so loaded too.

"For the next book."

"Slow down," Cam says. "The next, *next* book can wait. Surely?" She's surprised by the sentiment: Adam took almost seven years to deliver the second book. She can't pretend she wouldn't like the third sooner, but . . .

He catches her eye. "It's been seven years?" he says, a guffaw escaping. "*Slow down*—isn't the agent's advice usually to speed up?"

Charlie's brow begins to furrow, wondering perhaps if he ought to be privy to this sort of strategic conversation between agent and client.

"Well, yes, but . . . I mean, by all means, write your third if you're happy to!"

It's Adam's turn to frown now. "What?" he says. He downs his drink, and Cam suddenly wonders if he might think she's baiting him or something. Maybe he doesn't want to discuss his long break in books here and now, is embarrassed to do so.

She waves a hand as Stuart drifts by, talking to somebody in foreign rights. "Let's talk about something else," she says. "Whatever you want."

"My third?" he asks. "I haven't written my second." He says it slowly, like she is an idiot.

Cam stares at Adam, dumbfounded. "You posted me your book?" she says. "Your crime novel . . ."

"No, I didn't," Adam says.

"Oh," Charlie says awkwardly. "Someone else, maybe? Something unsolicited?" he says, clearly trying to smooth things over.

Adam blinks, perplexed and—clearly—ashamed.

"But . . ." Cam says. "It was sent in a jiffy bag. Like you did with the first. In Baskerville," she adds lamely, though it occurs to her that this is a common font. "I said *Thank you for your book* at the bookshop launch!"

"I wondered what you meant by that," he says. "I thought you meant my debut . . . I didn't send you a book, Cam," he says.

And distantly, in Cam's mind, she's aware she's committed a social faux pas. But she doesn't care. Can't seem to. Because of the implications of what he's saying.

He didn't write that anonymous book.

Somebody else did. And they wanted her, and only her, to see it.

49

Niall

Niall next checks the tracker on Deschamps's email: it's remained there for the entire seven years, as is the case with wanted and dangerous people, but it yields nothing. Deschamps must've turned off the confirmation from Text Anon, so only the website itself knew about it. He's ditched the burner phone.

There is no trace of him.

Niall hunts around in the surveillance file for other activity, but there isn't any. He is on borrowed time here. He ought to tell the Met what he knows. But he wants more information. He wants hard evidence of why Deschamps did what he did.

If he tells them Deschamps is very likely alive and well, they will throw the full force of the state into finding him. And incarcerating him. Or worse.

"How are you feeling about Viv?" Jess asks mildly.

"Haven't had a chance to think about her," Niall says. Downstairs, the bakery hums with activity. If Niall has a morning session it smells of bread. Lunchtime, sausage rolls. And now, near to evening closing, a mishmash of leftovers. You can get a cinnamon swirl for ten pence if you time it right, which Niall very often does.

"I don't buy that," Jess says.

"OK—I have, but . . . I . . . I don't know," he says carefully, thinking how funny it is that for his entire career, he's been trying to make people

open up, and now it's him. It's him who's got to do it, and Jess, *his* negotiator, is sitting in front of him. "It's weird, the Deschamps case resolving."

"They're tied for you in your brain."

"Well. It was the same day," he says. "Obviously."

"But—beyond that?" she probes. "That day when your man shot the
hostages, and then you went home and Viv had gone. What, for you,
stands out about then?"

In his mind, Niall turns away from the warehouse, and, suddenly,
he's in their flat in the Barbican, largely as it is now, except with a better
kitchen, a more colorful one. He walks around their preserved apartment. Viv's teapot out on the counter, the ceramic one she painted herself. Pasta in jars—the sort of thing she did, not him.

She didn't take much stuff with her. He turns around in their kitchen
and looks into the hallway, where she's standing in his mind. Bags
packed. A large suitcase and a small hold-all too. Her fucking birthday.
How could he have been so stupid? The mistake is so tangible, it makes
his regret bitter and black. If only, if only.

"It's this," Niall says, his eyes popping open, the kitchen and the hallway suitcases disappearing. "I missed it."

"That the hostage taker would shoot?"

"No. That, all the while, I was focusing on the case, and she was leaving me. Picking which clothes to take, which to leave. Taking her book
from by the bed, her toothbrush . . . I was negotiating with the wrong
person," Niall says, blinking back tears. "Fucking futile. All of it."

Jess is looking at him, her expression somewhat sad too. He isn't too
surprised: all good negotiators feel too much empathy.

"I put her bin back for her. The other day."

"Her bin?" Jess says with the practiced, professional expression of
somebody who has been told everything any human could ever admit.

"She hated doing the bins. Her worst chore. Used to leave it out until
the next week, easily. So I passed her house—legitimately, for work—
and I just dragged it back up for her, put it in the bin store."

"Why did you do that?" Jess says, but she doesn't say it with criticism
or judgment. Sometimes, Niall wonders whether she is paid to be on his
side or if she really is.

"I thought a lot after our last session," Niall says, and he's surprised to find his cheeks are burning. "About what Viv actually said to me, and perhaps—what she really meant."

"Right—good," Jess says with a wide and genuine smile. "And what do you think she meant?"

"I did put work first. I did. It's undeniable. It wasn't just about a birthday."

"And so the bin . . ." Jess says, her tone dispassionate, and Niall suddenly wonders if she goes home to her husband and moans about counseling ordinary men about ordinary occurrences. *It was a whole session on bins today*, she will say. Niall frowns at the thought of it.

"What?" she says. "What's that—" And then she scrunches up her face, a rough imitation of his.

"Nothing. Just feel—I don't know. Embarrassed to be telling you this stuff," he says. "It's so—quotidian."

"Doesn't seem it to me," she says lightly. "The bin, for you, is: *I see you.* You see Viv. What she likes to do, what she doesn't. What she finds hard, or boring. And you did it for her."

"Yes."

"Do you think there is a way for you to do what you do for a living but not have it be top priority? Above all else?"

Niall thinks of the Inner Temple with Camilla, finally getting her to talk, betraying his own employer to do so. It had never even crossed his mind that it was out of hours, overtime. Some people tot up their time off in lieu, and those people are not police. "I don't know," he says honestly. "When I'm chasing something down . . . when I'm negotiating . . . it's like I can't even see anything else."

"So you could say you would be conflicted about entering another relationship."

"I don't want another relationship if I can't have her."

"We know you are a bit of an all-or-nothing guy."

"Maybe so."

"And so, naturally, you obsess over your work," Jess says, leading him faithfully down the road she wants them to travel through.

"Precisely," he says. "I feel like she made me feel guilty for working at all. And then didn't even say anything. Didn't give me a chance to put it right. Just—left."

"Maybe she felt you wouldn't change."

"Maybe I wouldn't," Niall says honestly.

"Maybe she'd already said it."

Niall says nothing to this. Jess waits a beat, then asks outright: "Had she?"

"Sort of," Niall says, and she had, hadn't she? "Yes."

"Right." Jess leaves a loaded pause, clearly hoping he will fill it.

"Look," he says. "Hostage negotiating—it takes it out of you. Emotionally." He knows he shouldn't defend himself, but he wants to. Doesn't want to be consigned to the pool of untreatable maniacs.

"Are you still getting the dreams?"

"Yes."

"Still every night?" she says: so she knows he lied about the frequency.

"Pretty much," he says. "I've had breakthroughs on that case, now, but I don't know. I think it's a different trauma."

"The trauma of Viv."

"Exactly."

She sighs, just slightly, but then steers him to policing, instead, perhaps a kind distraction. "What kind of breakthroughs?"

Niall gratefully fills her in about what Camilla told him. About Madison Smith, and Alexander Hale and James Lancaster, and everything else. "The thing is, I looked," he says. "I looked, that night in April 2017, for signs of where Deschamps had been, and now it turns out there was a double murder. I just can't understand how come I didn't spot that on that day."

Jess turns her mouth down. "I mean—I don't know how policing works," she says. "At all. But . . . it doesn't strike me that you're the type of person to miss something."

"I am. I mean—the two hostages are dead because of me."

"Two men who came to kill Luke."

"Yes, but even so."

"Is it possible that it wasn't there that day?" she says to him. "This— entry on the database for the double murder?"

Niall closes his eyes, thinking. Checking HOLMES, sun slanting into the Wetherspoon's, urgency in the air. Was he rushing—or had something else happened?

And that's when the answer arrives, as easy as if it's nothing at all: his brain supplies the solution, right there in fucking therapy. His eyes open and meet Jess's. "You've got it," he says, rising to his feet, even though they're only halfway through the session.

"Have I?"

"Yes. You've cracked it." He's at the door now, his hand on the knob. "I didn't miss anything," he says to her. "I didn't. You're right. Someone took it off. That must be it: the double murder wasn't on the system. The hostages had no identities *on the system.*"

Niall's mind is racing, the way his brain speeds up sometimes when information is coming at him, piece after piece after piece slotting neatly, not being jammed or forced. He's landed on it. He knows he has. "Someone could have removed information from the police computer," he says. "The only person who was connected both to the hostages and to the police," he says. "A man called George Louis, Isabella's husband. They weren't victims: they were perpetrators."

50

Cam

Cam makes her excuses to Adam and tries to leave, weaving her way across the rooftop, past authors and agents and people serving drinks.

"Shit," she says under her breath to Charlie.

"I know—really awkward," he says.

Her mind is reeling.

All this time. All this time. That book's been in her house. She tells herself it's a general submission, some author who's found her address.

But she doesn't think so.

The kid selling the drugs. From a crime family.

One of the murdered teens. The double murder.

The other teen, from a rival crime family.

The Hales and the Lancasters.

The man who killed the narrator's killer accidentally, in trying to help. The good Samaritan returns to the scene and is spotted.

Luke, driving that night to Whitechapel. Using more fuel than she expected. Covering up his locations. Crying over onions. Attending a funeral.

The family of one of the dead teenagers finds out who he is.

Luke, who had people break in, to ID him, in a burglary that wasn't. Luke, who had two men sent to kill him.

She opens her eyes. Could it be? She didn't notice. She'd been so sure it was Adam's manuscript. And maybe this was his aim. A dead narrator. The story not told from Luke's perspective. A disguise.

It could be about him.

It could be *from* him.

She.

Has.

Got.

To.

Get.

That.

Book.

And if it's his . . . he was definitely alive to deliver it to her. She blinks. This thought is too huge, like she's staring at a close-up and can't see the whole picture.

She needs to get out of here.

"Shall we go?" she says to Charlie.

"Definitely," he says, oblivious to her internal turmoil, not having connected the dots himself.

"Are you going?" Stuart says to her as they're on their way out, unaware. "Can I introduce you to one of my newest authors?" He is standing with a woman in her mid-thirties, wearing a long slip skirt and a nervous expression on her face.

"Sure," Cam says, distracted, not wanting to leave work things early again, not wanting to appear still unhinged, still stuck in the past. "Hi," she says. Charlie's arm is around her waist, and all she can think about is how she can renege on their plans, her child-free night, and be alone with that book.

"What are you writing?" she asks Stuart's author mechanically.

"Well," she starts, but Cam doesn't listen to the rest.

She stands there, rictus grin, thinking, My husband wrote his story down for me.

". . . hoping to reach readers who like Lisa Jewell," the woman finishes, and Cam is smiling and nodding along. A rights assistant joins them, and Stuart tells her Adam's delivered his manuscript, and Cam can't bear to correct him.

Stuart pats her on the shoulder as she leaves, and she's glad of him, her colleague of over a decade who's never once asked too much of her.

Cam is silent on the walk from the Tube to her house. She hasn't found a way to tell Charlie he isn't coming in after all. She needs to find an excuse, and quick. She'll tell him she's changed her mind about everything.

At her front door, she turns to him, but he's looking behind him. "What was that?" he says.

"Huh?"

"I'm sure I saw someone go into the alley behind yours."

Cam's back goes cold. Her face feels numb with fear. All those times she thought she was being watched.

"Will you look?" she says, the book temporarily forgotten.

Charlie nods once, expression serious, and Cam lets herself inside, stands nervously in the hallway, waiting for him. Hoping he's wrong.

"Couldn't get them. I saw someone leaving, but they ran," Charlie says, letting himself in five minutes later, cheeks red with exertion.

"So weird."

"Really."

He pauses, then says, "Coffee?" and she thinks, Yes, OK. He can stay and keep her safe. The book is more valuable than she could have imagined. Somebody might want it.

And as she joins Charlie in her kitchen, all she is thinking is what better way for Luke to tell her his side of the story—if he remains in danger—than to disguise it in fiction? It even fooled her. Names changed for legal reasons. Her husband, writing it from the perspective of a teenager now deceased. She should've guessed: her husband, the ghostwriter.

51

Niall

Niall gets to the car park after Jess's session and knows he only has to make one phone call to confirm George's involvement. It's the evening, London's lights scattering glitter around and above him, and he breathes slowly as he dials Claire in the communications team.

As he waits for her to answer—she always diverts her desk phone to her mobile after hours—he leans against the railings of the multi-story. "I need somebody who can mine for information," he says when Claire picks up. "Ideally now. Busy?"

"At the boys' five-a-side, but not busy," she says. "I've got my phone, so I can help."

"Great," Niall says. "I think something was deleted from HOLMES in 2017. And I think two people had their DNA taken off too."

Claire pauses. In the background, he hears a whistle blow. "Those are big claims," she says.

Niall paces the length of the car park. "I'm trying to work a few things out before I accuse anybody, before I go on-record." And it's funny, it's so funny that this sentence has, somehow, become true. He was off-record because his appetite to solve the Deschamps case was insatiable, to atone for his own mistake. And now he's off-record because he suspects there's a copper at the heart of it. It's almost like he knew, in some big, wise part of himself that was always in charge, even when he didn't know it.

Down below, wide streets are lined with ugly roller shutter doors that remind him of Bermondsey. A hot breeze whips in between the layers of the multi-story. "I can't—Niall . . ." Claire says.

"Please just look at the system. Look up the name Andrew Smith. He's one of the hostages. His details were removed from the system," Niall says. He is not privy to this information, available only to the telecoms team.

"Give me five—I can't do it on my phone while talking. Hang on," Claire says. "There are loads of Andrew Smiths."

Niall waits in the car park, walking back to his car and then away from it, past puddles that could be rainwater and could be God-knows-what. It's virtually empty, almost quite tranquil in a weird way, and he walks and thinks about Viv and Deschamps and how some things just take their time to work out, to sort out. He leans on the railings again where a light rain splatters his knuckles, and tries to exhale the way Jess taught him to.

Niall's body begins to slow down in a way it has never before been able to. Funny, he thought being on the go, anxious, addicted to various things, was what fueled him, but actually, it got in the way. Now his mind is calmer, he is all the more able to think.

He avoided what Viv wanted most in the world—him, and his time— because it was easier to face other people's problems than his own.

That's the truth of it, he thinks, breathing still slow. And he has to live with that. The true mistake at the heart of the Bermondsey case.

His phone blares after just a couple of minutes, Claire's extension, and he answers it.

"Entry deleted by George Louis, on twenty-first June 2017," she says. "The records show he deleted a second, too, for a man called Pete Arbuthnot. The other hostage, I am guessing. This is why they never flagged anything on the system: they were no longer there. He also deleted the Alexander Hale and James Lancaster murders, but reinstated them a few days later."

Niall nods: reinstating them prevented anybody from ever knowing. At some point, deleted entries that stayed deleted would've been noticed, and officers are regularly audited. This way, he only hid them for the minimum time period.

"Thank you," Niall says, tilting his face up to the rain and almost smiling. He was right. He'd worked it out.

"So the accidental hostage . . ." Claire says, and Niall suddenly and vividly recalls Isabella's vulnerability, her shock, that she wet herself in fear.

All made up. That article in the *Mail* Niall read years ago about her inner trauma. Obviously sold to them. A clever bluff.

This case continues to invert and invert, like a sand timer tipped this way and that, the grains falling one way and then completely the other.

And this way around, it makes perfect sense. The Louises owned the warehouse. A shabby, unassuming place to siphon their wealth into. They arranged to kill Deschamps in it, a place that has a back lift, somewhere they could control, and dispose of the body. They sent two men to do it for them, and Isabella to oversee it. The only error they made was that they forgot about their tenant having hired a remote security guard, who streamed it. Their private, criminal act that went so badly wrong when witnessed, and when Deschamps retaliated.

Niall shivers with it, remembers all those years ago, the way George blew the siege. Of course he did: he and his wife organized the killers, and it went wrong.

They weren't caught up in it. They were it.

The only question that remains is why?

Does he have enough to hand this right over to the Met, knowing how they will respond? Maybe. Maybe.

52

Niall swings by the Louises' house on his way home, debating phoning in George Louis's corruption but unable to resist just observing this family, for a little while, to see what secrets might reveal themselves.

He doesn't want to act rashly. He wants to think. What does George Louis have to do with Deschamps's murder? Why would he order it? And how does the Whitechapel murder feature? He takes his phone out and makes a request to Claire to dig into any familial connections, any work connections, that George has. He trusts that she won't escalate it up to management yet.

You can do a lot with information, but the most important thing is to try to get more of it before you act. What really happened? Who are the heroes and who are the villains? Sometimes—just sometimes—you can get information by observing people, unseen, from the shadows. If the Louises are criminals, as he suspects they may be, then an admission is helpful. He can charge them with much more than corruption.

Niall's skin shivers as he waits near their house, as though God himself has reached a hand down, passed it over his body, and said, *Keep going. You're almost there.*

Niall stands there, a detective alone on a quiet London lane, glad of the police-issue pistol in the boot of his car, looking up at the buildings.

George Louis's flat is in the basement, number 68B, one of the nicer ones. The street is leafy, that summer-sharp tang of plants in the air. There are sleeping policemen on the road, a cycle lane just to the left with a few bits and pieces of litter, dusty and wilted from the summer heat. The front door is wide and painted white, new paint. The kitchen is at the front, one of those half-and-half flats that are partly recessed but still have natural light. As a result, it's easy for Niall to look down into it.

A white-walled kitchen. A light is on somewhere, casting it all in citrus colors. All Niall can see is a kitchen table. Huge, pine, four chairs around it.

Niall loiters on the street outside, appraising it. They're not rich. That's his first observation. Theirs is—maximum—a two-floor flat, a kind of maisonette, worth perhaps half a million: it is absurd but true that this buys you a completely average London home, no off-street parking, no office in the garden, nothing else except cramped conditions, too-close neighbors, and rubbish on the street outside.

It's late, and the air starts to deepen to black as Niall observes. He wants to watch and wait: if you are more patient than anybody else, you are eventually rewarded. He can't risk being seen by the Louises—Isabella in particular would recognize him immediately—and so he walks slowly up and down the street, ready to turn and leave at any moment.

He hides in the shadows of the flat above the Louises'. It has five white stone steps leading to a front door, and they're either in bed or away, the house shut up and silent. He hopes for the latter.

He peers down. He can see wrought-iron railings and the tops of the Louises' bay windows, but nothing else. Can hear nothing.

Quarter past eleven, half past, twenty to twelve.

He stays very still, watching and waiting for nothing.

Until it becomes something. Isabella and George are leaving the flat.

"Uh-huh," George says, phone held close to his ear, which lights it up, a white seashell. "Janet says just to go in," he adds to Isabella. "Door's open."

Niall reels. Janet. Janet Hale. Alexander's mother.

"Sure," Isabella says to her husband.

"Thanks, sis," George says into the phone.

And there it is. They're siblings. George Louis and Janet Hale. No surname in common, thanks to her marriage.

A pact made between family, who will do anything to help each other out. The Hales, whose child was killed, with a vendetta against Deschamps.

And the Louises, who arranged his murder.

But why? Did Deschamps kill their child?

53

Anonymous Reporting on Camilla

I have information, I text him.

My phone rings immediately, and I reject the call. *Text*, I type to him, though my brother doesn't often like to deal in writing.

He reads it and doesn't reply. *Deschamps has contacted her*, I type to him. *I'm here in her house. I'm going to get hold of what he's sent. I've made up a reason I need to stay here a while.*

Thanks, Charlie. Knew you'd crack it when we dispatched you in.

You're welcome, George.

54

Cam

Charlie is making them coffees and all Cam can think about is that her husband's story lies on her sofa in her living room. It seems to glow and throb in there like an ancient talisman. Cam is desperate to read it but doesn't yet want Charlie to leave either, in case somebody is waiting for her outside.

"I used to be able to have caffeine and go to sleep," Charlie chatters, "but I just can't, after turning forty. Will be up all night."

"I used to drink buckets of the stuff with Luke," Cam replies, her husband's presence so vibrant in the room with her that she can't not mention him. "Hardly do now."

In the living room, Charlie turns on the lamp himself, fingers scurrying up the pole to find the switch by the bulb. Something about it momentarily unsettles Cam, but she's distracted by the light it provides, which illuminates the bound manuscript, right there on the sofa. Bright-white pages, black text. So mundane. The perfect disguise.

Neither of them mentions it, even though Cam is itching to. Charlie overheard the conversation but has clearly decided not to pry.

Darkness fully closes in outside. Charlie beckons Cam toward him on the sofa. "Anyway," she says, injecting a note of finality into her tone. "It's been so nice. Let's have the coffees and then I think I need to get an early night."

Charlie's face betrays some strong emotion Cam hasn't seen in his eyes before. A flash, like the lightning just after the thunder. Blink and you'd miss it.

"I thought I'd stay—at least for a while," he says. "That person outside, I . . ."

"Really, it's fine," she says, thinking only: the book, the book, the book.

"Let's see how you feel when I've finished." He raises the mug to her. He takes a sip, his eyes on her. "Wait—I forgot to stir it." He grimaces as he swallows.

"I'll do it," she says, taking the cup.

In the kitchen, the tiles are cool underneath her feet, the window cracked open, a long strand of wisteria attempting to snake its way in. It's a female kitchen, with a pink toaster that Polly wanted. A paperback proof Cam has been reading is splayed on the side. She misses, suddenly, a man's touch. A discarded tie, a wallet, a set of cufflinks. She stirs Charlie's coffee, staring at the swirling topography of the bitter blackness and milk as they mix. Is she delusional? Is this book merely nothing? An unsolicited manuscript, meant to be packaged up and sold, nothing more than that?

Charlie is sitting where he was in the living room when she brings in the coffee, inclined back onto the cushions, his legs crossed at the ankles on the table.

But the book. The book, so central in Cam's mind it may as well be the North Star, the book has moved. At least a foot along the sofa, its pages slightly rifled-looking, the front cover sheet now skewed: he's read something in it.

Her footsteps slow. Charlie turns his head to her.

And their eyes connect. He tilts his head, just a fraction. The slightest movement. You'd miss it if you weren't looking for it.

55

Niall

Just as they're leaving, George evidently receives a text, then relays it to Isabella. Niall, in his position in the doorway, strains to listen.

He moves backward, pressing himself against the front door. Twigs from a bush that arches overhead sharp-scratch his skin, leaves grazing his arms and neck, but he knows he needs to be hidden and he knows he needs to hear.

"Deschamps sent a book to Camilla. Charlie's read some of it. Deschamps has written down the whole thing as Alex. How Alex killed James. Names changed. And how Deschamps saw, then killed Alex, trying to get him off James. He's written all about our family—he must've found other people to talk about us. Says at the end of the book that he's in Dungeness. We need to go ourselves. Now."

The night is so silent around Niall that the air seems to throb with it. Distant traffic, a pulsing siren somewhere, but nothing else, only the low, muted voices of people who do not want a casual observer.

He nods, just once, to himself. It makes sense. It makes sense now. A peaceful feeling comes over Niall. He can do anything, even scary things, if only he knows the why. And he does. Deschamps was caught in a crossfire that night, witnessing a murder, trying to intervene, trying to be good, going about it the wrong way. And now has enemies, one crime family, at least. The Lancasters' child was murdered by Alexander Hale. But Hale was then killed by Deschamps: making him the enemy.

And to a copper too. No wonder. No wonder he had to disappear once he had killed their lackeys.

He'd had no chance.

The Louises don't want a follower, but that is precisely what Niall is going to be. He checks his phone, wondering whether to contact Cam and tell her, but decides not to. She is not in danger: he is with her enemies.

He can debrief with her afterward. Once he's solved it. Once he's rescued her husband and brought him to her.

56

Cam

"Why has the book moved?" Cam says.

"What book?"

"The book? The book . . . that Adam . . ." She points to it. "Did you read it?"

"The jiffy-bag book?"

"Yes."

"No," Charlie says, his expression a perfect picture of mild curiosity. And he's a good liar, Cam thinks. Exceptional, in fact. But he is lying. Because the book has moved. And there is only one person in the room who could have moved it.

"Shall we watch something?" Charlie says, perhaps too quickly. "I've got the jitters already from one sip of coffee! I need to relax."

His neck is flushed, a corned-beef pattern creeping across it. Cam's never seen that before on cool, collected him.

She stares mutely, not saying anything, a hundred thousand thoughts happening internally but none making it out of her mouth and into the real world. Maybe he was only curious. Maybe he's embarrassed by that. But why, really, would he lie like this? Why would he flush so red?

"Sure," she says, buying time while she thinks.

He fiddles with the remote control. "First the boiling-water tap, then your telly," he says, jabbing buttons.

Cam blinks, looks back down at the sofa. There's the book, and, just along from it, his phone. As she's staring at it, it lights up.

She takes a step toward it, her body full of fizzy and sharp adrenaline, thinking that the world is upending in the most domestic of settings, the way it always seems to do for her.

The text previews, and she can just about read it, standing behind the sofa, squinting at it.

GEORGE: *Thank you. We're heading to Dungeness now. Keep Camilla there.*

A hundred spiders walk their way up Cam's spine. She takes a step backward, two, her teeth chattering like she has a fever.

Keep Camilla there.

We're heading to Dungeness now.

Charlie's been sent to keep an eye on her. To infiltrate her. All this time.

He looks up at her, perhaps oblivious, perhaps only pretending to be. And Cam realizes, the truth slowly falling into place, that she can't leave. He may be her Charlie, in his burgundy shirt, fiddling with her television, so his presence seems benign—but it isn't. She is not tied up. She is not bound and gagged. But she is his hostage, no doubt about it. And, meantime, her husband is in danger.

Her husband is alive and in Dungeness.

And Cam is trapped here. She's got to get to him. But she's got to save herself too. If she lets on, who knows what Charlie might do? And what he might tell Luke's enemies?

She doesn't try to look at the book. In fact, she plays an Oscar-winning role at being normal while she summons all of the thrillers she's ever read to try to work out how she is going to get out of here and go to Dungeness.

She doesn't know whether Charlie saw her read the text message, but they talk about his prior relationship again, and about Libby. Neither of them mentions Luke or the book. And perhaps it's the lack of mention that is more damning than the text: Charlie knows. And he knows Cam knows too.

She's on borrowed time. She's got to leave.

And it comes to her as she thinks of the book, Luke's book, his private love note to her, and then she knows. She knows what she is going to do to get out of this.

"Bed?" Cam says, and she's sure Charlie looks at her in surprise. But she has a plan.

Cam undresses in the bathroom, the way she sometimes does with him. She doesn't know if Charlie has tracked her phone, so she contacts nobody. When she emerges in a T-shirt and shorts he is lying on her bed, on Luke's side. He's stayed over only a few times, his presence unfamiliar, and now sinister too. She sits down next to him, her Judas, her enemy, the man whose job it is to keep her here.

"All right?" he says, turning to her. And he's going to want to . . . Cam begins to shiver, the skin on her body tightening, hairs rising. Her limbs, her nerves: they know she is in danger.

She lies facing him, and he runs a hand along her hip, as soft and as tickling as a feather. Won't he know if she doesn't . . .

Cam stares down at his hand, those square, neat fingernails. She knows them so well, but, it turns out, she doesn't at all.

He's staring at her body, his eyes wet pools.

Cam looks back at him, and she knows she should, she knows it will help her, knows he might fall deeply asleep afterward, but she can't, she just can't do it. Not with him. Not now she knows. And not with Luke—perhaps—alive somewhere . . . relying on her to get this right.

"Ah, maybe tomorrow morning," she says to him, trying to imbue her rejection with wry humor, but it doesn't work, the tone of it is all wrong, hitting a flat note when she meant a sharp. "I had too many canapés."

"Oh, for sure," he says, withdrawing his hand and avoiding eye contact.

"I'm just—I also keep thinking about work," she says. "I feel like . . ." Her mind spins, trying to make up something credible. "I don't know. Just a bit like I don't fit in there anymore." She's bubbling, killing time. Faking intimacy.

"How come?" Charlie says, and they're still half-clothed, still lying on her bed facing each other, but something indistinct has settled between them like a mist they can sense but not see. *Does* he know? Does he know she's worked it out?

"Just—maybe it's time to make a move to another agency," she says, though she doesn't feel this whatsoever.

"Maybe," he says, and she slides under the covers and places her back to him, even though every single animal instinct in her tells her not to do this. Some limbic alarm system, *Do not turn your back on him*, on the enemy. But she does it, and he puts his arms around her, and she tries not to think of them as a trap. Tries to relax and slow her breathing down.

"What do you think?" she asks. "It's just . . . I've been there so long, and Luke is never coming back—I don't know, I . . ."

As the words leave her mouth, she feels it. His body tenses, just for a microsecond, then relaxes again, and he draws her closer. His warm thighs against the backs of hers. The ticking of a clock out in the hallway. She's been here so many times, felt so safe and, all the while, he was her antagonist.

"Maybe moving would be good," he says. "Moving house and moving job." He is mumbling, his voice sleepy, and Cam drops her shoulders, exhales slowly, willing him to tip over into unconsciousness and release his grip on her so she can figure out what to do.

She thinks back to how they met. Him walking into her agency. A new research assistant who didn't—actually—seem to have much idea of how publishing worked. A man in his forties embarking on a job like that. It's all . . . so obvious. He was a stooge. Sent to infiltrate her life.

But why? And why then? She is forced to wait half an hour, mind whirring, until Charlie's breathing becomes, finally, even. He is not asleep, she doesn't think, but he at least has stopped anticipating her escape.

Cam lies next to the man sent to capture her and watches the shadows fast-moving across the ceiling like shapes at the bottom of the ocean. Charlie rolls onto his back, but she feels his hand come near to her wrist. If he shifted just a little, he could grab her arm. Stop her from getting out of bed. Stop her . . . She wonders if he fell in love, even just slightly. She wonders if she meant anything at all to him.

And then she remembers it. The paragraph in Luke's book that made her shiver. She hadn't quite known why, at the time, but . . .

If anything . . .

The same phrase he used on his final note to her. *If anything.* Was this his final clue to her?

That, if anything . . . if anyone ever wanted to escape the family business, the weapon I always used was buried in the garden.

Luke's book isn't only an explanation: it is a series of instructions, encoded just for her. He said once, if she were ever drowning, he would rescue her. And he is trying to.

And everything that has been leading up to this moment lines up like dominos, their rectangular bodies so perfectly arranged that they fall one after another after another. The book. His words. The upside-down house she has been so afraid of is her final savior. There is a door, right there, to the garden, less than two feet from her. The person watching her isn't outside: he's in. It's all ready for her. She just needs to do it.

Fast or slow, she has to decide, and in the end she goes with fast. She vaults out of bed, running, in just a T-shirt and shorts, thankful for a pair of flip-flops by the door, and for the endless summer heat, and wrenches open the door. Within seconds, he's on his feet, too, alert, but her head start mattered.

She turns on her phone's torch, looking for disturbed earth. But Charlie's right behind her, grabbing at her waist. He misses, and Cam lunges randomly.

And she sees it. A mound, by one of her rosebushes. Luke must have been here the night the security light clicked on. Knew that sending the book was a risk. Knew she was endangered by him. Protected her, the way he will always have wanted to do.

It's a pistol, barely buried. Loaded and heavy, the metal cool and just becoming dewy. She is lying stretched across the lawn with her hands on it. And all she is thinking is that she was right, he is alive.

Cam takes it, lifts it, her body knowing what to do. She turns around and Charlie sees it. He gives up, lets his arms fall to his sides, looking at her in the security light's white-hot beam.

"Cam . . ." he says, and his voice becomes pleading.

"Stop!" she shouts. "How could you?"

"I was—I was told to. It wasn't . . ."

"Why?" Cam says. "Why then?"

Charlie drops his head, seems to deliberate, then speaks: "He started getting careless," he says. "When you started to look into selling the house. He knew about it. He came back . . . he came here one night, and one of our associates doing a drop-off saw someone matching his description. We were on his tail within moments. We thought he might try to contact you again. And he did . . . with the coordinates. You told me yourself."

And that's what makes Cam do it. Not the danger she's in. Not how he lunges at her as she cocks the gun, but because of how coldly he said that. That her husband, alive and well, was going to come back for her. That he tried to.

And as though it was always, always going to end this way, consequences be damned, Cam shoots, just once.

Her aim is true.

57

Niall

Following somebody is an art, not a science, and a skill Niall hasn't recently practiced. He hasn't done it for years: he is brought to his hostages: they are captive, he is free. But this is different. He has a pistol on his front seat and a task to complete.

Two cars for cover. That's right. He lets George leave, pulls away, too, but looks for two cars to keep between them once they're on London's main streets. They take it slow, so Niall does too.

He keeps thinking about everything Isabella told him during the siege and its aftermath. Her trauma had felt so real, and perhaps it was. Who knows the precise nature of what somebody's been asked to do by their family? And how wrong things can go?

Their nephew dead. Grief drives people mad, Niall thinks as he follows them, feeling both sympathy and revulsion. And so does guilt: in a crime family, kids don't die for no reason. They die because they're in crime. Because their parents got them into crime.

The reason Alexander was murdered is because he murdered somebody else. And the reason he murdered somebody else is because his family schooled him in crime. Maybe they even demanded it. George Louis, probably one of the heads of the crime family. Alexander brought up hopelessly into it.

Their car rises and falls gently over the speed hump, and Niall tries to act naturally. No disguises, no turning your lights off: you have to behave like a normal driver, else people notice.

And so, two minutes later, when they go through an amber light, he doesn't gun it at the red, but waits, instead. Keeps his eyes on the horizon, watches them indicate left, up ahead, and the second he gets a green, he goes, glad for his car's electric engine that doesn't rev too loudly. He guesses their route, takes a shortcut through an estate, and catches up with them: hopes they have no idea.

They collect the Hales from Sarah Carpenter House. Then over the river. Through Greenwich. Niall knows where they're going by the time they signal to get onto the A2. It's busier, nighttime but in summer, people out enjoying the end of the day, and Niall closes his gap to one car.

They're going to Kent.

Has Deschamps stayed there all this time? He must have a good hiding place. Somewhere, or with someone, he trusts.

As Niall drives, he tries to think of somebody he could call to help him. Not work, not now that time's against him. Say he told them about George: they'd open an official weeks-long fucking corruption inquiry, all the while Deschamps's enemies drive to kill him.

Or they'd come and—you know what?—they'd do the thing they wanted to do seven years ago: they'd shoot Deschamps. Get the truth later. He's currently the fugitive, he's the killer of the hostages, he is the killer of Alexander Hale.

But he is good.

The A2 rises and crests, gently hilly, and Niall uses these as vantage points, the way he always did when he was a copper on the beat. You can drop way back, prevent them from becoming suspicious, use the hills as a long-range view, before coming back into sight. If you can leave it long enough, they'll never realize you were the same car driving close to them earlier.

The road is lit with red lights this way, white the other, the sky black, and they're headed to the coast. It's easy to follow somebody in London in the evening. A rural road at night is another story.

Niall presses his foot to the floor, thinking that he can't tell Camilla now—not when it isn't safe—but that, hopefully, at the end of this, he will bring Deschamps home to her.

And that is what matters. This is why, Niall thinks. This is why his job reigns supreme. Not because of the information, because of the mystery-solving. Not because of knowledge. For forever, he thought this was his thing, the thing he wanted above all else. But it isn't.

It's this. *I miss you I miss you I miss you.*

And now Niall sees, burning bright on the horizon like the moon, why he does this job.

Cam and Luke love each other and deserve to be together. And so Niall does it for the humanity of it: he does it for love.

58

Cam

Cam has shot a man in the thigh and she has run away from him. This is a fact that she knows to be true but that her mind won't yet let her care about.

She's out on the dark street and she's running and she knows exactly where to go.

Her husband. Returned from the dead, after seven years. Her husband, nearby, all this time.

She can't think about it. Usually, Cam thinks too much, worries too much, but not right now. Now her mind narrows to almost nothing, a single focal point, lit by a streetlamp: Luke. Luke. Luke. Nothing else. The past doesn't exist. Seven years' estrangement doesn't exist. All she has is him, in her sights. At last. Her long-lost husband. She knows she ought to think about Polly, but she doesn't. She thinks only of him, right in this moment. She will do her best, for Polly, to survive. But right now, on this weekday evening in London, the night belongs to Luke, and to her, and to their love story. Forget Charlie's betrayal. Forget it all. Nothing matters but this.

She takes the shortest way there, running fast, flagging down the first taxi she sees, the streets a blur.

She wonders how this is going to work, but she doesn't dwell on it. Life has been leading her here for seven years. She didn't know it, but it was. She's just left her house but, really, she set off seven years back, on that hot June day that seemed to last forever.

And how strange it is, Cam thinks in the taxi, gun held close to her body in the waistband of her shorts as her destination looms into view. All along, she was looking for the heroes and the villains, and she had them the wrong way around. At the heart of this mystery was a book that solved everything for her, the way they always do. A story that made sense of the chaos of life. All sides of it, written down in her husband's careful hand. For her, so that she understood it.

She tells the driver to speed, pays using her phone and reaches the quiet of what she is sure is her husband's hiding place. The book said it. All along, the book revealed it to her.

A simple tap on a simple door. It opens just a crack, and she's brought inside, willingly so, by hands as familiar to her as her own, as their daughter's.

He takes her into the darkness, closes the wooden door behind her.

And—

And—

It's him. It's Luke. She has reached him before everyone.

Her husband.

The missing love of her life. Her mouth parts, and her body stops all functions, or so it feels, and she's right in front of him—real, warm-bodied him—and everything has slowed way down like it did that first day, the day it all began.

Luke's eyes meet hers.

She holds his gaze for two seconds, three. His hair is darker than it was and he's so thin and she cannot, cannot stop looking at him. Here he is. Returned to her.

He stares back at her and he makes a gesture, bringing his hands together across his body as if in prayer. He holds them there for several seconds, palms on his heart, just looking at her, and that's how she knows it.

She knows everything she needs to: that he's been wanting, needing, all this time, to come back to her, trying as hard as he can, but because of these people surrounding him, could not. He wrote to her instead. A one-hundred-thousand-word love letter. An explanation.

She breaks eye contact, casts her eyes downward. Thinking, *Thank God.* Thank God he's good. For her, and for Polly.

Their fingertips meet, and then their hands, and then, finally, their foreheads touch together, just once, their eyes locking together, reunited.

Later, five minutes, ten, Cam doesn't know, he speaks.

"I owe you—an explanation," Luke says.

"You wrote me a book."

"I know. I . . ." He leans back. They're in a tiny, wooden room. Inside is a dirty old pillow, a sleeping bag, and a gun. There's no natural light, only what filters in from the streetlights outside. A slice catches Luke's blue eyes that sheen gray. His eyes. There they are. She'd forgotten the precise shape of them. They had been lost to time, like everything. Photographs couldn't conjure them. Nor could her imagination.

"I've been living here since I sent the book. Hoping you'd figure it out."

"I did."

"Does anyone know we're here?" she says, glancing behind her to the door. "I—Someone knows about that book, I think. Your enemies."

Luke's entire face turns white. "Do they?" he says.

"They . . ." She doesn't know where to begin to explain about Charlie. "They have the book."

Luke's head sinks to his chest, a condemned man.

"But we can help you," she says. "Please . . . if you explain. We can help you." She doesn't elaborate on who, not yet.

He grabs the pillow and passes it to Cam, who sits on it in the tiny wooden cubbyhole. She strains to listen, but she can't hear anything. Nobody approaching: they're alone. For now.

"Talk. Fast," she tells him.

"I took Polly out," Luke tells her. "A night in April. She wouldn't sleep. It took so long, I ended up in the middle of London."

"Yes. I got this from the book." She scoots her body close to him. And somehow, although the truth is about to unspool in front of her, she feels deep within her that their time is borrowed. His body looks fragile, too thin. But there's something else too. The hard wood of the room they're in. The metal gun. And that body, soft and vulnerable. He's made it this far, she tells herself, but it can't stop the feeling of foreboding.

"I saw two kids, youths. I later found out they were enemies from rival families. One shot the other, right there in front of me. I vaulted out of the car without thinking and pulled him off, shoved him roughly to the ground. He hit his head on a bollard I didn't see. He was out cold. I took his pulse after a few seconds—and . . . nothing. I mean . . . I just stood over them. Two bodies. One bleeding from a gunshot to the chest. The other with a head injury. And I thought . . ."

"God, Luke," Cam says, stunned. The pieces of the book tessellate with his story, and here it is. The answer she has craved for so long. And it's nothing buried in his work or deep in his past. It's just a chance encounter on one night that changed his life forever.

"I just stood there and—Cam, I just didn't know what to do."

"I bet."

"I thought: No one will believe me. Who do you believe killed the two dead people? The alive one. Right?" he says, and, even now, seven years on, his voice catches on the words, like somebody losing their footing.

"I left the scene, but then went back."

And Cam is pleased about this. The reasons are so deep and murky she can't tell why, but she is, even though it caused everybody seven years of pain. His conscience, there in the past, in good working order.

"And I thought about phoning the police . . . handing myself in. But then someone saw me. The father of one of the victims. He just *looked* bad. Powerful, clearly concealing a weapon. We locked eyes, and I fled. Just left. Later, he said he only knew his son had died when the police knocked on the door, but it wasn't true. How awful, to leave your son's body to stage your surprise, to leave him to go home: to ensure that you could go after the perpetrator yourself, lawlessly. Later, I found out on the dark web that Alexander had been asked to kill a dealer *by* his father."

Luke's book is springing to life, right there in front of Cam. She can't believe she ever thought it was Adam's. No one can write like Luke.

"And then I looked them up, and they're all over the dark web. Two warring, awful families. Two heavies for fathers. I thought I had managed to get away with it, for a while. Couldn't sleep with the guilt, but no one yet had found me. But then I did something awful. I had this dream that I went to hell. The devil was next to me, saying I was a murderer. A killer. His skin was blood-red, he had a pitchfork—it was . . . I woke up in a panic. I had to atone. I found out it was the funeral. So I went. I spent the day in turmoil, then went hours after it had finished. I thought I'd just visit the grave, afterward. Like an idiot. But he was still there. And he saw me.

"He must have followed me home. A few days later, he, or someone he sent, broke into ours, to check it was me, looked at my ID. Later, a note through the door: the warehouse address. They were toying with me, these mafia. The warehouse, the date and time: I knew it was my death warrant."

"Go on," Cam says, but Luke stops for just a few moments, perhaps overcome. He slows his breathing in a deliberate way Cam doesn't remember him doing before.

"Do you know the maddest thing?" he says. "I can count on one hand the number of conversations I've had these past seven years. I hardly use my voice."

Cam closes her eyes in sadness. Her husband the extrovert. The man who couldn't stop chatting at work, sent away to live alone because of something he did that was right.

She thinks of that morning, the day of the siege, when she woke up alone. Far worse happened to Luke that day.

"I had no choice but to go. I left you the note to . . . I didn't know what would happen. I wanted to say . . . it *had* been so lovely with you both."

"It had," Cam says sadly, thinking of the lemon-drop summer morning, her ignorance, that she had no idea what was to come. That there wouldn't be another normal morning for seven years. She hesitates on that thought.

Maybe tomorrow will be the first.

"I knew your note meant something."

"I started to say *if anything*, but I didn't want to incriminate you. I didn't want there to be any risk it appeared you might know what I was doing, and could have stopped it if it should end badly. So I left it. I'm sorry. My head was . . . in a scramble."

"I know." The note. The note that, in the end, meant nothing.

"But in the end," he says, his voice brighter, "it was a good phrase to put in the book—I knew, years on, you'd pick it out." He smiles a wan smile. "My agent."

"Your wife," she says, thinking really of his final note to her: his book.

"I turned up. Knowing it was over, really. An arrest was the best I could hope for. Inside was the kingpin's wife, Isabella, and two heavies with their faces covered. After a few minutes, they put her in a balaclava too. I knew it was over, then, for me. All I could think about was survival, and you and Polly. I watched and waited. I was late. Eventually, the hit man put his weapon on a table, and I used the opportunity. Sprung in. Took the gun. Directed them into chairs. Didn't know about the CCTV. Or that it would only capture part of the room. How it would look . . . I tied them up. Was going to call the police myself and confess."

"And then—the hostage negotiator."

"Right. The phone goes. Isabella says to me if I let her answer it, and let her go, she will tell me how to get out of there without the police or the hit men catching me. It was—I was so scared, Cam. My system was in overdrive. I took her up on it. Only, when I released her fully, she untied the hostages, so quick, ordered them to wait, then overpower and kill me once she'd left. They came for me. I had no choice but to shoot. The first then the second, quickly, close range, had them in a headlock." He holds Cam's gaze. "In self-defense." He pauses, eyes glazed. "I was surprised by how small the holes were. I kept thinking about it, years later."

And—it's the way it ought to be—only Cam knows how he truly feels, and what really happened. Once more, she knows her husband's innermost thoughts. The world watched the siege, the police tried their best to solve it, and Cam read the BBC live feeds and felt humiliated. But here, only she knows the full truth of it, thanks to his book, thanks to his last words, just for her. The way it should be: intimate communication between husband and wife restored.

"Then?"

"Then I left. A fugitive."

"And you never came back," she says.

"I had enemies everywhere. The police. The Louises. The Hales. I was a dead man walking."

"I know."

"But I did come back. I tried to come back. That night. I waited and waited in the Lewisham house. Did the police tell you about Harry?"

"Yes. Rightmove. They found it on your phone."

"Ah. He lists it on there perpetually but never sells it. Uses it as a location for clients. Anyway, that night, the police were on your tail. I had to tell Harry to deny he had me. He let me out of the bathroom window, right before they came in and searched the house. You were right there, out on the street, and I couldn't get to you."

"Oh, Luke. You were there."

"I was. And you came for me."

"Tried to," Cam says, thinking of all of their missed chances, missed connections. How close they were, really, all this time. He in the warehouse; she outside it. He in Harry's house; she waiting on the street below.

"I know. I know you did," he says.

"I lived in Kent for a while, working for cash in hand, living virtually off-grid. Each month, I swore I'd sort it out. I was on the dark web all the time, trying to find other enemies of this family, people who might help me bring them down. The Lancasters, even, but I was too scared to involve other criminals. Trying to pluck up the nerve to go to the police. To tell my side of it. And then . . ."

"And then what?"

"You started to enquire about moving house. Months ago. You asked for a new mortgage valuation, the bank sent it to my email too. I had to log in at internet cafés, using shields to block it, so no one would know. But I got addicted to it. To knowing what you were doing. There were only ever emails about joint things, but it was like . . . a connection to you. Out there in the ether," he says with a self-conscious little laugh. "So I came back. One night. But someone in a hood saw me. A shit coincidence, I think, though my enemies are criminals, and have footmen everywhere. He followed me a little, until I ran, and I was too scared to try to physically return. So I started to think about other ways I could tell you."

And Cam closes her eyes in such exquisite pleasure. All this time, all the time she thought she saw him on the Tube and at the school gate, those times she wished for him at parties, the moments when she looked into the sky and thought of him, he was doing the same about her.

59

Niall

Dungeness. A jut of land at the very bottom of England, sticking out like the crest of a tiny wave. The A-road turns coastal.

Niall's speed slows even more. A bleak, postapocalyptic tarmac road cuts through desert-flat headlands dotted with occasional huts and shops and pubs and lighthouses.

The car slows to a stop in front of an abandoned-looking hut, the nuclear power station in the background, lit up and blinking like a spaceship.

The air is warm and dark and the sea rushes elsewhere somewhere. Otherwise, all is quiet, the power station a sentient being in the background, the cars abandoned.

Is Luke in there? Niall stares at where the Hales and the Louises are heading. They can see Niall now, and they're running. They know he's about to act.

They head to a lighthouse; Niall follows them. They must know his precise location. It must be in that book, the book that they have taken. After a second, Isabella turns around and looks at him for just a moment. Their eyes meet and, suddenly, he wonders if she is the enemy after all, or just forced into crime by George.

The lighthouse is tall and striped black and white, windows boarded up, illuminated only at the top, throwing light and shadow onto the surrounding pavement. The windows of the hut are shut up, dark, nothing happening.

The Hales start to try to break into the lighthouse, pulling the wood away from the door. And it makes sense: the police never checked it. It looked boarded up, uninhabitable. Niall shakes his head.

Noise breaks out all around him. "You killed our boy!" somebody yells. It's Janet Hale.

"Come out," George Louis commands. He reaches into a pocket and pulls out a gun. A small pistol that he handles as easily and as familiarly as a mobile phone.

He cocks it, and Niall touches his own weapon and thinks of Luke, in there, alone and waiting.

George hasn't turned around to acknowledge Niall yet.

"Police!" Niall barks.

George moves his body slowly, head fixed, to stare at Niall.

"Put your hands in the air," Niall says, and his instruction goes ignored. Immediately, George whips back around and begins to try the door of the lighthouse, but it doesn't budge.

Niall thinks of Cam. And he thinks of these people, who will never listen. Who will never accept their role in their child's murder. Some people cannot be negotiated with. The truth is too painful for them.

George shoots at the mechanism of the door. The noise reverberates all around the quiet coast. Niall flinches with it. He didn't know it would escalate so quickly. The second time he's been surprised by gunshots.

"Deschamps!" George shouts. "Open up!"

"Stop!" Niall yells, and George whips around, the gun still trained. In his entire career, Niall's never once looked into the barrel of a gun aimed at him. The round metal seems to fill his vision, a circle of menace.

"No," Niall says, knowing it might be one of the last things he says. "You've got to stop this—Deschamps is—"

"*He* would still be here without Deschamps," George says, and pain constricts his words like tight laces.

"No, he wouldn't," Niall says. "You can't bring someone into crime and not pay the consequences . . ." but his voice trails off. George is not listening. "What do you want to achieve?" Niall says, but this is no negotiation. It's not a two-way street. "You've killed, haven't you? To try and avenge?"

"She was going to break confidence," George replies.

"What do you want?"

"Revenge," George replies simply, and he's turned away from Niall, and he's got the door open.

The world becomes silent and distant as Niall realizes what is about to happen. He holds his own weapon close to his body and seems to rise up above and outside himself. As he surveys his body language, he realizes, with all of his training and knowledge, that he is about to shoot: he has the agitated posture, he is aiming.

George Louis finally heads into the lighthouse and points his gun. And Niall gets there first. He pulls the trigger, and sound explodes all around him. And that's when he realizes it: the dreams weren't the gunshots from the past; they were from the future. From now.

Afterward, after everybody is maimed, tied up, his hostages, Niall opens the door to the lighthouse while he waits for the police. But it's empty: no one there. He was protecting no one.

60

Cam

The book has taken everybody to Dungeness, but only Cam could read between the lines of what her husband wrote to her in his secret manuscript, in what he felt might be his last words to her, the explanation from one lover to another. *That if anything . . . if anyone ever wanted to escape the family business, the weapon I always used was buried in the garden. That important items were in a lockup under my name.*

Cam remembered it. *A lockup under my name.* She took a chance that he meant St. Luke's, came here, and it paid off. They're alone. They've got some time. They hope.

"What made you send the book?" Cam asks.

"I thought if you sold the house, I'd lose you forever. I don't know. It's so symbolic, isn't it? It wasn't that I couldn't find you. It was, to me, evidence that maybe you'd moved. On." He holds her gaze here, and she decides not to mention Charlie. Not yet: there's time for that.

"Then you filled the form in, to declare me dead: I got an alert on my email as part of their automatic procedure. And it was the final thing. I sent the coordinates here almost immediately. They went wrong—I was here, in this lock-up, the entire time. I had been researching the Hales on the dark web, and I began writing when you started to try and sell the house, typing day and night on a beat-up old laptop I bought for cash. I finished it that night."

"I see," Cam says softly, thinking of all of the years past, how many times they had just missed each other, the danger he was in, how if Luke hadn't been out that night, if Polly hadn't been awake, if, if, if . . . "And you put the story in the book. Their story. And the clues for me to find you."

"You were always good at reading me," he says simply. "And my words."

He looks at Cam, his eyes full of love. "What is she like?" he asks, and Cam knows just whom he means: their daughter, Polly, the only witness to Luke's crime. The person who, all along, knew the score, but didn't know it too.

Act IV

SEVEN YEARS
AFTER THE SECOND
SHOOTING

61

Niall

Niall waits for the phone to be answered. It rings two times, four, six, eight, but, today, he knows they're going to pick up.

"Six hundred thousand," says a voice, a deep register, accented. Niall turns away from the payphone. He's inside a bar in Bogotá. Outside on the street, yellow taxis rush by. There's graffiti outside, a white Colombian sky, close weather, a McDonald's opposite—aren't there more McDonald's restaurants in the world than anything else, or is that some sort of myth?

"I can't do six hundred," Niall says into the untraceable payphone. "Trust me when I say I don't have the authority to." This is the language he is careful to use: he wants to comply but can't. He's governed by forces beyond his control. Not his fault, he's just the messenger.

Niall is fully freelance these days, but this is the weirdest job for a little while. He tilts his head back on the phone, listening and thinking. "What can you go to?" the voice says, downbeat, no question imbued within it.

"Half that."

"No deal," the voice says, and hangs up the phone. Niall rubs his head and sighs, walks away from the phone. He sips his drink—a virgin whiskey sour—and waits.

From the back room of the bar, the man arrives.

"No deal," he repeats, a broad smile on his face.

"Right," Niall says, turning with him to face the group of hostage negotiators in training looking up at them. "That's what happens when you talk figures too early," he says as his Colombian friend nods.

"Exactly," he says. "No deals."

"More tomorrow," Niall says. He checks his watch. It's five o'clock: finishing time.

If there's a McDonald's on every street corner in the world, there may also be a Patisserie Valerie. Or, La Patisserie de Valerie, as it's known here. And outside it, there is Viv, holding a box.

"Hello," she says to him, her face immediately brightening up like somebody has animated her. God, her eyes. "All done? Up-and-comers all educated?"

"Not really," Niall says with a laugh. "Sometimes, I actually think you can't teach this stuff."

"Oh."

"Which is good," he adds sarcastically. "As—now—a teacher."

"Oh dear, struck off from the Met and now from teaching?"

Niall smiles a half-smile, thinking of what led him to be struck off. The siege, the events afterward, that night when Camilla found Deschamps. The second Deschamps sent the book, he went to sleep rough in the little lockup that Niall had peered inside. Waiting for her. He was there when Niall checked, hiding in the back, in the shadows. And he was there, too, on that night.

The whole time, Deschamps and Camilla were not in the lighthouse at all. He'd left another clue in the book. Leaving Niall free to shoot, alone.

Deschamps and Camilla had come to Dungeness that night when he'd asked them to and had lied for him. Said they'd seen the shooting, that he had needed to do it. That it would have saved them, hiding in the lighthouse. Niall had got away without being charged, but he'd lost his job for withholding information. For acting alone. The Hales and the Louises he'd wounded had gone to prison.

"No. Just done for the weekend."

"Well, I *happened* to buy four cakes," Viv says. She opens a second box, held in a bag by her side that he didn't see. "And oh my God, a teapot."

"Only you would come to Colombia and buy a teapot."

"Shush. Take your pick. I have no idea what the cakes are."

Niall nods as he remembers the day she came back to him. Knocked on his door out of the blue. Asked if he wanted a tea. He'd said yes. They'd had five each. Whiled away an afternoon together, and only when the sun descended had they got on to the important stuff.

It's evening, now, again, and Colombia bustles around them. Hot and colorful and only slightly dangerous—it's best for his trainees to learn on the ground, and this week's course is all about Bogotá and its varied practices. Viv walks more closely to him than at home, and Niall's glad she came. He wouldn't have come if she hadn't wanted to.

"It's coffee and walnut," Viv says, taking a bite, "old-fashioned but nice."

Niall gazes at her. Perhaps she no longer thinks about back then, their separation, their reunion, but Niall does, every single day. Viv comes first, work second, and that's the natural order it has to be.

She shows him the other slices, and Niall thinks there could literally be a piece of shit in that box and he would still eat it with her.

"What do you want to do tonight, and until we go home?" Niall asks.

"Don't mind," she says. "But—about home. There're a few stray cats waiting for us . . ."

"Uh-oh," Niall says. "How many is a few?"

"A good number. Four." Viv leans right up against him, head on his shoulder, and Niall looks into the distance. They still have the one-eyed cat.

Niall thinks about that stupid cat, and the others joining them soon, and muses that it's funny: all this time he was trying to reunite Deschamps and Camilla, his own two strays. Deschamps wrote that he had spent seven years living in a boarded-up lighthouse on the Dungeness estate, coming out only at night, but really, he had been cleverer than that. He'd worked cash-in-hand, no ID needed. Couch-surfed, slept rough, paid for motels and short-term lodgings all over the southeast, in notes he was paid with that left no trace. He'd only ever gone to Dungeness to ping the mast, should anyone have intercepted his book.

Niall worked so hard to bring them back together, but it took a lot of time, and a lot of therapy, for him to realize that what he needed to do was give that to himself. To reunite himself with whom he loved most.

62

Cam

They're about to leave the house; Polly has a musical theatre performance. She's nearly fifteen, tall and thin and blond, just like her father.

"Ready?" Luke says, a hand on the doorframe, watching Cam.

"Sure," she says. "I was just thinking about . . . everything." She looks at Luke's printed-out memoir on the shelf. Charlie survived—and Cam wasn't charged: his account of events matched hers, and the CPS said she'd acted in self-defense. He'd gone to prison for harassment. She wonders if he'd backed up her story out of kindness, guilt, or something else. She hasn't ever quite told Luke how close she'd come to falling in love with somebody else: he doesn't need to know.

"What's new?" Luke says with a dimpled smile.

"Right. I know. I never change. You get your work done?" she asks him.

"No," he says, the way he always has. "Not enough." He grins at her, and it's a dark sunburst of a smile from her husband, who she once wished was law-abiding, meek, and less fun. No longer. "Fuck it," he adds, though it is not as humorous as he once was.

He doesn't write much any longer. Does odd writing jobs, online, is all. The last book he wrote was his memoir, written just for her, *Famous Last Words*, the one he delivered to her in the jiffy bag. They called it that to replace his infamous note the papers got hold of. She printed and bound it at work, added a back-cover blurb for them to keep. No one else ever saw it. She wouldn't want them to. Sometimes, even now, Cam lies awake at night thinking that her husband has killed three men. It has changed him, she thinks. Hardened him into something perhaps more serious. Bleaker, sometimes, his humor darker. His view of his self fractured.

Polly strides in, in full orange makeup, glittery costume—it's *West Side Story*, but seems to be some sort of lurid, modern version of it. Cam can't help but beam at her, though—secretly—she'd rather stay home and read. Once an introvert, always an introvert.

"Can you French-plait me?" she asks, and she comes to her mother over her father. She is still this way. Was tentative with Luke for years, as though he were a stepfather or stranger. And he was, to Polly, though it pained Luke to know that. He didn't move in with them for a year and, even then, there was a self-consciousness to it when he eventually did. He still knocked on the door sometimes, sat stiffly on the sofa, never made himself a drink. It has taken years.

Polly first called him Dad only three years ago, when she was eleven. Until then, he was Luke. And she still favors Cam. Always will. Sometimes, you pay a price for happiness. It's worth it, but you still pay it.

Luke averts his gaze from Polly going to Cam, and she tells herself that this is just being a mum, though she knows it isn't true. If Luke had never gone out that night, he might be plaiting her hair right now. She knows he would have been that type of father: involved, not a stereotype in sight.

"Sure," Cam says, and she begins to weave her daughter's mane together, and it could be Luke's. Thin and straight and shiny, natural blond highlights move like silk underneath her fingertips. Sometimes, she thinks the family resemblance helped father and daughter to knit back together.

"Is Libby coming?" Polly says.

"Yes, of course."

"Is Bobby?"

"He's too young to sit for that long," Cam says. Bobby, born three years ago using a surrogate, looks just like her sister; Cam hadn't realized she could ever love a nephew almost as much as she loves her own daughter.

"Even though it's the best performance he will ever see?" Polly says, doing a little jig.

"Even though," Cam says, while Luke snorts. He's grasped his daughter's personality easily, these past seven years, but he still doesn't quite know it like Cam does. Sometimes, she finds herself wanting to exchange a glance with somebody else, somebody who isn't there: the Luke who never left. Other times, Cam feels he never did. It's complicated, she supposes.

She finishes Polly's hair, and they head out the back way of the upside-down house that they still live in, do not, now, want to move from, no longer afraid to sleep by the patio doors. The three of them walk through the bedroom, which is no longer divided into two halves. It's come together, whole once more. His and hers.

Acknowledgments

————

I t's been quite a year. Sixteen months, in fact. This book took a little longer than the others, because I had a baby in the middle of it. Please know that I had such an amazing time, night feeding and thinking about hostage situations, as one does. I wouldn't change a moment.

My huge thanks, as ever, go to my agents Felicity Blunt, Lucy Morris, and Rosie Pierce for their always insightful edits, handholding, and guidance.

This book is dedicated to my editor, Maxine Hitchcock, to whom I owe such a great debt. From 2017, she has guided my career from book to book, being a sounding board for plot and character. But the most important quality she has is that she is happy for me to do the thing that authors must do mid-career: take a risk. I trust her and she trusts me, and that, to me, is so wonderful.

My huge thanks, too, go to the wider team at Penguin Michael Joseph: Ellie Hughes, Ellie Morley, Emma Plater, Richenda Todd, Clare Bowron; and, at Curtis Brown, Tanja Goossens, especially. My huge thanks, too, to my film and TV agents, Jason Richman and Mary Pender. You guys are quite the agents!

To the team at William Morrow: Emily Krump, Danielle Dieterich, Hannah Dirgins, Lisa McAuliffe. You are slick, dynamic, and so brilliant to work with: I'm so lucky. And to Ariele Fredman, too, my U.S. agent: thank you for all you do.

I am very much indebted to Martin Richards who answered numerous questions in this novel about hostage negotiations and even took me on a Zoom course. All errors are (I hope) deliberate, and mine, and please know that sometimes reality has been distorted for entertainment. Thanks, too, to my cop and friend Neil Greenough who is always on hand for esoteric questions from me ("Morning. What does a RIP round sound like?").

Thanks to my close and intimate circle of friends. In this business, it's wise to have people to keep your secrets, and you do for me. Thank you to my father for his endless plot chats on this one, his character suggestions, and his close listening skills. Our relationship is one of the highlights of my whole life.

Thank you to Dana for her kind companionship, to Sarah Carpenter of Sarah Carpenter House fame, to Jess, and penultimately to David, without whom I wouldn't write love stories, wouldn't know how to (albeit those featuring hostages).

Final thanks go to my son, now eighteen months. Right before I gave birth, someone said to me, "the love of your life is inbound," and they couldn't have been more correct. (Thank you also for napping well as requested.)

And a real heartfelt more-than-thanks goes to my readers. I get to live a strange and wonderful life because of you, and I don't thank you enough.